Lash's Hurricane

Iron Punisher's MC 4

Ciara St James

Copyright

ISBN: 978-1-955751-61-2
Printed in the United States of America
Editing by Mary Kern @ Ms. K Edits
Photograph by Jessica Johnson Photography
Book cover by Tracie Douglas @ Dark Waters Covers

Blurb:

A club ride and an almost overlooked glimpse along the road bring Lash and his club to a halt. They might be bikers, but no one who knows them will say they're not men who help others and right wrongs when they can. After that ride, Lash is more determined than ever to do it.

A woman shrouded in mystery grabs hold of him, and she won't let go. As he spends time with her and she settles into life at the compound, he's more than certain that she's the one he's been waiting for his whole life. Sure, they have a couple of things to resolve, but who doesn't?

As they seek answers, a misspoken accusation leads to more pain and then danger. Will Lash be able to keep the woman he loves and wants to spend his life with while punishing those who deserve it?

Troian never imagined what she would find when she woke up. She's surrounded by strangers in a world she doesn't know. As she regains her strength, she falls under Lash's spell. Only Troian thinks she doesn't have a chance with him.

As feelings are revealed, there's hope and joy until an unfounded allegation threatens to tear them apart. It's not just Lash and Torian who are battling things either.

In the end, how will Lash win his Hurricane and resolve their issues? Or will it all come crashing down? Come find out in Lash's Hurricane.

Warning

This book is intended for adult readers. It contains foul language and adult situations and discusses events such as stalkers, assault, torture, and murder that may trigger some readers. Sexual situations are graphic. If these themes aren't what you like to read or you find them upsetting, this book isn't for you. There is no cheating or cliffhangers, and it has a HEA.

Iron Punishers Members

Holden Grier (Reaper) President w/Cheyenne
Creed Donovan (Maniac) VP w/ Lark
Jamison Tyrell (Mayhem) Enforcer w/ TBD
Killian Hardison (Ratchet) Road Captain w/ TBD
Damian Tatum (Crusher) SAA w/ TBD
Austin Kavanagh (Ink) w/ Alisse
Derrick Tatum (Lash) w/ Troian
Vance Halliwell (Tinker) Treasurer w/ TBD
Aidan Priestley (Spawn) Secretary w/ TBD
Carter McKnight (Sandman) w/TBD
Braxton Russo (Shadow) w/TBD
Dante Braun (Remus) w/ TBD
Dillion Braun (Romulus) w/ TBD
Colt Langley (Gravel) w/TBD
Rhaines Dallesandro- Prospect

Reading Order

For Dublin Falls Archangel's Warriors MC (DFAW), Hunters Creek Archangel's Warriors MC (HCAW), Iron Punishers MC (IPMC), Dark Patriots (DP), & Pagan Souls of Cherokee MC (PSCMC)

Terror's Temptress DFAW 1
Savage's Princess DFAW 2
Steel & Hammer's Hellcat DFAW 3
Menace's Siren DFAW 4
Ranger's Enchantress DFAW 5
Ghost's Beauty DFAW 6
Viper's Vixen DFAW 7
Devil Dog's Precious DFAW 8
Blaze's Spitfire DFAW 9
Smoke's Tigress DFAW 10
Hawk's Huntress DFAW 11
Bull's Duchess HCAW 1
Storm's Flame DFAW 12
Rebel's Firecracker HCAW 2
Ajax's Nymph HCAW 3
Razor's Wildcat DFAW 13
Capone's Wild Thing DFAW 14
Falcon's She Devil DFAW 15
Demon's Hellion HCAW 4
Torch's Tornado DFAW 16
Voodoo's Sorceress DFAW 17

Reaper's Banshee IPMC 1
Bear's Beloved HCAW 5
Outlaw's Jewel HCAW 6
Undertaker's Resurrection DP 1
Agony's Medicine Woman PSC 1
Ink's Whirlwind IP 2
Payne's Goddess HCAW 7
Maverick's Kitten HCAW 8
Tiger & Thorn's Tempest DFAW 18
Dare's Doll PSC 2
Maniac's Imp IP 3
Tank's Treasure HCAW 9
Blade's Boo DFAW 19
Law's Valkyrie DFAW 20
Gabriel's Retaliation DP 2
Knight's Bright Eyes PSC 3
Joker's Queen HCAW 10
Bandit & Coyote's Passion DFAW 21
Sniper's Dynamo & Gunner's Diamond DFAW 22
Slash's Dove HCAW 11
Lash's Hurricane IP 4

For Ares Infidels MC

Sin's Enticement AIMC 1
Executioner's Enthrallment AIMC 2
Pitbull's Enslavement AIMC 3
Omen's Entrapment AIMC 4
Cuffs' Enchainment AIMC 5
Rampage's Enchantment AIMC 6
Wrecker's Ensnarement AIMC 7
Trident's Enjoyment AIMC 8
Fang's Enlightenment AIMC 9
Talon's Enamorment AIMC 10

Ares Infidels in NY AIMC 11
Phantom's Emblazonment AIMC 12
Saint's Enrapturement AIMC 13
Phalanx & Bullet's Entwinement AIMC 14
Torpedo's Entrancement AIMC 15

For O'Sheerans Mafia

Darragh's Dilemma
Cian's Complication
Aidan's Ardor

Please follow Ciara on Facebook. For information on new releases & to catch up with Ciara, go to www.ciara-st-james.com or www.facebook.com/ciara.stjames.1 or www.facebook.com/groups/tenilloguardians or https://www.facebook.com/groups/1112302942958940 or https://www.facebook.com/groups/923322252903958

Russian Dictionary

Babe- detka
Bastard- Svoloch'
Bitch- cyka
Cock- petukh
Cocksucker- khuyesos
Does the name Razin ring any bells?- Imya Razina vam nichego ne govorit?
Do you think I'm a slut?- Ty dumayash', ya shlyukha?
Forgive me- prostite menya
Fuck you- poshel na khuy
Fucker- podonok
God- bog
Goddamnit- proklyat'ye
Hello- Privet
Hello Kirill, what did you find out, cousin?- Privet Kirill, chto ty uzna, cosuin?
Hello sweetheart, my name is Crusher- Privet, dorogaya, menya zovut Krasher
How do I know Russian? -Otkuda ya znayu russkiy?
How're you doing, babe?- Kak dela, detka?
Hurricane- Uragan
I hate you- ya tebya nenavizhu
I love you- ya tebya lyublyu
I'm doing great, Crusher- U menya vse otlichna, Krasher
I'm not a whore/slut- Ya ne shlyukha

I'm sorry- mne zhal'

Let go of me, you son of a bitch- Otpusti menya, sukin sin

No- nyet

No, I'll be fine, Thank you. If I do, I'll let you know.- Nyet, yabudu v poryyadka. Spasiba
            yesli ya eto sdelayu. Ya dam vam znat'

Oh God- O bozhe

Oh, I know a lot. You're full of shit- O, ya mnogo znayu

Please- pozhaluysta

Pussy- kiska

Put me down, bastard- polozhi menya, ublyudok

Queen- Koroleva

Quiet- tikhiy

She speaks Russian?- Ona sovorit po-russki?

Son of a bitch- sukin sin

Sweetheart- Dorogoy

Sweetheart, where do you hurt?- Milaya, gde u tebya bolit?

What's your name?- Kak tebya zovut?

Troian: Prologue

They knew. I could tell by the way they were constantly watching me. When they thought I wasn't looking, their faces were full of rage and hate. Oh God, what should I do? As much as I feared what this might mean for me, I didn't regret what I did. It was beyond wrong, and I had to stop it, stop him. Surely they could understand that. Would every single one of them have turned a blind eye to it if they'd been the ones to find out what Andrik was doing? I hoped not.

I almost didn't keep it a secret at first. I assumed they'd rally around me. However, a tiny voice in the back of my head told me not to do it, so I didn't. I thought I was lucky that my part in it was kept secret. All I did was provide leads and proof I'd found. Well, I thought it had been a secret. How had they found out? Andrik didn't even know. The tension and the vibes told me that I was in danger. My survival instinct was screaming at me to get out and run.

Pasting a fake smile on my face, I eased out of the living room, making the excuse I had a long workday tomorrow and I needed sleep. As soon as I was clear of their gazes, I hurried to my room. Shutting the door, I locked it and then dragged my suitcase out of the closet. I wouldn't be able to take much, but even a little was better than nothing. I'd wait until they were all asleep for the night, then I'd sneak out.

I had no idea where I'd go, but I'd figure that out after I got away from here. Anywhere was better than staying where I felt like I was in mortal danger. I knew for years they weren't the most loving people on the planet, but this was ridiculous. Maybe they were more heartless than I knew, like Andrik. I'd spent too many years being at their beck and call and trying to repay them for giving me a place to live when my parents died all those years ago. My obligation was repaid, and then some. It was time to get a life and maybe one day find happiness of my own.

As the hours passed, I became more and more anxious. No one had bothered to come check on me, which should've made me feel better, but it didn't. It made me worry more. People were in and out of the house for hours. I could hear the murmur of their voices and the thumps of footsteps. It was well after midnight before the house became quiet. I waited another hour to be sure everyone was asleep before easing my door open. I listened but didn't hear anyone. I tiptoed down the back hall, carrying my suitcase so it wouldn't make any noise. Leaving out the back door, I sprinted to my car. I'd be able to coast it down the long drive for a good way before I had to turn it on. I was gonna make it.

I was almost to my car when I was grabbed from behind. I couldn't help but cry out in fright. Hard hands bit into my arms, and I was shaken hard. "Did you think we'd let you go, *cyka,* bitch? You're gonna pay for what you did," Zandro's angry voice hissed in my ear.

"Please, don't—" I didn't get to finish my plea

before something hard hit me in the back of the head, and then everything went dark.

Lash: Chapter 1.

It was early October and still hot and sunny in this part of Virginia. There was just enough of a drop in the temperature to make it bearable. Summer was always hot and humid, so fall made this perfect riding weather, and the whole club was taking advantage of it. The ride we'd taken today had been along a section of the Claw of the Dragon. We accessed it from Marion, which was about forty-five minutes from Bristol. The Claw was one of the best scenic back roads that looped through the Blue Ridge Mountains and was in Southwest Virginia. Many motorcycle riders rode it, making it a popular ride.

We hadn't made the entire three-hundred-and-fifty-mile loop, but it had still been great. It had totaled a three-and-a-half-hour ride. We stopped to break it up and spent time checking out the local scenery and grabbing a bite to eat. It was late afternoon now, and we were almost back home.

We'd left Interstate 81 behind and were taking the lesser traveled roads. This one took us past the Mendota Trail, a hiking area that connected Bristol, our hometown, and nearby Mendota. It was one of my favorite hiking trails. The lush green trees and the wild undergrowth flashed by. The air was filled with the scent of greenery and earth. I drew in a lungful. I never got enough of that smell.

Reaper and Cheyenne were in the lead. As president, it was his spot. Directly behind him and to the left were our VP Maniac and his woman, Lark. Crusher, our sergeant-at-arms, was on the right. Behind them were Ratchet, Tinker, Mayhem, and Spawn, our other officers, and then the regular members like me were behind them. Ink and his old lady, Alisse, rode beside me.

Out of the thirteen patched members in the club, only three had old ladies. It wasn't because the rest of us didn't want one. Sure, some weren't ready yet, and the rest of us hadn't been fortunate enough to meet a woman who made us unable to think of anyone but her and held our hearts in her hands. Believe me, if I had, I'd have her riding on the back of my bike, too.

I'd begun to wonder over the past few years if there was such a woman out there for me. To be honest, I'd started even before that when I saw how our friends in the Warriors MC chapters settled down over the years. I was thirty-nine. If there were such a woman, she'd better show herself soon. I didn't want to be sixty and find my old lady. I wanted as many years as I could get with her, plus I still had hopes of having a family one day. That desire grew as the three little ones we had so far joined our family.

Lilly, Reaper and Cheyenne's daughter, was fifteen months old and into everything now that she could walk. Arya, Ink and Alisse's little girl will be a year old next month. Flynn, Maniac and Lark's son was the oldest at five and a half. He was the little man around the club who took his role of protector for the two little girls seriously. He'd settled into his new life with us and became more outgoing. It had been slow going at first when Lark and Maniac had adopted him after the murder of his biological parents. However, with lots of love and attention, he'd blossomed. Today, to give the couples time away, Annie, a close friend of the club, had all three of them for the day. She had been overjoyed to get alone time with them and urged us to take our time.

Thoughts of the kids and my lack of romantic prospects were pushed from my mind when Alisse pointed off to the side of the road. She was saying something to Ink and lightly slapping his arm. I glanced over to see if I could see what had caught her attention and got that kind of reaction out of her. She had a disbelieving look on her face.

Off among the high weeds and other plants, I caught a flash of something light, and then it was gone. Ink signaled to me and those behind us that he was pulling over. I followed him. Those in the lead would either circle back or stop and wait for us to catch up. I signaled the ones behind us to keep going. There wasn't any need for us all to stop. They nodded and sped past me. Circling back to where Ink had backtracked, I stopped my bike. I shut it off like Ink had his. Alisse was scrambling off it.

He grabbed her. "Stay here, Whirlwind," he ordered.

"Hurry," she pleaded.

"What's wrong, Alisse?" I asked as I got off my

bike.

"I saw something over there under those trees. I swear it looked like clothing."

"Clothing? Maybe someone threw out a piece of furniture, like old cushions from a couch or something. People litter along these roads. I hate it, but they do it all the time. Why they can't take shit to the dump is beyond me. Lazy, I guess," I grumbled.

Ink was off his bike now. He grabbed her hand to get her attention. She was peering off into the trees. "I want you to stay here and let us go see what it is. Probably, it's what Lash said. I don't want you to get bitten. There are snakes in these woods, and the plants hide them."

"Okay, but hurry. I saw it over there," she said as she pointed.

Deciding to go with him, we headed in that direction. I heard the roar of multiple bikes as we did. It looked like the others had decided to come back and see what we were doing. Ink and I walked side by side. The plants were halfway to our knees. As we got further in, I saw some had been beaten down. As we neared the spot Alisse had pointed at, I saw the fabric she had spotted. The shape seemed wrong to be a cushion.

"What the hell is that?" I asked Ink.

"Hell, if I know. Let's get this checked, then get on the road. It'll be dinner time soon."

"Fine by me."

It wasn't until we were almost on top of the object that it registered what it was we were looking at. When it did, I took off running. Ink was right behind me. I dropped to my knees and reached out, but then stopped myself. Doubts assailed me. I shouldn't touch it. I didn't want my prints on anything.

"Jesus Christ," Ink muttered. As he did, a low, barely above-a-whisper moan came from the lump. This changed my mind. I touched it lightly.

"Can you hear me?" I asked. I couldn't believe what I was looking at. The supposed cushion was, in fact, a body. We could see what looked like a tarp had been rolled around the body. There wasn't anything showing to tell us if it was a man or a woman.

"What is it?" Reaper shouted from the road.

"It's a body. Christ, get Colt to bring my bag," I shouted.

Colt was one of our two prospects. We'd brought them on in the past year since we patched in our last two, Remus and Romulus. They'd been following us in the crash truck in case we broke down or had problems. They were stopped behind the bikes. My medical supplies were in the truck.

Not getting more than a moan from the person, I decided to touch the light-colored tarp again. Slowly, I rolled the body onto what I thought was a back. As I did, the tarp parted, and I caught a glimpse of the person inside. My heart skipped a beat. Long red hair spilled out onto the ground. Despite the bruising and the swollen face, I knew it was a woman. Someone had beaten her savagely. She moaned but didn't open her eyes. Ink looked at me, stunned.

The sound of footsteps running up to us had me turning around to grab my bag. Colt was wide-eyed as he handed it to me. Coming toward us from behind him were the rest of the guys. I sat it down and unzipped it. Leaning closer, I asked the woman, "Miss, can you hear me?"

She didn't make another sound or open her eyes. I didn't want to risk hurting her more than she already was, so I took the knife I always carried in a sheath in the back of my pants and carefully sliced from one end of the tarp to the other. I went slow so I wouldn't cut her. When I was done, I eased the material back.

"Shit," Ink breathed.

The woman's face wasn't the only thing that had been beaten. From what we could see of her arms, legs, and upper chest, so had the rest of her. Angry black and blue bruises were everywhere. There were superficial cuts as well. Her clothes, which were a t-shirt and a pair of shorts, were torn, wrinkled, and dirty. Her hot pink toenails stood out to me as being at odds with the rest of her.

Despite her having bottoms on, there was no way to know if she'd been sexually assaulted. Her thighs were heavily bruised, so it was a distinct possibility. Bile rose up as I looked at her. The thought of her having suffered that, along with a savage beating, made me sick.

"Is she alive?" Reaper asked from over my right shoulder. He had crouched down beside me. Ink was on the other side of her.

"She was. She moaned a couple of times. Let me check her out."

"Do you want us to go ahead and call for an ambulance?" he asked.

Typically, I would immediately say yes, but something held me back this time. Call it a gut instinct or whatever, but something told me that wasn't what was best for her. I shook my head. "No, hold off on that. Let me see what we're dealing with first."

I removed my stethoscope and blood pressure cuff from my bag. First, I listened to her chest. Thankfully, her chest was moving up and down, so I knew without checking her pulse she hadn't died on me. Her lungs were clear, and I heard a surprisingly steady heartbeat. Next, I gently put the cuff around her arm and inflated it so I could check her blood pressure. As I expected, it was low, but not so low that I feared she'd die at any moment.

"Lash, is she gonna be alright?" Cheyenne asked softly.

She, Alisse, and Lark were huddled together not far away. I knew at least Cheyenne and Alisse would understand me when I told them, "Her pressure is ninety over sixty. Her pulse is sixty, and her heartbeat is rather strong." I watched as the two of them sagged in relief.

Lark whispered to them, "Is that good?"

"It could be a whole lot worse," Alisse told her.

My touching her and our voices must've reached the woman somewhere in her unconscious state because she suddenly jerked and cried out. Her words made me want to put my fist through something, or more likely, someone.

"Please, stop. Don't. I'm sorry. I don't want to die," she whimpered as she tried to move away. She moved like she was trying to put up her hands to protect herself, but she was too weak to do it. I heard my brothers swear.

I leaned closer to her and put a hand on her shoulder. "No one's gonna hurt you, sweetheart. We're here to help you. We need to get you to the hospital," I told her.

Suddenly, her eyes snapped open. Her dark brown eyes bored into mine. I saw fear and panic in them. "Please, don't. They'll find me. Don't let them kill me," she pleaded. Tears swam in them and then spilled down her face. I wiped them away carefully.

"I won't," I told her hoarsely. As soon as I did, her body relaxed and her eyes closed.

For a moment, I panicked, thinking she had died, until I saw her chest rise. As my heart settled, I stood up. I faced the others. They were all watching me expectantly. Making a hasty decision, but one I thought was the best one under the circumstances, I began to issue orders.

"Rhaines, get a blanket out of the truck. We're gonna load her up and take her back to the compound with us. Until we know more, I don't think we should call an ambulance or the police. Whoever hurt this woman left her for dead. I need to get her to where I can examine her more closely and see what we're dealing with."

It was a testament to how much my club trusted me that no one objected. Reaper nodded. I continued, "Colt, I need you to ride my bike back." He gave me a startled look. "Don't wreck it, or your ass is mine. Hear me, prospect?" I growled. He gulped, then nodded.

I heard mutters of surprise from the others. Only in extreme emergencies did a biker allow another biker to ride his bike. For me, this was one of those times. I needed to be in the back of the truck with her. Sure, I could've asked Alisse or Chey to do it. They were both medical assistants, and Alisse was in nursing school, but I didn't want them to do it. It had to be me.

"I can ride with her," Alisse offered.

"No, it needs to be me. But thank you."

By the time these few conversations were done, Rhaines was back with the blanket. I took it and settled down next to her. I gestured to Ink. "Stay on that side. I'll roll her over, and then I want you to tuck this underneath her. I'll roll her again, and then we'll wrap her up. I want this tarp taken with us. There might be evidence on it. Shit, here, put on these gloves," I muttered as I got both of us a pair out of my bag. As soon as we had them on, he got the blanket ready.

Slowly and as gently as possible, I rolled her onto her side toward me. I heard him hiss. "What's wrong?" I asked hastily.

"Her back is a mess. There's blood all over it," he snarled.

"Just be careful. There's nothing we can do until we get her home."

It took us a couple of minutes to get her situated. After we did, I slid one arm under her thighs and the other under her shoulders. Lifting with my legs, like I was taught, I hoisted her up into my arms. As she settled against my chest, I tried to ignore the crazy thought that she felt right in them. She didn't weigh anything compared to what I carried when I was in the Navy. Some of those sailors and Marines had been big bastards, and carrying their asses out of a hot zone along with my equipment hadn't been an easy feat. Even all these years later, I still kept myself in peak shape so I could do it if necessary.

By the time I got to the truck, everyone else was back on their bikes. Rhaines held open the back door for me. Thankfully, it was a dual-cab. It had plenty of legroom in the back seat. He slammed the door shut once we were inside, then ran around to the driver's side. I didn't bother with a seatbelt. Although there was room to lay her on the seat partially, I didn't.

The ride back to the compound, although it wasn't too terribly far away, seemed to take forever. Every time he hit a bump, I swore at him to watch it. I couldn't help it. I watched her face the whole time to see if she would wake up or give any indication she was in too much pain. As I studied her, more details became noticeable to me despite the bruising and dirt.

She had very light-tanned skin, which was at odds with her red hair. Her eyes, when she had opened them, were a deep, dark chocolate brown, not blue or green like you might expect. Her face was delicate, with a slim, straight nose and full lips. Her chin was slightly pointed. I noticed her lashes were really long and tinted darker red than her hair. Her brows were the same color. That told me she was a natural redhead, not that it mattered.

She was of average height, which I estimated based on her length. I couldn't tell a whole lot about her body other than what I'd seen. She appeared to be fit. What struck me even more was despite the dirt and blood smell, I could still catch a faint scent of her skin. She smelled like rain and the wind to me. I inhaled deeply. Gently rubbing my thumb along her cheekbone, which was high, I whispered to her, "Who did this to you, love? Who wants you dead and why?" She didn't answer me, of course.

By the time we pulled through the gate at our compound, I was more than pissed and ready for answers. Whoever did this would be found and made to pay. I had no doubt she was innocent. I was positive that if she were an evil person who deserved this, my gut would've told me. Instead, I knew she was a victim in need of justice and maybe revenge. I waited impatiently until my door was opened. It was Sandman who opened it. He reached in.

"Here, give her to me," he said.

"Get the hell back," I snarled at him before I could stop myself. He gave me a shocked look, then stepped back with his hands in the air.

"Whatever you say, Lash."

"Sorry," I mumbled as I got out. Feeling and acting territorial wasn't like me. He was only trying to help so I could get out more easily. However, I couldn't help it. I clutched her slightly closer, even though she was plastered to me. I had to make myself ease my hold. I didn't want to risk hurting her more.

I walked briskly toward the clubhouse. I had a room set up inside as a treatment area, for lack of a better word. I'd been working on it for years. Since Alisse came along, she'd helped me to outfit it even more. Thankfully, the club had the means to do it. We might not be able to afford an X-ray machine, MRI scanner, or other high-end diagnostic equipment, but it did the job. If someone needed those or surgery, then they had to go to the hospital.

Alisse raced ahead of us. When I got to the room, she had a sheet thrown over the exam table. I lay my precious cargo down gently. The others either crowded in the doorway and hall or in the room. I faced them. "I need you all to scram. I need to examine her, and she doesn't need a bunch of witnesses."

"I can stay and help you," Alisse offered.

"Okay, thanks, that might be best. I'd hate for her to wake up and find some strange man taking her clothes off or touching her."

"We'll be in the common room. Let us know what you find," Reaper said as he shooed the others out. He gave me one last look before closing the door.

Not wasting time, Alisse and I washed our hands before we slipped on gloves. Taking it slow, I unwrapped the blanket. She shook her head. "Who would do something like this? God, why're people such animals, Lash?"

"I don't know. I think the first thing we need to do is get these clothes off and clean her up so we can see what we're dealing with. Will you get a basin of warm water and a washcloth, please?"

"I can do this part if you want."

"No, I need to do it so I can assess as we go."

Even though she was training to be a nurse, I had a lot more training than her. I'd been an Independent Navy Corpsman who served alongside sailors and Marines in the field. An IDC was equivalent to a physician assistant in the civilian world. It was an intense twelve-month training program beyond the basic corpsman training program. That schooling called A school was fourteen weeks long after basic. Even though I had a paramedic license—I could've gotten a PA one—I'd been happy with doing that. If I'd been planning to work a full-time job in healthcare, then I would've reconsidered. Despite that, I kept my skills and training up. My full-time job fulfilled my other passion. I worked at our home restoration business, Iron's Rehab, with Tinker.

While Alisse got the water, I cut away my patient's top. I used another sheet to preserve her modesty as much as possible. I'd never looked at a woman who I was treating and ever had a physical response to her. In a medical setting, she wasn't female. However, when I removed this woman's top and bra and her breasts were exposed, I noticed them. She wasn't huge, but she had more than enough.

Trying to redirect my thoughts, I covered her and then quickly cut off her shorts. She had on a tiny pair of bikini underwear, which I tried to ignore as I cut them away. I saw red curls before I hastily covered her. *Jesus, what the fuck was wrong with me?* I noticed she was female. What a sick bastard. Maybe I should let Alisse handle this. As soon as the thought entered my mind, I rejected it. I could do this.

When Alisse came back, she had two washcloths. We worked together to wash as much of the dirt, blood, and grime away as we could so we could see her injuries. She was covered in bruises underneath her clothing, just like she was on the exposed parts I saw before. There were more superficial cuts, although not as many. I examined those closely. So far, I didn't think any of them would need stitches, maybe a butterfly bandage or two. While she was out, we worked to remove the grime in the wounds. It was painful, so we might as well do it while she was unconscious.

I put off cleaning and examining her most private area. Instead, we rolled her over. I saw what Ink cursed about at the scene. Her back was raw. After we got the blood and dirt removed, it appeared to me as if someone had dragged her along on her back. There were cuts that were deeper there. Those I'd end up gluing together. Hopefully, they wouldn't scar. As we finished cleaning her, I guessed that when she was dragged, they had her legs and bottom in the air since she wasn't torn up there.

There was no escaping it. We had to do the last part. I gestured to Alisse. "You clean her down there. I don't want to violate her anymore. When you're done, we'll do the exam."

She gave me a nod before she got to work. While she did, I looked away and tried to think of something other than whether she'd been raped. Just because she had her clothes on didn't rule it out. Whoever did this could've raped her first and then got her dressed before doing the rest. Acid bubbled in my gut. I wanted to throw up and scream at the same time.

It had always bothered me when I saw a woman hurt, especially that way. I'd grown up in a tough neighborhood, similar to what Maniac had grown up in, although I hadn't dealt with the gang issues he had. It was too common to see girls and women forced, in some instances, to become prostitutes. Some did it because they didn't see another way to survive. Others did it because a man in their lives forced them to do it. It could be a father, brother, boyfriend, or husband sometimes. It had infuriated me and was one of the things that made me want to help people so much. When I went to the Navy, it was natural for me to enter the medical field.

"Okay, I'm done, Lash. I don't see any trauma, but

you take a look," she said softly.

Taking a deep breath, I looked down. I was able to ignore the fact I was looking at her pussy. She was right. There wasn't any obvious trauma, although it could be on the inside. Swallowing, I knew that I could do an internal exam, but I wouldn't. Not until she was awake and could either tell us she hadn't been raped or that she agreed to let me do the exam. I hurried to cover her up.

"Let's get her a hospital gown and get her covered. I'd like a blanket, too. I think I'll start an IV. She's probably dehydrated. We don't know how long she's been out there. Fluids won't hurt her. If she starts to show signs of pain, I'll give her some pain medicine through it, although I prefer not to do that until we know whether she has any allergies. Same thing for antibiotics."

"Sounds good. After I get her dressed, I can stay with her."

"Nah, you need to be with Arya. She's probably wondering where her mommy is. I'll stay. If I need a break, I'll let you know."

She didn't argue. While I got the IV inserted and the fluids going, she got her covered. Before she left, after we were done, I asked her one more thing. "Will you send Reaper and Maniac in here, please? I need to talk to them. They have to be going crazy wondering what's going on."

She smiled. "They all are, I bet. Sure, let me get them, and don't hesitate to call me if you need me. Ink can stay with Arya, and if he can't, Chey or Lark are more than happy to do it."

"Thanks, sweetheart," I told her. She squeezed my bicep before leaving.

I sat down beside the table. Seeing this woman on that hard table made me get back up. We had a couple of hospital beds in the room. I picked her up and juggled her IV while I moved her over to one. At least it would be slightly more comfortable. Retaking a seat, I took her hand in mine.

Her bones felt so delicate underneath her skin. I rubbed my thumb back and forth, hoping it would convey comfort to her. I wish I had a cardiac monitor. Maybe we should make that the next piece of equipment we bought. It would be helpful as hell. My mind was taken away from that thought by a soft knock at the door. "Come in," I called out.

The door opened, and my president and VP strolled in. They both looked serious. They came straight to the bed. "How is she? Alisse said you'd fill us in." Reaper immediately got to the point. That was him, Mr. No-Nonsense.

"She's bruised and cut to hell. Her back is the worst for cuts. I think someone dragged her. I had to glue a few of the lacerations. She's gonna be sore as hell when she wakes up. I'm waiting to see if she regains consciousness before I give her anything for pain or antibiotics. I don't want to give her something she's allergic to."

"Makes sense. What about, you know..." Maniac asked, then hesitated.

"Outwardly, no signs of trauma, but we won't know for sure until she can either tell us or I do an internal exam. I didn't feel right doing that when she was out. Guys, whoever did this, they intended to kill her. I have no doubt. This was beyond someone just getting upset and beating her."

They exchanged a look, and then Reaper spoke. "We've been talking. It might be best if we call the cops and let them handle this. They can take her to the hospital for that exam and hopefully find out who did this. The hospital can give her meds and call her family."

Instantly, my hackles went up. Before I could stop myself, I snapped at him. "Like hell, we will! She's staying here where I can take care of her and protect her."

A grin spread across his face. He looked at Maniac, who was smiling too. Reaper held out his hand to him. "Pay up. I told you so."

"Screw you, Reap. I didn't take the damn bet. I knew it, too, just like you and Ink did. It's those other idiots out there who don't have a clue who were saying that shit," Maniac retorted.

"Knew what? Why would you suggest we do that? We protect people from monsters, so why not her?" I asked. I was ready to argue my point. *What was wrong with them?*

"True, but we've also had a few times we let the law handle shit. As for what we knew, we knew there was no way in hell you'd let anyone take her from you.

It's good to see, brother," Reaper said.

"What's good to see? You're talking in riddles." I said in exasperation.

"It's good to see another one of us find the woman meant to be his. We need more of us, and the old ladies will welcome the company," Maniac said with a smirk.

I held up my hands. "Whoa, hold on there. No one said anything about her being anyone other than a hurt woman. You're way off base," I quickly told them, although my heart jerked as I said it.

"Oh really? Our bad. Well then, you won't mind letting one of the others sit with her. I mean, just because you're not interested in her that way doesn't mean they aren't. Several of them were talking about how attractive she was, even with all the cuts, bruises, and grime. You won't lack volunteers to play her nursemaid," Reaper added.

"Like fuck they will! Who's saying that shit?" I barked. I fisted my hands at my side.

Both of them burst out laughing. It was all I could do not to punch them. However, as they laughed, I realized what I had said and how I was acting. I took a moment as they got themselves under control to examine my knee-jerk reaction. Anger was coursing through me. The idea that any of my brothers would look at her sexually and want to be with her pissed me off. On the heels of that thought came the realization that I was the only one who needed to see her that way. Jesus Christ, they were right! I was starting to fall for a woman I didn't know a damn thing about. One I'd only exchanged a few words with.

"He's getting it," Maniac said as I sat back down.

"Shut up. You bastards don't need to be so damn happy about it. Shit, I'm insane, aren't I? I don't even know her name, and I'm acting possessive. I'm not like this," I mumbled.

"You're right, you normally aren't like this, but you're not insane. I instantly knew Chey was more the moment I laid eyes on her. The same goes for Ink and Maniac. We're just lucky that way. We know when we meet the one meant for us. Whatever brought her to this point, I have no doubt she didn't deserve it, and we'll take care of whoever did it. Right now, concentrate on getting her to wake up and on the road to recovery. We need to know who did this, so we can teach them a goddamn lesson they'll never forget. Or should I say, one that's permanent?" Reaper growled.

"Permanent," was my immediate response.

"That's what I thought. Okay, do you need anything for her or you right now?" Reaper asked. I shook my head no. "Good. If you do, let us know. Make sure you utilize the others to help watch over her. You'll need to get some sleep," he added.

"No. I don't want any of the guys in here."

"Lash, we were messing with you. None of our brothers were talking smack. A few did wonder if we were gonna call the cops, but that's it. None of them said anything about her," Maniac tried to assure me.

The problem was I knew as soon as they got

a good look at her, especially after the swelling and bruising went away, they'd notice. She was more than pretty with those marks. Without them, she'd be gorgeous. The thought that she might prefer one of my brothers tied my gut in a knot. "Still, I should stay here. She's not out of the woods yet. I'll call Alisse or one of the other women if I need a break. There's another bed in here. I can nap on it. I've slept in worse places."

They didn't argue. "We need to have church in a few. Let me get one of the ladies to sit with her. We won't take long, but we do need to discuss this as a club," Reaper reminded me. I nodded. As they left, I sat back to think about what I'd just discovered. *God, was she the one I'd been looking for? Was it that easy to find her?*

Lash: Chapter 2

I was antsy as everyone gathered for our emergency church. We usually held church on Monday nights, but this was too important to wait two more days. Everyone was gazing at me with questioning expressions. I guess Maniac and Reaper hadn't told them much, if anything. They were leaving that up to me.

I drummed my fingers on the table. Reaper's amused look made me stop. Once everyone was settled, he started the meeting. "Alright, I know everyone is ready to continue relaxing after our ride, but we have something important to discuss as if I have to tell you that. Lash, I'll turn it over to you. Fill the guys in on what you found and what we discussed."

"Sure. The woman we found has bruising all over her body. Someone beat her, and from the looks of it, they wanted to kill her. She's got cuts, too. The worst is on her back. It looks like they dragged her. Alisse and I got her cleaned up and the wounds patched. She's still unconscious. I'm waiting to see if she has any allergies before I give her meds. I'll be staying with her in the treatment room. We'll know more once she wakes up, and I can ask her questions."

"Was she raped?" Tinker asked. He grimaced as he

asked.

"I can't say for sure. She had clothes on, and there were no outward signs of trauma, but we didn't do an internal exam. I hope she'll be able to tell us when she wakes up," I told him. This set off a round of grumbles and swearing.

"So what's the plan besides waiting for her to wake up? Are we calling the cops? If we do, won't they want her to go to the hospital? You know they'll think we had something to do with it. You know how they are," Ratchet said with a sneer. He wasn't wrong. Most local cops distrusted us, but not all. If we could guarantee we got the ones who didn't, that would be one thing, but we couldn't.

"I don't think we should call the cops. Even after she wakes up, I don't know if it'll be safe for her to go home. Whoever did this could find her again. I think the best bet is to keep our mouths shut for now. The longer the animal who hurt her thinks she's dead, the better. It'll give us time to find him and kill the fucker," I growled.

"Do you think it was just one person?" Shadow asked.

"I can't say. I did notice her knuckles were swollen, bruised, and scraped up. She fought back," I told him.

"That's all we know right now. Until we know more, we'll keep her here. The ladies will be helping Lash to keep an eye on her," Reaper jumped in to add.

"We can help, too," Mayhem said.

"That won't be necessary, but thanks," I said quickly. I hoped that I could leave it at that. I should've known Ink, Maniac, and Reaper wouldn't let it slide. They grinned, and then Ink cleared his throat. I glared at them. It didn't work to keep their mouths shut. I swear to God, nothing was sacred in this damn club.

"In case you haven't noticed, Lash is a little possessive. We'll have to cut him some slack. He's not liking other men around his woman," Ink said as he winked at me.

I gave him the finger and mouthed *fucker*. Goddamn it, they had to go there. It wasn't like I'd wrapped my head around the possibility they were right yet. Couldn't they give a guy a break? As I thought that, while the guys started to make their teasing comments, I remembered I hadn't been that restrained with them. Shit, payback time. I hated when stuff came back to bite me in the ass.

"Oh really? He's already claiming her? What the hell? What if we want a chance?" Romulus asked. The other remarks were more razzing me. I narrowed my gaze on him. He smiled at me. He was closer to what I thought her age might be.

"What if I want to shove your head up your ass to see if you can find your brains?" I shot back.

The cocky asshole laughed. "You can try, but I think I can take you, old man."

The bastard! I was only a dozen years older. I was

hardly Methuselah. I went to stand up. Before I got all the way out of my chair, his twin, Remus, smacked him on the back of the head. "Shut it, dumbass. He's gonna kill you, and then I'll have to tell Mom. She'll blame me for not stopping you."

"Hey, I'm only yanking his chain. You know I'll never go there if a brother has claimed a woman. Is that what you're doing, Lash? Should she be considered spoken for?"

"Don't you think she should have a say?" Crusher asked.

I wanted to protest, but I couldn't. Everyone was getting ahead of themselves. There was no guarantee she was even single or interested. It was insane to be talking like this.

"Enough. No one is claiming anyone. We'll let Lash get back to work, and we'll see what happens after she wakes up. Until then, we'll keep our mouths shut to outsiders about her and our eyes and ears open to see if anyone says anything about a missing woman. Alright, get your asses out of my sight. I've looked at you too long today," Reaper said.

I was out of my chair, out the door, and headed to the treatment room like a flash. They called after me, laughing. Like I said, bastards. I was halfway back to her when I heard yelling and a scream from the treatment room. I took off running. I heard boots thundering behind me, but I didn't stop or look to see who it was.

The door was open. Lark was coming out when I got there. She looked relieved when she saw me. "She's freaking out. All we were doing was sitting with her," she said hurriedly.

I gave her a chin lift as I passed her. Inside, I saw Alisse with her. She was trying to get her to calm down. It wasn't happening. The redhead was climbing out of the bed despite the look of agony on her face. She was slapping at Alisse's hands as she tried to get the agitated woman to lie still. Rushing the bed, I gently moved Alisse aside and reached out toward the woman. I swear I saw relief on her bruised face.

"Hey, hey, there's no need for that. You're safe. No one's gonna hurt you. We've been worried about you. It's good to see you awake."

As my hands wrapped around her upper arms, she sagged. Her eyes rolled in the back of her head. I caught her. As gently as I could, I lowered her to the bed as I called out to her. Nothing. As soon as she was down, I grabbed my stethoscope and cuff by the bed where I'd left them earlier to be accessible. Working fast, I checked her vital signs. Her pulse and blood pressure were higher than they had been, but that wasn't unusual after the screaming and fighting she'd done. What the hell had made her faint? Was she that terrified, or was it something more?

"I'm sorry. I tried," Alisse said. She wrung her hands together.

"It's alright. She's confused and scared. Imagine waking up to strangers in a strange place," I told her.

I grabbed a penlight and opened her eyelids to check her pupils. They responded sluggishly. Fuck, I'd been so busy checking the rest of her earlier I hadn't thoroughly examined her head. Dropping the light, I began to feel gently all over her head. It wasn't until I got to the back of it, on the left side, that I felt the lump. Shit, it was a big one. She was likely concussed, or at least partially. Some damn medic I was. "Fuck," I swore.

"What's wrong?" both women asked. I vaguely noticed that the guys were watching us from the open doorway. A few were standing just inside it.

"She's got a knot back here. No wonder she's confused and fighting. Alisse, get me the smelling salts. We need to see if we can wake her up. If we can't, then we might need to have her seen at the hospital after all."

It was the last thing I wanted to do, but we weren't equipped to test her for a brain bleed or to treat it here. As much as I hated the idea of letting someone else take care of her, I would if it was best for her. Alisse handed me the ampoule. I broke it and then waved it under her nose. She moved away with a frown on her face. I did it again. The second pass had her opening her eyes.

There was confusion and panic in them. She locked eyes with me. *"Pozhaluysta,"* she whispered hoarsely, then she closed them again.

I wasn't sure, but it sounded like she was speaking Russian or another Slavic language. I didn't know any of those. I glanced over at the door. I spotted Crusher. He saw me looking at him. He came into the room and walked over to the bed.

"She said please. Obviously, she's either partially

Russian or knows the language. Do you want me to ask her something in Russian?" I knew he'd understand and be able to communicate with her. His mom was Russian. He grew up speaking the language. I was his cousin, but not on that side of his family.

"She spoke English before, but sure, why not."

"*Kak tebya zovut?*" he asked her. Her eyes flew open, and she stared at him in shock. I thought it would ease once she realized he knew her language, but instead, it changed to fear. She tried to move away from him.

"What did you say to her?" I snapped.

"I asked her, 'What's your name?'"

"Why would that scare her? Hey, beautiful, look at me. You have nothing to fear from us. What's your name? Mine is Lash."

Her gaze landed on our cuts. Her eyes widened more. She began to shake her head and held up her hands. "No, please. I'm sorry."

"You have nothing to be sorry for either. All we want to know is what to call you and what happened to you?" I told her. She moaned as she moved again.

"Hold still. You're beat to hell. I can give you something for the pain, but not until you tell me if you're allergic to anything. But first, tell me your name. Surely that's not too much to ask." I smiled when I said it, hoping it would make her see that we meant no harm to her.

"You don't know me?"

"No, we don't. We found you along the road..." I let it peter off, indicating I needed her name.

"My name is Troian," she said softly. She pronounced it try-yan. I'd never heard it before, but I liked it. It was unusual, and something told me she was too.

"It's a pleasure to meet you, Troian. Do you have any allergies?"

She frowned and shrugged. I decided to ask another question before getting her anything for pain. "Tell us who did this to you. We're here to help, but we have to know who to go after."

She didn't say anything for several moments. As I waited, I noticed her frown grew worse. She shook her head. "I don't know."

Well, hell, that made things more difficult. "Okay, tell us your last name and where you live. Do you live here in Bristol?" I'd never seen her before, but it was possible I'd merely missed her in a town of over forty thousand. If you counted the Tennessee and Virginia sides together, it was a possibility.

Her frown grew, and she rubbed her temple. "I-I don't know. Bristol? Where's that?" she asked softly and hesitantly.

"We're in Bristol, Virginia. You're at the Iron Punishers' compound. We're a motorcycle club. Are you saying that you don't remember your last name? Tell me. What do you remember?"

She looked around the room at all of us. It had to be intimidating to be faced with so many people she didn't know and for them to be mainly big bikers on top of it. God knows we scared the shit out of people all the time.

"Let's clear out of here and give her a chance to think. Go, I'll let you know what I find out. Crusher, I'd like you to stay. Reaper, Maniac, you can too if you want. Ladies, if you would stay too. It will be more comfortable for Troian." I smiled at her. She gave me an ever-so-faintest one back.

Once the others were gone, I silently waited as she thought. You could almost see the wheels turning in her head. She frowned hard. I couldn't resist reaching over and rubbing the lines on her brow. "Don't force it. It'll come when it's ready. Do you recall anything, sweetheart?"

"I remember you. And loud, angry voices, darkness, and pain. So much pain, but that's it. What's wrong with me? Why can't I remember?"

"You have a big lump on the back of your head. I think you were hit. It's likely you have a concussion. Trauma like that can make you forget things. Your body and mind have been through a lot. Don't panic. Try to relax."

"Will my memories come back, or will I never know who I am and what happened? How can I know that my first name is Troian but nothing else?"

"The brain works in funny ways. I'm not an expert, and we'd have to do tests, but I think you might have retrograde amnesia. Your recent memories are affected first, then the older ones. I'm not sure why you remember your first name but not your last. You know how to talk and move. I assume you know how to dress yourself and walk."

"Of course I do."

"Good. It could take hours, maybe days, or weeks, to get them back. It's a very, very tiny number who don't. I wouldn't worry about that. Right now, we want you to heal. I can give you something for the pain. I'll do that first to be sure you don't have a reaction since you don't know if you have allergies. Once I know you're good, I want to put you on antibiotics."

"Why antibiotics?"

"You have several cuts and scrapes. We cleaned them as well as we could, but I don't want you to get an infection," I told her. She shifted and then cried out, rolling onto her side.

"Your back is pretty raw. It looks like you were dragged. Try to stay on your side. Here, let me get the pain meds," I said as I hurried over to unlock the cabinet where we kept them. My brothers and their old ladies were trustworthy, but there were people in and out of the clubhouse on party nights. You could never be too careful.

As I drew up the medicine in a syringe so I could inject it into her IV, Crusher moved closer. I had to stop myself from telling him to stay back. He was giving her a tender look. "*Privet, dorogaya, menya zovut Krasher.*"

"*Privet, Krasher, priyatno poznakomit'sya. Menya zovut Troyan,*" was her immediate response. I hated not knowing what was being said. She gave him a startled look. "*Otkuda ya znayu russkiy?*"

"Hey, English for those of us who don't understand," I asked.

"Oh, I'm sorry," she said contritely.

"It's okay. I just like knowing what you're saying."

"I told her my name is Crusher," my brother explained.

"And I told him it was nice to meet him and my name is Troian. Then I realized I understood him and was speaking Russian. I asked him how I knew Russian. Shouldn't I have forgotten that too?"

"Again, it's probably one of your first memories. Those stick with you longer," I explained again.

"Your English is almost flawless. You've obviously been speaking both since you were a baby. It's good to speak Russian again," Crusher told her with a smile.

"How do you know it?"

"My mom is Russian. I grew up speaking both, like you. People rarely know I do unless the rare word comes out or I've been talking to my mom. Then it makes my accent pronounced."

As they talked, I injected the med. It would take

effect fast. I knew it was petty, but I broke their bonding moment. "I hate to interrupt, but we need to talk. This medicine will probably make you sleepy, so we have to be quick. Crusher, you can go now. She obviously understands and speaks English. If she slips up, I'll just ask her to translate."

I heard a snort. I think it was from Maniac. Crusher gave me a knowing glance, then nodded. "Sure, no problem. It was nice to meet you officially, Troian," he said as he made his way to the door.

"You too, Crusher," she called out.

Right before he left, he looked back at her. "Anytime you want to chat, just let me know. I'll be more than happy to do it." He winked at her and smirked at me before shutting the door.

I swear to God, if he were trying to move in on her, I'd kill him, family or not. Maniac and Reaper were trying not to grin. I glared at them. The ladies were turned away, so I couldn't see their faces. Troian gave me a puzzled look. I pasted a smile on my face. I leaned closer. The next part would likely make her uncomfortable, but I had to ask.

"Troian, I hate to ask this, but it's important. Alisse, over there, and I were the ones to clean you up and examine you. I treated your wounds. However, there was one thing we didn't do, and I hope we won't need to." I hesitated for a moment, then just told her. "We didn't see external evidence that you'd been violated, but there could be internal signs. In order to treat you effectively, we have to know. Were you raped?"

She instantly shrank away from me and lowered her gaze. The guys and Lark moved further away to give us privacy. Even though I said it quietly, they heard. Alisse stepped closer and gave her an encouraging smile. Fuck, she had been. I wanted to roar out my rage.

"I don't know if I have or not. I don't think so, but..." she whispered.

I sat down on the bed and took her hand. "Okay, I know this is embarrassing, but we need to know. I'd like to examine you. Everyone but Alisse will leave. She's going to school to be a nurse, so she's my assistant."

"Are you a doctor? Is that how you know all this?"

"No, not really. I was a Navy corpsman, which is like a physician assistant. I've been trained to do most things a doctor can do. I promise I know what I'm doing. I'll make it as quick and painless as possible. If you have been, I'll take samples. I have a friend who can run tests to see if we might be able to identify who did it. It'll allow me to know how to treat you so you heal. I can give you the morning-after pill, just in case." It was bad enough thinking she'd been raped, but to be pregnant and have to deal with that, would be even harder.

She shook her head. My heart sank. She wasn't gonna let me do it. Then she spoke and surprised me. "I can't take that pill. I don't believe in it. If I'm pregnant, then it is God's will. The baby isn't to blame for what its father did. Go ahead and do the exam before I chicken out. I'm terrified to know but more terrified not to."

Her answer stunned me. It took me a couple of

seconds to get my ass in gear. Once I did, I started by clearing the room, although it was hardly necessary. Reaper, Lark, and Maniac were already headed for the door. Alisse went to prepping my equipment. It was sad that as part of the training I did with her, so she could learn and assist me better, I'd shown her how to prep for a rape exam.

There had been too many women we knew and called friends who'd suffered that awful crime and others we helped to rescue. Plus, when I was in the Navy, I hated to admit that I'd performed more than a few. Sometimes, it was a fellow sailor or Marine who did it, and other times, it was civilians. Regardless, it was always uncomfortable and embarrassing for the woman.

Alisse draped the covers over Troian and placed a stool at the bottom of the bed. I could move her to the table again. It had stirrups that pulled out, but I didn't want to hurt her. I could do it here. Taking a seat, I gave her an encouraging smile. "I'll be fast. You tell me if anything hurts, okay?"

She nodded, then closed her eyes. Alisse came closer and gathered her hand in hers. I saw Troian squeeze it. Taking a deep breath, I prepared myself. I hated the thought of examining her for this reason. I wanted to stay impassive and unemotional, but I couldn't. The longer I was around this woman, the more she was pulling me in. It felt like my brothers were right. I'd be claiming her if she'd allow it. Who knows if she'd ever let a man touch her, especially if she'd been raped?

"You'll feel my hand on your knee. I'm just running it up your leg so you get used to me touching you, and then you'll feel me touch you between your legs. I have to insert a speculum so I can see. It might be uncomfortable. Try to relax."

She answered me by relaxing her legs wider. Running my hands up her thighs, I noticed, despite the bruising, how toned they were and how soft her skin was. *Get your mind out of the gutter,* I lectured myself. I wasn't totally impersonal as I looked at her. She had short dark red curls protecting her most private place. I swallowed as I parted her folds. Working fast, I inserted the lubricated speculum. She hissed and flinched but didn't tell me to stop. Widening it, I turned on the small light I had clipped to it, an OptiSpec. Looking inside, I froze.

I took a quick second look before withdrawing it. My heart pounded. I glanced up at her. She was now looking at me with fear on her face. "Did they?" she asked. I shook my head no.

"How do you know for sure?"

"Oh, I'm sure. You haven't been raped, Troian. There's no need for testing or medicine."

"Maybe there was no damage. What if they gave me something?"

Her fear made me say what I didn't want to say. How did you tell a woman what I'd just discovered? I had no experience with this. "I know because you're still a virgin. You have a hymen." As soon as I said it, her face turned beet red, and she gasped before looking away.

"That's a good thing. We know for sure no one hurt you that way. Everyone is a virgin at some point," Alisse told her with a smile. She patted her hand. "Come on. Let's get you straightened up. How's your pain? Is the medicine working yet?" She went right into nurse mode. I was proud of her. She put Troian more at ease and allowed me time to gather my scattered thoughts.

The last thing I expected was to find out she was untouched. My first response after the shock was satisfaction which was a total possessive and asshole thought. I couldn't help but be pleased that no one had ever touched her. As my satisfaction wore off, the disbelief came. I didn't know how old she was, but my guess was mid-twenties. For a woman to get to that age and still be a virgin was almost unheard of, especially one who looked like her. The bruises and swelling couldn't disguise the beautiful woman underneath. What the hell? Had she been raised in a strict religious community like Cassia, Blade's woman, down in Dublin Falls? Or was there another reason?

Those thoughts kept running amok in my head as I cleaned up the equipment and let Alisse settle her. Troian yawned. Deciding I'd procrastinated long enough, I walked over to her. Her cheeks were still pink when she looked at me. I ignored it. "Why don't you rest? I need to go take care of a few things. Alisse, can you stay with her, or should I ask Lark or Chey? Arya might want her mommy."

She shook her head. "She's fine. She's all about her daddy, anyway. I'm just the one who carried her for nine months, spent hours in labor birthing her, and he's the one she goes to. It's not fair. She even said Dada first. Little ingrate," she said with a laugh.

Troian giggled. "They do seem to like to do that. Moms always get the raw end of the deal." As soon as she said it, she jerked. "How do I know that? God, this is frustrating. I hope my memory comes back soon. I don't know if I can stand this. I feel stupid."

"You're not stupid. Pushing yourself will only make it take longer. Rest and I'll be back soon. If you need me, text me," I told Alisse. Before I said something I shouldn't, I got the hell out of there. I took a detour and went into my old room at the clubhouse. Even though I didn't live here anymore, I had the space if I needed it. Sinking down on the bed, I got to work on trying to figure out my thoughts and feelings. I'd update the others in a bit.

Troian: Chapter 3

Three days. Three days without a clue who I was or what happened to me. Sure, I knew my name was Troian, and I'd been badly beaten. It terrified me to think someone or several someones out there hated me enough to want me dead. And I had no clue who they were. How could I protect myself from them when I didn't know?

I talked about my fears with the ladies. I'd found that the Iron Punishers weren't what I thought a biker club would be like. Where my knowledge came from, I had no idea. I just knew it. Just like I knew the answer to trivia questions on the game shows that I watched as I lay in bed. It kept my mind active, at least. I hated not doing anything. The women were nice enough to bring me books to read, which I enjoyed tremendously. They helped to keep me still.

When I attempted to get up yesterday, Lash had a fit. He ordered me to stay in bed and rest. I knew he was only looking out for me, but I didn't care if it hurt. I had to move, or it would take longer to get better. Again, how I knew that, I didn't know. Well, it had been long enough. I was getting up today, no matter what he said.

I'd at least gotten them to let me be alone for short periods of time. I argued I had a way to call if I needed help. Besides, they had other things to do. Cheyenne, Lark, and Alisse all had small kids. The children needed them more than I did. I could get to the bathroom on my own, even if Lash thought I needed to be accompanied. The first day, he insisted on carrying me, which I found uncomfortable and exciting at the same time.

I was uncomfortable having a stranger help me do something so private. I was excited because being around Lash made my heart beat faster, and this energy, like an electrical current, buzzed through me. I knew it was wrong, and I should put a stop to it. He was my doctor, nothing else. He was unfailingly kind and helpful, but I got no indication he saw me as a woman. Why I wasn't happy about that, I didn't examine too closely. I had other things to worry about, like staying alive.

I'd met with Reaper and the other officers. They were an intimidating bunch. They informed me that until they thought otherwise, I would be their guest, and they'd keep me hidden. They were eager to find out who had done this to me and make them pay. I wasn't sure what they meant by making them pay. Reaper told me I was in their compound and I'd stay there, inside the fence, where it was safe. The outside world wasn't.

Lark was aiding my escape from the confines of the bed. She seemed to understand my need to move more than the others. Maybe it was because she'd been bedridden herself. I noticed she walked with a cane. She saw me staring at it and explained her history. It was heartbreaking yet inspiring at the same time. I cried when I heard about her son Flynn and how they came to adopt him.

Due to my bruises and cuts, she brought me a dress and a pair of flip-flops. We were the same height, and the dress was a loose, flowing one, so I knew it would fit okay. We were both about the same size on top, even if she had more curves on the bottom than I did. I was jealous of her. While I was fit, I kinda wished I had a defined hourglass shape.

I was dressed, which was a struggle, but I'd never admit it. I sat on the edge of the bed to catch my breath and steel myself. Lash had switched me over to pain pills. I tried not to take them because they made me sleepy. I wanted to be awake and to remember. When I slept, all I did was dream these crazy, horrible dreams. Never did I see who hurt me, but I knew the dreams were from that night.

Taking a deep breath, I stood up. The room didn't whirl this time. That was a good sign. Walking slowly and using the furniture as I went, I walked toward the door. When I opened it and stepped into the hallway, it was a major accomplishment for me. I wanted to cheer, but I didn't. Keeping a hand on the wall to steady myself, I looked both ways. I could hear voices coming from the right. I moved that way.

When I entered the room where everyone seemed to be, I was a little overwhelmed. I'd met some of the club members over the past few days, but not all of them. Seeing them all together and dressed in their leather cuts and sporting tattoos was rather terrifying. Any one of them could crush me with one hand. Was I crazy to put my faith in them? What if they were just playing with me because... A quick flash of a face came to mind as I was thinking of someone telling them to keep me here. It made my head throb. I cried out despite trying not to. Who was that man in my head? Was he a memory?

My cry got their attention. I heard one of them swear. "Goddamn it. What's she doing up?"

Someone else said, "We'd better get her back to her room before Lash sees her."

My pain spiked, and more images of that angry man's hate-filled eyes glaring at me flashed through my mind faster. It made me feel sick. Suddenly, I felt hands on my arms. I lashed out without thinking. All I knew was I had to protect myself. I had to get away. I screamed as I hit someone. It didn't do me any good. I hit a chest that felt like a brick wall, but I didn't dare stop. I had to get away. They were gonna kill me. Voices were coming from far away. They sounded garbled, but they were loud. The hands wouldn't let go.

I screamed again and fought harder. "No, I won't let you do this. He deserved it!"

Abruptly, one voice came into focus, and I could understand what was being said. I even knew who it was. All those hands disappeared, and new ones grabbed me. I was hauled against a hard chest. This one, I didn't fight. I knew I was safe. It was Lash. I somehow recognized his touch and the smell of him. I sagged against him.

"Troian, it's Lash. You're safe. No one's gonna hurt you. Do you know where you're at?"

All the other voices had gone quiet. Slowly, I lifted my head and glanced around. People were standing everywhere, staring at me. Shame filled me. I buried my face in Lash's chest. What the hell just happened?

"I'm sorry," I mumbled.

"You have nothing to be sorry about. What're you doing out here? You should be resting. Let me help you back to your room."

I lifted my head again to look at him. "No, I don't want to go back there. I'm sore from lying around so much. I need to move. That's why I came out here. I'm not sure what triggered that. I didn't recognize any of you, and then I saw him." I whimpered a little at the end.

"If you won't go back to your bed, then at least sit with me. Here," Lash said as he gently led me to a nearby table. He pulled out a chair and gestured for me to sit. I refused to admit I needed it. My legs were weak. Once I was seated, he sat next to me.

"Who did you see?" he asked with curiosity in his voice and on his face.

"I don't know! All I saw was a man's angry face. He was yelling. I was scared and knew he was gonna kill me. I don't know his name or who he is. God, when will I get my memory back? I can't stay here forever. Someone could be missing me."

"It's okay. Don't push it. It's only been three days. Yes, someone could be missing you, but if they are, they haven't reported you missing," he told me.

"How do you know that?" I snapped.

"Because our brother, Spawn, has been looking," he said.

"Looking? How? If you don't know my last name, how do you know who to look for? Or where? I might not even be from Virginia," I protested. I wasn't sure why I was arguing with him.

"Troian, may I join you? We haven't met yet. I'm Spawn. I think I can explain what Lash means," a super tall, handsome man said. He was standing near the table. I nodded. He came the rest of the way over and pulled out a chair on the other side of me. I turned so I could see him. I noticed he was carrying a laptop. He opened it and tapped on the keyboard.

"Give me a second, and then I'll explain," he said. I waited. When he was done, he glanced up at me and smiled. "So, what Lash meant about me looking is that I've been searching the police missing person reports for not only Virginia but all the states surrounding us. No one has reported anyone named Troian or matching your description as missing."

"Maybe I'm from another state. How in the world are you able to search police reports?"

"I've considered that possibility, so I started to expand it to other states. To speed things up, I asked a friend of ours to help. He can do it much faster than I can. Also, he has contacts and resources I don't."

"I appreciate you doing that. Thank your friend for me. You still haven't explained how you can do it.

Do you work with the police or something?" If he did, what did he think of the club not reporting my assault to them?

He laughed. "No, sweetness, I don't work for the cops. They wouldn't want someone like me helping them. The reason I can do it is because I'm a hacker. I've got my fingers in a lot of places. It's what I do. What I love."

"Motorcycle clubs have hackers?" was my immediate response. Those standing around all chuckled. I was glad that I amused them. What I was thinking must've shown on my face because Reaper spoke hastily.

"No one is laughing at you, honey. We're laughing at your astonishment. Yeah, it might sound odd, but all the clubs we're friends with, at least, have someone who's an expert on computers and performs duties as needed for their club and others. The friend he referred to is named Smoke. He's part of the Archangel's Warriors. They're down in Dublin Falls, Tennessee. Their sister chapter is in Hunters Creek, Tennessee. Anyway, Smoke is more than a hacker. He works with the government at times, although we don't exactly know what he does for them. His old lady, Everly, is like him. I don't think there's anyone like those two in the world. Don't get me wrong, Spawn here is no slouch, but they're royalty in his world."

"Hey, I'm not offended. I learn something new from them all the time. Anyway, while that's happening, I've been searching for something else." He glanced at Lash and then Reaper.

"What?" Lash asked sharply.

"Well, even though we don't have a last name or town, her name isn't exactly common. I did a search of the US Census Bureau for everyone in the country named Troian, even if it was their last name. I set some parameters. There were only three women in her age group. I believe I've found you. I was coming to tell you guys when I heard the commotion."

He grinned as he turned his laptop to face me. On the screen was my face. I gasped. Quickly scanning it, I saw my last name was Kriska. I was twenty-six, and the address, if it was correct, said I lived in Richmond, Virginia. I tried out the name in my head. Troian Eva Kriska. It had a nice ring to it, but it didn't stir any recognition. I hit the table with my fist. The guys gave me a surprised look. Lash reached over to rub my upper arm.

"Sweetheart, there's no need to get upset. I take it the name doesn't ring any bells?"

"No, it doesn't. I can see it's me in the picture. How is it that even with all this, I don't recognize my own goddamn name? Ugh, think," I said mostly to myself as I hit the side of my head with my fist. Lash growled and grabbed my arm before I could do it a second time.

"Stop hitting yourself. I won't sit here and let you do that shit. That's not gonna work anyway. We know you're frustrated. I'm sorry. But at least we've got stuff we can work with now. With this name and the address, Spawn can find out about your life and your friends and family. We'll figure out why no one has reported you missing, and hopefully, we'll be able to determine who did this to you."

"What if you can't? You're assuming it's someone I know. It could've been a stranger. A crime of opportunity or whatever," I argued.

"Or a crime of passion. Maybe it was an ex. He got jealous you were with someone else, and he took it out on you," another man suggested. I scanned his cut. I'd learned that was what their leather vests were called. Cheyenne had taught me that. I knew for the guys, on the front was their road name, or what I called a nickname. I squinted to bring his name into focus. I saw it read *Ratchet*.

The ladies wore one, too, but it was a property cut, and the name on it was the name designated by their man. It was confusing since most people didn't call them those names like they did the men. They used their actual names. On the back, it had the name of the man who claimed them. They were proclaimed as property, which had made my hackles rise, but all three women had explained it wasn't as bad as it sounded. I had to take their word for it.

"Why would you think that?" I asked him.

"Because a woman as beautiful as you would drive a man to do a lot of things. Of course, I'd never beat you. I'd beat the hell out of the guy and warn him to stay the fuck away. You, I'd keep cuffed to the bed and sexed up until you saw the light," he said with a huge smirk on his face.

He wiggled his eyebrows, which made me laugh rather than get offended or scared. I thought he was kidding. Apparently, Lash didn't. I heard a loud growl come out of him, and then he was on his feet with the front of Ratchet's shirt in his fist. He jerked him close and was right in his face.

"You need to back it the fuck off, brother, before you get something you don't want," he warned him.

"Lash, stop. He's only joking," I told him. I got to my feet and wavered. He instantly let go of Ratchet and swiftly put an arm around me. He eased me down on the chair.

"Are you okay? Do you feel dizzy?"

"Just unsteady for a moment. Why did you do that to him? He was joking."

"He knows why. I'll explain later. Right now, let's talk about whoever beat you. They either brought you here and beat you or drove you here afterward to dump you. Richmond is almost five hours away. We should see if anyone has noticed strangers hanging around town or someone asking questions. If I dumped a body, I'd be anxious to hear if it was found or not."

I shivered at the thought. It was weird to know he was referring to me as the body being dumped.

"You know who might know? Jonas. That boy knows everything and a lot of it is shit he shouldn't. I can ask him when I see him this week at the Fortress," Maniac said, causing me to jump. "Sorry, did I scare you? I didn't mean to."

"You're fine. I was just in my head, and you startled me. Who's Jonas, and what's the Fortress? Is that code for something else that's biker-ish that I don't know? I swear, I need a manual to keep up."

This made the guys laugh. "That's a good idea. We should think about putting one together. That way, when we find a new old lady, we can just hand it to her and have her read it," Maniac said.

"Or an old man. Don't forget Tiger and Thorn and Bandit and Coyote," Crusher said. He sat down on the other side of me and flashed me a smile. I couldn't help but smile back. I felt comfortable with him. I think it might be because we had a common background of being Russian. Kriska was, for sure, a Russian surname.

"Dare I ask who they are? And you still haven't answered my other questions," I reminded them.

"The fortress is the Fortress of Bravery. It's a youth outreach center that Lark created in town. They help kids who are the most at risk to join gangs or have other challenges. Jonas is one of the teenagers who goes there. He's about to turn eighteen soon. He lives in one of the worst areas. Even though he's been able to avoid joining a gang, he knows a bunch of people who are in them, and they talk to him. He might be able to find something out.

"Now, as for who's Tiger and Thorn. They're two Warriors club brothers in Dublin Falls who ended up claiming a woman, Neriah, but they also claimed each other. They're all together in one of those throuple relationships, or whatever you call it. I get confused about which one has the guys sexually involved and which isn't. Anyway, they are definitely sexually involved. In the same chapter are two other brothers, Bandit and Coyote. No one knew they were together either. There's no woman in their relationship. We have to make it for either sex," Crusher said matter-of-factly.

I was stunned. I would've thought these very alpha, macho men would be against anything that dealt with couples or throuples containing the same sex. They didn't seem to have a problem with it. Or was it because it wasn't their club?

"Oh, don't forget, they have Steel, Hammer, and Regan too. In their case, Steel and Hammer are only sexually involved with Regan. Damn, that's crazy when you think about it. What's in the water down there?" Ink mused.

"The same thing that has them popping kids out as if their lives depend on it. They're fertile as hell." Reaper chuckled.

"Hey, give us a few more women, and we'll be competing with them. Hunters Creek is the same. It's just our superior biker sperm," Mayhem joked. Or maybe he wasn't joking. He had a satisfied look on his face.

"Wow, you certainly have interesting friends. They'd be fun to meet, I think. As for Jonas, as long as he won't get into trouble or anything for asking, please do. If we can be sure no one is lurking around waiting for my body to be found, I can leave the compound."

"Leave? And go where?" Lash asked sharply.

"Well, I can't go back home. There's no telling how long it'll take to find out who did this to me. I'll have to make a living, which means getting a job and a place to live. I can only do that if I can freely move around town."

"You have a place to stay. Here. If you need something, just tell me. I don't want you pushing yourself to get a job. Your memory hasn't returned, and your body has a long way to go to heal. You need to rest. Besides, we can't be too careful. Even if whoever did this isn't in town now, they could show up at any time," Lash argued.

I hadn't thought of that, but I knew I couldn't stay here forever. Going home to family, assuming I had any, wouldn't be wise. Something in my gut told me that to do that would be a huge mistake.

"True, but I'm not staying here and freeloading off you guys for weeks or months either. Spawn, how long will it take to find out if I have family or friends in Richmond?"

"I doubt long, but it'll still be too dangerous to contact them, Troian. We don't know if they're involved," he warned me. I wearily closed my eyes for a moment. I was suddenly running out of energy. I needed a nap. What the hell?

"That's enough for now. Spawn, you let me know what you find. In the meantime, Troian needs to rest. She's tired. Come on, I'll take you back. Before you go to sleep, there's something we need to talk about," Lash said as he stood up and pulled my chair back. As I rose to my feet to follow him, he surprised me by picking me up.

"Lash, I can walk! There's no need to carry me."

"I'm not taking a chance you'll fall. I'll see you guys later," he told them before striding off. I heard them call out that they'd see us later. I waved since he wasn't giving me a chance to say goodbye. I watched his face as he carried me. God, he was so handsome. I could stare at him all day, although I'd better not. Instead of thinking about him, I needed to think about what I had forgotten.

Lash: Chapter 4

I could admit it. I hadn't reacted well to Ratchet's comment to Troian. I hadn't liked Crusher sitting next to her either. Christ, what was wrong with me? I'd never in my almost forty years been possessive of a woman. I didn't just get territorial but wanted to growl and mark her. If this was what Reaper, Maniac, and Ink felt like all the time, I needed to apologize and get them a lifetime supply of Valium or something. Here was the biggest kicker. My brothers weren't giving her vibes like they wanted her naked or anything overly sexual in nature.

What the hell would I do if some guy did that? Fuck, orange wasn't my color. Well, okay, it was, but I didn't want to live in it twenty-four-seven. I'd have to either get control of myself or make sure I was the slickest, sneakiest motherfucker on the planet not to get caught when I killed them. I'd need stock in Home Depot to cover the shovels I was gonna need. Maybe a backhoe would be better. Yep, it was official. I'd gone around the bend, and there was no hope for me. This conversation with myself in my head said it all. Shit, there I go again.

Shaking my head to clear out the chatter, hopefully, I went back to working on the custom cabinets I was making for one of our current restoration jobs. They were going to be used in a house built in

1900. The new owner wanted it to be brought back to its original look, only with the modern conveniences. I was also making a China cabinet that would be built into the wall.

Usually, working with wood and my hands allowed me to become calm and blank out my mind. All I concentrated on was the feel of the wood, the grain, and what the piece said to me. Sometimes, I had to make it to match a specific design request, and other times, I could get creative and see what happened. I made things so that if they didn't end up in a house rehab we were doing, we could sell them in our storefront. I wasn't the only guy who did that. People were willing to pay big for custom work. Iron's Rehab made a nice profit for the club. Add onto my cut the bulk of the money paid for my custom work, and I did more than alright.

I'd never imagined my love of wood and making things that I developed as a kid from watching my grandpa work would help me make a living. He taught me what he knew. My house, while built by others for the framing, walls, and construction, had my cabinetry and furniture in it. It truly felt like home. I loved it.

It was my house that I had thought about before, which led me to think of Troian. After we left the common room the other day and I took her to lie down, I brought up her moving out of the treatment room to somewhere more comfortable. That had been an interesting, if frustrating, talk.

She lay on the bed, staring back at me. I was slightly anxious about what I wanted to talk to her about. The thought had been in the back of my mind since yesterday, but today, it solidified the need to talk about it. She was becoming mobile. The reality was I didn't want her wandering the clubhouse when I wasn't here. God knows what she might see or hear. What if one of my brothers did decide to see if he had a chance with her? Sure, they knew I was interested, but she hadn't been claimed. Technically, she was a free agent. Nope, I couldn't go there.

"What did you want to talk about, Lash? I can see it's making you restless. Is there something wrong that I don't know?" she asked with a cute frown on her face. The swelling had almost gone away. She was still bruised, but that didn't disguise her beauty.

"No, no, nothing like that. I want to talk to you about getting out of this room. It's not meant to be a permanent place to stay. You're healing, and I don't think we need you to stay here."

"Oh, well, I can move. That's not a big deal. Which room do you want me to move to? I won't be taking one of the guys' spaces, will I? I won't do that. I'm here as a guest. This is their home." She sat up as if she was planning to do it right now. I held up my hand so she'd stop.

"I didn't mean right this second. As for where, no, you won't be taking one of my brothers' rooms or, in fact, any of the rooms in the clubhouse."

"Then where? I can't stay in town, right? You said it's not safe. Do you have some kinda guest housing or something here?"

I needed to stop dancing around it and just tell her. "No, we don't have that, although we need to do it. With us adding old ladies, some might have families who want to visit. *Plus, our allied clubs do come to visit, and they have families. There are empty rooms here that can be used. Anyway, I have a house that I just recently built on the compound. It's got more than enough room, and I thought you could move there. That way, if you have medical needs or need help, I'm close. It would get you somewhere quieter, more private, and the bed will be a helluva lot more comfortable than this one,"* I said in a rush, then held my breath, waiting to see if she'd say yes. If she didn't, I had more reasons why she should.

Her eyes widened a little, and her mouth slightly opened and then closed. She blinked a couple of times and then found her voice. "Lash, I can't thank you enough for all you and the club have done for me, and you, especially. You've barely left my side. I can never thank you or repay you adequately, but I don't want to invade your privacy. That's too much. I'll be fine in one of the extra rooms. The bed in it has to be more comfortable than this one. I have to agree with you on its lack of comfort. I can move right now. It's not like I have a bunch of things to pack," she said with a smile.

Her last remark made me look at her dress. I recognized it as one of Lark's. I should've thought of it myself and gotten her some clothes. She didn't need to be borrowing someone else's. I'd take care of it later. Right now, I had to get her to consent to moving in with me.

"You don't have to thank me or the club. We hate to see people abused and hurt who don't deserve it. We're happy to help. You won't be invading my privacy. During the day, I'll be working a lot as soon as you're okay to be left alone. At night, if I want privacy, I can hang out in another room. Most of the time, I'm here with my brothers. As for *your lack of belongings, we'll take care of that. Please, it would make me feel better and less anxious if you stayed with me." I wasn't above making it sound like she was doing me a favor. Was I a dog? Yeah, I was, but it was for a good reason.*

"Oh no, please, don't think that was a hint to buy me things. Lark was nice enough to loan me this, and she said she had more. Once I get back on my feet and can work again, I'll replace mine. Or if I can sneak home, maybe I can get what I have there. Hmm, I wonder how hard that would be?"

"Troian, I need you to move to the house," I told her firmly.

"If it makes it easier for you, although I don't see myself needing your care, and you're sure I won't get on your nerves, then I'll do it. Just let me know when you want to bring someone over, and I can hang here or something." She blushed as she said the last bit.

Jesus, she thought I'd bring a woman home when I had her there? Fuck, she had no idea the only woman I wanted was the one in front of me. I'd be focusing my efforts on winning her heart, not fucking other women. The thought of touching someone else turned me cold. Shit, I hadn't been with anyone in a couple of months, even before we rescued her. They'd been too much effort and drama.

"Sweetheart, I don't bring women home. That's my sanctuary. It won't happen."

"Oh, okay, well, if you change your mind, let me know. I don't want to cramp your style or whatever. So, when do you want to do this?"

"Right now, if you want," I told her. *I decided not to remark on her cramping my style.*

That was how I got her in my house, and I spent long-ass nights awake, thinking of her and how I could win her. Which led to me almost being late for work almost every morning since. I fell asleep in the wee hours every night. I'd gotten Alisse, Lark, and Chey to promise to check on her while I was at work.

"Hey, Lash, how are those cabinets coming along?" Tinker's booming voice from behind me made me jump.

I swung around to glare at him. "Do you have to sneak up on people? For a big bastard, you're stealthy."

He laughed as he shrugged his massive shoulders. He was built like a bull. "What can I say? I'm a ninja, and you're just jealous. Looking good, man. These are gonna look fantastic in that house. Hey, I know you got Troian to move into your house last week. You're taking your doctoring duties way too seriously, aren't you? She's recovering. If you wanted her out of the treatment room, you could've asked me. I'd share mine with her," he said with a smirk.

A growl came out before I could stop it. I pointed the awl I was using to make decorative lines in the wood at him. It was sharp and pointed like an ice pick. "Don't make me use this on your ass," I warned him.

He burst out laughing. I scowled at him while he got himself under control. He was so loud that others looked at us with curiosity.

"Shh. Stop laughing like a damn hyena," I hissed.

"Hey, no need to get pissy. I'm just joking. Come on, I'd be an idiot not to see how you feel about her. You practically piss on her and savage anyone getting too close to her. I had to jerk your chain. How long do you think it'll take to close the deal and make her your old lady?"

"Christ, she's not even healed yet. We don't know if she's even interested in me. She might just see me as her doctor," I tried to insist, although deep down, I prayed that wasn't the case.

He snorted and rolled his eyes. "Man, you haven't seen the looks she gives you when she thinks no one is looking. She's attracted. All you have to do is make her see the benefits of being yours."

"And what are those?" This should be interesting.

"Protection, cherishing, and endless orgasms," he said with a wink.

"I'll remind you of this amazing pep talk when you meet someone one day."

His smile fell away. "The woman for me wouldn't want to put up with my ass. It would be nice, though. If you find her, hogtie her and bring her home to me."

"Tink, I'm sure she's out there, and you're gonna meet her when you least expect it. Look at me. No way would I have imagined how I met Troian. You'll know. I had the same immediate reaction and knowledge that she was special and mine as soon as I saw her, just like the others told us. Now, enough about our love lives. Did you need something, or were you just wasting my precious time? If the boss sees us, I could get fired." I joked to get him out of the sudden funk he went into talking about his future woman, whoever she was.

His smile was back. "Fuck the boss. I wanted to see if you wanted to grab lunch. I'm starving. I was thinking either Stacked for a deli sandwich, or we could go to Annie's."

"Is that really a choice? Don't get me wrong, I like a mean deli sandwich, but you know it's Wednesday. Annie will have pot roast today. I can't say no to that."

"Damn, you're right. Leave in ten?"

"I'll meet you out front."

"Will do," he said before he walked off. I spent those ten minutes washing up and getting some of the wood chips and dust off me. When I walked outside, he was straddling his bike with his helmet on. I hurried to do the same, and then we took off. It wasn't far to Annie's diner. My mouth was watering thinking about it. She had pot roast as her daily special on Wednesdays.

The parking lot was crowded when we pulled in. We parked in the special spot reserved for bikes. Annie was our friend through Reaper. We came here a lot. She liked to have designated parking for bikes close to the door. The rest were reserved for disabled parking. Walking inside, we were greeted by one of the regular waitresses, Bonnie.

She gave me a flirtatious smile. I wanted to groan,

but I didn't. I kept a friendly, although not too friendly, smile on my face as she took us to a booth. Bonnie was an attractive woman in her early thirties. She'd worked here for a long time and had always flirted with me and my brothers. I resisted what she was offering for a long time, then stupidly, nine months ago, I got lonely and went there with her. I had hoped she might be someone special if I gave her a shot. We had fun one night, and then we were done.

She knew going in I wasn't promising her anything beyond that, and she agreed. After being with her and hanging out, I knew she would never be more than a hookup, even if I were secretly looking for that. So, I didn't lead her on. I left it at once and told her we weren't doing it again. Only she didn't want that. She kept hinting at how good we were together and how good we could be as a couple. I'd told her more than once it wasn't gonna happen, but she persisted. I should've called to see if she was working before I came. I'd avoided Annie's when I knew she was on because of this reason.

After sitting down, when she handed out the menus, she made sure to press against me. I edged away. "What can I get you guys to drink?" she asked in a sugary voice that put my teeth on edge. Why hadn't I noticed that before? It irritated me and always had when women used that particular tone.

"I'll have ice water, no lemon," I told her without looking at her.

"I'll take a Dr Pepper, no ice," Tinker said.

"I'll get those right out and then take your order. I don't want you big, strong men to starve. You have to keep up these muscles." As she spoke, she squeezed my bicep. I wanted to tell her to keep her damn hands to herself, but I didn't. I didn't want to start something in Annie's place. She'd kill me. She was already upset with me for sleeping with Bonnie. I'd heard all about it. Bonnie had gone to work and told everyone.

Once she was out of earshot, Tinker muttered, "Jesus, she's like a damn dog in heat. You better never bring Troian here, or there might be a catfight. She's determined to stake a claim on you, man. Glad I didn't sleep with her. Believe me, I thought about it. Glad it's you, not me."

"Thanks, fucker. I hate it, and no matter what I say, she won't listen. She's gonna have to get used to disappointment because I'm determined to have Troian as my old lady. And I will bring her here, so Bonnie will have to learn to behave herself."

"Good luck," he whispered as he shifted his eyes to the left.

I looked up and saw Bonnie approaching. She batted her lashes as she set the drinks down, then continued to try and press against me as she took our orders. I breathed a sigh of relief when she went away, only to groan softly when I saw Annie coming toward us. She looked upset. She shoved my shoulder, so I slid over. She plopped down beside me. She elbowed me in the ribs.

"Ow, watch that bony elbow, Annie. That hurt," I

told her as I rubbed my ribs.

"Hurt my ass. You're hurting me."

"How?"

"By making me watch that twit make like a panting bitch every time she sees you. I swear to God, Lash, if you sleep with another one of my employees ever again, I'll kill you," she hissed at me.

"You don't have to worry about that," I told her.

"Why? You have erectile dysfunction already? I mean, I guess almost forty isn't young, but damn," she said with a fake sweet smile. Tinker burst out laughing.

"Don't laugh, asshole. You're two years older than me, remember?" I reminded him with a grin. His laugh became a scowl as he looked at Annie, who was smiling like she won the lottery.

"No, thanks for the concern, but everything works perfectly down there. I meant that you won't ever see me with one of your people," I told her.

"I'll believe it when I see it."

"If he does, then his woman will dump his ass and give one of us a chance," Tinker chimed in as he smirked at me.

"His woman? What woman? Why am I the last to hear this? Since when have you claimed someone and not told me? I have to approve of her, you know. What if she's a bitch or a user? You need to tell her she's not claimed until I can meet her," she ordered immediately.

"I haven't officially claimed her yet, but I'm doing my best to make it so. And you don't get a say. She's the one. You actually met her, or at least know of her. Her name is Troian. She's the woman we brought home that Saturday when you watched the kids while we did the ride," I explained.

Her mouth fell open, and her eyes got bigger. "You mean the one beaten almost to death? That's the woman you plan to claim? Oh my God, you guys do have a type, don't you? You have to be rescuers. I heard she woke up and has no memory. What if she already has a man?"

"She doesn't," I said firmly.

"How do you know? Not wearing a ring doesn't make it so," she argued.

Annie was like an older sister to us, which made us want to hug her half the time and strangle her the rest. She thought she could boss us around, even Reaper. It was because of him that we claimed her as family. She'd been his mom's younger sister's best friend. Say that five times really fast. Unfortunately, his aunt Lonnie died several years ago, but Annie stayed friends with Reaper and, subsequently, the club.

"I know. No one has reported her missing. Spawn figured out who she was and where she was from. There's been no police report filed. If she had someone, he would've reported her missing by now. That, along with other stuff, makes me sure she isn't involved," I mumbled.

"What other stuff?" she demanded.

"None of your business."

Tinker was watching us like it was a tennis match. His head and eyes bounced from one of us to the other, then back again. He wore a satisfied grin, the asshole.

"Tell me. If you don't, I'm gonna tell Bonnie you want to see her again."

Her evil smile told me she would do it. "You evil witch, you would, wouldn't you? God, I can't believe this. Lean over here. I'm not announcing it to the world or Tink. He's a gossip," I said. Tinker gave me the finger. She leaned over so I could whisper in her ear.

"She's a virgin. I found out when I had to examine her to be sure she hadn't been raped."

She gasped and jerked away. "She's a virgin?" she almost shrieked. Heads turned all over the dining room. I slapped my hand over her mouth and glared at her. Tinker choked on his drink.

"Jesus Christ, do you have to tell the whole fucking town? I swear, I'm muzzling you. Tinker, you didn't hear that, and you won't mention it to anyone else or to Troian. She was embarrassed when I told her what I found."

"I cross my heart and hope to die, stick a needle in my eye, promise. Wow, you would get a virgin. Lucky asshole," he muttered.

"What are we, five? Stick a needle, I swear. And

how is that lucky?" I asked.

"Have you ever been with a virgin?" Annie asked.

"That's none of your business," I told her.

"That would be a no. Tell you what. If you get her to say yes, come talk to me. I'll give you tips so you won't muck it up, and she might get off," she said with a grin.

"I don't need help in getting a woman off," I growled.

"That's for sure," I heard said from behind us. I closed my eyes and prayed for strength. It was Bonnie, back to ruin my appetite.

She set our plates down. Annie whipped her head around to glare at her. "Bonnie, that's not proper talk for work. Get back to your job if you want to keep it," Annie barked. Bonnie walked off, pouting.

"Thanks."

"You're welcome. But you know, you'll have to face Bonnie one day when she hears you're taken. Be prepared. Now, when can I come over and meet her? I know. I can come tomorrow morning around ten. Oh, we should throw a party to welcome her. Well, as soon as I make sure she's suitable. I can cater it," she babbled excitedly.

"You did hear the part where I haven't officially claimed her, right? And that you have no say? I'd like to introduce her to some more people, but not until we know she's safe from whoever tried to kill her. As for you coming to meet her tomorrow, let me see if she's feeling up to it. She's still healing. If she says yes, you have to behave yourself and not tell her anything you heard today," I warned her sternly.

She waved her hand at me and rolled her eyes. "Pleeease, as if. She'll want to meet me. She has to be bored to tears lying in that bed at the clubhouse. I'd go crazy if it was me. I'll come to entertain her."

"She's not in that room anymore," Tinker said.

"Where is she? In your old room at the clubhouse? Did you sanitize it first?"

"Remind me why we're friends, and I don't strangle you. No, she's not in my old room. I'll have you know. It didn't need to be sanitized. I'm not the manwhore you seem to think I am. She's been made more comfortable at my house. It makes it easier to keep an eye on her."

"You have her in your house already? Oh well, I say the claim has been made. I can't wait to meet her. See you tomorrow. Bye," she quickly said before she popped to her feet like a jack-in-the-box and rushed to the back. I wanted to hit my head on the table. She was gonna come whether I said yes or not. Once she got something in her head, there was no stopping her.

"You might as well stop trying, man. You know Annie. She's coming. Just do your best to prepare Troian for her and pray. You know, I often think we should find Annie something to do, you know, in her off time. A hobby or something," Tinker said between bites. I took a bite of mine before it got cold. I wanted to moan. It was so good.

"You mean she needs a man, don't you?"

He cringed and shook his head no. "Hell no, that's not what I meant. The last thing we need is for her to have some man trying to muck up her damn life. We'd have to kill him. Forget it." He sounded disgruntled by the thought.

It was true. In the past, any mention of Annie having a man had made all of us object and shoot the idea down, but it didn't seem fair to me that she didn't have someone in her life. She'd had boyfriends over the years, although it had been a while since the last one. She'd been married when she was young. From what Reaper shared, it had been a less-than-pleasant marriage. Most of her time, as far as I knew, was spent here or at home doing God knows what. Probably thinking up ways to drive us insane.

We enjoyed our meal, but I didn't linger. Bonnie stayed away unless we waved her over to refill our drinks or get something else, although you could tell she didn't like it. Tinker kept chuckling every time he saw her sour expression. We left enough money on the table to pay for the food and leave her a decent tip. As we left, she called out goodbye and said that I needed to call her. I didn't acknowledge her.

Back at work, I finished off my day and then headed home. I was anxious to see how Troian was and to let her know she was having a visitor tomorrow. I'd cleared it with Tinker already that I wouldn't be in. He was fine with it because I'd been ahead of schedule before Troian came and still was, even despite the few days I lost. I'd texted throughout the day with Chey, who was off and checked on her for me. She said she was doing great. I wanted to be able to text Troian directly, but she had no phone and had been refusing to let me buy her one.

Well, tomorrow, a new one would be coming in the mail for her, and she'd have to accept it. Just like she'd accepted the clothes I bought for her online. She refused those, too, and wouldn't pick any out, even though she did check some out on the website. Since it was in my account, I was able to go back and see previously viewed items. I was able to get her sizes and what caught her interest from her search. I'd ordered those for her. They were due tomorrow as well. I anticipated an argument, but there was no way she could do for long on the few outfits she'd been given, and we couldn't sneak to her home in Richmond to get any. That was a whole other mess.

Spawn had been hard at work investigating her life there. He'd found out she was self-employed. He'd held off digging into her work life more so he could check out her personal life since it was unlikely her work led to her beating. Her personal life had left us with more questions than answers.

She appeared not to have much of a social life. There was no boyfriend or even recent dating history. He said she wasn't one to be posting her life all over social media, so that made it harder to confirm she hadn't been at least casually dating someone. She didn't seem to have friends she went out with. Her life was mainly spent at home. She worked from home and lived in a house filled with extended family. She had several second cousins and their families in her life. They all worked a variety of jobs.

With there being no real friends to speak of, it left us with the burning question still—who'd hurt her? It was looking more like it had been random rather than an acquaintance or friend. Had she just been in the wrong place at the wrong time? Had she seen something she shouldn't have? Or was there something in her work that was the cause? That question had sent Spawn digging today into her work history.

Despite knowing she had so much family, we didn't feel we could let them know she was alive. They would be happy to know it, I didn't doubt, but whoever did this might know them. There was still a slight chance of that. I refused to risk it. Selfishly, it meant she had to stay here with us, with me, and that would allow me time to win her over. Tinker's assertion that she was attracted to me made me feel better about it.

I parked my bike in my garage. I didn't waste time getting off it and into the house. I was anxious to see her. I found that my day wasn't complete unless I could see her every morning and every night. That, if nothing else, told me I was a goner.

Troian: Chapter 5

I was nervous. I was waiting for a woman I didn't know to show up to meet me. I had no idea why she wanted to. I wasn't anyone. When Lash came home from work yesterday and said I was to have a visitor the next day, I'd questioned him up and down about who she was and why. I understood his explanation that she was a close club friend. Her desire to meet me, I didn't. Unless she was afraid that I was taking advantage of the club, which I felt like I was.

Despite my requests to help around the place or be allowed to venture outside the gate, I was repeatedly shot down. It was deemed too dangerous. I deemed the risk to my sanity by not doing anything was too dangerous and possibly dangerous to others as well. When I told the ladies this, they'd been sympathetic and gave me a task, well, not really a task. I'd call it a gift. They said if I was feeling up to it, I could come over and play with the kids as much as I wanted, even if they were at work.

Lark often had Flynn with her at Fortress. I wanted to visit it so much. She said once the danger had been taken care of, she'd give me the full treatment. She talked about the kids there so much that I felt I already knew them. I was dying to meet them. In particular, Benji and Jonas intrigued me. As for Lily and Arya, they had found a wonderful woman named Becca who watched them at the compound. She took turns doing it at one house or the other and kept both kids. On the days Flynn didn't want to go to the Fortress, he was there too. I was more than willing to help her out.

Babies and small kids were so curious and filled with joy. They made other people happy. I had a blast on the days I got to spend time with them. They were mobile enough to play with. Flynn was able to talk, so we had even more fun. It made me wonder if I had kids in my life, although Spawn had said I didn't have any of my own, which my virginity would support.

His discovery of my home life and lack of friends had saddened me. I wondered why my life was so lacking. Was it my preference or some other reason? I hoped it meant I was close with the extended family they said I was around and lived with. However, thinking about that being true made me hate not telling them I was alive and well. They had to be suffering. But if so, why didn't they report me missing? Was it because they were worried it would bring the attention of my attacker or attackers to them?

All this thinking about the possible reasons for my beating and who did it made my head hurt. At night, I would have to meditate to get my head to stop pounding and my mind to stop running in circles so I could sleep. If I weren't worried that I'd keep Lash awake, I'd get up and pace or go for a walk. I didn't do the latter because he'd insist on going with me, and he needed his sleep so he could go to work.

I couldn't lie to myself. Thoughts of Lash kept me

awake as much, if not more, than my lost memories and worry. I was fighting an intense attraction to him. One I didn't want him to know about. How humiliating would that be? The woman you found thrown out like trash, who you helped out of the goodness of your heart, thinking there's a chance of more than friendship and human kindness from you? I'd die of mortification if he ever found out my thoughts and fantasies.

As my body healed and the pain lessened, the more desire I felt. I wasn't sure if I'd felt it in the past since I couldn't recall. If I had, it must not have been strong, or I wouldn't still be a virgin. My virginity was another embarrassing thing for me. For him to know that I was one mortified me. Even if he could be attracted to me, why would he want to be with someone who didn't know anything or who no other man had deemed pretty or sexy or attractive enough to have sex with? I had a hard time thinking it was merely due to me not finding a man attractive. Maybe I was being too hard on myself, but I couldn't help my thoughts.

I jumped when I heard the front door slam. He'd gone to the clubhouse earlier. I was at his house pacing and worrying. I quickly sat down before he could catch me doing it. He'd be all over me, asking what was wrong and if I needed anything. He'd done more than enough for me—both him and his club. The clothes and phone which came first thing this morning proved it.

I'd told him I wasn't accepting them, that there was no need. He'd argued there was and said we had no idea when I could get my own back in Richmond. My response was if he wanted to get me clothes, then go to the thrift store. He'd looked offended when I suggested it. He muttered something about being able to afford new stuff for me. Deciding to leave it for the moment, I handed back the phone. He insisted it was already paid for, and he had me on his plan. I told him he could drop me off his plan, and he could either sell the phone, keep it himself, or give it to someone else who needed it. That's when he'd said he needed to go to the clubhouse and he'd be back. I was pretty sure it was so he wouldn't strangle me for no other reason.

I gave him an innocent, unconcerned look when he walked into the living room. He wasn't scowling like he had been when he left. He smiled at me. "Troian, are you ready for Annie? She's here. I had them hold her at the clubhouse so I could come warn you. She's chomping at the bit, so no promises on how long they can hold her back. I tried to tell Crusher to tase her if he had to, but he's too scared of her to do it," he said with a chuckle.

"Should I hide? Why is she so insistent on meeting me?" I asked in a slightly bigger panic.

He hurried over to me and sat beside me. "No, you shouldn't hide. I promise Annie is nice. She only wants to meet you since she's our really good friend. She's like a big sister to all the guys. Just don't let her push you. She has a strong personality. Sometimes, people take her the wrong way. She tells you if something is bullshit and expresses her opinion. She tends to intimidate people who're afraid to do the same."

Well, that just made me feel more ready to run. I jumped to my feet. "If that was a pep talk, you need to change your damn definition of one and give me a car so I can get the hell outta here. She sounds like she's here to judge me and then run my ass off. If that's the case, I'll save her time and energy. I don't know enough about myself to know what my opinions are, and I'm not willing to express the ones I have."

He reached over and grabbed my wrist. "Stop it. You'll do great. She's high energy. I'll be right here, and I won't let her get out of control."

"I don't need or want you babysitting me. I'm an adult."

He opened his mouth to say something back but was interrupted by a loud, brisk, no-nonsense knock at the door. I tried to go toward the back door. He held on to me and got up. I had no choice but to let him lead me to the front door. My knees were weak as he threw it open. I gulped when I saw her standing there. I'm not sure what I expected, but it wasn't her.

First of all, she was taller than I expected. I was of average height, and she was a few inches taller than me. She wasn't overweight, but she had curves. She had thick, shoulder-length blond hair, lightly tanned skin, and pretty light green eyes. Lash had said she was older than him, but she didn't look like it. I was instantly insecure around her. Why wasn't he or one of the others with her? She was definitely the kind of woman I expected guys like them to be with. My mouth went dry as she walked in, hugged him, and then pushed him out of the way.

"Move it or lose it, Lash! Quit hiding her like you think I'm gonna steal her or kill her. Only if she really pisses me off will I kill her. And only if she can give me the best sex of my life or I think she needs rescuing will I steal her," she said to him.

"Annie, behave yourself. She's already worried about you. Don't make me send your ass back to the clubhouse," he warned her gruffly.

She snorted. "As if you could. You might've been eating your Wheaties, big man, and I'm a woman, but I can still put your ass down. I have skills. Don't forget it. Hello, I'm Annie. I hear you're keeping this guy on his toes. Good. He needs it. If you need advice or a cohort in crime, assuming I like you and don't need to kill you, give me a call. I'd be glad to help put him in his place. I live for that shit."

I had to laugh despite her mentioning it twice within a minute or so that she might kill me. I wasn't sure if she was crazy, sarcastic, or funny. Maybe a combination of all three.

"Hello, it's nice to meet a friend of Lash's. I'm Troian. Believe me, there's no reason for you to have to kill me. I don't plan to piss you off. As for needing a rescue, I don't think I do, and the best sex of your life, I'm not sure I swing that way. No memory, remember?" I said back.

She burst out laughing, then hooked her arm through mine and tugged me with her. She steered me into the living room and over to the couch. She pulled me down to sit with her. I gave Lash a helpless look. He rolled his eyes but followed us.

"Why don't you get us something to drink while

we get to know each other?" she ordered him. I couldn't say she asked him even though it was phrased like a question. The way she talked to him struck me as equal amounts amazing and surprising. Even more surprising was the way he took it. He might chastise her a bit and roll his eyes, but he didn't get upset or ugly about it.

"Annie, mind chilling a bit? You're ruining my biker image with your shit talk. Anyone listening to you would think I was a scooter-ridin' snowflake without a reputation to uphold," he grumbled.

"Lash, honey, I hate to break it to you, but everyone already knows that's what you are."

As soon as she finished saying it, he was out of his chair and grabbing her. He got her in a headlock and rubbed his whisker-covered face against her cheek and neck. She let out a sharp squeal and fought him. "Stop!" she shouted.

"Nope, not until you take it back and tell her what a badass I am," he told her as he grinned at me.

"Okay, fine, you're a god among badasses. Now, will you get us a drink, please?"

He gave her a kiss on the cheek and, as he stood up, said, "Sure, iced tea, okay?"

We both nodded. My stomach made a funny flipping motion when he kissed her cheek. I didn't like it, but I wasn't about to admit why, not even to myself. He could kiss whoever he wanted. It wasn't any of my business.

As he got the tea, she faced me again. I could see the redness on her cheek and neck from his whisker burn. "He's not really a god. I just told him that because I'm thirsty. Don't tell him," she whispered, and I giggled.

"What's she saying now?" Lash asked from the nearby kitchen.

"I'm not saying anything. You're getting paranoid in your old age," she quipped back.

"Well, if I am, you certainly are since you're older than me."

She gasped. "I can't believe you said that! You never talk about a woman's age, no matter what. Those are grounds for murder and burying a body. I thought I taught you better."

"You haven't taught me anything other than how far my sanity can be stretched. Here you go," he said as he handed us our tea. He sat down across from us with his.

"You don't need to hang here with us. We'll be fine on our own," she informed him.

He shook his head. "I'm not taking any chances with you. Troian, babe, if she gets too crazy or annoying, just wink, and I'll throw her ass out."

I smiled at him. "I'll keep that in mind."

"I'm ignoring you, mister. Okay, so I know you lost your memory. Have you had any memories come back? They obviously found out your name. How?"

"I woke up remembering my first name but nothing else. I have no idea why. It was Spawn's sleuthing skills that put a last name to my first and gave me some history about myself. It's weird to know nothing about yourself but know who the president is and how to walk, talk, and do other stuff. Lash said I have retrograde amnesia and that my memories are most likely to come back any day, or it could take weeks or months. There's no way to tell. I hate not knowing because that means we have no clue who hurt me or why. I can't go home to Richmond—that's where I'm from. I can't get a job or anything. They say the danger is too much. I hate taking advantage of them like this."

"How many times do I need to tell you you're not taking advantage of me or anyone else here? We're more than happy to help. You getting killed is the last thing I want," he barked sharply at me.

"I know you have, but I don't know how I can't be. Your whole life is turned upside down. You have some strange woman living not just in your compound but also in your house. You've had to take care of me and act as my doctor. You're clothing, feeding, and protecting me. I don't think anyone else would do that. All I can do is help watch the kids once in a while. You won't even let me clean your house or do your laundry as a thank you."

"You're not a damn maid. You don't need to do those things. And there are a lot of people, guys I know in other clubs, who would gladly do it, too. I don't want to hear anything like that again. Now, relax and enjoy Annie's company until she annoys you too much, and then I'll run her off." He said the last bit with a smile.

I didn't want to fight with him, especially not in front of her, so I shut up. As time went by, I found that I liked Annie a lot. She was witty, smart, and full of laughter. She made Lash laugh several times, which made me not want to like her, but I fought that unwarranted feeling. We talked about so many different things. I found out she owned a diner in town, which was quite popular. He told me the food was amazing no matter what it was.

By the time she informed me it was time to go, I was sad to see our time together end. She broke up the boredom, and after I relaxed, she was a lot of fun. She made me laugh, especially when she'd snipe with Lash. They held nothing back. I was still trying to figure out why they weren't together or if they'd ever been in the past. I didn't get that vibe, but I could be wrong.

We walked her to the door. She gave him a hug and then gave me one, which surprised me. "I'll see you later. Call me if you wanna chat," she ordered. She'd given me her number earlier when we were talking about the phone Lash had bought me.

"I will. It was great to meet you, and I had such a good time. Drive safe."

"I will." She waved as she walked off his porch. I watched her get into a car in the driveway. I'd been so anxious when we answered the door I hadn't even noticed it there. Lash closed the door once she was on her way. He gave me a probing look.

"What?" I asked.

"How was it? I know she's intense, but we love her. I hope she didn't offend you too much or scare you."

"She didn't offend me, and after I relaxed, she didn't scare me. She's fun. I like her." As I told him this, we walked back to the living room and sat. I hesitated and then thought, what did I have to lose?

"Can I ask you something personal? You don't have to answer if you don't want to." I had a hard time maintaining eye contact with him.

"You can ask me anything. I don't get offended easily, and I doubt you can ask me anything too personal for me to tell you." His gaze seemed to be extra intense as he spoke.

I hoped he meant it. Here goes nothing. "Have you and Annie ever dated or whatever? And if not, why not?"

He sat straighter, and a slight frown marred his face. Shit, I had offended him. I hurried to retract it. "Never mind, don't answer that. It's none of my business, and that was rude of me."

"Troian, I'm not mad at you. I need to ask you something before I answer, okay?"

I nodded. I mean, I couldn't say no.

"Why would you think that or ask it?"

I glanced down at my hands. I was twisting them together. I stopped and tried to relax them. After I uncurled both, I took a breath and answered him. "She's a very pretty woman. Gorgeous, really. She's got a great personality, and she seems smart and has herself together. She's the kind of woman I imagine you and the other guys like. She's your type. If you haven't been with her, I wondered why. Is it because you don't want to ruin your friendship?"

"What do you mean by my type? I'm not sure I understand. I agree she's all those things, as well as a great friend."

"You know. She's sexy, and she has what men want. It can be rather intimidating for other less confident women when they meet someone like her. She's bigger than life. I can see her not standing for crap. That's what I think, although in a slightly quieter way, Cheyenne, Alisse, and Lark are." I wasn't sure if I was explaining myself well.

"Yes, she's sexy, and I guess lots of men want that. And the old ladies are various degrees like her. Let me ask you something. Do you see yourself as being like her?"

"Oh no, I'm not like them at all. I may have been more outspoken in my previous life, but it's the other things that I can't really see myself as. I was just wondering."

"I've never had anything but a friendship with her, and that's all I've ever seen myself having. She'd make a good old lady as long as her man was strong enough to handle her without taking away her spirit. As for what you said about yourself, you're so damn far off the mark it's not funny," he said with a growl to his tone.

"How?" I asked in confusion.

"You're smart, sexy, beautiful, and you have strength. Look what you've survived in the last two weeks. Any guy would be lucky to call you his, especially me. Don't ever sell yourself short like that again. Anyone who tells you differently, have them come talk to me."

"Really? You see me like that?"

He got up from the chair he had sat in all morning. He came over and sat next to me on the couch. My heart skipped a beat when he said a man would be lucky, especially him. I wanted to hope for more than his friendship, but I was too scared. I hated the idea of being friend-zoned like Annie. He had to be crazy not to go there with her. Unless he wasn't in for a serious relationship. Just because a few were in relationships, it didn't mean all the rest of the guys were. That must be why. He raised his hand and touched my cheek. He was gentle. I knew he was concerned he might cause me pain, but my pain was quickly going away. Although the bruises were still there in a variety of colors.

"Baby, I absolutely see you that way. God, I have to ask this, and I pray it doesn't make you uncomfortable. Is there anyone here that you're attracted to? You've had time to meet everyone."

I wanted to tell him yes, then confess I thought that way about him, but I couldn't. I'd be so embarrassed when he told me he only saw me as either a victim or a friend, despite his last remark. He didn't mean it the way it sounded. I shrugged and glanced at the floor. I could feel my cheeks getting warm. He used a finger to lift my chin.

"Tell me." This time, he wasn't requesting I tell him something. He was ordering me to, and I knew without a doubt if I didn't, he wouldn't let it go. Maybe I could hedge it.

"Yes, there's one, but I don't think he'll see me as anything but a friend. Can we please stop talking about this so I can save myself from mortification?" I pleaded. I wasn't above begging.

"Who is it? I have to know. Tell me," he ordered tersely.

"Lash, I can't!"

"Like hell, you can't. Why not? Surely you're not afraid of me."

Before it could get any more tense, I quickly broke down and told him. He'd back off then. "Fine, if you must know, I'll tell you, but if you laugh at me or tell anyone, I'll murder you."

"I won't. But before you do, I want to ask you to do something for me," he asked firmly.

"Okay, what?" I was wary of what he wanted me to do, but I agreed.

"When we're alone like this, I want you to call me Derrick."

"Derrick? That's your real name, isn't it? Why would you want me to do that?"

"It is my real name. It's actually Derrick Tatum.

It's because I want you to, especially if the answer to my question is what I pray it is."

I didn't have enough spit in my mouth to swallow nervously, but I did anyway. I threw all sense out the window. He deserved a laugh. I prayed he wouldn't pity me. "Since you insist, if things were different, the guy I find myself attracted to... God, this is hard. Okay, the guy would be you. Okay, moving on," I said quickly.

I expected him to laugh or get this sad look on his face before he told me he only saw me as either a victim or a friend. Instead, an expression of what looked like satisfaction spread across his face. He didn't say anything. Instead, he moved like a flash, and the next thing I knew, I was pressed against him, and he was kissing me. I wasn't able to hold back my moan. His lips were firm and insistent. As he kissed me, his tongue probed between my lips.

I couldn't remember if I'd ever been kissed. I assumed so, but if I had, I knew they'd never been anything like this. I was instantly sent into a full-body meltdown. Heat infused my body. My nipples tightened as my breasts tingled. There were other tingles lower down, too. Slight dampness came with it. I gave in to his insistence and opened my lips. His tongue thrust its way into my mouth, and I met it with mine. He groaned long and deep.

I didn't know how long we kissed. I was lost in pure sensation. Suddenly, he tugged me harder against him. Where his arm just happened to be was where one of my worst and most painful bruises was on my back. I inadvertently cried out in pain. He let go of me so fast, that I fell back. He was on his feet like a shot, and then he started to ramble.

"I'm so damn sorry. I shouldn't have done that. I didn't mean to hurt you. I need to go. I-I've got things to do. I'll see you later," he said before practically running for the door. I was too stunned to say anything until after he was gone. What the hell just happened? Did he not mean to kiss me? I thought, based on that look, he was happy that I was attracted to him. I sat there, not knowing what I should do, feeling lost and embarrassed. This wasn't good.

Lash: Chapter 6

I ran like a pussy. That was all there was to it. I'd never run from a woman, even one who I should've run from, like Bonnie. That would've been the time to do it, not after I'd found out the woman I was the most attracted to in the world found herself attracted to me, and I kissed her for the first time. I should be right there still talking more about us and hopefully doing a lot more kissing. Instead, I was hiding at the clubhouse, drinking a beer, and wondering if I went too far, too fast.

That was the real reason I ran. I panicked over the possibility I was moving too fast for her and had scared her off. I didn't want her to worry about her safety. Who knows what she might think, especially after what she'd gone through? If I was her, I'd be leery of everyone. Sure, you hoped that, by now, she would know that she had nothing to fear from us, but who's to say?

I'd been here drinking the same beer for an hour, staring off into space. There was no one in here when I first arrived, but I vaguely heard a couple come in. I didn't bother to turn and see who it was. I had more important things on my mind, like how could I make this not bite me in the ass. The thought that I might've ruined something that would be amazing before it ever started made me sick to my stomach. A body hitting the stool next to me made me turn my head. I had to at least say hi.

I was surprised to see Ink. It was still the middle of the day. He typically would be tattooing during the day. His stuff was in high demand. People came from all over to get him to do their ink and would wait months to get in to see him. That was no slight against the other artists at his shop. They were really, really good at what they did, but he was a level above.

"What're you doing at home in the middle of the day?" I asked.

"I had a big piece scheduled, but he had to back out at the last second. I decided to come home. I was checking in with Reaper when I saw you sitting here, lost in your own little world. Why aren't you at work? What's wrong?"

"Well, where would you like me to start? First, I took the day off because Annie informed me yesterday that she was coming today to meet and approve of Troian."

He groaned in sympathy. I continued, "So, I asked Tinker if I could take the day off so I could be here. No way I'd let her face Annie alone, no matter how much I love that woman. Troian was so damn nervous it wasn't funny."

"Did it go that bad? Is that why you're sitting here drinking a beer at this time of the day? Where's Troian?"

"No, the visit ended up going well. That's not why I'm here. The bad part came after Annie left. We got into a discussion, and Troian ended up mentioning being attracted to someone here."

"There's no way it was one of the others. No damn way. I've seen how she looks at you," he immediately defended.

"No, she didn't say that. After a lot of prodding, she confessed that she was attracted to me. She was embarrassed to tell me."

"Ookaaay, so what's the problem? You should be jumping for joy and be with her right now," he asked with a confused frown.

"I ended up kissing the hell out of her then I realized I practically attacked her ass. She doesn't know me or any of us. I'm freaked out that I scared her, and she'll not want anything to do with me now. She was attacked, for God's sake. Sure, whoever it was didn't rape her, but still."

"Did she tell you she was scared or that she was upset that you kissed her?"

"No, because I didn't give her a chance to tell me."

He groaned long and loud. He closed his eyes and shook his head. "Please tell me you talked to her about it and didn't run out of there like your ass had gasoline farts being lit out of it."

"Gasoline farts? We've obviously led different lives in our youth," I tried to joke before sobering up again. "Yes, I did leave her at the house. I thought she needed space, and I needed time to figure out what to do. What if this ends any chance of there being an us?"

"What probably has the poor woman thinking that she wants nothing to do with you is the fact you're a colossal dumbass for running off after rocking her world. She's sitting there thinking there's something wrong with her. I guarantee it."

I hadn't thought of that, and the idea of it made me sicker. "Shit, do you think?"

"Nope, I don't think. I am ninety-nine percent certain it's a definite. You need to get your ass back to that house. Tell her what a boneheaded jackass you are. Apologize for running out. Beg her to give you another chance and let her know that as a mere mortal man, you're learning. You'll think of shit to say. Just be prepared to grovel a lot and to work extra hard until the next time you mess shit up. It's what I do. Believe me, our women have options. We can never let them doubt what they mean to us even if we do mess up."

"What if—" I started to say, but he cut me off.

"I've seen how she looks at you. This isn't gonna make her not want to be with you. You didn't beat her, treat her like dirt, or cheat on her. She'll just need reassurance that she wasn't the issue and that you'll keep evolving. Let's face it. We're not too far from Tarzan mode in some ways. If they're attracted to us, there's a part of them that likes it, as long as we temper it with other things. Now, stop talking to me, get your ass up, and go home."

I didn't wait to be told twice. I jumped to my feet, slapped him on the shoulder in thanks, then beat ass out the door. I'd walked to the clubhouse rather than rode, even though, in the scheme of things, it wasn't that far away. I wish I'd rode now so I could get back faster. By the time I made it to the house, my ass was sweating, and I was stroking out from the heat. Taking a moment to breathe and compose myself, I walked inside.

As soon as I hit the living room, which allowed me to see into the kitchen, I saw she wasn't there. She must be in the bedroom. I hurried to hers. She wasn't there. Frowning because I couldn't think of where else she might be, I quickly rushed from room to room and called her name. Nothing. All that greeted me was dead silence. My heart beat like a drum. Surely, while I was at the clubhouse wallowing, she hadn't left the compound? What if she did? Was she out there walking alone and unprotected alongside the road, where any weirdo or pervert could snatch her? Or where the ones who hurt her to begin with could get her again?

I hit the front door at a run. As I ran, I called Colt. He was at the gate the last I saw. He picked up after three rings. "What took you so goddamn long to answer?" I snapped.

"I-I'm sorry, Lash. I was running an errand for Reaper. Whatcha need?" You could hear the nervousness in his voice. I fought to calm down. It wasn't his fault unless he let her out the gate.

"Before you left the gate, did Troian come to you asking you to let her leave?"

"Nope, and if she did, I wouldn't have let her. I know what the penalty is for getting one of the old ladies hurt. Hell no. Why?"

"I can't find her. Is Rhaines at the gate now, or is it unmanned?" We couldn't keep someone on it twenty-four-seven. She could've slipped out.

"Yeah, he took over for me. Do you want—?"

I abruptly snapped and cut him off, "No," then hung up on him. I'd apologize later.

I pulled up Rhaines name and number and hit the dial button. He answered after only two rings. "Yo, I'm at the gate, but as soon as I'm done, I can do anything you want."

"Good, you're still there. Has Troian come to you and asked to be let out of the compound?"

"That would be no, and if she had, I'd have called you. I know the drill. When was the last time you saw her?"

I had to look at my phone. I was shocked it was over two hours ago. I didn't think I'd sat there that long. "Over two hours ago," I confessed.

He didn't make a comment about that. He just threw out suggestions. "Did you check if she went to the clubhouse? Or maybe she's at the house with one of the other women. I think someone is off today. Could she be taking a walk?"

All were solid possibilities. "She wasn't at the clubhouse. I just came from there. I'll go check to see if Alisse, Lark, or Cheyenne are home and have seen her. If that's a bust, then I'll search the area. Thanks. Call me if you see her, and under no circumstance is she to be allowed to leave," I warned him.

"Got it. I'll call as soon as I spot her. If I do, that is."

"Thanks," I said before hanging up. Rather than running around to each house individually, I brought up my text messages and typed a message to send to all three old ladies.

Me: Are you home? If so, is Troian with you?

It was torture to wait for them to answer me. I was about to say the hell with it and go to their houses anyway when the first one answered me.

Cheyenne: No, I'm at work. Why? What's wrong?

Me: I came back to the house, and she was gone.

Suddenly, I got another answer.

Alisse: Chey said you can't find Troian. I'm at work, too. Sorry, I was with a patient. Let's see if she's with the sitter at my house. What happened?

I knew they wouldn't let it rest until they found out, but I didn't have time for this right now, so I kept my response short.

Me: Let me know if you find her.

Then my phone dinged, and it was Lark.

Lark: I'm off but running errands in town. Why are you looking for Troian? Aren't you at work? Isn't she answering her phone?

I groan. I forgot all about her phone. Shit.

Ignoring Lark for the moment, I hurried to bring up Troian's number and called. It started to ring, and that's how I found out she left her phone at the house. I heard a muffled ringing. I walked around until I could hear it more clearly. Searching the couch, I found it wedged between the seat cushions. There went my next idea... to have Spawn track her using her phone. My phone alerted me to another message.

Cheyenne: What the hell is going on? Lark said you messaged her, too.

Me: It's nothing. She must've gone for a walk. I thought she was with one of you. It's fine. See you later.

I sent that one to all three of them. I barely tucked my phone back in my cut before I was out the door like a shot. I wasn't sure where to search first other than away from the houses and the clubhouse. I headed toward the back part of the property. My house was the only one built this far back to date, so there was nothing behind mine except grass, trees, and the storage buildings we had back there. Underneath the storage buildings were bunkers.

Walking that way, I scanned the area and called out her name. I'd pause my yelling to listen. Nothing. As I walked further and got no answer, I began to panic. What if she was hurt and couldn't answer me?

Abruptly, my phone rang. I jumped since it startled me, and then I answered it without bothering to see who it was. "Did you find her?" I asked urgently.

"No, and why the hell am I hearing from my old lady that you've lost yours? You should've called me.

What the fuck is goin' on?" Reaper barked.

I held in my groan. I should've known Chey would call him. "I didn't want to bother you, Reap. It's nothing."

"If it's nothing, then why are you calling and jumping on prospects, asking if they saw her or let her leave, and then messaging the old ladies asking if they know where she is? And why do you sound panicked? Talk to me."

Sighing, I confessed what I did and then what I found when I came home to fix my fuckup. He groaned as Ink had. "Jesus Christ, no wonder you're going in circles. You're a bonehead. If the prospects say she didn't leave through the gate, I doubt she climbed it. She's gotta be somewhere on the compound. Let me rally the troops. Where are you right now? We'll need to split up. Did you try calling her?"

"Her phone was stuck in between the cushions of the couch. I'm not too far behind my house. I've been calling out for her, but she's not answering. What if she's hurt?"

"I doubt she is. She's probably mad at you and wants peace and quiet to decide what she's gonna do. Keep your phone with you, and give me a few minutes to see who's around. Don't go imagining the worst."

Before I could thank him, he hung up. I kept searching and calling out for her. It was maybe five minutes before I heard the sound of bikes coming toward me. I stopped walking and watched as Reaper, Ink, both prospects, and Spawn came riding up. They shut off their bikes and got off them. They came at me as a pack.

"We need to split up and search along here. The grass is higher back here, so in case she's on the ground, look and don't just call out. Move the grass. And don't freak on me, Lash. I'm just saying that as a precaution. If you find her, call out. Stay within earshot of each other. I got the others who can get away coming," Reaper commanded.

I was so thankful to have help that I couldn't seem to say anything, and they didn't appear to expect me to. Spreading out like you see those people on television do when searching for someone, we began where I left off and started walking toward the back acreage. We didn't run, but we did move at a brisk pace. Each of us scanned the area around us and called out her name as we moved the tall grass. After each call, we'd wait to see if we could hear her.

As we worked our way back, we got closer to the trees and the storage buildings. How our compound worked was there were small clusters and individual trees all over the place. Most of us with houses had at least one or more outside in our front yards. It wasn't until you got toward the back section where the storage buildings were that there were two thick woods on either side of the road that ran through the middle of the property. That was intentional, to help hide the buildings with the bunkers and our escape routes.

Our land had been part of a military installation years and years ago. As such, we had bunkers. We'd intentionally built the storage buildings on top of the bunkers. This was in addition to the safe room built into one of them now, as well as the one we had in the basement of the clubhouse. Back in the day, the club had been into less-than-legal things, and we had more enemies. We'd been prepared for anything. With us now settling down and having kids, it was even more imperative we could keep them safe. Anyone storming us would be in for a rude awakening. We had firepower, heavy-duty weapons, and more. We wouldn't go down without a fight.

It wasn't long into the group search before more engines were heard, and three more guys rolled up— Maniac, Tinker, and Ratchet. They got off their bikes without saying a word. They took up positions at each end of our line and started working with us. This was the shit that made being in an MC such a family, as long as you were in the right kind. I'd seen and heard of plenty that didn't have this kind of unity. I could never be in one of those. Plus, some of them were into shit I never wanted anything to do with.

I was about to lose it. It was fifteen minutes later, and there was still no sign of her. We were now in the woods, and the going was slower. I was about to call all of us together and devise a new search plan when Troian came out of the trees. She seemed to be walking fine with no sign of injury. She was looking at her feet and hadn't spotted us. I shouted her name and took off running toward her. She didn't look up. As I got closer, I shouted her name as loud as I could. She wasn't gonna fucking continue to ignore me, no matter how pissed she was at me. Her head snapped up, and she froze. Her eyes grew round, and she looked around in utter shock. Hastily, she reached up and jerked. I spotted the earphones in her ears.

She'd confessed a few days ago that she liked to listen to music. She didn't know how she knew that or the fact she liked to use earbuds to do it. The next day, I brought her the best noise-canceling ones I could find and a small MP3 player so she could find and download music.

When I reached her, I grabbed her upper arms and tried not to squeeze too hard as I gave her a shake. I didn't do it hard, but just enough to get her to focus on me since she was looking at my brothers. Her eyes snapped to mine as I half-shouted, "Where the hell have you been?"

She blinked twice before she answered me. "I-I was taking a walk. Why? What's wrong? Why're you shouting and shaking me?"

"Why? Because you took off, and no one knew where the hell you were or how long you'd been gone. You could've been lying somewhere, hurt or dead, for all I know. You shouldn't have taken off without telling someone where you were going. Even better, you should've kept your ass at the house," I snapped.

I heard a groan, and then someone muttered, "Dumbass." Her worried look changed to one of anger in a flash. She shook to get me to let go, but I didn't. That's when she let me have it.

"If you don't let go of me this instant and back the hell up, I'm gonna do damage to you that you won't be able to walk off. If you have any hopes for future children one day, they'll be a dream," she growled softly. Her eyes snapped fire at me.

Now, the really fucked-up part was that as worried and angry as I was, seeing her being so fiery made me half-hard. A smart man would've done what she said. I must've been a stupid one because not only did I not let go, but I crowded her. "Oh yeah, if anyone is getting punished here, it's you for worrying me to death. Goddamn it, woman."

Her knee was coming up and toward my crotch. I shifted my leg to protect myself as I dropped my hands to cover my cock. I realized my mistake when she punched me in the gut and then kicked me in the side of my knee, almost buckling my leg and putting me on my ass. She moved away from me.

I tried to reach for her, not to hurt her but to reassure her. She took up a fighter's stance with her fists up, ready to punch. Reaper was the one to defuse the situation. "Troian, sweetheart, he's a dumbass, but he didn't mean anything by his remarks. He's not gonna hurt you, and he's only been worried about you when he had no idea where you went."

"Bullshit, he didn't know. I left him a note. I wasn't told that by staying here, I had no right to even leave the damn house and take a walk. He walked off when he wanted without an explanation, so why can't I? Even though I did say where I was going, unlike him. I waited for over an hour for him to come back, and when he didn't, I decided to get some air," she snapped.

Reaper looked over at me. He mouthed, *fix this,*

then he turned to the others. "Let's give these two some privacy. We're heading back. If you need us, just call. Troian, I wouldn't leave you with him unless I trusted him not to hurt you. You're more than safe with him. Just talk to each other and get this mess cleared up. There are so many misunderstandings floating around, it's almost painful."

Before she could protest or thank him, he circled his finger, and the others all turned and began walking away briskly. I knew I'd hear about this later. As they got further away, I faced her again. She was watching me through narrowed eyes. Shit, where to begin?

Troian:

I was ready for a fight. After sitting in his house for over an hour, waiting for him to return, and he didn't, I knew I had to get some air and think. I'd left him a note, in case he did come back, telling him I went for a walk. When I left, I remembered to grab my music and earbuds but forgot my cell phone. When I discovered my mistake, I was far enough away not to want to go back for it.

I'd wandered the woods and the back part of the compound for a long time. The music and nature helped me to get into a better frame of mind. It took a while. I had no idea how long I'd been gone. I'd explored the area, including the two buildings I found, though I couldn't get inside them. When I was feeling much calmer, I headed back the way I came. I was shocked to see him running toward me and several others with him. To have him chastise me, shake me, even though it wasn't hard, and then threaten to punish me had made me issue my own threats and then react.

I wasn't sure where the fake-out followed by the punch and kick came from. It was like it was automatic. That made me wonder what my life had been like before coming here and what led to me knowing how to do that. If I knew how to do that, why had I been beaten and left for dead? Did that mean there was more than one attacker, or had I been surprised and incapacitated? Or had I known them, and they got the drop on me? So many questions were whirling through my brain, along with the ones I had about Lash.

He was watching me warily. I wasn't saying a word to him. I was thinking. Close to the top of the list was why he had run. Was kissing me that terrible and a turnoff that he had to get away? If so, why come looking for me? Was he here to tell me that I couldn't stay here any longer? That thought made me sick to my stomach, but I refused to show it. I wouldn't beg anyone to stay where I wasn't wanted. I'd had too many years of feeling like a burden and obligation. Wait. Where did that come from? I tried to concentrate on the brief flash of an image of faces, and then it was gone.

He cleared his throat. "We need to talk. Will you come back to the house with me? We need to be comfortable for this, and it might take a while. I swear I won't touch you. I'm sorry I shook you and grabbed you like that. Are you alright? I didn't hurt you, did I?" he asked worriedly.

As much as I wanted to be a bitch, I couldn't make him think he'd hurt me when he didn't. His grip nor his slight shake had hurt. I shook my head no. He held out his hand. "Will you come with me?"

I didn't take his hand, but I did move over next to him. His face fell for a moment, and then he straightened and led the way. He was quiet the whole way back. It wasn't a quick walk. I hadn't been aware of how far I'd come. When we finally entered his house, I was hot, and the cool air inside felt so good. I sank down on the couch, but he kept going into the kitchen. He still had the ever-slightest limp. I saw my phone on the table, so I picked it up and put it in my pocket. He got us both water, then came back to me. He set it down. Then he sat down in the chair across from me. I gulped half my water down. He sipped his. When I was done, he spoke.

"I'm sorry I reacted the way I did. I had no idea where you were. I didn't see the note. I thought you were upset with me and that you left the compound. When I discovered that it was unlikely and that you weren't with any of the old ladies, I panicked more. I went searching for you. Reaper and some of the guys found out I was looking for you, so they came to help me. We'd been searching for a while and calling for you when you came out of the woods. I was relieved and upset at the same time. I didn't handle it well. I was terrified you were lying somewhere hurt or worse, dead."

"Lash, that's all well and good, but I think we should back up and talk about why I was out there walking in the first place. You obviously have something to say to me. I think we should get it out of the way. No need to beat around the bush. Based on the fact you were gone over an hour before I left and who knows how long afterward, you're upset about the kiss. I want you to know I understand."

"What do you understand?"

"That you regret it, and to continue to stay here with you would be awkward, to say the least. I get it, and I would never expect you to let me continue to stay. You don't need to feel bad about asking me to leave. I don't want to stay where I'm not welcome or wanted. All I ask is to borrow enough money to get me out of town on the bus. Once I find a place to lie low or go home, I'll repay you the money and for everything else you've bought me."

He came bounding to his feet. His face was red with what looked like anger. "You think I fucking want you to leave? That I regret the damn kiss? Jesus Christ, did you not listen before? I'm so damn attracted to you that I can't think. I can't spend a moment with you that I don't want to kiss you and do a whole lot more. I left so I wouldn't push for more than you're prepared to give me. I was upset that I scared you, and it would ruin my chances with you. Hearing your confession that you're attracted to me made me lose my shit."

"I-I…" I stuttered.

"If you think for a second I'll let you get on a bus to go God knows where or to go home, you've got another thing comin'. If I have to put a guard on you twenty-four seven to keep you here and safe, I will."

"Lash, you're—" I tried to speak, but he cut me off again.

"And if you call me Lash one more time when it's just us, I'll have to remind you in a way you'll remember to call me Derrick."

I came to my feet. I stomped over to him. I poked him in the chest with my finger. "Listen here. Let me talk goddamn it. You're not the boss of me. I'll call you whatever I please, and I'll do what I want. You have no say over what I do," I smarted off. I knew what I was doing, but I didn't care. I wanted to see what he'd do.

Did he yell at me more? No. Did he hurt me or hit me? No. Did he throw me out? No. What he did was yank me against his rock-hard chest, fist my hair, although not painfully, then he kissed me. I thought the first kiss we shared was amazing. This one was phenomenal. He kissed me like a man who was starved and had found his first meal in weeks. He nibbled, licked, sucked, and everything in between, not only my lips but also my tongue. All I could do was hold on and try to follow his lead. Hungry moans and growls came out of both of us.

He backed me up until my back hit the wall. He hiked one of my legs up by the knee so it was partially hooked around his thigh. I whimpered in need as he pressed his hard cock into my throbbing core. I was wet, and my breasts throbbed. I fisted my hands in the back of his hair. His hips bucked, and I cried out as I humped him. I tried to stop, but it was impossible.

I didn't know how long we went at it before my whole body tightened, and I came. As I did, I screamed into his mouth. I was equally thrilled and mortified. Oh my God, I just came from a kiss and humping a guy like a dog in heat! I was so embarrassed. I tore my mouth away from his and shoved him. He stumbled back drunkenly. I had to get out of here.

Lash: Chapter 7

I was on fire and felt like I was drunk as I staggered back after Troian caught me off guard with her shove. I wanted to ask her what was wrong, but my brain didn't seem to be sending signals to my mouth. My mouth was open, but nothing came out. She gave me a red-faced look, and then she took off.

I tried to grab her, but my legs still wobbled. Jesus Christ, if a kiss did this to me, what would sex do? Kill me? I stumbled after her as she ran upstairs. She was headed to her bedroom. I finally found my voice when I reached the bottom of the stairs. She was almost at the top. I swore I heard her sob. My gut clenched hearing it.

"Troian, come back. Babe, please," I pleaded. When she didn't slow down or stop, I pounded up the stairs. My legs were back, and I had to make this right. However I fucked up, I would make it right.

Her door slammed shut before I got to it. I heard the lock engage. I pounded on the door. "Troian, open the damn door and talk to me. What did I do?" I asked.

"Nothing. Go. Away. I want to be alone," she said hoarsely. I could hear tears in her voice. Her voice cracked, and she sniffed. She was crying.

"I'm not gonna do that. Nor am I gonna talk to

you through the door. I swear, I'll stay across the room, and I won't touch you again." I wasn't sure if I could keep that promise, but I'd do my damndest to do it.

She didn't respond, but I could hear her moving around, and there were thumping noises coming from her room. Shit, was she packing? I just knew it. I frantically searched for a way to get in. I could kick in the door, but that would scare her and damage more than the door. The frame would likely be destroyed. That was the quickest way. However, the smartest and least destructive was to use the tiny Allen key that was above the door on the frame ledge. Most houses, at least modern ones, had some placed there in case the doors accidentally got locked and you had to open them from the outside. I felt along the ledge until I found it. Taking it in hand, I gave her one more chance to open it on her own.

"Baby, I need you to open up now," I ordered her. I didn't think it would do me any good, but I tried. The noises halted for a couple of seconds, then resumed. She didn't answer me.

I inserted the key in the small hole in the doorknob and worked it around for a few seconds. I heard the soft click when it released the lock. Putting the key back, I twisted the knob and opened the door fast. I stepped inside. She didn't see me because she had her back to me. I was right. She was packing. On the bed was a large duffle bag one of the old ladies brought stuff to her in. It was the click of the door closing behind me that got her attention.

She whirled around, and her eyes widened when

she saw me on this side of the door, blocking it with my body. My arms were crossed over my chest. She hesitated, and then her spine straightened. She narrowed her gaze at me and pointed at me.

"Get out this instant, Lash. I'm not talking to you, and I don't want to hear what you have to say. I'm done. This isn't gonna work. If you refuse to give me money for a bus ticket, then hopefully Reaper will. I'm waiting for Cheyenne to answer my text with his answer."

Anger filled me. She wasn't running. I wouldn't allow it. Whatever I had to do to keep her here, safe, and nearby so I could find a way to win her heart, I would do. "His answer will be no."

"You don't know that."

"Like hell, I don't. I know it because that would be what I would tell his woman or any other woman here who belonged to one of my brothers. There's no way on earth I'd help the woman one of them wanted as his to leave him unless he was abusive to her."

"So you mean every time you guys meet a woman you want to have sex with, you don't care if she wants you or not," she said, outraged.

"No, that's not what I mean. Although the women who come here looking for a good time don't care who they get some from, so it's never been an issue. Those aren't the ones I mean. I'm referring to the women who we want to be ours forever and not just for a night or two."

"Oh yeah, well, how many of those have you had

that you ended up keeping prisoner until they did what you wanted? Ten, twenty, a hundred? How long do they last? A week, a month, six months?" she shouted.

The pain I saw on her face shattered my control. I was across the room, and I broke my resolve not to touch her. I wrapped her in my arms and tugged her against me. She immediately began to struggle and swear at me. It was in Russian. I knew it was swearing by the way she spit out the words.

"*Otpusti menya, sukin sin! Ty dumayash', ya shlyukha? Svoloch'.*

"I don't know what you're saying. Say it in English," I ordered.

She spit it out in English. "Let go of me, you son of a bitch. Do you think I'm a slut? Bastard," she hissed.

I gave her a small shake. "I know you're not a slut. I may be a bastard and a son of a bitch, but I've never been tempted to keep a woman for myself, ever, not until I met you. You, I want to keep and not for a week, a month, or even a year. I want you for the rest of my goddamn life, Hurricane. All I need is for you to stop running, fighting, and thinking the worst. I need you safe. I want you to trust me. I need you to let me kiss you without either of us running. Fuck, I just need..." I trailed off and then did what I wanted. I kissed her.

As my mouth took hers, she tried to resist for a few seconds, then she moaned and gave in. I grabbed behind her thighs and hoisted her in the air. She wrapped her legs and arms around me. That put her pussy in direct contact with my achingly hard cock.

I groaned as I walked her to the bed behind her. The movement had her rubbing over me in the most delicious way. I shuddered. Fuck, she could have me coming from just that.

She was eagerly kissing me. I didn't let go of her mouth as I lowered her to the bed. I went with her and was cradled between her thighs. I buried my hands in her hair so I could slant her head to give me a better angle. Our tongues were twining together when our lips weren't kissing or our teeth weren't nibbling on each other.

God, I wanted her naked and my cock buried so deep inside of her that she'd never get rid of me. If this didn't convince her to stay and be mine, I might just have to tie her to the bed and pleasure her until she said yes. It was humbling to realize I wasn't above it or begging. It didn't matter that she and I had only known each other for a couple of weeks. I knew without a doubt she was born to be mine.

Her hands yanked my shirt out of my waistband, and then they slid up my naked back. Electric tingles raced through me. Her legs wrapped around my waist, and she rocked against my erection. She tore her mouth free and arched her neck, pushing her head back. Her eyes were squeezed shut. She was panting. Fuck, she appeared close to coming.

Wanting to give her that again, I rocked my pelvis and pushed up her top. I hastily pushed the cup of her bra aside so I could latch onto her breast with my mouth. A quick glimpse of her breasts told me she had the most beautiful, perfect breasts I'd ever seen. Out of respect, I hadn't let my gaze linger on them when we cleaned her up that first day. I sucked hard, which made her cry out, then I bit down on her nipple, tugging it gently.

"God!" she screamed, then she came, shaking and whimpering. I didn't stop thrusting or sucking until she went limp. It took every ounce of my strength not to come in my jeans. I was so damn close, it hurt. I eased off her and flopped down beside her. I had to close my eyes and breathe deeply to keep from coming. I fought for control.

I had to work on it for a while. When I finally thought I had myself under control, I jumped. The faintest, tickling movement ran the length of my denim-covered cock. My eyelids flew open to find her raised up on her elbow next to me. Her face was still dreamy looking, and she was staring at my erection, pressing out my jeans. Her hands were lightly touching me. I grabbed her hand. She glanced up at me.

"Baby, if you keep doing that, I'll blow."

"What if I want you to come? You made me. I think it's only fair if you do, too," was her husky reply.

"As much as I'm dying to come, I don't want to do that in my pants."

She sat up more. She bit her bottom lip for a moment, then blew me away. "Then don't. You can take them down, can't you?"

"Troian, babe—" I couldn't say it. As much as I didn't want to push more than I already had, I wanted nothing more than to take my pants down and have her touch me or even touch myself. I hurt, but she wasn't ready, and I had to remember she was a virgin. Hell, she might've never even seen a cock. The thought of me being her first and hopefully only made me get harder, which I didn't think was possible. I groaned softly.

Suddenly, she was undoing the button on my jeans and then began to tug down the zipper. I tried to grab her hand, but she smacked my hand with her other one. I drew back in shock. She eased down my zipper. She did it slowly so as not to catch anything, thank God. As she spread the two sides back, she reached inside and rubbed the palm of her hand over my length through my underwear.

"Fuck," I moaned.

"Can I?" she asked.

"Can you what?" I asked gutturally.

"Can I take it out?"

I gave up. I was too weak and racked with need to say no. "Yes."

I had enough brain cells left to lift my ass and push down my jeans to my thighs so she could get to me easier. I watched in rapt anticipation as she slowly peeled down my underwear until my cock and balls were exposed. Her gasp made me proud. I was more than decently hung. When she licked her lips, I went from proud to begging.

"Touch me. Just be aware that I don't know how much I can stand before I come."

She ran her finger down my length, making it jump, which made her jump. She gave a startled giggle, then did it again. Her finger circled the head, gathering precum on her finger. I wanted her to taste it even though I didn't expect it. Imagine my shock when she put her finger in her mouth. I inhaled and waited to see what she'd say or do. Some women hated the taste of cum and wanted nothing to do with it. Just like some hated giving blow jobs regardless of whether the guys came in their mouths or not. Troian's moan made my heart speed up. She didn't look disgusted.

Her hand came back down, and she wrapped it around me as far as she could and slid her hand up and down once, then stopped. She looked at me. Her face was red. "It feels soft and hard at the same time. Am I squeezing too hard?"

"No, you can do it much harder than that. Here, let me show you," I told her as I put my hand over hers and showed her. Her breathing picked up. I let go, and she kept slowly jacking me. Her rhythm wasn't a practiced one, but she was causing me to get close to blowing my load just because it was her. To try and stave it off for a bit longer, I distracted myself by asking her a question. "Baby, how did you like that taste you had?"

"It wasn't like I thought it would be," she answered. She was mainly watching her hand, but she did glance at me when she responded.

"Really? What did you imagine?"

She wrinkled her nose. "I thought it would taste

awful, to be honest. I heard women say it was."

"What did it taste like?" I asked, curious. I'd never cared enough to ask a woman who tasted my cum what it tasted like. They either did or didn't like it. As long as I got off and so did they, I hadn't given a damn. In Troian's case, I wanted to know. If she never wanted to taste me again, I'd live just as long as I had her. There were plenty of other things we could do.

"You're salty with a tiny bit of sweetness. Not horrible at all."

Her hand sped up. I had to take a deep breath before I could speak. "Does that mean you're willing to taste me again?"

She nodded her head as she gave me a shy glance. Jesus, she was a damn siren. "I'd love to taste you, only..." she trailed off.

"Only what? Don't be afraid to tell me what you want and need, baby."

"Can I put my mouth on you? Is that something you like?"

I almost blew just hearing her ask. "God, yes, you can. I'd love that, but only if you want to do it. Don't just do it to please me."

She answered me by lowering her head and opening her mouth. Her tongue came out, and she swirled it around the head, taking my breath and sanity. I moaned. I had to clench my fists to keep from gripping her head and pushing her down on me. She hummed, then opened wider and sucked me inside. At first, she only sucked the head and swirled her tongue, then she took more. My balls were drawing up. I grabbed the base and squeezed.

"Am I hurting you?" she asked as she lifted up.

"Fuck no. I'm close. Being in your mouth is heaven, Troian."

The pleased smile on her face morphed into heat again as she lowered her mouth as I held the base. This time, she took me to the back of her throat. She gagged, which made me hiss. I thought she'd stop, but I was wrong. She took me deeper. Despite gagging, she kept sucking and swallowing. My hand came up to hold the back of her head. I didn't force more inside. I merely held her. "Shit, that's it. Swallow my cock, babe. It feels amazing," I whispered hoarsely.

Her hand came down, and she gently kneaded my balls as she bobbed up and down on me faster and tightened her magic mouth around me. I couldn't stop the tightening in my balls or lower back. Motherfucker, I was gonna die. I issued a warning. "Baby, I'm close. You have to stop before I come. There's nothing I'd love more right this moment than to come in your mouth and have you swallow my cum, but that's too much for your first time. Hell, that's if you even want that. If you don't, it's all good," I rambled.

Everything tightened, and my hips flexed. I shouted a warning since she hadn't stopped what she was doing. In fact, she sped up and gripped me tighter. "I'm coming!"

She shocked me by swallowing me deeper. I

exploded and groaned as I filled her mouth with squirt after squirt of my cum. She took it like a champ. Never once did she pull away or stop swallowing despite gagging a couple of times. By the time I stopped coming and wilted boneless into the mattress, she lifted up, then wiped her mouth with the back of her hand and smiled up at me.

Gripping her jaw, I tugged. She took the hint and raised up until we were face-to-face. Pressing on the back of her head with the other hand, I slammed her mouth down on mine. She gasped, and I speared my tongue inside. I could taste my cum. She was right. It was salty and sweet. It wasn't gross as I expected. I eagerly French kissed her. She whimpered and kissed me back just as eagerly. This was the first time I'd ever done that to a woman after she gave me head or had tasted my cum. I took my time before breaking it off.

She was flushed, and her gaze was heated. She squirmed slightly and closed her legs, which told me she was turned on. I smiled at her. "Thank you, Troian. That was the best blow job of my life."

She rolled her eyes. "I doubt that, but thank you. I promise I'll get better if you'll let me practice."

"I don't lie. That was the best. Being practiced at doing it isn't all that counts. You actually wanted to do it and enjoyed it, which made it great for me. I didn't expect you to swallow. I'll be more than glad to have you practice whenever you want. And I agree that the taste isn't what I expected either."

Her surprise was evident. "How can you not

know what you taste like when kissing a woman after she, you know?"

"You're the only woman I've ever kissed after a blow job. See, it's not just firsts for you. I think we'll have a lot of those. Now, I have a question for you."

"What?"

"Can I help you with that ache between your legs?" I asked, giving her a smoldering look. She was squirming, which told me she was turned on. She got redder but didn't answer. I decided to take control. If she didn't want me to do it, she'd have to tell me to stop. There was no way I'd watch my woman suffer if I could do something about it.

I sat up and then lowered her onto her back. She didn't fight me. Her breathing hitched. Her pants were the kind with an elastic waist. As soon as she was flat, I didn't waste time teasing the skin above the waistband after I pushed her top up to expose her belly. She shivered. Watching her expression, I slipped my finger under the band and ran it back and forth. She watched me.

After a couple of passes, I pushed the band down an inch. When that got no protest from her, I went for it. I eased my hand underneath the bands of both her pants and her panties. I moaned when I felt her soft curls. Jesus Christ, she was soft down there. I had to bite my lip to stop from demanding to see her pussy.

"Open your legs," I ordered. She did it without a single protest. I could feel the heat coming off her before I slid my finger down her slit. She cried out as I stroked over her hard, distended clit and down her slit to her entrance. I groaned. She was soaking wet and so hot.

I teased her folds and her nub. She shook. I withdrew my hand after several strokes and put my honey-covered finger in my mouth to taste her. I moaned. All good intentions flew out the window. I sat up and intently stared at her. "I want to see you and taste you fully. Can I take your bottoms off?"

It took her a few moments to nod yes. As soon as she did, I didn't waste time. I sat up all the way, tugged my jeans and underwear back up, then quickly lowered hers together. I didn't just lower them to her thighs, though. I took her clothing all the way off and tossed it to the floor. She tried to cover herself, but I wouldn't let her. Gently but firmly, I pressed her legs apart. Her pussy beckoned to me, along with her wetness and tantalizing scent. Growling, I lay down on my stomach and swiped my tongue from her entrance to her clit where I paused to suck it into my mouth. I worried it with my tongue.

Her scream was loud and long. I smiled and then kept going. Her pussy tasted better than any I'd ever had. Her responsiveness was the best, too. Hell, everything so far about her was the best. I sucked, lapped, and teased her without mercy. When I slid my finger into her hole, she came. I lapped up her honey and started to push her toward another orgasm. The first one was intense, and I wanted her to come again.

As I worked her, I made sure to rub my finger over her G-spot. That got her to babbling. "Oh God, Derrick, oh God. Please, I can't stand it. You have to stop," she pleaded brokenly.

I shook my head with her clit lightly clenched between my teeth as I flicked it with my tongue, and I thrust another finger inside of her, picking up the pace. She had to come again, maybe even twice more. Not only was I loving the response I was getting out of her, but she was making me hard again. I removed my mouth long enough to answer her.

"No, you need to come again. Give it to me. I need more of that sweet honey of yours. Fill my mouth and strangle my fingers. Goddamn, you're the tightest thing I've ever felt. Come for me, Hurricane. Come now," I ordered her.

I barely got my mouth back on her before she came again. She flooded my mouth and the bed. Her wails were loud and music to my ears. Her grip around my fingers made me growl. Her hand landed in my hair, and she pressed me tighter against her. I happily drank her cum down and wanted more. The taste of her was an addiction.

As she began to relax, I reared up and moved up until I could reach her mouth. Lowering mine down on hers, I kissed the hell out of her. I made sure to share her taste with her to see if she liked it. Her shuddering moan and the way her tongue frantically played with mine told me the tale. She didn't mind tasting herself. It was too much.

Lifting up until I was erect on my knees, I shoved down my jeans and underwear again, then fisted my cock. It was hard again. Like a possessed man, I stroked my cock with one hand, and with the other, I finger fucked her pussy, using my thumb to rub circles on her clit. She wailed and bucked her hips off the bed. I watched her with hot eyes as she got louder and wetter. My balls were tight, and I was close in no time.

I clenched my teeth so I wouldn't come until she did. It only took a minute or so for her to throw back her head and scream. Her whole body convulsed as she cried out my name and came. A couple of heartbeats after she began to come, I shouted, then started to shoot my load all over her belly and mound. I grunted with each jet of it. I coated her in my seed, and as it ran down her pussy, I wished it was inside of her. I had to fight not to thrust it inside where it belonged, but I couldn't do that. There was a chance she could get pregnant from it. And as much as I wouldn't mind getting her pregnant, I wouldn't take her choice away.

I slumped over her and stared deep into her slumberous eyes. "No more talk about leaving. You're mine, Troian. I'm yours. This seals it," I told her gruffly.

She gave me a shy smile as she caressed my face. "Okay, no more. I'll stay."

"And be mine."

"And be yours."

I sealed the deal with another intense kiss and then lay down beside her to regain my senses and feeling in my legs. Goddamn, she was likely to kill me, but it would be so worth it.

Troian: Chapter 8

It had been a few days since the whole thing blew up with Lash over the kiss and him running off, then me taking a walk and freaking him out. Or maybe it was my packing and talking about leaving that pushed him over the edge. Whatever it was, I was thrilled it happened because the man had shown me he definitely wanted me, and in a spectacular way.

I was not only pleasured almost out of my mind, but I had gotten to do things I'd never done. I didn't know how I knew that, but I did. One, I saw a cock in person and got to touch it. Two, I was shocked that I had been bold enough to touch him and give him a blow job. My untutored moves and responses had been enough to get him off, and then later, I turned him on enough to get himself off. The sight of him stroking himself to completion had been hot as hell.

Afterward, we cuddled until he got up and came back with a warm, wet cloth to clean me up. I tried to take it from him, but he gave me a stern look and told me that was his job. That was also the end of me sleeping in his guest room. He'd carried me to his room and the next morning, told me to move my stuff into his. I'd given him token resistance which earned me a kissing session that made me crazy and a smack on the ass. I might just have to resist all the time if that was my punishment.

Over the last few days, I tried to keep busy with cleaning the house, cooking, and spending time with the kids and old ladies. It helped, but I was still bored. I might not remember my past life, but from Spawn, I now knew I'd edited books. I wanted to know for whom and if there was a way I could still do it. When I suggested it, Lash had said it was too dangerous. What if they said something and it got back to my attacker? He had a point, although if I did it all online, I didn't know how it would.

The club was no closer to figuring out who had hurt me. Lash and Spawn had been here last night talking about it. I joined them. It had been frustrating. I wasn't upset with Spawn. I knew he was doing everything he could.

"You checked out every business contact she has?" Lash asked Spawn again.

"Yeah, I have, twice. As far as I can tell, and remember, I can't get into everything. None of them appear to have a reason to hurt her. The authors she works with love her work. They're the extent of her professional interactions. She doesn't interact with other people in the business. As for friends, I told you, she appears to stay isolated and only associates with her family. I did a search to see if there's any violent offenders in her town who might've fixated on her."

He paused, letting Lash ask, "And did you find any?"

"I did, but only a couple hurt women, and none of them appear to have crossed paths with Troian. They don't

go to the same stores, coffee shops, libraries, or anything. I can't be one hundred percent sure, of course, but as far as I can tell, it's a no. We have to consider it was purely random. She was out for whatever reason. Someone saw her, and she fulfilled their dark need to hurt someone. If that's the case, we'll likely never know who did it. Sorry, Troian," Spawn said with a sympathetic look.

"It's not your fault. I appreciate all you're doing to find out who did it, but at this point, it looks like we'll never know. Which means that hiding me here isn't necessary. Whoever did this was in Richmond and dumped me here. I doubt they're hanging around, waiting to see if my body is found. They might've been for a few days, but it's been almost three weeks. I should be okay to leave the compound."

"You're not going back to Richmond! I thought we talked, and you understood your place is here with me," Lash barked.

"We did talk, and I didn't say anything about leaving Bristol, crazy man. I'm only wondering if I could go to town and see where I'm now living and maybe find a job. And if there's a way to get my stuff from home."

"Give it another week or so, baby. I want to be sure you're truly safe. Even when you start going out, you're not doing it alone. As for a job, I hate for you not to be able to do what you were doing. Let me think about that. Now, the whole 'get your stuff from home thing,' I don't want that," Lash said.

"Why not?" I asked.

"Because we have no idea about them. Why haven't

they reported you missing to the cops? Spawn, have you started diving into them?"

"I haven't. Sorry, there was stuff Reaper had me do. I started with the most likely culprits first. I promise I'll do them next. I agree. It's weird that they haven't called the cops."

"They've never trusted the cops. Back in Russia, most were crooked," I said out of the blue. I jerked in surprise.

The guys both froze as they stared at me. It was Spawn who spoke first. "How do you know that? Did you remember something?"

"I-I'm not sure. It's not like I had a flash of memory. It was more like it just popped into my head and out my mouth like something I've always known. Like I know that I hate cooked spinach."

"That's good. It means more things are starting to come back. Can you remember anything else?" Lash asked eagerly.

I closed my eyes and concentrated. There were just flashes of a bedroom and a laptop with words on it. I opened them again. "I saw a bedroom. I think it might be mine. And a laptop with a bunch of words on it. It might've been me editing one of those books. That's it. Sorry."

"There's nothing to apologize for, sweetness. Just keep Lash informed of anything you remember, no matter how small, and he'll let me know if he thinks anything needs to be drilled into. I'm confident your memory will return when we least expect it," Spawn said sweetly.

I smiled at him. "Thank you, Spawn. I just want you

to know you're very sweet. How haven't you been snapped up by some woman by now?"

He burst out laughing. Lash let out a growl, and he was frowning. He tugged me onto his lap. Up until then, we were sitting next to each other. He cupped my jaw, so I had to look at him. "Hurricane, you do not say shit like that to anyone, not even my brothers. He's not sweet, and you're not allowed to think that. You're taken."

I huffed. "Really, you wanna act like a caveman? I was only complimenting him, not propositioning him for sex! I know we're together. I guess that's what this is called. Anyway, I wasn't flirting or trying to have sex with him. And what's up with this Hurricane name you keep calling me?"

"I am a caveman, and you love it. As for complimenting him, don't. He doesn't need a big head. His is big enough."

Spawn flipped him off. He sat there with a big grin on his face. When he saw me looking, he winked, which made Lash growl. Lash continued, "Wink at her again, and I'll pluck those eyes outta your head, brother. Troian, you're supposed only to see that I'm awesome. As for the nickname, that's what you remind me of. You came into my life like one, and when you get going, you remind me of one. You mix me up like one, too."

"Ahh, that's kinda sweet, I think. Unless you don't like me mixing you up."

"I love it, babe. Now, behave, and later, I'll show you how much I love it. Right now, we're entertaining this smiling fool. Don't look at him for the rest of his visit. He's

preening like a peacock. I might need my gun."

That made me laugh. The rest of the visit was filled with them talking about what else they could do, and Spawn got rises out of Lash by flirting with me. It was fun.

However, all that was in the back of my mind. I had something else to worry about today. The club had decided at the last minute, a couple of days ago, that they would have a party. However, it wasn't just them who would be there. It was their friends from both Warriors' chapters, and another club called the Ruthless Marauders. Lash had explained that the Warriors came out of Dublin Falls and Hunters Creek, Tennessee, and the Marauders were from Knoxville, Tennessee. Apparently, it had been a while since they saw each other and longer since it had been here.

I'd asked him what the club was celebrating. He said I'd see. The good thing was I was busy helping the ladies prepare for it. The prospects were put to work cleaning the clubhouse so it was spotless. I learned the extent of what their duties were, which was anything they were told to do. They did it without complaint. That impressed me.

The women weren't the ones who would make all the food for it and do the shopping. The prospects shopped for anything they needed, and Annie was providing some of the food. I learned she did that for most of their bigger get-togethers. The rest, the old ladies did, and I was more than happy to help them. I'd learned that I knew how to cook, and from what Lash said and now the ladies when they tasted what I made, I did it well. That made me happy.

Now that everything was prepared and the actual day was here, my nerves were out in full force. I had things to distract me from them over the past few days, but not anymore. I had gone back and forth a dozen or more times on what to wear. Thankfully, I finally broke down and asked Alisse, Lark, and Chey what to wear. They helped me and even lent me a top. It was sexy but not slutty. It was one of Alisse's, and they all swore it was perfect. With it, I was pairing jeans and a pair of heels that Lash had insisted I needed when he did the massive clothing order after I first got here. They were about three inches tall, strappy, and, of all things, red. The top I was loaned happened to be red, too. I'd shown them the shoes, and Alisse had giggled and gone home to get the top. All three insisted it was exactly what I had to wear.

Along with that, Chey lent me earrings and a bracelet to go with them. They were silver and black and had cool skulls on them. Just what you would expect a badass biker babe to wear was what she told me. I tried to argue I wasn't one, but she rolled her eyes and said yes, I was.

I forgot my nervousness when I was with Lash. He had to work during the day, but once he got home, it was all about us spending time together. We talked about so many things—him more than me since I couldn't remember much. That frustrated me to no end, but he was content to wait. He told me he had no doubt I'd remember, and if I didn't, then we'd learn together.

He and I learned about the kinds of shows and movies we liked, as well as music. I didn't do straight-out horror shows, but most other things I liked. Even the ones you'd think were for guys only, the explosion-and-shoot-'em-up kind. He was sweet enough to sit through romantic ones with me even though they weren't his thing. I tried to do horror with him but ended up hiding my face the whole time as he held and teased me.

Music-wise, we were both into country, rock, and heavy metal. He was more surprised by the last one than I was. I tried out opera and rap. Those were a hard no. He didn't listen to those either, so we were safe. While we were discussing music, I found out some of the guys in the club were musical and played and or sang. He quickly told me he wasn't blessed with that gene, but Reaper, Ink, Spawn, and Ratchet were. They all played an instrument, and in Ink and Reaper's cases, they also sang, as did Lark. I was hopeful that they might do it today.

Along with all this, there was a lot of special time. He kissed me repeatedly. When we woke up, he left for work, he got home, and before falling asleep was a given, he said, and I didn't disagree, but those weren't the only times. I'd be cooking or watching television, and he'd pull me closer and lay one on me. I got lost in him every time he did.

In bed, he'd make sure before I went to sleep to give me a few orgasms. He didn't go without either. I was diligent in learning about his body and what he liked. I was perfecting my oral work and hand jobs. The way he got off told me he more than liked what I did if his words left me in doubt. The only thing we hadn't done was go all the way. He never asked to do that, and I was hesitant to ask for it. Maybe he was waiting until he found out more about me, or I regained my memories. I knew he said I was his, so I assumed eventually we would.

If it were only my choice, I'd no longer be a virgin. He was driving me insane. I wanted to know what it would feel like to have him inside of me. It was that frustration, if you'd call it that, that had me voicing my concerns to the old ladies this morning when I was talking to them without him. They'd asked if we'd had sex yet. I figured they all knew from Alisse that I was a virgin. Remembering their responses made me smile and want to laugh.

"I don't think Lash is ready to have full-on sex yet with me. We've fooled around, but that's it. Maybe it's because he wants to know more about me or for me to recover my memories first. He insists I'm his, but I don't know."

"Girl, there's no way that man doesn't want you. Get that out of your head if you think that. As for waiting for you to get your memories back or until he knows you better, I can't see it," Alisse said immediately.

"I agree. Once these guys claim a woman, hell, even before they do, they go after what they want. I don't see Lash giving a damn about whether you have your memories back or that he has to know everything about you first," Chey added.

"Have you told him you're ready to go all the way? He's likely waiting for you to indicate or tell him you are," Lark responded.

"I haven't said it, but I thought that my willingness to do what we have done would show him that."

"Do you think he's holding back because of your condition?" Alisse asked delicately.

"Condition? What condition?" Chey demanded.

Alisse gave me an apologetic look. That told me she hadn't shared what she knew from my exam. I didn't see a reason to hide it from the other two. "She means the fact that at my advanced age, I'm still a virgin for some reason. He found that out when he did my rape exam."

"Girl, there's no reason to be embarrassed about that, no matter your age. I was twenty-five and still one when I met Reaper. He was happy as shit I was, the damn Neanderthal. Lash might not want to push you. I think the way to go is to just tell him and seduce him, and I have the perfect thing for that," Chey said with a grin.

Her perfect thing was hidden in one of my drawers. I planned to reveal it and my request after the party tonight. We all giggled and called it "Operation Deflowering." I might've not had friends back in Richmond, according to what Spawn had found, but I felt like I had them already here. It was wonderful.

I was over at Chey's getting ready with her, Alisse, and Lark. The guys were busy doing something, and the kids were either playing on the bedroom floor or napping. Flynn was out with Maniac. He was his mini-me. We'd told the guys we'd meet them at the clubhouse. We'd heard the roar of numerous bikes over the last twenty minutes. I had no idea who we might still be waiting on, but we were ready. I took one last look in the mirror.

The top was one that had chains holding it up. From there, it was open, then ended down on the arms in short cap sleeves. The front unzipped partially down the front, so you could control how much cleavage you showed. It was unzipped all the way since the girls insisted that I do that. Checking out their tops, I knew I wasn't exposing more than I should. Some would say that a redhead couldn't or shouldn't wear red. I didn't subscribe to that idea, and neither did they.

I left my hair long and straight. I was blessed with thick hair that looked great that way. They lined my eyes in dark charcoal gray shadow and black liner and coated my lashes in black mascara. On my cheeks, I applied only a faint blush to them since my lips were red. Thankfully, it was a long-wear formula that wouldn't rub off or have to be reapplied every fifteen minutes. I felt good, and the girls all whistled when they saw me.

Walking over to the clubhouse with them and the kids, I checked out the people milling around. There were guys, women, and kids all over. As we got closer, people began to notice us and call out to the other three while I got curious looks. I was looking for Lash when I heard Alisse mutter.

"If Lash doesn't want some of these guys over here trying to claim you, he'd better get out here and show them you're taken. Without a property cut, they have no way of knowing you're his. I see the dogs getting ready to come running and they're drooling."

I knew the leather vests they wore that had the names of their men on them were property cuts. I thought they were amazing, and secretly, I was jealous they had them. They just completed the biker chick look. The other two women laughed. I gave Alisse an amused look. "I hardly think they'll do that."

"Girl, are you blind? You're beautiful, and they can see it. See, here one comes. He's single, and I bet he'll turn on the flirting charm as soon as he gets here. Oops, make that here they come," Lark said with a giggle.

I watched wide-eyed as three men came toward us. I couldn't help but notice they were all very attractive men. I mean, I had eyes. They might not attract me like Lash did, but they were still nice to look at. They were all smiling as they joined us. The other women had stopped to wait for them to get to us. One was in the lead, and he was the one to speak.

"Hello, ladies. Do your men know how gorgeous you look?"

"Why, thank you, Jinx. We haven't seen them yet, but I'll be sure to tell Reaper you said so," Chey told him.

"Of course, you will. You want me to get killed, don't you? Why don't you introduce us to your friend?" He looked at me as he asked. He had the greenest eyes I'd ever seen.

She laughed. "Troian, this is Jinx. He's the president of the Ruthless Marauders. These two are King and Beast, two of his club brothers. Guys, this is Troian."

Before she could say more, Jinx stepped closer and held out his hand. He had a sexy smile on his handsome face. King and Beast were smiling, too. When I held out my hand automatically, he took and held it.

"It's a pleasure to meet you, Troian. Why don't we get better acquainted?"

"Hey, don't hog her," King said. Cheyenne had pointed out who was who when she introduced them.

"I wouldn't take her anywhere if I were you," Alisse said with a grin.

"Why not?" Beast asked.

"Because he might kill you," she added as she pointed behind them. I glanced up to see Lash bearing down on us like a bull. He had a determined look on his face.

Jinx didn't turn around and just sighed. "Who's your old man, darlin'? Damn it, why can't I ever meet one of you first? I get why Agony whined for so many years. Maybe if I start that, I'll find someone like he did."

"Agony?" I asked.

"He's the president of the Pagan Souls in Cherokee, North Carolina. He bitched for a few years until he finally met Eliana," Jinx added. King and Beast turned to look over their shoulders.

"Shit," Beast said.

"Goddamn, it would be him," King muttered.

"Just tell me, gorgeous. Don't make me turn

around," Jinx said with a sexy pout.

"She's mine, so get your grubby paws off her," Lash growled as he reached us. He bypassed them, came to stand beside me, and wrapped his arm around my waist, molding me to his side. He gave them a narrow-eyed glare.

Neither Jinx nor the other two seemed too concerned at his growl. Jinx didn't let go of my hand, though. Lash stared hard at our hands. Finally, Jinx sighed and dropped mine. "Lash, how did someone as mean and ugly as you get someone as beautiful as this? And why the hell haven't you put a property cut on her? If you don't want her carried off, you'd better do that soon."

"You let me worry about that. You just make sure it's not your ass I have to bury out back," he grunted.

I was getting worried about them going at it. I was about to say something when they all grinned and then started to laugh. The next thing I knew, Lash let go of me and was hugging and slapping them on the back. He came right back to wrap his arm around me again when he was done.

"Babe, these three are cretins, but we do consider them friends. Don't let them charm you either," he said with a grin.

"Cretin? Look who's talking. Where did he find you, darlin'?" Jinx asked.

I gave Lash a panicked look. I didn't know if they wanted me to tell their friends anything or to keep it a secret. Catching my look, they tensed and exchanged speaking glances.

"Is that something we shouldn't ask?" Beast asked.

"No, you can ask. The club was on a run three weeks ago, and on our way back, Alisse saw something off in the grass and weeds along the road. When we went to look, we found Troian."

"What the fuck? You mean she was standing there, right?" Jinx barked.

Lash shook his head. "No, she was rolled in a tarp. Someone had beaten her and left her for dead. We assume they dumped her body thinking she was dead."

This set off a series of swearing out of all of them. They were so loud they attracted the attention of others. I watched as more men and a few women started our way. Oh Lord, it looked like I was gonna meet a herd all at once. I gulped. Lash saw them coming, and he waited before saying anything else. The new bunch held six men and six women. I had no idea which clubs they were with since I couldn't see the back of their cuts.

"You gotta hear this shit. Tell 'em, Lash," Jinx demanded.

"This is Troian. She's my old lady. I was telling Jinx and the guys how we met. The quick explanation is we found her left in a tarp along the road. She was beaten and left for dead."

This made the women gasp, and the men swear. I

was turning red from the attention. One of the women reached out and took my hand. "Oh, honey, that's terrible. Please tell us you took care of whoever did this." The last part she said to Lash firmly and with a scowl.

"Let me make introductions before I answer that. Baby, this is Jocelyn. She's married to this guy. His name is Bull, and he's the president of the Hunters Creek chapter of the Warriors as well as the entire charter. These other guys are all his. This is Demon and Zara, Payne and Jayla, Tank and Brynlee, Joker and Raina, and Outlaw and Tarin. Now, to answer your question, no, we haven't because we don't know who did it. Troian has lost her memory. Until she remembers or we find something out from Spawn's digging, she's here, and we'll keep her within the compound. No one knows she's alive so keep it to yourselves. Even though she's from Richmond, we don't know if the culprit or culprits are still hanging around."

I was warmed to my soul when the offers came from all of them to help. Beast was first. "I'm good with a computer. I'll be more than happy to help Spawn with the work on this. If Reaper is okay with it, I'll get with Spawn while I'm here."

"I'm more than fine with it. I believe he did talk to Smoke, but you should check with them," Reaper said from behind me. I jumped and glanced around to find not only him but also Ink and Maniac. They were quickly claiming their women.

"I'm available too," Outlaw said. Bull nodded his head.

"Wait, I'm confused. What can you all do to help Spawn and this Smoke guy?" I asked.

Beast smiled at me and winked. "Babe, I'm a hacker like Spawn is. I'm not up to Smoke's level. None of us are, or his woman Everly's, but we're not slackers either. Outlaw is one, too."

I looked at Lash. "They're the hackers in every MC you told me about."

He laughed. "Not everyone has them, remember, but in the ones we know and claim as extended family, yes. We have three more besides these two if we want, and the Dark Patriots have people, too. I just didn't think we'd have to use them. Beast, stop winking at my woman."

Beast laughed. "I can't help it. I see a beautiful woman, and I have to flirt. Come on, you can't deny me that. It would be cruel and inhumane. I might die."

"You keep it up, and you might die anyway," Lash retorted.

"I think she's worth it," Jinx added as he winked. King, not to be outdone by his brothers, smirked, then gave me two winks. I couldn't contain it. I had to laugh too. I patted Lash's hard chest. "It's alright, honey, I can handle them. I promise their flirting won't go to my head."

"I know, but I'd still feel better beating their asses then killing them if they keep it up. I have to stay sharp and in practice, you know." He appeared very stern, then grinned at the scoffs and remarks he got back.

We spent several minutes chatting with them. Thank goodness it wasn't about my situation. The other women made sure to welcome me and tell me about themselves and their kids. It seemed their kids were here and off with other members or playing. After a bit, they let us go so I could meet the others.

Everyone was warm and welcomed me. There was more teasing and flirting from the single guys in the other clubs. I found out that other than a few prospects, all the guys in Dublin Falls had settled down. Over half of the ones in Hunters Creeks were, too. The Marauders were all bachelors. They had a lot of fun teasing me and telling me that I had options. We were talking to two of them, their VP, Animal, and a new member, Crow. He informed me he'd patched in barely a year ago. I'd met another one named Cujo, who had been patched in just over six months ago.

As we were talking, Crusher came up to us. He bumped my shoulder and asked, *"Kak dela, detka?"*

I smiled at him asking me how I was doing and calling me babe in front of Lash. I told him I was doing great. *"U menya vse otlichno, Krasher."*

I saw Animal's eyes widen, and he jerked. A huge smile spread across his face as he leaned closer. I was the one to be stunned next. *"Ona govorit po-russki?*

Before either Crusher or I could answer, Lash interrupted us. "Hey, speak English or at least translate. You know the rule, Crusher."

"Sorry, I keep forgetting. It's so unreal to have

someone I can speak Russian with. I had no idea how much I missed it. I asked her, how are you doing, babe? She said I'm doing great. Animal responded, asking 'she speaks Russian.' I see we surprised you with that one," he said to Animal, who was staring at me in awe.

"Surprised my ass, more like stunned. Goddamn, now you really have to leave Lash. You're my dream woman. Or you will be if you can also cook."

"She sure can. I taste-tested some of the stuff she made for today," Crusher said with a grin at Lash.

"I swear, if you don't stop trying to get her kidnapped by Animal or one of these other horn dogs, I'm gonna kill you, brother."

To my astonishment, Animal fell to one knee and took my hand. "Will you marry me? I promise to shower you with jewels, treat you like a queen, and give you all the mind-blowing sex you could ever want or need. Plus, I'm a club officer, unlike this bastard," he said with an adoring look on his face. I blushed. I wasn't sure what to say, even though I knew he wasn't serious. I settled on teasing him.

"Animal, you'd better watch doing that. What if you say that to the wrong woman?"

"I'm only saying it to you. I never thought I would find my very own Russian *koroleva*, queen," he informed Lash.

"Too bad. She's my queen, and no one is taking her." Lash growled at him.

Animal sighed and hung his head, then got to his

feet. He gave me a pleading look. "Please, tell me you have a single sister or cousin."

"I don't think so, but there could be. I don't remember my past, so I can't be positive."

Apparently, he hadn't heard my story yet, so this led to a ten-minute discussion with him and Crow, plus Crusher adding his thoughts. When we moved on to the next group, Animal gave me a mournful look and blew me a kiss before laughing and running. I hugged Lash.

"Honey, I like all your friends. They make me laugh and they sure know how to make a girl feel good. You're lucky to have them in your life."

"I'd like them more if they weren't trying to steal my woman away," he groused.

"You know, they're only playing. I think it's funny and sweet. As attractive as they are, they don't hold a candle to you, Derrick," I whispered so only he could hear me.

He stopped walking and took me in his arms. The kiss he laid on me would leave no one in doubt that I was his. I got lost, and, honestly, if he'd told me to take off my clothes right there and then, I wouldn't have remembered we weren't alone. That was even with the hollers and hoots we received. When he let go of me, my panties were wet. I let him know.

"You just drenched my panties. I need to change them."

"No, I want you to stay like that. Let me think about that all day, and later tonight, I'll peel them off and taste your sweetness. Fuck, I want to eat your pussy right now," he groaned in my ear. I shuddered. "Fuck it, come with me." He took my hand and hurried toward the clubhouse, which was only a few feet away.

"Lash, what're you doing?" I asked breathlessly.

He didn't answer. He took me into the clubhouse. People greeted us, but he didn't bother to return them. I waved as he practically dragged me down the hall. The next thing I knew, he pushed into a bedroom, then he slammed and locked the door. His heated gaze landed on me. I could see the erection he was sporting, trying to push through his jeans. I knew how big his cock was, and I wanted my hands and mouth on it. Hell, I wanted it inside of me.

"Strip and get on the bed," he ordered. He was tugging off his cut and shirt.

I hesitated. "Honey, we have guests."

"I don't give a fuck. If I don't taste your pussy right now, I'm gonna die. Do it." His words were partially an order mixed with a plea. I couldn't resist. I took off my top and wiggled out of my shoes and jeans. In the time it took me to do that, he stripped off everything. He stood there, fisting his erect cock and stroking it as he watched me. He licked his lips, which made me flood my panties more.

"Get the rest off and get in the center of the bed. Hurry," he growled.

I tore off my bra and flung it aside, then shoved down my panties. I barely straightened up before he was on me. He lifted me and threw me on the bed. His body came down on mine, and his mouth took mine again. His cock ground into my mound. I so wanted to widen my legs and let him slip inside, but he had them pinned. Instead, I thrust my hips up. He groaned and eased back from our kiss.

"Hurricane, you gotta stop that. I'm on the edge. I can't have our first time be in my old room in the clubhouse where anyone could hear or interrupt us."

"Then eat my pussy and let me suck you off so we can get through the day and evening. Then, tonight, you'd better make me yours, Derrick, in every way. I need you inside of me. Please." I was over waiting or being shy to voice my wants.

"Jesus Christ, please tell me you're not just horny and saying this," he pleaded.

"I already decided to ask you tonight well before you got me all crazy and hot. I'm yours for the taking, Derrick."

He answered me by rolling over onto his back, taking me with him. "Turn around and give me that beautiful pussy. Straddle me so you can reach my cock. Hurry. I need my appetizer for tonight's main event."

Giddiness filled me as I got myself situated. He grabbed my hips and jerked me back. He latched onto me, and I cried out. He wasn't playing around. Deciding to show him I wasn't either, I gripped the base of his huge cock and licked the head once before engulfing him, taking him as deep as possible. He grunted.

I'd discovered that I loved sucking his cock and making him come. The taste of his cum was like a drug for me. In addition, I loved having him eat me out. The man had seriously talented fingers, lips, and tongue. He made sure I came at least twice before he would let go, no matter how hard it was for him. I hadn't told him that my goal was to get him to blow after once and, eventually, him first. Hey, a woman needed goals.

I'd like to say I lasted forever, but I didn't. He had me shaking with the first one within a couple of minutes. The next one wasn't a whole lot longer than that. It was then that he let himself come and filled my mouth with his yumminess. As I went limp, I smiled and sighed in contentment.

Lash: Chapter 9

The hours since our side trip to my old room at the clubhouse seemed to have been days ago. I was about to lose my mind. All I could think about was getting Troian naked in our bed, in our house, and sinking my cock into her for the first time. I knew it would be the best sex of my life. What we'd done so far, even if not a lot, had been the best. She made me harder than any other woman ever had just by talking or being in my thoughts. Her hands and mouth on my body made me wilder than anything. I got off harder than I had ever in the past, with or without a partner.

We'd gotten smiles and smirks when we left my room, although no one outright said anything. I think it was her blush that stopped them. I didn't give a shit who knew what we were doing. I dared any of them to resist their woman. I knew my brothers would sneak off whenever the mood struck them. The intervening hours were filled with more talk, laughter, drinks, and food. Troian seemed to be fitting in well and enjoying herself.

It was getting late, and there was still something I needed to do before people either left or got into the more serious partying. The families would cut out early, and the single guys would have the bunnies and hang arounds show up to entertain them. Some of the couples might stay. It was their choice. I wasn't planning to do that. So far, Troian hadn't been exposed to those women, and I wanted to keep it that way for a while longer.

I knew it wouldn't be a pleasant discussion. I'd seen it with Lark and Alisse. Chey was slightly different because her dad had been part of the life, so she knew about them. Didn't mean she liked them any better, but they weren't a shock. I knew I'd have to warn Troian and get her to see that they would be around but not a part of my life. My cock belonged to one woman, her. However, I could understand not liking to have women who might've been with your man in your face. If she had prior lovers or one-night stands, I would fucking hate them to be near her.

Reaper, Maniac, and Ink had taken me aside the other day and asked if I'd explained about them yet. When I told them no, they cringed and suggested I do it before today. I knew they were probably right, but I didn't want anything to put a damper on today or ruin it. It was special for more than just introducing her to some of our friends, and that reason was about to be revealed.

I signaled Reaper. We'd agreed ahead of time when I wanted to do it. We were gathered outside in the barbeque area. He jumped up on a picnic table as Maniac cut the music. They weren't planning to play live music tonight, but it might still happen later. People looked around to see why and then got quiet when they saw him. Well, the adults did. The kids kept talking and playing, or in the case of the babies, some cried, but you could still hear his booming voice.

"Zip it. Lash needs your attention, you animals," he bellowed with a grin before gesturing to me. I took Troian's hand and led her to the table. She had a puzzled look on her face, and she asked me what was going on.

"Just come with me, and you'll see." When I got to the table, the others moved back. "Stay right there. Don't move," I told her before I stood on the seat of it. The grins and smiles told me the others knew what was about to happen, even if she didn't. It was a familiar scene that played out many times with those with old ladies.

"I've heard over and over today that I should make sure no one, least of all you slobbering dogs, steals Troian out from under me. I've been told that she shouldn't be running around without a property cut. Well, you're damn right she shouldn't. I would've made sure she had one before you all got here, but I wanted to present it to her with you all as witnesses."

I jumped down to stand beside her. She had her hands over her mouth and a shocked look on her face as Maniac handed me her cut. I raised my eyebrow. "What do you say, Troian? Are you willing to wear this and be my old lady? I know it's fast for you, but you and I already know what we want. This is the first step to making that permanent."

I waited nervously as she said nothing at first. God, had I made a mistake in doing it this fast? Should I have done it in private? What if she said no? I didn't think she didn't want to be mine, not if she was allowing me to touch her sexually and wanting to go all the way tonight. Finally, she lowered her hands, and a huge smile was on her face. She nodded yes as she said, "I'd love to have that, Lash. Of course, I'll be your old lady."

Before putting it on her, I had to grab her and give her a passionate kiss. The crowd hooted and hollered, then clapped and stomped their feet. I took my time with the kiss, then reluctantly broke it so I could put on her cut. She held out her arms when she saw I wasn't handing it to her. The sight of our club emblem on her back and the words, *Property of Lash* made me even more restless to get her alone and naked. She caressed the front of it, and then her head snapped up. She looked over her shoulder at me.

"Hurricane? Is that what everyone will call me, too?"

"Not all the time. Sometimes, if we're with others, they might. It's your club name, baby. I can't think of one that suits you more."

She smiled. "I love it. Now, I know we have to stay and be sociable, but as soon as we can sneak off, I want to go home and put this on with nothing else for you," she whispered softly.

The image of her like that hit me hard and low. My half-hard cock began to harden more. Fuck it, the others could get along without us. I let out a loud growl, and then I bent and hoisted her over my shoulder. She squealed, then laughed. The gang cheered and whistled. It would take too long to walk to the house. My bike was out in front of the clubhouse. I headed for it. Along the way, we were subjected to congratulations and ribbing about what we were off to do. When we got to my bike, I lowered her onto it and then got on. It took moments to get it started and moving. It was a quick ride to the house, only three streets down from the clubhouse. When we got there, I could hear the partying noise lessened. I didn't care. I was on a mission.

Parking, I shut it off and got off, lifting her again. I carried her to the house. Inside, I locked the door. No way did I want someone interrupting us. I carried her straight to our bedroom, and only when I got her there did I lower her to the ground. "I want you to take it all off except the cut and those red shoes. Leave those on. I've been fantasizing all day about those."

I started to strip as I told her that. She laughed. "So that's why you were so adamant I get them," she teased as she removed her cut to remove the rest of her clothes. My cut I hung up, but the rest of my stuff I shed, not caring where it fell. My boots were kicked into the corner. I'd pick shit up later. I beat her to naked by several seconds. As I stood there, I couldn't tear my eyes away. She was so damn beautiful.

It was obvious she had kept herself physically fit. Her defined, though not bulky, muscles were apparent. Now that her bruising and her soreness had gone away, she was starting to exercise. She told me it made her feel better. I had no issues with it. Even though she worked out, she still had curves in all the right places. I was never a fan of women who looked like a straight board or ones that were thin as a stick. Even though she was fit, she wasn't one of those stick figures either.

She had a nice plump ass, and her breasts, while not massive, were more than a mouth and handful. After pussy, I loved to have my mouth and hands on a woman's breasts. A nice ass was a close third. The cut gave tantalizing glimpses of her breasts and pussy when she slipped it back on. Those shoes made her legs look even longer and sexier. She gave me a shy, sexy smile, then ran her hand from her throat to just above her mound. That was it. I rushed her and took her down to the bed. She giggled and then moaned as I attacked her neck, biting her.

"God, Derrick, that feels good," she said softly.

"Oh, baby, I have so much more than that to make you feel good. I want you to lie there and only do what I tell you. Can you do that?"

"I think I can do that. What're you gonna do?"

"You'll see. Just know, if it's something you don't like, tell me, and I'll stop. Or, if you're not sure, tell me, and we can slow down. I know this is your first time, so it'll hurt. I'll go as slow as possible. I don't want to hurt you more than I absolutely can't avoid."

I hated the thought of hurting her, along with using condoms, but I knew I had to. She wasn't ready for a baby, although I did want her bare. That would be a first for me. "Later, we can talk about getting you on birth control. I don't want to keep using condoms if you agree." Maybe not the sexiest thing to discuss, but I wanted it out there.

"I have the shot," tumbled out of her mouth. I

reared back in shock. By the look on her face, so was she.

"When? How?" I asked.

"I-I don't know exactly when. It feels like it was recently, but it just flashed in my mind when you said that. I remember getting it, though. I saw someone giving it to me. How can I remember that but not the rest?"

"Babe, the mind works in crazy ways. You know that. Are you sure you got it, and it was recent, like in the past three months?" I asked eagerly. I didn't focus on why she had gotten it. If there was a man who she was thinking of sleeping with, he was a thing of the past. She was mine. Her heart, mind, soul, and body belonged to me just like mine did to her.

"I don't know how I know, but yes, it's been less than that."

"If that's the case, can I take you bare? I'm clean. I've always worn a condom, and I got checked not long ago. I haven't been with anyone but you since then."

Her answer was to reach up and pull my head down to hers. Right before she kissed me, she said, "I'd love to feel nothing between us, Derrick."

That was the last restraint on me. It broke, and we kissed hungrily. She ran her nails down my back as we kissed, making me hiss, but I loved the bite. Something told me between that and how she'd reacted to our previous play, she was gonna be a wildcat in bed. I fucking loved the thought. I liked my sex rough, wild, and, if she was willing, kinky.

I soon broke and had to leave her mouth so I could taste the rest of her. Before I let loose, I eased off her cut and shoes. I tossed the shoes to the floor but made sure to lay the cut on the bench at the foot of the bed. I kissed, licked, nibbled, and touched her, starting at her chin and all the way down her neck to her breasts. Once there, I focused on pleasuring her by loving her breasts for a bit before moving to her stomach. She was whimpering and impatient, pushing my head lower. I stopped and looked up at her.

"Put your hands over your head," I told her.

"W-what?" she stuttered. Her passion-glazed eyes were unfocused.

"You heard me. Hands over your head. Don't touch me unless I say you can. I need to concentrate on you, and your hands distract me."

"But I like touching you?"

"I'll let you later, but for now, I need you to do this for me. I want to make this the best experience possible for you, baby. You'll find that I like to be in control a lot of the time in the bedroom. Can you live with that?"

If she said no, I had no idea what I would do. It wasn't about being bossy. It was about bringing enjoyment to my partner and me, and, in her case, I could see myself being even more dominant since she meant everything to me. Her pleasure was an absolute must. She thought before she answered, which I liked. She wouldn't make a promise she didn't mean. Finally, she nodded her head.

"As long as I get chances to be in control and to touch you, then yes, I can do that. So, what're you waiting for? Take control," she told me as she raised her arms over her head. I groaned, then nipped her tummy with my teeth before pushing her legs apart and homing in on the prize between her legs. Her scent hit my nose and made me crazier to taste her, to have her come on my tongue and fingers, then my cock.

I traced a finger down her slick center, causing her to moan. Just that one swipe coated my finger in her wetness. I ran it back up and circled her hard clit. It was begging for attention. Her breathing was already speeding up. I smirked, then put my tongue to work. She cried out as I laved her folds, sucking on her clit between making circles. She became even wetter.

I stuck to that for a minute or two before inserting a finger inside of her. Shit, her tightness made me wilder. My cock throbbed with the need to bury itself in her and come, but not yet. I had to make her ready to take me. I wanted to cause her the least amount of pain as possible.

I made sure to rub across her G-spot with each thrust. She whimpered, and her hips came up off the bed. I growled when I caught sight of one of her hands coming toward me. She jerked it back over her head. "Good girl. Baby, have I told you how incredible you taste? And how much I love to make you come?" I asked as I paused to stare up at her.

She looked dazed as she met my gaze. It took her a few moments to answer me. She shook her head. "No, you haven't, I don't think. I don't know. I can't think," she moaned.

"Well, you do, and making you come is one of my favorite things to do. Now, come for me," I growled before lowering my head again. I attacked her with everything I had. It took barely a minute for her to tense up and scream. She gushed, filling my mouth with her sweetness. I growled louder as I lapped it up. However, I didn't stop when she stopped coming. I kept at it, pushing her toward another one.

It took even less time to get her there the second round. When she went off this time, I didn't wait until she was fully recovered before rearing up on my knees and lifting her bottom from the bed. She was panting as I notched the head of my cock to her entrance. I was so goddamn turned on that the head of my cock was almost purple. I eased the tip inside. The feel of her surrounding me like a tight band made me groan. I stopped. Fuck, this was gonna be harder than I thought. I was fighting not to just thrust all the way inside and pound her pussy until we both came.

I jumped when her legs came up to encircle my waist, and she tugged me close. I slid another inch deeper. "Babe, I don't want to hurt you. Don't," I warned her.

"You're hurting me more by waiting, Derrick. I need you. Take me," she pleaded. When I didn't, she growled at me. "Fuck me, please, baby," she cried as her back arched.

It was the look of desperation on her face, the

heat in her eyes, and the plea in her voice that did it. Letting out a roar, I thrust all the way into her, breaking through her barrier and planting myself deep. She tensed and moaned as I took her virginity. I had enough brain cells left to halt and give her time to catch her breath and let the pain hopefully ease. Motherfucker, she was so damn tight. She was like a skin-tight glove around me. I blew out my breath and held myself rigid.

I was afraid I was about to break and move when she gave me a sexy smile and told me, "I'm good. Move, honey. I need to know what it feels like to come on your cock and have you fill me with your cum."

I'd like to say that I took her slow and easy. I'd like to, but that wasn't what happened. Sure, I didn't rut into her like a complete animal, but it was close. I pulled back my hips, and when she gave no sign she was in true pain, I snapped my hips, sinking deep again. She whimpered. As I thrust in and out, I told her hoarsely, "You can touch me."

Instantly, her hands were running over my chest, teasing my nipples and then gripping my shoulders and back. I kissed her mouth hungrily, then latched onto her breast. I sucked and flicked her nipple over and over. I wasn't at it long before her nails bit into me, and she squeezed down hard on me. Shit, it was like a vise. I somehow held off from coming as she wailed and came. I didn't stop stroking in and out. In fact, I sped up. I was so close, but I wanted her to come with me.

Deciding I needed her in a different position, I pulled out. She sobbed and reached for me. "No!"

"I'm not stopping. I want you on your hands and knees, Troian. I need to go deeper," I snarled.

She whimpered, but she was quick to roll over and get up. She was barely in position before I was on her again, sliding in. Goddamn! I held onto her hips and used them to slam her on and off my cock as I powered in and out of her. She was sobbing and then screaming, and it wasn't in pain. She was wetter than any woman I'd ever been with. I felt her start to tighten moments later. I leaned over her and gently bit her shoulder. She detonated. Her screams almost hurt my ears. I let go, and as I came for the first time inside of her, I roared, "Fuck!" and then grunted with each jet of cum I gave her.

As she drained me, I couldn't help but wish she wasn't on birth control. The thought of giving her my seed and making a baby excited me. However, I knew she had things to resolve in her life before we could talk babies. But once we found and took care of whoever hurt her, I'd be having a talk with her.

She sagged to the bed. I followed her so I wouldn't slip out. I was drained, but I didn't want to lose the connection yet. I slumped over her but kept my weight mostly off her with my forearms. I kissed the back of her neck. She had her head turned to the side, her eyes closed, and a smile on her face. I nudged in to claim her mouth as much as I could reach. She turned her head more. When I broke our kiss, I whispered to her, "That was incredible, Hurricane. Are you alright? I didn't get too rough, did I?"

Concern filled me as the heat of desire eased. God, I'd gone at her like a beast. I started to ease out of her, but she protested. "No, don't move yet. You're right, it was incredible, and no, you weren't too rough. It was so hot. I never imagined it would be that good."

I growled and nipped her shoulder. "It's not that hot with anyone but you and me. No one can make you feel like that other than me," I warned her.

She giggled the minx and told me, "I wasn't suggesting they could or that I was planning to find out, caveman. You're who I want."

"And this is forever. I want all your love and affection, baby. You might think it's too soon for me to say this, but I love you, Troian. I've never told a woman that. I'll work my ass off to make you fall in love with me."

She wiggled like she wanted to move, so I reluctantly pulled out and lay down next to her. She rolled on her side and gripped my face between her hands. She gave me an intense look and then blew my mind. "You don't have to work to do that because I already love you, Derrick." She sealed that declaration with a heated kiss. I slipped into bliss as I kissed her back.

Eventually, we came out of our love-and-lust-filled haze. That's when I snapped into caregiver mode. I got up off the bed and held out my hand. She groaned, "I don't want to move."

"I know, but you need to get cleaned up, and I

want you to take a bath. A long soak will help with the soreness. Come on, I'll get in with you," I promised.

She crawled over to me. It was sexy as hell and made me want her all over again. In order to stop my erection from coming back, I picked her up bridal style and stalked to the bathroom. She squealed in surprise. I sat her down on the side of the tub so I could get the water hot and fill it.

While I worked and put bath salts in the water, she kept stroking her hands over my tattoos. Just that made me start to harden. She saw it and smirked. I pulled her to her feet and smacked her ass before stepping into the filling tub. "Behave. You're not getting me to do anything until you soak." I sank down and brought her to rest between my legs. I made sure to put in a tub big enough for two in the hopes that one day, I would share it with someone.

She sighed as the heat hit her. As she relaxed back against my chest, she looked over her shoulder and wiggled her eyebrows. "Does that mean as soon as I soak for a little bit, we'll repeat that? Because if you say no, I may cry."

I laughed and gave her a peck on the lips before I answered her. "Yeah, it means we can do that again, as long as you're not too sore."

"Yay!" she said with a grin and clapped her hands.

That made me laugh. "Nut," I said before settling in to wash her while she relaxed. I sure hoped she wouldn't be too sore to repeat that soon. I hadn't lied. It was the best sex of my life. I had no idea what I did to deserve her, but I was damn thankful I had.

Lash: Chapter 10

The past couple of days with Troian have been unbelievable. And it wasn't just because we were having sex. I loved every moment I spent with her, even if all we were doing was watching television or having a meal. I should've known something would dampen things.

I was at work when the call came in. I fumbled to get my phone out of my pocket. I tensed when I saw it was Spawn. There could only be one reason I could think of for him to be calling me at work. I answered swiftly, "Whatcha got?"

"I'm not sure yet, but I think we should talk. I'm not far from Iron's Rehab. I'll be there in five."

"Sure, see you in five."

He hung up. My nerves jumped. I didn't bother to keep working on the table I was making. I went to clean up. By the time he strolled in, I had some of the sawdust and wood chips off me, and my hands were clean-ish. I pointed to Tinker's office. He was out at a jobsite, so we'd be good to use it. As he took a seat, I closed the door. I got in the mini-fridge we had in there, got a bottle of water for us both, and then sat down. He gave me a chin lift when I handed him his.

I rolled mine between my hands. He had papers in

his hands. "Tell me," I said.

"So, I finally got started on really digging into Troian's family like you asked. I don't know for sure if this means anything when it comes to whoever beat her, but it does make me want to look at them closer. It seems about six months ago, her second cousin, Andrik, went to prison. His family is the one she lived with. He's the oldest."

"What did he do?"

"He was found guilty of forcing women into prostitution. He had a whole stable of them working for him."

"What the hell? Please tell me none of them were underage." The idea that any were forced was abhorrent to me and the whole club, but if any were teenagers or kids, I'd lose my shit.

"Not that I've found so far. The ones who testified against him were all over eighteen."

"So, they got the courage to turn him in. That's good. Was it only him, or were there others involved?"

"That's the thing. I don't think the women were the ones to go to the cops, at least not at first. I'm reading the official court transcripts, and something seems off. I'm working to get my hands on the prosecutor's personal notes on this case. They had details that those women shouldn't have known about the business side of things. Sure, they would know how he forced women and locations where they worked and who the customers were, but not the other stuff. They had enough to bury his ass. They got him for pimping and pandering, which is a class-four felony. That's typically a two to ten-year sentence and or a hundred thousand dollars in fines. He got the max fine and the max of ten years. As far as they knew, he was the only one involved."

"But you don't think that's true, do you?"

"Honestly, no, I don't. I have to wonder if there were other family members and maybe friends involved in it. They found a couple of accounts with a lot of money in them, but based on the number of women he was running and the prices, it didn't seem to jive."

I didn't want to ask my next question, but I had to. So far, we'd assumed Troian was a victim. What if she was a perpetrator who someone punished for her involvement in her cousin's business? I wanted to vomit at the thought. "Do you think Troian was involved in his business, and someone found out and was seeking justice?"

"Lash, don't go there, man, not yet. I don't think she was. She's too sweet to do that," he protested.

"But we can't be sure she wasn't. It might just be that her memories are gone. Shit, do you think I want to believe that? It's making me sick to even suggest it, but we have to be sure. Or, what if she never really forgot? This could be her way to hide out." I had to swallow the bile that came up the back of my throat.

"If you ask her that and it turns out not to be true, she might never forgive you. Let's talk to the guys and see what they think. I'll get Smoke and the others working on it, too. The sooner we find out, the better."

"Do it. I want this done today."

"On it. Just stay calm and don't go off half-cocked," he warned me.

After he left, I couldn't forget what he told me or my concerns. I was worthless to work, but I didn't want to go home. I wasn't ready to face her. I wasn't sure I wouldn't tell her what we found and what I needed to know. Time crawled by until I got the text telling all of us to get our asses to the clubhouse for church within the hour. Shit, maybe I should've talked to Reaper myself rather than asking Spawn to do it.

I rode into the gate, feeling like a lead weight was in my stomach. I saw several of the guys were already there. I parked and walked inside. They were gathered in the common room talking. You could tell they were discussing what the hell was goin' on. I didn't stop to talk. Instead, I went straight into church. Reaper was there. He stood up.

"Don't go there, Lash. We don't know if that's true or not," he warned me like Spawn did.

I sat down and put my head in my hands. "I don't fucking want to, but I have to consider it might be possible, Reaper. Jesus, what if she's involved? I love her, goddamn it! I want to spend my life with her!" I practically screamed.

Rustling made me look up. I saw a few of my brothers coming in. They'd heard me and were giving me worried looks. Sandman was the one to say something. "What the hell are you yelling about? Why can't you spend your life with Troian?"

"Sit down, and we'll explain," Reaper ordered everyone. They did, but you could see they wanted answers now. As soon as they were all seated and the door was shut, he got right to it.

"Spawn found out some stuff today about Troian's family. Now, I want you to listen to him and not jump to conclusions. We don't know anything else yet."

I sat in misery as Spawn swiftly told them what he told me earlier. When he was done, there was muttering and several incredulous looks. Maniac shook his head. "There's no fucking way she's involved in a forced prostitution ring. That's what you're thinking, isn't it? That she was hurt due to her involvement being discovered. Come on, Lash, you can't believe that."

"I don't want to! I've seen nothing that indicates she is, but what if her memory loss is masking something?"

"Or she's faking memory loss to hide out. If you think it's even remotely possible she was involved, then you have to have thought that's possible too," Tinker added.

I came bounding to my feet. "Nope, fuck it. I refuse to believe it. No one is that good of an actress. Her memories might be gone but her personality isn't. Spawn, tell me you'll figure this out soon."

"Brother, I already have the others working on it. One of us will get our hands on the truth. Just don't say anything to her. If you do and she's innocent, you'll crush her."

"I don't want anyone to say anything to her. Do you hear me?" Reaper snapped.

"I don't either," I added.

"We won't," everyone echoed back.

"Do you think the other family members were involved?" Remus asked.

"I have no clue. That's something else we hope to figure out," Spawn told him.

The meeting didn't last long after that. When we filed out to the common room, I had to stop and grab a beer. I wasn't ready to face her yet. I needed some Dutch courage first. My brothers joined me and didn't say a word.

Troian:

Something was wrong with Lash. In fact, something was up with all the guys. For the past week, they'd been kinda stilted when speaking to me. I saw them laughing and joking less when I was at the clubhouse. The women seemed fine. I'd asked Lash repeatedly what was wrong. He kept telling me nothing, but I knew it was a lie. He was barely touching me and was spending less time at home. He insisted he was tired, and he stayed late at work, sometimes not coming in until after I was in bed.

I didn't want to think that he regretted claiming me and telling me he loved me, but I didn't know what else it could be. Or had he tired of me already? Fear made me sick. What if he came home and told me he wanted me gone, not just from his house but the compound? I had no job, and if I couldn't go back to Richmond, then I would have no place to live.

It was these fears that had me using his computer during the day. I knew they didn't want me to contact anyone from my former life, but I had to protect myself. That was why I'd reached out to a few of the authors I'd worked for. I found their names and emails on a piece of paper on his desk when I was searching for a pen and paper. I wasn't sure why he hadn't shown it to me, but I didn't ask.

I gave them a long apology for dropping off the radar and explained that I'd had a personal tragedy. Kindly, they forgave me. They expressed how sorry they were and asked if they could do anything. I told them I was wondering if they had any editing jobs they needed to have done. A few said no, but others said they were so glad to see me back, and they did have work. I agreed to take those and set deadlines to get them done and back to them.

As soon as he left in the morning for work, which was earlier than he had in the past, I got started. I worked all day and didn't stop other than to go to the bathroom until I heard him come roaring up to the house on his bike. When that happened, I shut it all down. I didn't have to worry about cooking him dinner since he was no longer home for that, and I had no appetite. The lack of which I already saw in the fit of my clothes. I was barely taking in anything during the day. I couldn't do it, though I needed to eat. Today, I'd gotten up and almost fainted when I got dizzy. I knew it was due to low blood sugar. I'd choked down an apple and a glass of milk.

Deciding I needed to do something healthy, I left the house to take a walk. It was the middle of the day. I had time to do it and make it back to do more editing. Aimlessly, I wandered around. Before I knew it, I was almost at the clubhouse. The sight of all the bikes and a few trucks caught me off guard. Why were they home in the middle of the day? Hurrying to see if something was wrong, I rushed to the door and went inside.

The common area was empty, but I heard the

rumble of voices down the hall. Curious, I went that way. I was almost to the room where they had church when I stopped. They were in a meeting. I knew those were private and not to be interrupted unless it was an emergency. Lash had told me that weeks ago. I turned to go back the way I had come when I heard my name mentioned. I crept closer. Why would they be talking about me?

"Smoke got the information. Troian wasn't involved in her cousin's forced prostitution ring like you feared, Lash. You can stop worrying about it or that she's faking her memory loss to have a place to hide out," Spawn said.

I had to cover my mouth and bite down on my lip to keep from giving away the fact I was out there. Unimaginable pain ripped through me. I bent over, trying to breathe. I knew I had to get away before they caught me. Somehow, I made it out of the clubhouse. Outside, I threw up in the grass. Gazing around in a fog, I spotted Lash's truck. He'd taken it to work this morning rather than his bike. I ran over to it. Climbing inside, I prayed his keys were in it like usual. I sagged in relief when I saw they were. Starting it, I threw it in reverse and backed up.

By some miracle, neither Colt nor Rhaines were at the gate when I got to it, and the automatic opener triggered. I squeezed out and took off. I hadn't been to town since I'd been here, but I knew the bikes and cars always turned right when they left, so I went the opposite way. As I cruised along, tears blurring my vision, all I could think about was what Spawn said and my thoughts. Oh my God, Lash thought I was involved in something like that? And that I was lying about my amnesia?

How could he say he loved me then think that? And what cousin were they referring to? As I drove, the pain began to compete with the anger. Fuck him. I was gone. I'd use his truck to get to the next town and then leave it. I'd find a way to get in contact with my family and let them know where I was. Surely, one of them would come get me. I never wanted to see his lying face again. If I couldn't find a phone number, I'd hitchhike my way back. I knew my address from the photo of my driver's license when Spawn found out who I was.

I was so caught up in my thoughts and escaping that my reflexes were slow. I rounded a turn and wasn't able to avoid the dog standing in the middle of my lane, frozen in fear. I jerked the wheel hard to the left to avoid hitting him. The truck fishtailed. I tried to correct it, but I overdid it. The next thing I knew, I hit the edge of the road, and the truck flipped and rolled. I screamed as I was thrown all over the cab. I prayed I would survive as I rolled down the embankment. When it came to a shuddering stop, I was gasping and in pain. I tried to get my belt off and get out, but when I moved, agony shot through me, and everything went dark.

I had no idea how long I was out, but when I came to, it was to lights, loud voices, people asking me questions, and pain. It took me a couple of minutes to realize it was police officers, firemen, and paramedics. They were asking me questions but I couldn't seem to form coherent answers other than to tell them my first name. In no time, they had me out of the truck, strapped to a gurney, and in an ambulance. As it raced to the hospital, I let oblivion take me again.

Lash:

My relief at knowing for certain that Troian wasn't involved in her cousin's prostitution business was immense. I'd known deep down it wasn't possible, just like it wasn't possible she was faking her amnesia, but it was great to know it absolutely. It had been hell staying away from her for the last week as I waited for the news. I didn't want to risk blurting anything out to her. It would hurt her to know that we ever wondered or had investigated further to prove it wasn't true.

Smoke's findings didn't answer other questions. One, were other family members involved in it? Two, had someone hurt her, thinking she was involved? Spawn told us he was still working with the other hackers to find out more. I was anxious to get out of there and go see my woman. I needed to hold her and make love to her.

We were about done when my phone rang. We'd gone on to discuss other stuff while we were here. Usually, I had it on silent when we were in church. Unlike some clubs, Reaper didn't insist we leave them outside. I took it out to silence it. However, when I saw the number, I knew I should answer it. It was one of the paramedics I knew and worked with. If he was calling, it must be important. I glanced at Reaper. He nodded.

"Hello, what's up, Perry?"

"Lash, do you know a woman named Troian?"

I went on alert. How did he know her name? "Maybe, why?"

"We're outside of town, about fifteen miles from your compound. We just found your truck and a woman was driving it. She said her name is Troian."

"What?" I shouted as I came to my feet. Everyone got deathly quiet. "What do you mean you found it and Troian?"

"I'm sorry, man, but your truck rolled, and someone called it in. We just transported the woman to Bristol General. When the cops said who the vehicle was registered to, I thought I should call and let you know. They'll probably be calling soon."

My legs gave out, and I slammed down into my chair. "H-how badly is she hurt?"

"We don't know for sure. She was unconscious when we got to the scene. She briefly woke up and told us her name. Then she was out again. You should get to the hospital. She's back with the doctors now. I take it she's important," he said hesitantly.

"Yeah, she's my old lady. Thanks, I'll be there. Let them know I'm on my way, and she's mine."

"Sure thing."

I didn't wait to hear if he had more to say. I hung up. As soon as I did, the guys all started talking. It was

Reaper who I ran into as I went to the door. "Lash, what happened to Troian?

"She rolled my truck. Fuck, how did she leave? When? Why? I gotta go."

No one tried to stop me or ask more questions. The thunder of boots behind me told me most if not all, were following me. Outside, I realized I'd have to go home to get my bike. Before I could take off running, I was grabbed by Tinker. He pointed to his truck. "Get in. You're in no shape to ride."

I didn't argue and got in. In a matter of moments, we were headed for the gate. I fidgeted as we waited for it to open wide enough to let us out. When we got on the road, he started talking. "She'll be alright, Lash. What did Perry say?"

"Someone found my truck rolled about fifteen miles outside of town. She was unconscious when they found her. She woke up and told them her name, then went out again. She's at the hospital. When he heard the cops say it was my truck, he called. Jesus Christ, what was she doing outside the gates, Tink? Why would she leave and go that way?"

"I don't know, but there has to be a good reason. You can ask her after you know she's alright."

"What if she isn't? Not staying awake is a bad sign. She's already lost her memory. Fuck!" I shouted and beat on the dash with my fist.

He reached over and grabbed the back of my neck, giving it a hard squeeze. I knew he was trying to convey strength and reassurance, but it wasn't working. The drive passed in a blur as I sat there imagining the worst-case scenarios. I prayed that she'd be okay. I couldn't lose her. It would destroy me.

When we pulled into the parking lot of the ER, he stopped long enough to let me dive out of his truck so I could run inside. I didn't wait for anyone else. The roar of their bikes was background noise for me. I went through the staff entrance. No way was I going to stand in the damn waiting area. Staff looked up, and when they saw me, they jumped into action. The doctor, an orderly, and a nurse all came hurrying over to me. I knew them all.

"Where is she? I need to see her," I snapped urgently.

"Lash, let's go sit down and talk," Dr. Sharma said.

"Doc, I respect the hell outta you, but I need to see my woman. I know she's here. Let me see her. What've you done so far? What's her condition? Have you started running any tests on her yet?" I barked.

"You can't be back here when the patient is family, you know that. We'll let you know as soon as we know something. She's been in and out of consciousness and in a lot of pain. She's having X-rays done at the moment. We're doing a PET scan next, then an MRI."

"She was hurt not long ago and lost her memory. I'm pretty sure it's retrograde amnesia. Did she tell you that?"

He frowned. "No, she didn't. Who treated her? I need her records."

"She wasn't treated."

He gave me a censorious look. "Don't. There was a reason she didn't come here. I'll explain it to you in private," I told him.

"Follow me," he said. I let him lead me to the dictation room that doctors used. I shut the door behind us. "Okay, we're alone. Tell me. Lash, you know I respect the hell out of you, but if I make an exception for you, I have to for everyone else who works here."

"I need to speak to her and find out why she was outside the compound. The reason she never got treated was the club and I found her in a tarp, badly beaten, and left for dead along the road. She can't tell us who did it. We figured it was better to keep her under wraps and safe than to risk whoever did it finding out she was still alive. If we went to the cops, that might've happened. This might be due to them finding her. My club can keep her safe. The police won't put a detail on her twenty-four seven, you know that."

He didn't say anything for a couple of minutes as he thought about what I said, and then he sighed. "Shit, you're putting me in an awkward position, Lash. However, since this is only hearsay, I don't technically have to report it. I didn't witness her condition. You're right. Even if the cops did know, they wouldn't put a security detail on her, and I know how you Punishers are when it comes to protecting people. Okay, you can stay for now. As soon as they're done with her X-rays, you can go see her. She's in bed seven."

"Thanks, Doc," I told him. He gave me a nod and then opened the door to let me leave. I went out by the cubicles and waited. I stayed out of the way and paced. Most of the staff I knew, so they smiled and spoke to me. I was at least with it enough to greet them back, even if I didn't smile. It was about ten minutes before Rosemary, one of the nurses I worked with more than a few times, came up to me.

"Hey," she said.

"Hey, yourself."

"I wanted to let you know your girl is done with her X-rays. You can go see her. They'll be up soon, though, to take her for her PET scan and MRI."

"Thanks, Rosemary. Is she awake?"

"She is. She's a bit groggy. She was thrown around pretty hard from the looks of her. She's banged up good and there are lots of cuts. Just don't freak when you see her."

My gut tightened. The thought of her hurt in any way, even if it ended up only being superficial, made me sick. "I won't. I'd appreciate it if you'd keep me informed of anything else you find out."

"I will. Go see her," she said as she patted my arm before walking off.

Rosemary was one of my favorites. She was steady, and nothing ruffled her. Of course, having a husband who was a fireman and five kids probably helped. I didn't waste any more time getting to bed seven. The curtains were closed. I eased them open. I had to bite my lip to keep the hiss from escaping.

Troian was lying there with her eyes closed. They had her hooked to monitors. That wasn't what got to me. It was the bruises already forming on her face, arms, and upper chest and the cuts. She had a white bandage wrapped around her forehead. "Baby, it's Lash," I said softly.

Her eyes flew open and landed on me. I thought I'd see relief and happiness in them. I was wrong. They were filled with anger and mistrust. As I went to open my mouth to ask what was wrong, she yelled, "Get out! I don't want you here, you son of a bitch! Nurse, nurse," she yelled even louder.

I rushed to her bedside. I tried to touch her, but she slapped my hands away. Jesus, she was confused and didn't know me. "Troian, sweetheart, it's Lash."

"I know who you are. Leave. I don't want to see you again," she snarled.

I fell back a step at her ferociousness. What the hell was wrong with her? This wasn't her. The curtain was ripped back, and there stood Rosemary, Dr. Sharma, and an orderly. I forgot his name. He was new. They were eyeing us in shock.

"Troian, what's wrong?" Doc asked.

"I don't want him or any of his club near me. If they don't leave, call the cops."

He gave me a stunned look. I tried again. "Baby,

you're confused. It's me, Lash, your man. Remember?"

"Oh, I remember, and I know exactly what I'm saying. I never want to see you or anyone from your club again. You're not my man. As soon as they say I can go, I'm outta here. I'm taking my fake amnesia and prostitution ring ass away from you and this town," she hissed.

My heart dropped. Fuck, she'd heard what was said in church. I felt sick. "Babe, let me explain," I pleaded. I took a step toward her again, and that's when she totally lost it. She screamed at the top of her lungs, grabbed the tissue box on her bed table, and threw it at me. More things came whizzing at me as she continued to scream. I ducked and weaved. More staff came running. She was totally out of control. Tears ran down her face.

Dr. Sharma grabbed me. "You've gotta go. This isn't good for her, Lash. We have no idea if she has internal injuries. This could cause more damage. Go."

"I can't leave her like this."

"If you don't, you could make her hurt herself, maybe even kill her if there's internal bleeding."

That made me reluctantly back away. They were trying to calm her. I saw one of the nurses injecting something into the IV they had in her arm. She was now just loudly crying with her eyes closed. It almost killed me to walk away. I was pushed toward the exit and then into the waiting area, where I saw several of my brothers standing there with worried expressions on their faces. As I reached them, I was grabbed and escorted through the waiting room to the outside. They took me around to the side of the building. I sank into a crouch and held my head.

"What the fuck was that?" Mayhem asked. The others were all muttering. I looked up at them.

"She heard."

"Heard what?" Reaper asked.

"What was said in church. She knows I thought she might be part of her cousin's prostitution ring and was faking her amnesia. She fucking heard, and I'm sure that's why she left. She hates my guts. Wants nothing to do with me," I muttered.

"Son of a bitch, are you kidding me?" Maniac asked. I shook my head no.

"Let her calm down for a few minutes, then go talk to her," Ratchet said.

"I can't. They had to sedate her to calm her. Dr. Sharma is afraid she might have internal bleeding. The way she was acting, it could make it worse, maybe even kill her if she has any." I tugged my hair. I wanted to rip it out by the roots and bang my head off the brick building. How the fuck had everything gone so wrong? How did she hear us?

"Okay, then wait until they make sure she doesn't have any serious injuries, then talk to her. We'll help you explain it," Ink said.

"You didn't see her face. She's beyond hurt. I'm pretty sure she hates me. She's leaving town once they release her," I told them in agony.

My insides were raw, and I was choking back tears. Surely, I hadn't found her just to lose her. Why the fuck did I ever voice those stupid worries? Even as I said them and I knew we had to check it out to be sure, I knew there was no way she was faking it or was involved. Christ, what if she left and I never saw her again? I curled over and slammed my hands on the ground. I beat them off it over and over.

Strong hands gripped my shoulders. I didn't bother to see who it was. They shook me, which made me snap my head up and around so I could glare. I saw it was Reaper and Maniac. "We'll find a way to make her listen. She loves you. Give her time. We won't let her leave and never come back," Reaper told me.

I tried to choke back my fear. I was about to ask what he would suggest we do when Alisse came running out and over to us. I came bounding to my feet. She looked scared.

"What's wrong?" I asked as I grabbed her upper arms. Ink growled low, making me realize I gripped her hard. I let go and gave him an apologetic look.

"A nurse came to find you. You need to get in there," she panted.

I didn't wait to hear more. I took off running. As I entered the waiting room again, I saw Rosemary standing at the entrance to the treatment area. I ran over to her. "What?" I asked.

"Stay calm, okay. She started having severe

abdominal pain. They're taking her in for emergency surgery. I thought you'd want to know."

"No!" I yelled. I tried to get past her, but she blocked me. I wouldn't shove her away.

"Lash, they already took her to the OR. You can wait in that waiting room. I promise someone will keep you informed, okay?"

I hung my head. She gave me a sympathetic look and a pat before closing the door. I heard the hard thump of boots behind me. I knew it was my brothers. I turned to face them. "She's having severe stomach pain. They took her to the OR to find out why. I'm headed to that waiting room."

They didn't say a word. Alisse and Chey wrapped their arms around me and led the way. I was numb. I knew too much about the possible reasons for her to be having abdominal pain. Many of them were life-threatening. All that ran through my head was that she could die. I barely made it to the new waiting area before my legs gave out, and I collapsed on a chair. Chey and Alisse sat on either side of me with their men next to them. The others sat, stood, or paced the room. There wasn't anyone else in there at the moment. Misery filled me as I waited to know if I would have a reason to continue living.

Lash: Chapter 11

Time crawled by. I swear the fucking clock stopped moving. If it wasn't for my club and family, I'd have lost my mind and torn the place apart hours ago. It had been three hours since they told me they took her to surgery. We'd been updated a couple of times that she was still in surgery and that the doctor would come to talk to us as soon as she was done. They didn't have any news as far as what they found or if she was gonna be alright. I knew they couldn't tell me that, but I still wanted to hear it. The longer it took, the worse I knew it was.

I was no longer sitting. I couldn't. I was pacing. Another family had come to the door but left when they saw us. If someone didn't come out soon and tell me what the hell was goin' on, I'd snap. Amend that. I was done. I stormed toward the door. I was getting answers no matter what I had to do.

"Shit," I heard one of the guys mutter.

"There he goes," another said.

"Get him." I think it was Reaper who ordered that. Chair legs scraped, and footsteps came for me. I gave them all my best "step back or die" glare.

"I need fucking answers, and you're not stopping

me," I snapped at them.

"We're fine for you to ask, but you look like you're about to explode. If you do, they'll kick your ass out," Tinker warned me.

"What would you do if that was your woman?" I snarled at him.

"Lose my shit and hope my brothers will keep me in check," was his immediate response.

He was shoved but barely rocked on his feet. Then I saw Annie squeezing by him and coming for me with a determined look on her face. She stopped in front of me with her hands on her hips. She gave me a stern glare. "You stay here, and I'll go ask. If you get yourself kicked out of here, I'll smack you myself. Sorry it took so long to get here. I was outta town when Alisse called."

"Where were you?" Tinker asked.

"None of your business, nosy. Now, let me go find out something before Lash's head explodes and he becomes a patient," she said with a wink, then she was gone.

It took almost everything I had not to follow her, but the guys diverted my attention by talking about Annie.

"She's been out of town a lot lately. I wonder what she's been doing?" Sandman mused.

"I think she's got a man," Crusher said with a smirk.

"A man? Why? What did she say?" Tink

immediately jumped in to ask. He was frowning hard. A few others grumbled a bit, but he appeared upset.

"Nothing, but she's been smiling more, and I saw her all dolled up one day. I asked her where she was headed, and she said out of town. That's all she'd tell me," Crusher said.

"And you didn't think that was something the rest of us should know? What if he's some creep or no-load user? We need to know who she's seeing so we can pay him a visit," Tinker snapped.

"Shh, she's coming," Shadow hissed. He was standing by the door, looking down the hallway. Alisse and Chey giggled and exchanged amused smiles.

When Annie entered, she wasn't alone. There was a man with her. He was wearing scrubs, and a mask was dangling from his neck. He looked about fifty. I also noticed his eyes were on Annie's ass. The growl that came out of Tinker had the man's eyes snapping up, and they widened when he took in the wall of leather, tats, and scowls facing him. He paled. His Adam's apple bobbed as he swallowed.

"This is Dr. Heatherton. He's the surgeon who performed Troian's surgery. I found him at the desk. This is her man, Lash. Give him an update before he goes apeshit," she ordered him. It was no surprise, as Annie ordered everyone around.

"U-uh, yeah, so your..." he petered off.

"My old lady, Troian," I prompted him. He wasn't filling me with much hope in his ability as a surgeon.

"Yes, Troian, she's in recovery. She should be moved into a bed in the next couple of hours. We're keeping her in the ICU overnight to be sure she's okay."

"I assume that means you found the source of the pain and repaired it. What was the cause?" I asked impatiently.

"The wreck appears to have caused a laceration to her liver. She was bleeding internally, and it was severe. I was able to repair it. Thankfully, she exhibited symptoms before it was too late to do something about it. I was able to patch up the laceration, and she seems to have stopped bleeding."

God, he was right. It was a miracle they caught it before she was too far gone. People died from this kind of injury more times than you would imagine, while others could heal without surgery. I had to see her. I needed to see for myself that she was really alive and on the road to recovery. "I need to see her."

"As soon as she's out of recovery—" I cut off his bullshit.

"Doc, I know all about recovery. I work here in the ER sometimes. You can let me back there," I ordered him.

He sputtered like he was about to say no, but then he took a closer look at my face and stopped. "Give me a few minutes, and then I'll send someone to get you, but only you."

"That's fine. I'll be waiting," I said.

He didn't waste time scurrying away like his ass was on fire. The guys snorted and laughed. Annie scoffed and glared at me. "Really? I get you someone, and you scare him into shitting himself."

"He's lucky that's all that happened to him. We should've blinded him for staring at your ass," Tink snarled.

She gave him a shocked look and then shrugged. "Hey, if he wants to look at my ass, at my age, who am I or you to tell him not to. Although I doubt that's what he was doing."

"Oh, he was," Ratchet assured her.

Her satisfied smirk had Tink growling deep in his throat. What the hell had gotten into him? If I didn't know better, I'd think he was jealous. Was that it? I glanced at him. When he saw me, he smoothed out his expression and stopped.

"What're you planning to say to her?" Chey asked.

"I don't know. She'll likely still be out when I get back there, but either way, I'm not staying away. I'll explain what she overheard, and if I have to grovel, then I will. If that doesn't work, as soon as she's good to go home, I'll kidnap her and show her that I'm sorry and that I'll never hurt her again."

"I knew it," Chey said and held out her hand to Alisse, who snorted and then put her hand in her purse. She pulled out a twenty-dollar bill and slapped it in Chey's hand.

"Neanderthal," Alisse muttered.

"Hey, I learned it from your old man and hers," I informed her with a grin.

"Oh, I know it. You all should get with the twenty-first century," she replied.

My brothers all had satisfied smiles on their faces, even the single ones. Laughter around the room helped to lighten the mood a little, which was needed. A few minutes later, a guy came to get me. I gave the others a chin lift as I followed him out of the room. He led me down the hall and through secure doors that he swiped his badge to open. The area was similar to the ER, with curtained-off cubicle areas. He took me halfway through the recovery area and then pointed to one with the curtain closed.

"Thanks," I said. He nodded and left me there. I took a deep breath before easing back the edge of the curtain.

She was lying there with her eyes closed and machines monitoring her. Her color didn't look as pale as before, but that might just be my imagination. I walked closer. "Troian, baby, are you awake?" I whispered. I reached out and took her limp hand in mine. I rubbed slowly and gently across the back of it. I picked the one without the IV in it.

She didn't answer or wake up. She must still be well under the influence of the anesthesia. The curtain sliding back made me whip around. A nurse came to an abrupt halt. She ran her gaze up and down me. She was a short thing. I estimated her to be in her late twenties or early thirties.

"Oh, sorry, I didn't know anyone was with her. They usually don't let anyone back here," she said as she smiled and came over to the other side of the bed.

"They don't, but they made an exception for me. How's she doing? Has she woken up since she got out of surgery?"

"Not yet, but she's only been out a short while. Her vitals are good. I'm Angela, her nurse. And your name is…"

"It's Lash."

"Lash, that's a different name. Is that because you're in a motorcycle gang?" she asked coyly.

I swear she fluttered her eyelashes at me. Shit, no goddamn way was she flirting over my unconscious woman's body. Was she? As I stared at her, I saw her check me out from head to toe, and her cheeks got pink. Her tongue peeked out. Jesus, she was.

"It's not a gang. It's a club. And I'd like to be alone with my woman if you don't mind."

She blushed. "Oh, sure, just let me finish checking her out. I didn't know she was married. I thought you were her brother."

"I don't know why you'd think I was her brother. We don't look a damn thing alike. As for being married, yeah, we are," I grunted. Her eyes landed on my left hand, then Troian's. I saw the disbelief there. Let her think whatever the fuck she wanted. In my mind, we were married. I'd claimed her as my old lady. To a biker, that made her my wife. My tone told her I was done talking, so she hurried through her assessment and then she rushed out.

I sat down next to the bed. I still had a hold of Troian's hand. I raised it to my lips and kissed it. "Baby, I need you to wake up and talk to me. I have so much to tell you and explain. First, I wanna say how goddamn sorry I am that you heard what you did. It sounded worse than it was. I didn't believe you were lying or involved in that shit. It was us being extra damn paranoid and cautious, despite knowing it wasn't true.

"You have no idea how terrified I was when I got the call that said you were here. Perry, he's a paramedic I work with sometimes, and he called me. The cops mentioned it was my truck you were in. I thought I'd have a heart attack before we got here. Then, to have you yell like you did, it tore me up. I know why you did it, I do, but I swear to God, I'll make it up to you. Add to it finding out they rushed you into surgery. It gutted me. Hurricane, I love you more than anything in this world. You're it. My heart, soul, body, and mind all belong to you. You have to forgive me for being a dumbass. If you don't, I don't know what I'll do."

She twitched, and I saw a slight movement, but she didn't open her eyes. I kept talking. I rambled about so many things it was impossible to remember them all. I wanted her to hear me and wake up. I sat there talking to her for the next ten minutes or so before there was a significant change in her vitals. The beeping of the machine sped up and caught my attention. Her pulse, respiration, and blood pressure were rising.

They weren't too high or doing it so fast that I was alarmed, but it meant she was surfacing. Her eyeballs were moving behind her eyelids, and she was moving in the bed. I stood up and leaned over the rail. I lowered myself more and kissed her lips.

When I raised back up, I saw her staring at me. I smiled at her. Only she didn't smile back. Instead, a weak punch to the jaw had me rearing back in surprise. She was glaring daggers at me. "Troian, baby, let me explain," I pleaded.

"Don't Troian, baby, me," she said hoarsely.

"You've got to listen."

"Like hell I do. Get out. I don't want you or anyone in your club near me. We're through, Lash," she hissed. She hadn't forgotten or forgiven me from earlier.

"No, I won't leave. This is all a huge misunderstanding. If you'd just let me explain, you'll see that. I love you. You love me. I'm not letting this come between us."

She didn't say anything for several moments. I thought it was a good sign. My words were getting through to her. I was dead wrong. She opened her mouth and began to scream, "Help! Help me!"

I heard feet running toward us as I tried to hush her. "Shh, baby, don't."

The cubicle was filled with several bodies within a minute. They all gave me hard looks and her concerned ones. "Sir, we need you to leave," a tall, older man told me firmly. He was a big guy, and according to his name badge, he was an orderly.

"I'm not leaving. She's upset because of a misunderstanding we had earlier. I'm not hurting her. I'd never hurt her," I barked back.

"Sir, we can't have the patient upset," a nurse, not Angela from before, insisted.

"Just give me a couple of minutes to explain to her."

They glanced at my cut. I saw unease on their faces. They then peeked at her. "Miss, what would you like us to do?" the orderly asked.

Troian met my gaze, and I saw her decision seconds before she answered them. "I want him out of here. He's not to see me or know anything about my condition. In fact, no one is. I'd like to talk to your security to make sure he and his club stay away from me."

"Troian, don't do this. I know you're mad at me, but don't be hasty. You'll regret it."

"The only thing I regret is ever meeting you."

The pain shooting through me almost doubled me over. I'd fucked it all up, and now I'd never have what I wanted most in the world, her. I was numb as they escorted me out of the recovery unit.

Troian:

I held in the tears until Lash was gone, and then the flood came. I had to hide my face in my pillow to muffle my sobs. God, it hurt so much. My heart felt like it had been ripped out. Telling him to leave was the hardest thing I think I'd probably ever done. I'd wanted to hurt him like he had hurt me, so I said my only regret was meeting him. That was a lie. I could never regret meeting him, even with how much he hurt me by not trusting me. The fact that I still loved him would be my secret.

Physical pain cut through me from the small incisions on my upper abdomen near my ribs. Before surgery, they told me they would be doing it robotically and would make three or four small incisions and where. I could tell where by the pain and the feel of the bandage covering it. I sucked in a shallow breath.

"Excuse me, Miss. I need to take a look at your bandage. I'm sorry," said a young woman's voice.

I uncurled from the fetal position I was in and wiped hurriedly at my wet face. I saw sympathy on her face. The last thing I needed was for anyone to feel sorry for me. I'd survive this just like I did the beating, and God knows whatever else happened in my forgotten past. Who needed a heart to live? I snorted at how stupid that thought was.

"That's fine..." I paused, not being able to see her name badge.

She gave me a sweet smile. "I'm Kimera. Everyone calls me Kim, though."

"It's nice to meet you. I think I'll call you Kimera. That's a pretty name."

"Thank you. I love your name too. I've never heard it before. Do you mind if I ask where you're from?" she asked as she lowered the sheet and lifted my hospital gown. She didn't remove the bandage, but she did study it closely. Talking to her helped me not to focus on my heartache.

"My family is originally from Russia, and it means trinity. How about your name?" That was another thing I just knew but didn't know how.

She shrugged. "I have no clue. I've tried to find out its meaning, but it doesn't seem to have one."

"Did you ask your parents?" I asked before I could think better of it.

"I don't have any. I grew up in foster care after I was ten. My granny who raised me didn't know where they got it. She wouldn't tell me anything about my birth parents, so I couldn't ask. Granny said I was better off not knowing."

"Well, they gave you a very pretty and cool name. How does it look?" I wanted to divert her mind from what I could see was an uncomfortable memory for her.

"I can't see the incisions, but the dressing is dry, and there's no bleeding through, which is good. You'll need to be careful. No bending or lifting. They did a robotic laparoscopic surgery, so you have three incisions. They've been stitched with dissolvable sutures and then glued together. For the next six to eight weeks, you'll have restrictions we'll review in a bit. Can I get you anything for pain? You're due."

I thought about it and decided it might help me sleep and I could escape thoughts of Lash. I nodded. "Yes, thank you, I'd like that."

"Okay, I'll be back in a minute. I just need to get the medicine. It'll go in your IV, so you'll feel it helps almost immediately. Hang on." I gave her a smile, and then she left. Tears gathered again, but I refused to let them fall.

She was back quickly, as promised. She fiddled with my IV and then injected the medicine into it. She stood there talking to me as it took effect. Wow, this was some good shit. "What is that?"

"It's oxycodone mixed with Toradol. The oxycodone is an opioid, and the Toradol is an NSAID, a nonsteroidal anti-inflammatory drug. It helps the pain med work better and reduces inflammation, which is common after surgery. They'll switch you over to oral meds soon, but until we get your pain controlled, this is what they want you to have."

"Thank you so much, Kimera—" I was interrupted from saying anything else by the arrival of a scowling, hulking biker. Thank God it wasn't Lash.

Still, I shrank back from him. He saw it, and his face fell.

"Don't do that, Troian. I'd never hurt you. I just need to talk to you," he said gruffly.

I didn't get a chance to say anything because Kimera was suddenly in front of him and invading his space. It was funny to see her looking up at him. Spawn was well over six feet tall. He was several inches taller than Lash's six foot one. She was maybe five feet four. She looked a tad shorter than me, but it was hard to tell. He gave her a raised brow.

"You need to back up and leave. She's in pain and recovering from surgery. She doesn't need to be any more upset than she already was. What's wrong with you guys? If you don't leave, I'll make you," she growled. I was shocked by her tone. Up until now, she'd been soft-spoken and sort of shy-acting. Not now. She'd turned into a growling guard dog ready to do battle.

I saw the corner of Spawn's lips almost turn up, and he got an amused twinkle in his eyes as he gazed down at her. "Whoa, calm down there, Hotcake. No need to go all chihuahua on me. I'm not here to hurt, Troian. I just need to talk to her for a few minutes. There's been a huge misunderstanding."

"Call me hotcake or chihuahua again, and you'll see what I do. Leave," she snapped.

"Babe," he said with a sigh. They were turned so I could see the side of her face. She narrowed her gaze on him. Her fists were clenched at her side. Shit, would she swing at him? I needed to put a stop to this before something happened. I didn't think he'd hit her, but she might hit him. That wouldn't be good.

"One," she said.

"One what?" he asked back. He was grinning at her now.

"Two," she said.

"Kimera, it's alright. I'll talk to him for a minute, then he'll leave. Won't you, Spawn?"

"Kimera? I like it," he told her with a wink.

"Like I care. Spawn, guess that's apt—Spawn of the Devil—no doubt. Say what you have to say, then get lost. She's gonna be asleep soon. I just gave her pain medicine." She crossed her arms after telling him that. From her stance, it was obvious she didn't plan to leave me alone with him. It made me feel better. Maybe if she stayed, he wouldn't get into too deep of a discussion. I wasn't up for it.

"One day soon, I'll tell you how I got that name, but I can't flirt right now. I need to talk to my brother's old lady." He walked past her and came closer to the bed. I heard the low growl in her throat as he did. She turned so she could watch him. I couldn't hold back my grin. He smirked at me.

"What do you want to say, Spawn? I can't think of anything we need to talk about. I'm tired. I want to sleep." That wasn't a lie. My eyelids drooped.

"I want you to know that I was the one who did the investigation and found out one of your cousins is in prison for running a prostitution ring. I'm sorry you heard what you did. It was just a precaution to check into you to be sure you weren't involved. We'd have done it with anyone who was involved with our club. Lash didn't believe you were. He's hurting, sweetheart. You gutted him. Don't be mad at him. If you have to be mad at someone, let it be me."

"That's bullshit. I heard you guys. You, as well as him, thought there was a chance I was involved and might even be faking my amnesia. All so I could do what? Hide out somewhere, I think you said? Use you and your club to expand my whoring business, perhaps?"

He winced. That told me more than I wanted to know. "You did. You thought I was gonna bring my prostitution ring to your territory, didn't you? That I pretended so I could get in good with you. Wow, I guess I know what you think of me. I'm not only a madam but a whore myself since I slept with Lash to lull him into doing whatever I wanted."

"Troian, no, don't. I'm sorry. Yes, we had to be sure. We had someone try to infiltrate our club when Cheyenne came to us. We don't know what would've happened if it hadn't been for her. It's made us more paranoid, I guess. Even while we checked, none of us truly thought you were any of those things. Lash loves you. He claimed you as his old lady. There's no going back from that."

"Maybe in your world, but in mine, I can do anything I want. It's over. Once I'm cleared to leave the hospital, I'm gone. I don't want to be with people who lie to me and think terrible things about me. I don't want to see or talk to any of you." Tears welled in my eyes again.

He looked like he was in pain. "Babe, where will you go? It's not safe. And you have to know, he won't let you go. He can't. Losing you will kill him."

I snorted. "He'll soon be back to screwing anything with a pussy. I was just a temporary diversion. He'll forget my name in a month. Now, I'm done. I need to sleep. Go." I closed my eyes. I heard him swearing, and then Kimera was hissing at him. I ignored them. Eventually, they must've left because it got quiet. I fell asleep crying.

Lash: Chapter 12

Three fucking days of utter agony. That's how long it had been since I saw my woman. I wasn't allowed in to see her or to ask how she was doing. The staff who knew me gave me sympathetic looks, but they were under strict orders not to say anything, or they would lose their jobs. I tried to sneak in to see her, but they had a security guard at her door. I could've gotten past him, but it would've led to trouble I didn't want at the moment. Sitting in a jail cell would push me over the edge that I was teetering on.

We all felt like shit that even for a second, we toyed with the idea she might be involved or faking her amnesia. We did what we did to protect the club but ended up hurting her. As much as I didn't want to acknowledge it, I could see her side of it. She was entitled to her hurt and anger. I just didn't know if she'd let go of it to ever forgive me and let me back in her life. If she didn't, I didn't think I'd be able to live without her.

Everyone walked around with sad expressions on their faces. Spawn looked like shit. He blamed himself for doing the investigation that found the information on her cousin. His attempt to talk to her had failed. He told me she planned to leave Bristol as soon as they released her. I couldn't let that happen.

I was lucky in one way. One of the admissions ladies loved me. She was an older widow, and I had helped her do repairs on her house a few times. She contacted me and said she'd let me know when she found out when they were gonna release Troian. She knew the charge nurses who worked the floor she was on. I thanked her profusely and promised to be her repair guy for the rest of her life. She laughed and told me it wasn't necessary, but I meant it.

I wanted to know how she was doing physically as well as mentally. Was her surgical wounds healing? Did the bleeding remain stopped? Was her pain bearable? I lay awake at night thinking of her. Missing her. It was amazing that she'd become so vital to me in such a short period of time. I had to find a way to earn her forgiveness and have her take me back.

Right now, I was waiting for church to start. It was Thursday, and we usually had it on Mondays, but with everything going on, Reaper wanted another one this week. I didn't know why, but I got up as he walked into the common room and twirled his finger, which was his signal to follow him. I took my beer with me. Maybe if I drank enough tonight, I could sleep.

Taking my seat at the table, I leaned back and stared at the beer in my hand. I peeled the label off it. Reaper rapping his fist on the table got my attention. I glanced up and found him staring at me. I straightened up. What had I done? He had a fierce expression on his face. Shit, was he about to call me out on my inability to do my job at the renovation business?

"I know shit has been tense this week. We're all worried about Troian and how she's doing, especially after she was hurt by what we did," he started out saying as he scanned the table.

My stomach flipped, and acid tried to make its way up my throat. I swallowed as he continued, "I never meant for it to hurt your old lady or you, Lash." He paused.

"Reaper, I know that. I was just as involved as any of you. I should've spoken up and said not to dig more. I should've been adamant that I knew she couldn't be involved or faking anything. We're all more cautious since the whole shit with the Soldiers of Corruption. I should've told her what we found out and that we would dig to be sure no one else in her family was involved. It's my fault," I told him.

"It's all our fault, and it's up to all of us to make it right and get your woman back here with you. Right now, she's in the hospital, and we can't get to her without causing trouble. As soon as she's out, we'll go to work," he said with a determined scowl.

"Speaking of that, I think we might want to reconsider waiting," Spawn said out of nowhere. He had a determined and sorta upset expression that made him look ferocious. I stiffened.

"Why? What did you find?" I asked.

"It was what Smoke and I found. It's not good. It seems the family has started to search for her. One of the authors Troian works with, Ciara, is her name made a stink when she didn't hear from Troian. It was so unusual for Troian the woman got worried about her. The cops went to the house to question her family. They came up with some bullshit reason that they didn't know she was missing because she went off to be alone so she could concentrate on work. They claim she's done it before and goes radio silent on them for weeks. They didn't think anything about it."

"There's no way in hell she'd do that," I immediately said.

"Exactly, which means they move up in the suspect pool for me. I think one or more of them might know what happened to her," Spawn added.

"As in, they had something to do with her being beaten and dumped?" I asked through gritted teeth.

He slowly nodded. "Yeah, I'm afraid that's exactly what I mean. They're hiding something. Maybe a fight got out of control. Smoke is almost into the prosecutor's personal notes that he keeps on his computer about her cousin's case. If anyone else was involved and they couldn't prove it, I bet he'll have it noted in there."

"Question. Do you think Troian might've been the one to help the police get evidence on her cousin and the others found out?" Crusher asked softly.

It was like a shock went through all of us. Jesus, why the hell didn't I think of that? What if she did help convict him and the others discovered it? What if some of them were involved in it all along? I came to my feet.

"Fuck! That's it. Christ, why didn't we think of

that? I want to know everything you have on those other cousins," I barked.

"I can get that. I do know that there are four other male cousins besides Andrik. They appear to be the ones talking to the cops and in control. There are a few women, but I don't think they're allowed much freedom or a voice. There's Zandro, Jarek, Laszlo, and Kaz. Zandro is a brother to Andrik. The other three are cousins," Spawn told me.

"Their last name is Kriska too?" Crusher asked.

"Nah, it's Gusev," Spawn said.

Crusher slammed his fist down on the table, making us jump. "Gusev? Are you fucking kidding me?" he snarled.

"Man, what the hell? No, I'm not kidding. Why?" Spawn asked.

"I need to make a phone call. Let me do that, and then I'll explain. Hang here," Crusher said. He didn't wait for permission to leave. He just got up and walked out. We all exchanged mystified looks. We had no idea why he reacted that way. It prompted Spawn to hop on his laptop.

It took everything in me not to follow Crusher and demand he tell me what the hell was goin' on. Why react like that to their name? Murmurs and side conversations broke out all around the table. I had to stand up and pace. It was about ten minutes of torture before he came back in. The scowl on his face told us that whatever his news was, it wasn't good. I retook my seat as he sat down.

"Mind telling us what that was all about?" Reaper asked.

"Sorry. I had to go talk to a member of my family. They have the knowledge I needed."

"Your family? I didn't know you had any other family than your mom and Lash?" Ink exclaimed.

"It's my extended family. When I joined the club years ago, I told Avenger my history. He said it didn't matter to him as long as it never affected the club, which it hasn't. I got so used to ignoring it that I never thought of mentioning it again. Did he tell you?" he asked Reaper. I was lost. What was there to know?

Avenger had been his dad and the old president of the club. When he died, Reaper was voted in as the new president. That had been over a decade now.

Reaper shook his head. "Dad kept things close, and I expect if he'd stepped down as president rather than died, he would've. Why don't you tell us now."

"My mother's family is Russian, as you know. What I didn't talk about is the fact that my mom's family is part of the Bratva back in Russia," he told us bluntly.

This caused a stir. We kept clear of the Mafia and especially the Bratva. We had many of them here in the States. He kept going after the murmuring died down some.

"My dad wasn't part of that. Mom met him when

she came to America to go to school. When they met and fell in love, the family wasn't happy. It was only because she loved him so much and they loved her that they didn't tear them apart and force her to marry for the advancement of the family. They were one of the few families that didn't do that shit in the Bratva. She assured them Dad wanted nothing to do with that life, and neither did she. In the end, they left them alone. Occasionally, they'd check in to see if they were doing okay or to warn them if there was a threat that could impact us. Over the past dozen years, I've maybe heard from them a half dozen times." He paused.

"Well, goddamn brother, way to shock the shit outta us," Ratchet said with a grunt.

"I know, and I didn't mean to make it a secret. It just wasn't important in my life. If I'd ever gotten a hint it might impact the club, I would've told you. Anyway, I heard enough growing up to know there were a few key families that Mom said were either in direct competition with or wanted an alliance with hers. One of those they hated happened to be a family with the last name Gusev. When I heard Spawn say it, I had to make sure it wasn't the same bunch."

"And is it?" Reaper asked.

"I gave my family the names you mentioned, Spawn. They said they have to double-check, but there's a group of the Gusevs in the States, and they have guys with those names."

"You've got to be kidding?" Mayhem growled. None of us looked happy. My gut clenched.

"If they're the same ones, then I seriously doubt it was only the one guy involved in the ring. They all have to be. If Troian helped put Andrik away and they found out, then there's no doubt they were the ones who hurt her. My family had nothing good to say about them. Kirill said they'd sell their own mother to the Devil."

"Can we ask who Kirill is and how soon they can confirm whether we have the right ones or not?" Ink asked.

"Kirill Razin is the head of the Razin family. He's my second cousin. He and my mom were close growing up. I was given his first name as my middle one when I was born. He's my godfather. He told me to give him an hour."

"Well, fuck. I don't know what to—" Reaper started to say but was interrupted by the ringing of a phone. We all glanced around. I knew it wasn't mine. We stiffened when Crusher took his phone out of his cut and answered it.

"*Privet, Kirill, Chto ty uznal, cosuin?*" He listened intently to what he said. He was growling and nodding as he did. He said an occasional word. The call only lasted a few minutes. At the end, he said, "*Nyet, ya budu v poryyadke. Spasibo. Yesli ya eto sdelyu, ya dam vam znat!*.

Thankfully, he hung up after that. He saw our faces and grinned. "I said, 'Hello, Kirill, what did you find out, cousin?' The last part was, 'No, I'll be fine. Thank you. If I do, I'll let you know.' He was asking if I needed the family involved with this. I hate to say it,

Lash, but it's the same Gusev family. They're lucky that when Andrik went down, the rest of them didn't, and their other illegal activities didn't come out. Troian's family are ugly, evil bastards. I'd say it's a safe bet that they did that to her."

Fear filled me. If they were getting questions from the police, they'd be worried if her body would be found. And if it was, could they be implicated? Her body dump was done hastily, and there was no telling if the tarp we saved had DNA or fingerprints that could lead back to them. I had no doubt they'd come looking, and when they did, we had to be prepared to take them out and protect Troian, whether she liked it or not. It would take planning since they were Bratva-connected, so nothing came back on the club.

"I want everything we can get on the Gusevs. Crusher, if we need to, I need to know if your family will give us information. Will they do that? And if so, what will they want in return?" I asked.

None of us wanted to be indebted to the Mafia, especially the Bratva, but if that's what it took, I'd do it. I'd give them anything they wanted, as long as it wasn't something that would hurt my family. I had to draw the line at that.

"They'll help. It was already offered. As for what Kirill will want, I'll ask, but he may do it simply because to eliminate them removes a snake from their world. It would negatively impact those at home in Russia, and he'll love that."

"Jesus, no offense, man, but if your Bratva family

calls them snakes and they're Bratva too, what does that say about them," Romulus asked after whistling.

"No offense taken. Kirill and the others aren't angels, not even close. They have no problem intimidating or blackmailing people or even killing them, but they do have some morals that other Bratva families don't. They don't go after wives and children. That's a big no with them. They aren't into human trafficking or prostitution, although weapons, drugs, and everything else is done," Crusher admitted.

"Why no prostitution and trafficking?" Ink asked. I wondered the same and figured so did the others.

"It goes back to our great-grandmother. It seems that she was stolen and was to be sold as a young woman. Our great-grandfather happened to come across her in his dealings, and the story goes, he fell head-over-heels for her. It was love at first sight. He rescued her from her fate and won her heart. He made sure that everyone involved in her ordeal was hunted down and killed by his hands. From then on, no one in our family was ever to kidnap or force women to sell themselves or be abused in any way. If they did, the rest of the family would kill them. He had a brother who didn't listen. He made an example of him. Suffice to say that none have broken that rule again to this day."

"Damn, it sounds like your great-granddaddy was a major badass," Maniac observed with a smile.

Crusher grinned. "He was, and he was a handsome devil too. I look just like him."

This earned him hisses and boos. It helped to

lighten the mood for a moment. I think he knew I was about to crack. I was still hung up on his guess that Troian's family were the ones to hurt her and that they'd come for her. Over my fucking cold, dead body, would they hurt her again. They quickly sobered, though.

"Lash, what do you want to do first?" Reaper asked.

"I want my woman out of the damn hospital and back here. Until that happens, the next best thing is to get a few of our men over to the hospital. Their security guards might stand outside her door, but they can't keep us from watching elsewhere. As long as we're not causing an issue, the hell with them."

"Okay, we can do that. Anything else?" Reaper continued.

"I don't know if this is possible, but can we get an alert or something that'll tell us if any of her family heads this way? It's not realistic to keep someone out near her dump site all the time on the off chance they go there," I asked. I directed this to Spawn.

He smiled. "Already working on it. Between us, Smoke and I can not only place alerts on bank and email accounts for the four key male cousins, but I might be able to set something up at the dump site."

"What?" Reaper asked before I could.

"No one would ever question a hunter placing a hunting trail camera in the trees along there. I mean, hell, deer frequent that area all the time," he said with a wink.

This earned him several chuckles and thumbs-up. I was impressed. I only had one question since I'd never used one before. "How long will the battery in one of those?"

"For any of the ones I'm looking at, it can last months. I'm just finalizing the comparison and seeing where I can get one. I don't want to order one and wait. With all the local hunting supply places in the area, we should have no trouble finding one in stock."

"Then we won't keep you. Get to it. Also, sit down with Maniac and work out the rotation for hospital duty before any of you leave. Now, before we tie this up, anything else we need to talk about first?" Reaper threw out.

I nodded. He gestured for me to speak. "It goes without saying, but I'm still gonna say it. When we have proof they did this to her, whether in emails or by one of them coming here, take them alive if you can. I want to spend some uninterrupted quality time with them. I think they should discover why I'm called Lash," I growled.

Every one of my brothers nodded in agreement and smirked. I'd earned my name in more ways than one. I wasn't a man you wanted to cross. There were a few out there more sadistic than me, but not a lot. It took a hell of a lot to get me to let that side of me loose, but when it was, look out.

With this said, there were no other questions, suggestions, or comments, so Reaper let us go. I went out to the common room to go to the hospital as soon as I spoke to Maniac about what I could do with the guard duty schedule. He sat down at a table and took out his phone. He waved me over.

"Okay, hit me. I know you'll wanna go to the hospital now. What days and hours do you want? And don't think I'm gonna let you have them every day. You still have to sleep and eat, plus work."

"Honestly, I don't care. I'll give my usual hours to Tinker, and if he doesn't need me for that much or if I get finished early, I'll let you know so someone else can take a break."

"Again, you have to sleep. Let us help you."

I gave him a chin lift and rattled off some shift times. I knew this would hopefully not be for much longer. Then the issue would be getting her to come back here so we could protect her or, barring that, to at least stay in town. If she insisted on leaving, I'd be hard-pressed not to kidnap her and lock her ass up. I was getting to my feet when my cell phone rang. Taking it out, I saw a number that I recognized. It was the hospital. With my heart pounding, I answered it immediately. "Lash speaking," I said.

"Hello, Lash, it's Mrs. Kendrickson. I hope I'm not calling at a bad time." Her voice trembled as she asked.

"No, it's never a bad time to hear from you, Mrs. K. Did you find out when my Troian is discharging?" The brothers closest to me all stopped talking and listened. They had hopeful expressions on their faces.

"My dear, I'm sorry. I hate to call you with this, but she's already gone. You didn't hear this from me, but the charge nurse was talking, and I guess your Troian discharged herself AMA, earlier today. They wanted to keep her another day or so, but she told them no. I called as soon as I heard."

"She what?" I almost bellowed. Her swift intake of breath had me calming my tone. "Sorry, I'm not yelling at you. Can you tell me what time she left?"

"Yeah, it was about two hours ago. Again, I'm sorry I didn't know sooner. If you need anything else, please let me know."

"I will, and thank you, Mrs. K. Let me know when you need me to come over. Don't wait."

"I won't, my dear. Goodbye, and I hope you get her to talk to you."

"Me too. Goodbye." As soon as I hung up, my brothers pounced.

"They discharged her?" Maniac asked.

"No, she signed out AMA, against medical advice, around two hours ago. Mrs. K. just heard the charge nurse talking about it. Shit, where would she go? How would she leave? She doesn't have any money or a car," I muttered.

"Let me check the security cameras outside the hospital. If she got someone to help her, I might see who," Spawn stated before rushing down the hall to his cave.

I began to pace as I racked my brain to try and think where she'd go. I came up blank. Other than us, she didn't know anyone local. A terrifying thought popped into my head. I took off running toward Spawn's office. I heard footsteps behind me. His door was open when I got to it.

He glanced up and raised his eyebrow. "What?"

"Is there a way you can check to be sure she didn't somehow contact her family? I know you're monitoring their emails. What about calls to their phones?"

"Fuck, let me get Smoke or Everly to check. They were working on setting that up for other reasons. Shit."

I waited as he placed the call. He put them on speaker. It took a couple of rings before Smoke answered. "Smoke the Magnificent. Whatcha need?"

"I've got Lash and just about our entire club in my office. It seems Troian left the hospital. I'm searching to see if I can find if someone picked her up when she left. Did you get those monitoring viruses set up on Lazslo, Zandro, Jarek, and Kaz's phones like we talked about? Lash is worried she might've found a way to call one of them. If she did, it's almost certain they're the ones who hurt her. We got new information, and I'll fill you in later on it."

"Son of a bitch! Okay, Everly and I did get those set up. Let me check if any calls have come from that area. I'll get right back to you. Lash, hang tight, man."

"Thanks, Smoke. I'm trying," I told him seconds before he hung up.

I sat down to wait. Some of the guys left, but not the officers. There wasn't enough room in Spawn's office for all of us. Mayhem asked, "What viruses?"

"It was Everly's idea. We get messages and notifications all the time on our phones. She suggested we send one to each of those guys' numbers. Embedded in it was a virus with spyware. As soon as they opened it, even if they didn't click the link, it would automatically download and infect their phones. It was slick, and they'd never know it. It would take an elite hacker to find it."

"Remind me to never piss any of you off. Goddamn, that's slick and ingenious," Mayhem said with a whistle of appreciation. Even as worried as I was, I had to agree and smile.

"Just remember that. Okay, let me get back to the cameras. I was checking starting about three hours ago in case Mrs. K's timing was wrong," he muttered.

We stayed quiet. I was filled with anxious energy. My leg was bouncing up and down like a pogo stick. I was about to ask him why it was taking so long when his phone rang. He answered and put it on speaker, so I knew it was Smoke.

"Tell me something good," Spawn said.

"I can tell you that no one from your area called or texted any of those four. Even better, my beautiful wife went a step further and sent the same thing to the phones of the women who are part of the family. None of them received calls or texts either. We feel confident she didn't ask her family to come get her," Smoke said.

We all sighed in relief. I leaned closer to the phone. "Smoke, don't take this the wrong way, but I love your old lady. She's getting a kiss from me the next time I see her."

"Just as long as you know, when I meet your woman, I'll be doing the same," he responded. A growl rumbled out before I could stop it. The fucker laughed. "See, now you know. I think Everly will be safe from your lips. If you wanna thank her, she loves dark chocolate with nuts. Now, let me get back to work, and we'll see what else we can find. Spawn, send me the info later on what you found out."

"I will."

"Thanks again," I told him.

"*De nada*," he said before hanging up. I knew enough Spanish to realize he'd said you're welcome.

"Well, that's good news. That means she's most likely still in town," Reaper said.

"Goddamn it to hell!" Spawn exclaimed, making us jump. He had a dark scowl on his face as he glared at his screen.

"What is it?" I barked.

"Sorry, I'm ninety-nine percent sure she's fine at least. Do you recognize her?" he asked as he turned the screen around. It took me several seconds to remember why the woman was familiar. When it clicked, I glanced at him.

"It's that nurse from OR recovery. What was her name?"

"Kimera Jordan," he grunted.

On his screen was a video clip of Kimera picking Troian up outside the hospital at the rear exit. They were both glancing around nervously as Troian got into her car. I swore. "Shit, we've gotta find her. Can you get a clearer picture of her license plate?" I asked.

"Yeah, give me a minute," he said. As he worked on it, I heard him mainly muttering under his breath. "Spank her ass." "Over my knee."

I didn't for a moment imagine he was talking about Troian. It seemed the little nurse had sparked something in my brother. It would be interesting to see how they acted together. It was close to ten minutes before he grinned. "Gotcha," he said. He glanced up at me. "I have her address. How much do you wanna bet she took Troian to her house? She lives outside of town."

I stood up. The others headed for the door. "Thanks, brother. Just send it to my phone."

Spawn stood. "Oh, no, I'm going. Little Hotcake and I have some talking to do," he said as he came around the table.

"Hotcake?" Crusher mused.

"Yep," was all Spawn said.

It didn't take long for me, Spawn, and an amused Crusher and Colt to head out. The others stayed behind. As Spawn led the way and Colt brought up the rear in an

SUV, I tried to decide what I would say to her and how we'd handle it if she refused to leave and the nurse gave us trouble.

Troian: Chapter 13

I was exhausted, and I hadn't done anything but sneak out of the hospital and into Kimera's car. I felt guilty for involving her in my problem, but she'd been the one to offer to help. I was surprised when she came to see me early this morning. She told me she had been wondering how I was doing and if I'd had any more issues.

"Hi, I hope it's alright that I stopped in. I've been thinking about you and wondering how you were doing," were the first words out of her mouth after she knocked on my door. I sat up straighter in my bed. I couldn't hold back the wince of pain. It wasn't as bad as it had been, but I still felt it when I moved the wrong way or too much.

"No, it's fine that you stopped by. Please come in," I told her, waving her forward.

She came in with a sweet smile on her face. "You look better than you did the other day. How's your pain?"

"It's better, although it's still there. It lets me know if I move around too much or the wrong way. It's so nice of you to remember me and to check up on me."

"I hated how things went the other day for you. I saw the guard outside your door. Is he here because of those men that day?" She worried her bottom lip with her teeth.

I hesitated. I didn't know how much to tell her. As mad as I was at Lash and his club, I didn't feel right talking about them to anyone either. Maybe mad wasn't the right word. It was more that I was hurt and felt betrayed by them. I thought he and I were building a future. Her anxious look made me answer her.

"I haven't had any of them try to visit me, but I don't know if that's because of the guards. I sent Lash and them away and insisted security be called and that no one here share information about me with them."

"Was he the cause of your wreck?"

"Not directly, no. I was upset over something I learned, and I was driving when I shouldn't have. A dog in the road caused me to swerve to miss it, and I overcorrected and lost control. I rolled his truck."

She winced. "Ouch, no wonder you were in so much pain and banged up like you are. Do you have any family nearby?"

"No, I don't."

"Is there anything I can do for you?" she asked.

"Not unless you know a way for me to get out of here and a place I can go that doesn't cost me a dime, and I don't need a car to get there," I said jokingly.

"I do, actually," she said.

"Really? Where?" I asked incredulously.

"My house. You can stay with me, and I'll drive you there. As long as you don't mind being out away from *people and having a dog for company."*

My mouth fell open as I stared at her in stunned disbelief. Surely, she was joking. She kept watching me and giving me a tentative smile. After a minute or so, I knew I had to answer her.

"I-I don't know what to say. It's so kind of you to offer, but I can't ask that of you. You don't know me, nor do you owe me that kind of kindness. I'll be alright. As soon as they discharge me, I'll figure something out."

"I wouldn't have offered it if I wasn't serious. You don't have anyone, it seems. I know what that's like. Please, it would ease my mind so much if you would."

"Why would you do this? It's more than me not having anyone. You have to have had a lot of patients who need help. Do you take all of them home with you?"

She shook her head no. "No, I don't. I feel a connection to you for some reason. I can't explain it. Add to that the fact that we women should stick together. Please, let me help."

From there, we talked for a while longer, and a plan was formed. She wasn't crazy about me leaving against medical advice, but I knew if I waited, the likelihood that Lash and his club might try to make me stay with them could be a factor. I couldn't take the chance that he hadn't washed his hands of me. Plus, I knew I wouldn't risk contacting my family. Something inside of me told me that wasn't the way to go.

Hours later, I was set up in her small guest bedroom. She had a small two-bedroom house outside of town. She didn't own it. It was rented, but she shared with me that one day, she wanted to be able to buy her own house, and if possible, she'd love to live outside of town. It didn't have to be on a huge piece of property, just something big enough to have a small yard, a decent garden, and room for her dog.

Her dog was a big Belgian Malinois. He was named Toro, and he was very protective. He'd eyed me suspiciously when she brought me in the door. After she told him I was a friend and gave him a command, he relaxed, wagged his tail, and came over to greet me. I was a bit afraid to present my hand to him to sniff, but I did. He licked my hand and then sat on the couch with me. It was calming to pet his coat. He looked a lot like a German Shepherd. He was the same fawn color with a dark mask around his snout, eyes, and ears.

I'd come into the bedroom to rest not long ago. I found just walking out of the hospital and sitting up in her car and then on the couch had drained me. I'd have to get over that soon. I needed to be able to get back to work. I knew I could use her computer to do my editing. She'd already offered it to me when I explained what I did. I had no idea how I would repay her, but I'd find a way.

My only concern about staying here, other than being a nuisance and using her resources and money, was it was too close to Bristol. I wouldn't be able to go into town freely. If I did, I'd run the risk of seeing Lash and the others. To avoid that, I'd have to work and get money sent to me here so I could help with expenses and hopefully start to save so I could get a place further away.

That thought made me want to cry. Thinking of Lash always did. I'd given him my heart in the short time we'd been together, and to know he thought such terrible things about me cut me to the bone. Add to it that the rest of his club thought it, too. I wanted to curl up in a ball and cry. However, I wouldn't do that. No one said life was fair or without heartache. I had to treat it as a hard-learned lesson. Be absolutely positive you know someone before you give them your heart.

A soft knock on my door had me wiping the tears from my cheeks. "Come in," I called out.

Kimera opened the door smiling. When she saw my face, she frowned. "What's wrong? Are you hurting?"

"No, I'm fine. Just being silly. Can I help you with something?"

She frowned but didn't argue with my obvious lie. "No, I just wanted to let you know that I'm taking Toro for a walk. If he doesn't get his exercise, he gets bored, and that means he can be sorta destructive. He creates his own projects." She laughed.

"Well, we can't have him doing that. Please do whatever you usually do. I'll be fine here. I think I might take a short nap. Later, when you get back, we can talk more if you like. I'd love to snuggle with Toro, too, if he'll let me."

He perked up hearing his name again and gave me a doggy smile with his tongue hanging out. He looked so lovable I couldn't help but laugh. He started to come to me until she called him to heel. He snapped to attention.

"He'll love that. It shouldn't be more than a half hour before we're back. There's a walking trail through the woods behind the house, and the neighbor who owns it doesn't mind us using it. Darn it. I just realized you don't have a phone. I hate to leave you here without one. What if you need me?"

"Kimera, go. I'll be fine. I'm not gonna expire just because I'm left here for a bit alone. I'm good. Go enjoy your walk and give this big guy his daily exercise. God knows I'm not getting much, so he's gotta get it for both of us."

She giggled and then waved before closing my door. I could hear her talking to him outside the house as they set out for their walk a few minutes later. I had something to drink, a television in the living room if I wanted to watch it, and a soft bed. I was set. Curling up on the top of the covers, I drew a throw blanket from the bottom of the bed up over me and closed my eyes. It didn't take me long to drift off.

I had no idea how long I'd been asleep when something woke me up. I didn't feel like it had been very long since I'd drifted off. I concentrated to see if I could hear what had disturbed me. The noise got louder, and as it did, I realized what it was. It was the roar of more than one motorcycle engine. I'd heard enough of them at the Punishers' compound to recognize that sound. My heart began to pound. There was no way it could be them. They had no idea I'd left the hospital, and even if they did, no one knew where I went. Kimera had met me outside in her car after I signed out.

I gasped as I tried to scramble out of bed and to the window. I moved too fast and pulled on my incisions. I had to bend over and pant through the pain. While I did, the sound became louder. *Oh my God, they were pulling up outside! Please, don't let it be them*, I prayed.

Hobbling to the window, I pulled just the corner of the curtain back. I gasped. I'd recognize that bike and Lash anywhere. Damn it, it was them. Dropping the curtain like it was hot, I went back to huddle on the bed. I needed to think. Maybe if I didn't answer the door, they'd go away. If that didn't work, then I'd have to take more drastic measures. Surely, they wouldn't bust in, but what did I know about them?

A loud knocking on the front door made me jump. I had to stifle my cry. There was a pause lasting no more than a couple of seconds before it came again. It wasn't until the third one that I discovered they weren't gonna leave, and then I heard Lash call out.

"We know someone is in there. Your car is here. Troian, baby, I just need to talk to you. There are things I need to explain and you need to know. It's not safe for you."

I slipped off the bed and tiptoed to the bedroom door. I eased it open and kept going toward the back door. I wasn't sure why I was tiptoeing. It wasn't like they could hear me. When I reached it, I unlocked it and slowly opened it. Scanning the backyard, I didn't see anyone. Sighing in relief, I eased out the door and shut it behind me. I'd head for the woods in the back that Kimera mentioned earlier. I'd find her and Toro and keep them away until they left. Once they were gone, I'd have to find a new place to stay. I had no idea where that would be, but I'd have to do it.

I was so busy trying to be quiet and watching behind me in case one of them popped around the house that I didn't pay much attention to what was in front of me. I didn't know anyone had already gone back there and was hiding behind one of the big trees until he stepped out. When I saw him, I screamed and tried to run. Only bare feet and recent surgery weren't conducive to that. I stepped on a sharp object about the time I jerked and sent pain crashing through my stomach. I stumbled and then fell to my knees, which jarred me and made it worse.

As I clutched my stomach and foot, I heard swearing and yelling. I was too miserable and defeated to care. Right now, I just wanted something to go right and for my pain to be a thing of the past. Arms slid underneath me and picked me up. I couldn't fight at the moment. I glanced up, and through my tears, I saw Crusher staring down at me with a concerned slash pissed look on his face. *How was it possible to be both at the same time?* I inanely wondered.

"*Milaya, gde u tebya bolit?*" he asked.

His calling me sweetheart and asking where I hurt made me want to curl up and cry harder. Hearing him speak my mother tongue made me want to let him take care of me, but I couldn't. He was the enemy, and I was mad at him.

"*Polozhi menya, ublyudok*," I snapped. Maybe it wasn't the smartest thing to say to him, to put me down, bastard, but it made me feel better. I scowled when he threw back his head and laughed.

"What the fuck is going on? Why did she scream, and why are you holding her?" Lash growled from behind us. Crusher turned us around to face him. I kept my eyes on Crusher, not Lash. Looking at him would hurt too much.

"Your *uragan*, hurricane, is being feisty. She called me a bastard and ordered me to put her down. Sorry, I can't do that. You've already hurt yourself once. If you get another scratch on you, my brother here will lose his damn mind, and then we'll all be dead."

"Give her to me," Lash ordered. Out of the corner of my eye, I saw him hold out his arms.

I shook my head hard. "No, I don't want him to touch me. For that matter, I don't want you to either. Put me down. I can walk," I snapped.

"No, you can't. You stepped on something and hurt your foot. Besides, if I did, you'd try to run again and get hurt more. You've just had surgery, Troian. Why don't we go inside and talk?" Crusher asked, sounding reasonable.

Before I could tell him where he could go, I saw Spawn coming out of the house. He was frowning. How did he get in there? When? He came marching over to us. "Where is she?" he asked.

"Who?" I played dumb.

"You know who. Your new friend who helped you leave the hospital against medical advice. The one who could lose her job for that shit," he snapped.

"Hey, don't you dare threaten to get her fired! She didn't do anything wrong. I was the one who decided to leave. She was just nice enough to give me a place to get back on my feet. If you cause trouble for her, I swear to God, I'll…" I stopped talking so I could think up a good enough threat.

The corners of his mouth twitched. The asshole was trying not to laugh at me. "And just what'll you do about it if I do?" he asked with an amused tone.

"She might not be up to doing anything, but I sure can," I heard growled from behind us. Crusher whipped around. There stood Kimera and Toro. He was on alert and watching the guys like they were his next meal. He wasn't growling, but he looked ready to attack at any moment.

"Hold on, let's not do anything crazy. I'd hate to hurt your dog, but if you give him the command to come after us, I won't have a choice. We're not here to hurt anyone. I just need to talk to Troian," Lash told her.

"Why don't you have your friend there sit Troian down and let her come to me? If she decides to talk, then we can all be civilized and move inside. However, if she doesn't want to, then you'll need to go. If you hurt my dog, I'll put holes in you," she said as she pulled a handgun out from under her shirt.

"What the hell are you doing with that?" Spawn

snapped at her.

"What kinda dumbass would I be to be a woman who lives alone and goes walking in the woods with her dog and doesn't have a gun? I don't know what bimbo idiots you're used to, but I'm not one of them," she replied, rolling her eyes at him.

"You can't get us all before we disarm you," Crusher informed her.

"No, but I can get at least one, if not two, of you. Wanna find out which ones it'll be?"

"Hold up. That's enough. No one is shooting anyone. You keep the dog under control, and we'll be fine. Like we said, we just need to talk to Troian. It's important. She's in more danger than she knows. She can't be out here," Lash said. I was finally able to look directly at him. His gaze was boring into me.

"Why would I believe a word you or any of your brothers have to say? You think I'm a conniving, lying criminal, remember? Go to hell, Lash. I'll take my chances out here. I'll get better treatment than with you behind those walls."

I swear there was hurt on his face for a moment, then I blinked, and it was gone. Instead, he was standing there with a grim expression on his face. "Troian, you can choose to believe what you want, but it's not true. I understand you're hurt. I get it. I'm sorry. A need to be one hundred percent sure my family and the other women and kids weren't in danger drove my decision. I refused to believe you were capable of that."

"He's telling you the truth. I was the one who did the investigation. You should be mad at me for agreeing to do it," Spawn added.

"Oh, don't worry. I'm mad at all of you. Crusher put me down. It hurts to be like this," I ordered him.

It pissed me off that he glanced at Lash first and didn't do it until he nodded. As soon as my feet touched the ground, his arms let go. I limped toward Kimera. One of the men must've moved because I saw Toro's ears perk up more.

"Babe, let me check your foot. What did you do?" Lash asked.

"Don't call me babe, and I can have Kimera look at it. How did you know I was here?"

"I'll answer that if we can go sit down and talk like civilized people. It's too exposed out here." he said.

"What do you expect? Someone to shoot me with a sniper rifle from a tree?" I asked, being a smartass.

"Don't fucking joke about that! You have no goddamn idea what you're dealing with. It's worse than we imagined."

He looked and sounded so sincere. Kimera must've thought so, too because she bent forward to whisper in my ear. "I know you're furious with him, but it doesn't look like they're gonna leave until he talks to you. You can't be blind to the threats out there. I'll stay with you, and so will Toro. If they don't leave after we're done talking to them, I'll get rid of them. If my dog and gun don't do it, I know who can."

I considered her recommendation for a minute, then whispered back, "Alright, let's get this over with. I need sleep."

I turned back to the guys. All three were watching us like hawks. I noticed that while Lash and Crusher were watching me, Spawn was staring at Kimera. "We'll talk, but when I say it's time for you to leave, you do it. Don't take this to mean anything has changed between us. And Spawn..." I waited until he glanced at me. "Don't you dare do anything to get Kimera in trouble at work. She doesn't deserve her life destroyed. One of us is enough."

"Troian, sweetheart, I know you aren't able to believe it yet, but we're not the enemy. We want to make it up to you for what we did and how it hurt you. As for your friend here, I'll behave. Well, I will as far as doing that anyway. Her job is safe." He smirked. When I shifted my gaze to her, she was glaring at him. I snickered when she gave him the middle finger. It caused the guys to laugh, even Spawn. He winked at her and then blew her a kiss.

She pointed to the backdoor. I took a couple of steps, and Lash was at my side. "Let me carry you, please," he uttered.

"No, I can do it. Go." He wasn't happy about it, but he didn't argue. Spawn and Crusher went ahead of us. Lash hung back and kept pace next to me. I limped, and my foot was hurting, but not as badly as the rest of me. I gritted my teeth and kept going.

Inside, I made it to the stuffed chair in the living room and fell into it. Before anyone could get started saying anything, Kimera bustled over to me. "I'm getting stuff to fix your foot. Don't argue. We don't need you getting an infection. I'll be back."

She didn't wait for me to answer or agree. She walked off and into the bathroom. I closed my eyes. The silence was deafening for several minutes. Suddenly, Crusher said, "That damn dog looks like he'd love nothing more than to eat one of us. Who do you think he wants the most?"

"My pick is Spawn," Kimera said, causing me to jump. I opened my eyes to find her returning, and she was smirking at Spawn.

"Hotcake, you can threaten me all you want, but it won't do you any good. I'm called Spawn because I'm related to the Devil. You know, Spawn of Satan. I can control your hellhound over there."

"Keep telling yourself that. Toro will take a chunk out of you if I tell him to, so behave and don't piss me off more than you already do. That means stop calling me Hotcake."

He just smiled bigger. She came over and handed me a glass and then put a pill in my hand. "Take that. It won't hurt to take another one, and I can tell you're hurting terribly. Let me get this taken care of." She hunkered down and lifted my dirty foot on her thigh. She brought out wet wipes and cleaned the bottom. She grimaced when she was done.

"You have a nice laceration here. I've gotta get the dirt and debris out of it. That means it'll hurt. Take a deep breath."

I nodded and did. By the time she was done cleaning it with some liquid that burned like acid and fire mixed, I was about to cry. She then applied some kind of cream and a bandage that stuck on its own. She patted my leg as she set my foot down gently. She picked up her supply bag and took it to the kitchen table, and then she washed her hands at the sink. One more stop at the fridge, and she came back carrying bottles of water. I guess hospitality dictated that even unwanted visitors were to be treated to a drink.

Once she sat, I looked at Lash. "Tell me what you think I need to know."

"You know that we dug into your background and family. We were trying to rule out that they were involved in hurting you."

I interrupted him. "Yeah, and you needed to prove that I was involved in my cousin's dirty criminal activities. Oh, and that my amnesia was faked."

"Jesus, we're never gonna get past this if you can't stop bringing that up! I know we fucked up. That I did. Christ, every time I open my eyes and don't see you in our bed or house, I know it. I'm fucking sorry, but that's not what we need to worry about. It's what else we found out since your accident."

"And what would that be?" Kimera asked.

"That her family, the Gusevs, aren't the people

she thought they were. It wasn't only your cousin Andrik who was involved in the prostitution ring. We're positive it was all five of your male cousins," he told us.

"And what are you basing that on?" I asked.

"What my family told me," Crusher said out of nowhere. He had a very grim expression.

"Your family? What do they have to do with this?"

"You know my mother is Russian. Well, most of her family is still back in Russia. I do have contact with them, although not a lot. My father wasn't involved in their business, so when my mom married him, they lived here and outside the family circle."

"What was your family's business?" Kimera asked. I was grateful she was helping me keep the conversation on track. I was tired.

"My family is Bratva," he blurted out.

The breath stilled in me. I might not recall my past, but I knew who and what the Bratva was. They were organized crime families, the Mafia, in Russia, and they were ruthless. God, did that mean his family worked with Andrik?

I began to shake at the thought of the Bratva being involved. Lash was up and over to me like a shot. He growled as he scooped me up. I tried to get down from his arms, but he carried me back to the couch and sat down with me on his lap. I smacked at his chest and wiggled to get away, but it didn't do me any good. A growl from Toro made me stop.

"Settle down and listen," he said.

"Hurry up," I snapped back.

"It's true they're not white knights or anything. They're involved in criminal stuff, but the one thing my family can't stand and won't do is be involved in anything that hurts women and kids. Human trafficking and prostitution do that so they won't go there, and they hate those who do. I was trying to find something, so I mentioned your cousin's last name, Gusev, to my family there. Kirill, my second cousin and head of the family, said there was a family in Russia in the Bratva who they hated and did shit like that. He checked to see if they were related. They are. Shit, Troian, we're sure more than Andrik was involved, and there's more," Crusher told me.

"What more can there be?" I asked as I tried to process what he had already told me.

"We're waiting for actual confirmation, but I think the reason you were beaten and left for dead is Andrik was convicted based mostly on evidence, not witness testimony, although there were a couple of people who did testify. That usually means an informant on the inside. We think you were that informant, and at first, no one knew it. Somehow, they found out and tried to kill you for putting him away and ruining a very lucrative business for them," Spawn said.

Immediately, my head was filled with flashes of what seemed like snapshots. I saw a man's face, followed by a dark night, a car, and then darkness. I recalled pain in my head. Then there was more pain and the sound of voices, and fists and feet hitting me over and over as I begged for it to stop. I couldn't see the faces of the people hurting me, but the voices belonged to men. I flung myself forward and vomited on the floor.

Lash swore. Toro barked, and I heard movement. All I could do was gasp and try not to puke again. My hair was pulled back, and Lash was at face level with me. "Just breathe and try to relax."

I tried to do as he said. As the nausea eased, I sat back. Kimera came bustling over with a bucket and mop. Thankfully, the living room had tile, not carpet. I went to get up. She didn't need to clean my mess. She stopped me. "Keep your butt right there. I got this. Puke doesn't bother me, and it's hardly the first time I've cleaned it up. It won't take more than a minute."

As she mopped, Spawn asked me, "What caused that?"

"I saw images. I remember a flash of a man's face, then pain in my head. It was nighttime. I remember voices and being beaten and kicked. I didn't see them, but it was men's voices, and I begged them to stop."

Lash rubbed my back. Spawn took out his phone and tapped on it. I had no idea why. I was about to tell them I was fine and Lash could stop rubbing me when Spawn handed me his phone. "Are any of these men the one you saw?"

I carefully scanned five men grouped together on one screen. They were just headshots, but I zeroed in on the last one. I pointed at him. "That's him."

All three men looked and then exchanged grunts. "You're sure?" Lash asked.

"I'm positive. Who is it?"

"That's Zandro. I think those male voices you recall are the other three, or at least a couple of them. Now, do you see why it's too dangerous for you to stay here? They'll be looking for you?"

"Why? They dumped me. They think I'm dead," I exclaimed. Lash tugged me close. By his expression, I knew he had more to tell me.

Lash: Chapter 14:

I was worried that any more surprises or blows would cause Troian to collapse. The vomiting concerned me. However, we'd come too far, and there was no way she'd let us get away without telling her the rest. Also, if I had any hope in hell of getting her back to the compound and safe, I had to tell her. Fear might be the only way to accomplish it, which made me feel like a bastard. But I'd be a bastard if it kept her safe.

"One of the authors that you work for became concerned when she didn't hear from you. Someone named Ciara. She knew that wasn't like you. When she couldn't contact you, she went to the police and reported it. They went to your home and spoke to your family. They claimed that they didn't know you were missing. They said that you often go away to work and go radio silent for weeks or more at a time," I explained.

I could tell she was thinking about it and trying to remember if that was her practice. I kept going. "From everything Spawn and Smoke could find, that wasn't like you at all. We think that now that has happened, they'll be nervous that your body will be found, and they might've left evidence behind that'll tie them to your murder. To be sure that doesn't happen, they'll have to come back and move your body. Hell, they could do more than that to hide what happened and to keep you from being found. When they see your body is gone, they'll know you're likely alive, and they'll begin to search for you."

She began to rock back and forth with her arms wrapped around her stomach. She'd gone so pale I thought she might faint. Tears leaked down her face. I couldn't stand it. I gathered her against my chest. She didn't pull away. In fact, she pressed closer and buried her face in my chest. God, it felt wonderful to hold her again.

"Shh, it'll be okay. We won't let them hurt you. You've got to let us take you back to the compound where you'll be behind a fence and have not only physical guards but security cameras and shit."

"Troian, I want to tell these guys to go screw themselves, but they're right. People like that are too dangerous to take chances on them not finding you. Even if you go somewhere else, there's no guarantee they won't find you. I can try to protect you, and Toro will help, but I'm not here all the time. I have to work. I have a suggestion if you're willing to do it. Oh, and if these guys can stay off my nerves." She said the last bit as she gave Spawn a challenging chin lift. He snorted, but I saw the gleam in his eyes. He was enjoying sparring with the outspoken nurse. Hmm.

"Let's hear your bright plan, Hotcake," Spawn teased.

She bared her teeth at him for the hotcake remark, but she didn't say anything about it. Rather, she surprised us. "I'd like to come with Troian. I can help her and make sure she recovers like she should. Toro will come, too. He's a trained guard dog. He'll be added protection for her. He'll tear anyone apart who tries to harm her or anyone else I indicate isn't a friend. He can be there even when I'm at work. Plus, I have a gun, and I know how to use it. If they somehow find a way into your place, I have no trouble putting them down like the vermin they are." Disgust was evident in her voice.

My first response was to tell her no. We didn't need her as a bodyguard, and putting her in that position didn't sit well with me. But as I thought about it, I realized it might get Troian to agree. Plus, the dog was a good idea. As for Kimera, there was no telling if someone saw her pick up Troian, and if so, and the Gusevs started asking around, it could lead them to her.

"Why don't you guys talk about it while I help Troian to bed? She's exhausted, and the pain meds should be starting to help her. Give us ten minutes, and then we can finish our talk. You can tell me all the reasons you want to say no, and I'll make you see you're full of it." She flashed a smile before she came over to me. I reluctantly let my woman get up. She slowly limped to an open door, and then it closed.

As soon as they were out of sight, I turned to the other two. "What do you think?"

"I think that woman needs a spanking," Spawn grumbled.

"Let me guess. You're not talking about Troian, and you're just the man to give it to her," Crusher teased him.

"Damn right, I am. She's got more balls than sense, but in this case, I think she's right. If she comes, it'll get Troian back home, and the dog will be extra protection. We can also keep an eye on her to make sure they don't find out she helped Troian," Spawn said. It was good to see we all thought alike. Crusher nodded in agreement.

"So, you think she can convince Troian to do it? Or do we need to bring in the big guns? Crusher asked.

"Big guns?"

"Yeah, the old ladies and Annie," he added.

"Only as a last resort. I don't want her to think too much about them or the kids. If she does, she might think she's putting them in danger and refuse to come," I warned them.

"It's always a chance, but no one will let the women or the kids go anywhere without an escort. We can keep them all covered even if we ask some of the guys from other clubs to help out. Am I to assume that once we get confirmation that the rest of her family are involved and did try to kill her, we'll take care of it ourselves, and in a way that we don't ever have to worry about them coming after her again?" Crusher asked with a smirk on his face.

"Really? Why ask? You know the answer," I said.

He gave me a thumbs-up. Spawn nodded in agreement. With that settled, we waited for Kimera to come back so we could finish persuading her and then Troian. If that failed, I'd have to go all alpha-dominant asshole on her and carry her off. Colt was still sitting outside waiting on us. He had the SUV to take her back. Recalling that, I sent him a quick text to tell him to just hang tight. I got a thumbs-up emoji back.

I had just finished reading it when the bedroom door opened. Kimera peeked out, then came out and closed the door. I was up and across the room in a flash. She held up her hand before I could open the door.

"She's almost asleep. Let her get some rest. She's overdone it. We can talk out here. Sit," she ordered.

I did it reluctantly. It was all I could do not to go be with Troian. I retook my former seat. I got straight to the point. "What did she say? Did you make her see reason?"

"Listen, I understand on one level why it's smart for her to go to your compound. She explained what it's like there. However, I see it from her perspective, too. She's hurt and feels like she's been betrayed and can't trust you. I don't blame her."

"Now, that's not exactly fair. Yes, we checked into her, but it was the right thing to do to ensure everyone's safety," Spawn protested.

"How about I go digging into your life and do it because I think you're lying and can't be trusted? And then I'll happily tell everyone I know that you're okay to be with. That wouldn't bother you or hurt you? Think before you answer," she warned him.

Spawn narrowed his gaze on her. After a minute, he shrugged. "I can see how that might upset me, but

Lash and her are in a relationship. You and I aren't."

I swore I heard him utter so softly, I barely heard him, "Not yet." Kimera, I knew, didn't hear it because she didn't respond by tearing into him. So, it seemed this little feisty nurse had grabbed my brother's attention. If I wasn't worried about saving my own happiness, I might be able to enjoy this more.

"Which makes it worse in some ways. Anyway, I did get her to agree to go back, but she'll only do it temporarily. She's convinced she'll be fine as soon as she finds a place to go where no one will think to look for her. The second stipulation is that both Toro and I go too, and she and I stay together."

"That's not a problem. You and your dog can stay at my house. I have room. Only he has to not try to eat me every damn time he sees me."

She giggled as she looked at Toro. "I make no promises. You try to harm either of us, and he'll rip out your throat. That's his job."

"Deal. As for her coming temporarily, you have to know, and so does she, that I'm not good with that. She's my old lady, and that means she and I are together until one of us dies," I inform her.

"Since I want her to be safe, I won't tell her that. If you can find a way while we're there to convince her to give you another chance, then so be it."

"Why're you involved in this?" Spawn asked out of the blue. Crusher was content to sit back and listen. I was waiting for him to comment soon.

"What do you mean, why am I involved?"

"You don't know her. You met her once for a couple of hours at the most in the recovery room. She's not your friend or a family member."

"Does someone have to be a friend or family in order to do something you know is right? Or for me to care that they're safe and not being hurt by someone? Or maybe I should sit back and assume she has a bunch of family who give a damn about her and will step in," she snarled back. You could see her defenses go up instantly.

"Who hurt you?" Crusher asked.

A surprised look flashed on her face, and then it was gone. She closed it down. "I don't know what you mean."

"Either someone hurt you, or you've seen shit. I'm willing to bet at least one man was the cause. Why else get involved this much and have a dog like that?" Crusher continued.

"I have a dog because I love animals," was her immediate response. I noticed she didn't answer his first question.

"You can love animals but not have a trained guard dog. Those don't come cheap," Spawn added. I saw the calculating expression on his face. His gears were turning, and he wouldn't be able to stop until he found out everything about her. She must've seen it, too. She scooted closer to the edge of her chair and stared hard at him.

"Go stick your nose in my shit and see what happens, Spawn. I have a guard dog because I'm a woman who works odd hours and lives alone out here. I'd be stupid not to protect myself in more ways than just my gun. I can't hide behind a fence with weapons and people at the ready. Some of us have to live out in the real, scary, and dangerous world."

Not wanting this to cause her to back out of coming and, therefore, cause Troian not to go willingly, I cut it off before it got ugly. "You have every right to protect yourself. We're not saying you don't. I'd like to get her there as soon as possible."

"Let her sleep for a couple of hours. That'll give me time to get our stuff packed, the house secured, and things loaded. We'll head back after that."

"I'll let Colt know to hang loose until we're ready, then he can drive them over and haul their stuff," Crusher offered as he took out his phone.

She whipped around to stare at him. She looked uncomfortable again. "There's more of you here?"

"Just one of our prospects. He brought the SUV. We didn't know what condition she'd be in and figured she wouldn't be up to a ride on the back of my bike," I explained.

"Send him back. We'll use my car. I can't be without it anyway. I have to work."

"It won't hurt to have him stick around in case you end up needing to take more stuff with you. We're not sure how long this will last, so bring plenty," Spawn told her.

"Make him come inside and wait," she replied. It came out as a demand, not a suggestion. I knew we all could see how uncomfortable it made her to have him outside. The question was, why?

"He's fine in the car. He'll entertain himself," Spawn told her.

She stood up. "Either he comes inside where Toro and I can keep an eye on him, or you all go."

"Goddamn, why the hell are you so damn paranoid, woman? He's not gonna go busting in here at gunpoint and decide to kidnap and rape you," Spawn snapped.

Suddenly, she went pale and swayed for a second. Instantly, Spawn was up and had his arms around her. Toro went on high alert and let out a threatening growl, then barked and showed his teeth. Spawn didn't let go of her.

"Call off your dog, babe. I'm not hurting you, and I don't plan to. You couldn't be safer than with me. I just want to know what made you react like that. We're not men who hurt women and kids. Yeah, we fucked up with my brother Lash's woman and hurt her emotionally, but that wasn't intentional. Tell me why you went pale and swayed. Did someone do that to you?"

She didn't answer him right away, but I did see her give a hand signal to Toro, which made him sit back down. He didn't take his eyes off her. The signal I recognized. Before I could ask her, she answered Spawn.

"I'm fine. My blood sugar must be low. That's all. If you'll let go of me, I'll grab a snack. Would you guys like something? Oh, and how about your prospect? Is he coming in, or are you all leaving?" There was a firmness to her tone that told me she wasn't about to budge on Colt staying outside.

"I'll tell him to head back if you're sure we won't need him," Crusher offered. I knew he didn't want to push her. Neither did I. I nodded so he'd know to do it. Spawn was in a staring contest with Kimera. I noticed he still held her in his arms. I fought back a chuckle. If he was going after her, it would be a wild ride.

"Thanks, cuz," I told him.

She turned her head to glance at me. "Cuz? You're blood-related, or is that another biker term I don't know?"

"We're second cousins on our dads' side," I explained as Crusher sent off a text to Colt. "Hey, let me ask you something. Did you happen to get Toro from Flynn Farm down in Tennessee? Seamus and Laura?"

She pushed Spawn's chest, and he reluctantly let go but didn't move back much. She faced me and gave me a surprised look. "Yes, I did. How do you know Laura and Seamus?"

"Well, shit. Our good friends, the Archangel's Warriors, and one of their brothers, Razor, married the Flynns' daughter, Talia. Their foster son, Bryce, is a Warrior, but he transferred to Hunters Creek. They call him Vex."

This got a small smile out of her, and the rest of the tension in her shoulders eased. "I've never met Talia or Bryce, but I've heard of them. Someone else trained Toro, and he was the one to work with me when I got him. Wow, small world."

"How long have you had him?" Spawn asked.

"Three years. I got him not long after I moved here," she told us as she moved off toward the kitchen. We leisurely followed. Toro didn't growl, but he did keep himself between her and us.

She opened the fridge and began to pile things on the counter. There was lunch meat, fruit, yogurt, and cheese. Next came condiments, tomato, and lettuce. Once she had those out, she opened a cabinet, brought out paper plates, and grabbed a few knives from a drawer. The last things she laid out were napkins before she pointed to everything as she grabbed a bag with bread in it. "Help yourselves."

We didn't say much as we all prepared ourselves a plate. I noticed she only took a small amount of cheese, fruit, and yogurt. When we were done, we all took a seat at her small kitchen table after she got us more water. You would've thought she was totally at ease, except I caught the glances she made at the front and back doors and even the windows. She gave Spawn a weird look when he pulled out her chair, too.

"Relax, he's gone. Didn't you hear the SUV leave? I promise there's no one from our club lurking around outside," Spawn assured her gruffly.

"Nothing says he couldn't have been told to go down the road and then sneak back on foot," she responded.

Crusher slid his phone out of his pocket, tapped on it, and then slid it over to her. "Here, you can see that I didn't tell him that. He's really gone, darlin'."

She read it and then nodded. I saw Spawn opening his mouth. Before he could start interrogating her again, I cut in and asked her how she liked being a nurse. This got her smiling and talking enthusiastically. We chatted about this and that while we ate. When we were done, we offered to put away the leftovers and clean up while she packed. She gave us a grateful smile and then went into another room. I assumed that was her bedroom. As soon as the door shut, Spawn whirled around to glare at us.

"There's something not right going on here."

"You mean more than just with Troian?" I asked, acting stupid.

He rolled his eyes. "Duh, yeah, that's what I mean, asshole. You know it is. The way she reacted to my snide comment about kidnapping and rape and the fact she carries a damn gun and has a dog that'll eat your ass. Someone either scared her or actually hurt her. Shit, I need to figure this out," he muttered. I saw his fingers moving like he was typing. I think this might've been as long as he'd been away from his computers in ages.

"Spawn, chill. You can't go diving into her past. You heard her. Why not see if we can gain her trust and then ask her? I agree it might be something ugly, or maybe she's just cautious like she said. Either way, if you're interested in her, she's not gonna like it if you go digging into her past," I warned him.

"Who said I was interested in her?"

Crusher snorted. "Brother, you almost pissed on her, for God's sake. She's got your attention. Don't lie. Now, if it's because you want to get your cock wet, forget it. That woman isn't one to go around sleeping with men to scratch an itch."

"I'm not just looking to—" he abruptly halted when he realized what he'd done. We both laughed at him. He gave us the finger. "Yuck it up, bastards. I'm not saying anything will come of it, but she's got my attention. There, now let's get this mess cleaned up and this show on the road."

We didn't give him any more grief. After cleaning the kitchen, Spawn said he'd be back. He wanted to check that nothing outside needed to be secured. I figured he needed alone time to process and to see what kind of security she had out there. He couldn't help but look at places that way.

By the time Kimera brought her first packed bag into the living room, Spawn was back. He marched up to her. Crusher and I let him do it, although we were all thinking the same thing. He scowled. "Hotcake, don't be lugging shit around. You pack, then we'll carry that shit and load it into your car."

"I told you, don't call me Hotcake, and I can do this. I'm not a weakling," she protested.

"It has nothing to do with your strength. It's manners. Women don't open doors, carry stuff, or pull out their own chairs around us. Give me your car keys so I can unlock it and put this in there." He held out his hand.

"How do you know it's locked?" she asked with a frown.

"Cause I tried the doors," he told her with a bland look.

"When did you do that?" she asked hotly.

"While you were packing. I checked to see if there was anything outside that needed to be secured or needed attention."

"And you thought my car did?"

"No, I was testing out a theory, and you proved it with the locked car."

"And what pray tell would that be?"

"That you're overly cautious, and one day you'll tell me why."

"Don't bet on it," she muttered as she smacked her keys in his hand, then turned her back and walked back to her room.

He gave me and Crusher a grin. "She's wearing down."

This made us both crack up and laugh. He kept smiling as he took her bag outside. As she packed more, we were pleasantly surprised that she didn't carry them out to us. She'd just indicate when she had another. She indicated a huge bag of dog food in her small pantry. I took it out to the car. We were at it for maybe an hour when Troian came shuffling out. We tried to keep our voices down and make the least amount of noise possible, but I wasn't sure if we woke her or not. She looked sleepy and was moving slowly. I wanted to pick her up and carry her, but I didn't.

"I assume we're still going?" she asked the room in general. We all nodded. "Okay, what do you need me to do?"

"You just rest," I told her.

"Lash, I don't need you bossing me around. I'm not helpless," she snapped.

I couldn't help it. I walked over and crowded into her personal space. I leaned down to whisper in her ear, "You know how much your being sassy turns me on. Keep that up and see what happens, Hurricane. Now, you wanna continue that, or do you wanna rest? I'm more than willing to take you back in that bedroom and make you purr," I growled. I had to fight not to get hard at the images in my head.

I knew she wasn't in any shape to have sex, but that didn't mean I couldn't make her feel good and ease her tension. She panted softly but didn't say a word. I smirked at her. It took all my restraint not to kiss her. I moved back when I felt something hit my knees. Glancing down. I saw Toro squeezing between us. He was giving me a "move your ass" look. Reluctantly, I moved. Not because of him but because I knew she was about to panic.

"Listen, you little cockblocker, step off," I told the dog. I swear the bastard gave me a doggy grin. Spawn and Crusher laughed. Kimera watched the whole thing with a curious look on her face. I wasn't sure why.

"I've got everything packed, I think. Why don't I come to help you get freshened up, Troian, and then we can go? These three can entertain themselves while we do that," Kimera offered as she steered Troian toward the room she just left. I wanted to be the one to take care of my woman, but I knew I couldn't. Not yet. She didn't protest as Kimera gently pushed her into the bedroom before she closed the door.

I blew out a deep breath and rubbed the back of my neck. A slap on the shoulder had me glancing up. Crusher was standing there, grinning at me. "She's got you all twisted up, doesn't she? It's good to see."

"Fuck you. Wait until the same happens to you. I'll tell you the same and see if you like it."

"Nah, that'll never happen. My woman will take one look at me, fall at my feet, and beg me to take her. We'll live in bliss for the rest of our lives."

Spawn and I laughed. It was Spawn who said something, though. "God, I can't wait to see how wrong you are. When she puts you in your place or on your ass, we want to be there. I want to record that, so you can watch it again and again and know how full of shit you were for saying this. Why would you get someone like that when none of us have or will? That's not our kind of woman. We need 'em with fire."

"You wait. I'll get an angel who'll never go against my advice when it comes to her safety, health, or happiness."

This made us lose it. We were still laughing when the women rejoined us. They gave us curious glances but didn't ask what we were laughing about. It was probably a good thing. As we escorted them outside, I had to stick close to Troian. I kept a hand at the small of her back, even though she tried to shrug it away. As soon as the door to the house was locked, we got them in the car, and then we straddled our rides.

Spawn indicated he'd ride behind them. As we took off, I couldn't help but keep glancing back into my mirrors to make sure they were still behind us. I knew Spawn was staying behind them not just for protection but to prevent them from bolting. I wasn't about to lose her now that I found her again. Nor was I letting this destroy our future.

Troian: Chapter 15

It had been five days since Lash found me at Kimera's house and talked us into coming back to the compound for my protection. Five days of second-guessing my decision. It wasn't because he'd done anything to make me think he wasn't out to protect me. That wasn't in doubt. Nor was it in doubt that the whole club was deadly serious about keeping me safe. They were so on top of it I couldn't walk outside the house without one of them popping up. I tried not to let it warm my heart, but it was impossible.

On top of it, they kept treating me like family. They insisted that Kimera and I come to celebrate Arya's first birthday. They had a party for her at the clubhouse. She didn't really know what it was all about, but she had fun and loved the cake. It was great to see them all making a fuss over her. They played with her and presented her with so many gifts. It was crazy.

No, what was making me second-guess things was how Lash was determined to make me believe that he loved me and never meant to hurt me. The man was constantly giving me light touches that made my entire body burn. I swear I was in a constant state of arousal. Even when he wasn't there, he'd text me or call to check on me. He loved to make teasing sexual remarks. Those, along with his touch, made me want to tear off his clothes and jump him. Luckily for me, I was still too sore from the accident and my surgery to act on it.

Kimera and Toro had settled in well. She was totally in awe of the compound, and Toro loved that he had so much space to run. She didn't have to worry about him getting lost or not coming back. I had no doubt he'd ever not want to come back to her. That dog adored his owner. Seeing how he was with her made me want a dog of my own.

When Lash wasn't working, he spent all his time around me. The only exception was when he was called to the clubhouse to attend meetings. I wondered what it was they had to discuss all the time. When I was here before, they only had it once a week. I didn't ask because I knew he wouldn't tell me. Kimera, on the other hand, did and got the standard "it's club business" explanation.

She'd asked me about that, and I told her what Lash had explained to me before. She rolled her eyes and huffed. I agreed with her. The old ladies came over to visit as much as they could, especially while church was happening. They were upset that I'd been hurt and were trying their hardest to get me to forgive everyone and not to leave. I didn't make any promises, but it was nice to spend time with them and the kids.

While Lash was out, I spent time working. I had editing jobs that needed to be done, and there was no way I could afford to leave unless I made some money. This I could do even if I was in pain and had to take breaks.

Kimera stuck close to me unless she was at work. She'd tried to tell the guys she didn't need anyone following her when she went to the hospital or came home, but they refused to pull the security detail off her. I didn't want her to get hurt because of me, so I insisted she let them do it. She reluctantly agreed.

This afternoon, she wasn't working, and we were sitting around the backyard on the patio, watching Toro run around. We'd throw balls for him, and he'd go nuts chasing them and bringing them back. I swear he could do that for hours. She'd explained that his breed needed lots of stimulation, exercise, and tasks to do so they didn't get bored. Boredom led to depression and destructiveness. I couldn't roughhouse with him like she did or run, but I could walk and throw a ball, although not hard or as far. He seemed to understand I was hurt. He was extra gentle with me.

We were laughing at his crazy expression as he gave us a doggie smile. Our giggling was interrupted by Lash. He wasn't alone. Spawn was with him, which wasn't unusual. He seemed to find a lot of reasons to come to the house. I knew it was due to Kimera, even if she didn't. Only this time, neither of them were smiling. I stiffened and straightened in my chair. Kimera jerked forward in hers and gripped the arms. Toro, sensing the change, charged over to us to stand between us and look at the two men.

"What's wrong?" I asked.

"Babe, we just found out something. I need you to stay calm. There's nothing to worry about. We've got you," Lash said firmly.

"Just tell me. What is it?"

"We've been getting more and more information on your family. There's proof that all five of your male cousins were in on the business Andrik was running, and there are other illegal businesses, too. What we didn't know was if they were, for sure, the ones who hurt you. Well, just a bit ago, Spawn received confirmation it was them. There was a text sent between them." He paused.

"Go ahead," I said past the lump in my throat.

"It said that they were coming to check if the body was found. If not, they'd have to make sure it would never be found. They're on their way to Bristol," Lash told me softly. He was watching me closely.

My first response was pain. It knifed through me as I realized my family had betrayed me for doing the right thing. Even if I couldn't remember them, it didn't hurt any less. For an instant, I wanted to deny it was them, but something inside of me whispered that it was true. I gasped and bent forward with my arms around my middle. Lash dropped to his knees in front of me. His arms came around me, and he held me.

"Baby, please, don't be scared. We're not gonna let them get near you. Now that we know it was them for sure, we can take care of this once and for all."

I pulled away so I could see his face. He had a hard look on his face. His tone told me he wasn't happy. My pain changed to fear, only not for myself. It was for him.

"Lash, don't you go doing something that gets you or the others hurt or killed. Do you hear me? They're not worth dying or going to prison for. They need to be the ones who go there."

He smiled. "Baby, you have nothing to worry about. We won't go to prison, and we'll go in loaded for anything, so we all make it back. This isn't our first rodeo with people like this. Surely, the old ladies told you their stories."

They had, and it shocked and scared me to know they did this kind of thing frequently. Their having experience didn't make it any less of a worry for me. "I don't care if you have done this before. There are no guarantees."

"True, but I could be hit on my bike tomorrow or have a heart attack or brain aneurysm and drop dead. There are never any guarantees. All you need to know is I will do everything in my power to come home to you."

I lay my head on his chest and closed my eyes as I thought about what he said. As much as I wanted to continue to argue, I knew he was right. His statement that he would do everything to come back to me struck me. He'd emphasized the "to me" part. His stare had been intense as he said it. He was trying to determine if I was going to stay. How could I answer that when I didn't know? There was a big part of me that was being pulled to forgive him and the club and stay. However, there was another part insisting that I go. It kept telling me he'd hurt me again, and what if it was worse?

He didn't say anything more. He just held me and

rubbed my back. I didn't know how long I leaned on him before I raised my head. Kimera and Spawn were watching us. I noticed he'd gone to stand next to her chair. I glanced back at Lash.

"I'm not saying that I can stay. I haven't decided yet. So if that's a condition of taking care of them, you now know it and can forget going after them."

"I want you to stay more than anything in the world, but whether you do or not doesn't change the fact that we will take them out. You're mine. That's for life, even if you leave me. I'll protect you, and taking care of them does that."

"So even if I move somewhere else and refuse to be with you, you'll still protect me? How?" I asked, feeling stunned.

"You'll have someone or something watching over you."

"And if I end up with someone else? Will you stop it then?"

I saw the anger enter his face, but he didn't voice it. Instead, he gave me a terse answer. "Even if you move on to someone else, I'll make sure you're safe. That includes from him. But I won't stop trying to win you back until you let someone else into your life and marry him. Short of marriage, I'll keep trying."

"Lash, you can't do that! What about your happiness? Having a wife and kids? You said you want that," I protested.

"I want that with you. If I can't have you as my

wife and old lady, and those kids aren't ours, then I don't want that."

I sat there speechless at his revelation. I glanced at Kimera. She gave me a speaking look, but I was too dazed to understand it.

She cleared her throat. "I think you've given Troian enough to think about. Tell me if I'm wrong, but you're okay with them doing what needs to be done to protect you. Right?" she asked me. I nodded yes.

"Okay then, why don't you guys go do whatever it is you do? Troian and I will fix something to eat. Are you hungry?" Kimera asked as she came to her feet.

"Why don't we bring something in rather than making you ladies cook?" Lash suggested.

"We could, but then the ribs we've been slow cooking all day and the pork we have cooking will have to wait. I thought barbeque ribs and pulled pork with beans and coleslaw would be a good dinner. Was I wrong?" she asked with a smirk. I almost laughed at the looks of stunned joy on their faces. She was telling the truth. We had made all that today.

"Hell no, you're not wrong! Tell me what you need me to do," Spawn jumped in to say.

"Stay out of the kitchen. I don't need you in my hair. Go plot with the guys or entertain Toro."

"I'd entertain your dog if he didn't look at me all the time like he was plotting ways to kill me and hide my body," he told her as he exchanged looks with Toro.

I swear the damn dog raised an eyebrow at him as if to say, "I am." I suppressed my giggle.

Kimera merely smiled at him. "Well, then I suggest you get to know him better, and maybe he'll stop plotting. Give us an hour, maybe an hour and a half, and it'll be ready. Shoo. We'll be fine." She waved them away. To my astonishment, they appeared to listen. But before Lash left, he laid a kiss on my cheek right next to my mouth. He lingered, then broke away and left. I watched him walk off with Spawn.

I ached to feel his lips on mine. My resistance was wearing thin. Did that make me a weakling? To forgive him so easily and quickly? The feel of his arms around me had been heaven. I hated going to bed without him.

"Girl, get that mooning look off your face. We've got work to do. And no, you're not weak for considering forgiving that man. I almost peed myself when he declared he'd always keep trying to win you back and even would protect you if you ended up with another man. Hot damn that made me melt," she said with a grin as she hooked her arm through mine and walked me to the back door. I let her lead me inside. Toro brought up the rear. As soon as we entered, he went to check the house. He did it every time.

We went to the kitchen, and she pressed me down on a stool at the counter. I knew she didn't want me on my feet much. She checked on the ribs and the pork, then got to work on making the coleslaw. The beans were done, and she took them out of the fridge and popped them into the oven with the pork shoulder we had marinated and cooked. The aromas in the house were amazing and made my stomach growl.

I hadn't had much of an appetite since the wreck. I had to be pushed to eat. It didn't seem to be the issue tonight. "Give me something to do besides sit on my ass," I told her.

She grinned as she grabbed items out of the fridge and pantry. By the time she was done, I had at least a dozen bottles, bowls, and spoons. She pushed a piece of paper toward me. "You can make the barbeque sauce to go on the ribs. Just follow the recipe."

I picked it up to find a handwritten recipe. Concentrating so I wouldn't mess it up, I got to mixing. It made me raise a brow when I saw the base of it was already a store-bought sauce. I had to ask. "Kim, why make one if we already have one from the store?"

She shook her head and looked at me like I'd asked her the most obvious thing. "I see you were raised where barbeque isn't a religion or at least a sport. Where I'm from, people are serious about their sauces. The only reason we're using this store-bought crap is because I don't have access to my usual base. It's at home. We can make do with this. Believe me, this will blow your mind. It has a bit of heat but not too much. I know Virginia is technically south of the Mason-Dixon line, but you're still not truly southern to me. I have to remember that you've been deprived all your life."

"Deprived, is it?" I teased her.

"Severely deprived. When you taste this, I expect you'll drop to one knee, declare undying love for me, and propose. Although I'll appreciate it, sorry, girl, but I won't switch teams for you, no matter how much you beg or bribe me."

This got me laughing. We had fun preparing the rest of dinner and joking around. It made me relax and got my mind off what the guys were doing. Exactly an hour later, they came into the house. We were almost done, so they set the table and got us all something to drink. I was used to that from Lash. I could see Kimera wasn't used to it at all.

The first bites after we got our food were just as amazing as she'd said they would be. I stood and walked to her chair. She had an amused look on her face. She knew what was coming. I lowered myself to one knee carefully, and then I grabbed her hand.

"Kimmy, I love you. Will you marry me?"

"What the fuck?" I heard Spawn ask.

"Hell if I know. Maybe she took too many pain pills," Lash said.

They made both of us burst out laughing and look at them. "I'm not high on meds. Kimera told me that after I tasted her barbeque sauce, I'd declare my love and propose. I was just proving she was right. She said she wouldn't switch teams to be with me, but I think I can convince her," I teased as I wiggled my eyebrows. She laughed harder, then choked it back so she could respond.

"Well, I guess I'll have to take it back. Let's run away with each other."

"Like hell, you're taking her away," Lash informed her as he came to help me up.

Spawn was studying her. He suddenly smiled. "Hotcake, you don't have to switch teams. If you want a proposal and undying love declaration for your cooking, I'm your man. When do you want to get married? I'd like at least three kids, so I hope you're on board with that."

She choked a bit before she could answer him. Lash and I stood there watching the scene unfold. I wasn't sure what she'd say or do to poor Spawn. They loved to spar with each other. "Well, Studcake, that's nice, but I believe Troian's offer is better. If you're good, I might let you come to the wedding. Do you want to be the ring bearer?"

He smirked at her. "Babe, you know you can't resist me. Keep trying. I know you'll see the light soon."

"Oh, great, so I'll be dying soon then because that's the only light I'll be seeing," she snarked back.

"I'm gonna rock your world," he told her. He said it with so much conviction that she didn't say anything back.

Instead, she pointed to his plate. "Eat before it gets cold. You two, too. I'll be pissed if you waste this meal Troian and I slaved over."

Lash helped me back in my chair, then retook his. I had to put them straight. "It was mainly all her doing, not mine. I mixed a few things and stuff, but she was the mastermind behind this."

"You both did a great job. I've never tasted barbeque this good," Lash said before digging back in. We ate in a pleasant silence. The only things to disturb it were the scrape of silverware and low grunts and moans. Those came from the guys. Kimera and I exchanged pleased grins. When we were done, she got up to get dessert, and they groaned.

"God, woman, you can't expect me to eat dessert too," Spawn growled.

"You don't have to. You can watch Troian and me eat it. It's just homemade banana cream pie. No biggie," she said as she shrugged her shoulders.

I thought Spawn was going to fall as he jumped to his feet. "I'll get the dessert plates. You need a knife to cut it?" She shook her head no as he practically ran to the cabinet. I looked at Lash.

He leaned over to whisper to me, "Banana cream pie is his favorite. I don't know if she knew that or not, but I think he'll be proposing soon."

I giggled. In no time, we all had a piece of pie. I knew she had made it, so I saved room. Despite their earlier groans and the way the guys inhaled it, they had room, too. I swear, listening to Spawn moan was almost sexual. Lash told him that.

"Man, you gotta stop moaning like that. It's indecent. You sound like you're having sex."

"Don't judge me. You have no idea what I'd do for a pie like this. Hotcake, who do you want me to kill? Or wipe their existence off the internet? I can make them disappear if you promise to make this once a week for the rest of our lives."

His teasing made her smile slip for a moment, and then it was back. I wondered about that. I know Spawn and Lash also saw it but didn't call her on it. Spawn kept going. "The wedding will be next month. That should give you enough time to find a dress. You never said if three kids are acceptable. I'm open to adoption if that makes a difference."

I was surprised when she went along with him. "Sure, three is fine, but I was thinking more like six myself. As for a month, that should be enough time. However, if I make this once a week, you might get roly-poly. I'd hate to do that to you."

"Woman, let me worry about that. I can exercise more to counteract that deliciousness. Where did you learn to cook like this? I knew Troian could. Lash bragged about it to the rest of us poor bastards enough, and we got to taste some at a party."

She got a tender expression on her face when he asked who had taught her. She smiled. "My granny taught me. She loved to cook, and I spent a lot of time with her in the kitchen when I was a young kid. She made sure I knew how to cook and bake."

"I take it she's gone? You used the past tense," Spawn said.

"Yeah, I lost her when I was ten. But I have my memories and a book filled with her recipes. She'd love to know people were eating them and enjoying it."

He reached over, took her hand, and gave it a squeeze. "She's dancing then because this is wonderful. Bet she's watching you from heaven with a smile."

She patted his hand. I decided to break the sad mood. "He's right. This is outstanding. I know I won't make it as good as yours, but I need this recipe. I already stole the barbeque sauce recipe. I hope that's okay."

"I know. I saw you jotting it down. It's perfectly fine. Granny would love knowing you have it. That was one of the great things about her. She never kept her recipes a secret. If someone wanted it, she gladly gave it to them."

"I think you'll be getting a lot of requests for them," Lash added.

We finished off the pie, and then the guys insisted they would clean and do the dishes. I happily let them. I was feeling tired and wanted to sit and relax. Kimera and I went to sit in the living room. I sat down, and we took turns petting Toro. He'd been given a small portion of the pork in his bowl before we ate. He was happy.

I rubbed absently across my stomach. Her eyes zeroed in on it. She frowned. "Troi, you hurting? Do you need me to go get your medicine? You didn't overdo it today, did you?"

I thought she said it low enough, but I was wrong. Lash was in the living room like a shot. He was frowning and bent over me. "Baby, do you need to lie down? Let me see your incisions. Are you sure they're doing alright?" He directed the last question to Kimera.

"They looked fine when I checked them last night. She hasn't been lifting. It might be a good idea to check them out, though. I'll go get her medicine from her room." She was up and gone before I could tell her not to do it.

I tried to fight Lash and keep him from pulling up my top, but he didn't let me. When he got it high enough to see my incisions, he ran a finger lightly over them. I shivered.

"They look good. These should heal well." He pressed on them gently. "Does this hurt?"

"It's a bit sore but not really painful. I'm fine, Lash. I'm just tired."

"I can't help it. I worry. You could've been killed, and the thought of losing you drives me wild. I couldn't handle that, Hurricane. I can't."

The pain on his face made me rub my hand along his jaw. He closed his eyes, sighed, and pressed against it. He wasn't fighting fair. His concern made me want to forgive him even more. Damn it. I would keep denying it a bit longer, but I knew I was going to forgive him. However, I'd make him wait a bit more before I told him. It would be good for him. We still had to go over some ground rules for our future before he was totally forgiven.

"I'm okay. You didn't lose me. I'm tougher than I look. Stop stressing so much. I'll take my medicine and feel better in no time," I told him as Kimera came back with not only one of my pills but the glass of water from my nightstand. I quickly took it so it would start to work. She smiled.

"How did her incisions look?"

"They look good. Nothing jumps out. She just needs to take it easier during the day. She thinks she's Superwoman," he muttered.

She bumped him with her hip. "Damn right, she is. We women are all superwomen. It's you mere mortal men who don't know that or conveniently try to forget it. It's why we have the babies. God knew what he was doing when he made that plumbing adjustment."

She winked at me. He couldn't see her do it. I knew she wanted to rile him up. It got him going a bit, but it was Spawn who jumped in with both feet. "Now, don't disparage the strength of us men, especially your future husband. I'll have you know, I'm tough, and I could have the babies if I was able to."

She laughed at him. "Have them my ass. As soon as you puked once or got an ache or pissed yourself, you'd curl up in the bed and refuse to get out even after the baby was born. Nothing would get done for your entire pregnancy, and you'd want to be waited on hand and foot. You'd want to be drugged to high heaven for the birth and whine for a solid two years afterward about how hard it was, and you'd never do it again. I worked labor and delivery before moving to OR recovery. Nope, you're not that tough."

Both of the guys puffed up. "Like hell, we couldn't. Yeah, there are guys out there that couldn't, but they're not bikers, baby. We're a breed apart," Spawn added.

Lash looked at me. "Tell her, Hurricane. Tell her that I'd be able to do it. Defend your man's honor."

I held up my hands. "Don't get me involved in this because it'll only hurt your delicate man feelings," I said with a smirk. I loved to jerk his chain a bit.

He gave me an outraged stare and then narrowed his eyes. He looked over at Spawn. "I think they need to be shown the error of their ways. I suggest we put on a show for them. It's been a while since we've had a fighting match. What do you think?"

Spawn fist-bumped him. "I think you're right, brother. Show these women what we're made of. I know the others will want to get in on this."

They both glanced back at us. They had serious looks on their faces before Lash added, "We'll work on getting the exhibition planned for as soon as possible. When we prove how much we can take and you have to eat crow, I'll expect a suitable reward."

"Me too," Spawn told Kimera.

"Oh really, and what pray tell is a suitable reward in your book?" I asked.

He smirked. "You let me do anything I want in the bedroom for one night. I promise I won't hurt you. All you have to do is relax and go with it. I'll make you scream harder and longer than you ever have."

Heat flashed through me at the thought. He'd already made me scream harder and longer than I imagined a guy could. Jesus, if he did more, I'd die. I was left speechless.

Kimera asked Spawn with a roll of her eyes, "And what's your reward to be, Studcake?"

He leaned closer and smiled at her. "Well, Hotcake, I think Lash has the perfect idea. So the same. I hope you don't have to use your voice for a while afterward, say a few days, because you won't have one when I get done with you."

She gave him a stunned look and didn't say anything at first, just turned pink, but she recovered quickly. "You talk big, but you have to prove you're tough, and it's not just Troi and me who'll judge you. I think the old ladies need to get in on this, as well as someone named Annie, whom I've heard about. That way, you can't blame biased judges when you lose."

"How the hell is that not biased? All women against the men! We should have a few men who've suffered major pain or maybe ones who are neutral to help judge," Spawn objected.

"And where would you get neutral men? None of the other clubs would be, and if they're regular friends of yours, they wouldn't be either. I think your best bet is to call it off now," I taunted. I was getting into the spirit of it. Kimera made me laugh and have fun. She had a wicked sense of humor once you got to know her.

"Hell no, we're not backing out. We'll let the guys know what's at stake, and they'll come through. In fact, we'll show you so well that even with six women judging, we'll still win. Sisterhood is one thing, but you can't beat brotherhood," Lash said.

"If you're that confident, why don't we put some money on the outcome? The winner picks the recipient organization that will receive the winnings as a donation. The losers have to double the ante amount, so it's a nicer donation," she suggested.

Both men nodded. "We can do that. Sounds like a good thing to do. Okay, give us a few days to get the others organized. Anything else you want to make a part of this before we do it? You can't back out after you agree because you get scared," Spawn taunted.

"We won't. You have a deal," I said. I held out my hand at the same time Kimera did. Lash shook hers as Spawn shook mine, and then they traded off. When Lash grabbed my hand, he kissed it after shaking it. He gave me one of his panty-melting smiles. The hot flash from just a couple of minutes ago came back with a vengeance. I only vaguely heard Kimera and Spawn bickering good-naturedly.

It took several minutes for them to calm down their trash talk. Once they did, Spawn reluctantly called it a night. "I gotta go, but I'll see you later. I've got work to do tonight. Later, Troian. Hope you feel better. Bye, Hotcake."

"Goodnight, Spawn. Don't work too late," I said.

"Night, man. See you tomorrow," Lash told him as they fist-bumped each other.

Kimera grinned at him. "Goodnight, Studcake. I know why you're really leaving. You have to start intensely working out for the fight, but it's no use. You'll still lose, so save the sweat."

He chuckled and shook his head. "You won't know what hit you, babe. Dream of me winning tonight."

I couldn't help but giggle as he flexed his way out the door. The man was a nut, but no one could call him a wimp. I settled back on the couch, and Lash joined me. Kimera excused herself to go check on the laundry she'd put in the dryer earlier. I was nervous, in a good way, being left alone with him. I'd see how well he behaved.

Lash: Chapter 16

I was on edge and knew everyone could feel it. I tried to hide it from Troian, but she knew it too. The past few days since we'd gotten confirmation that her so-called family was coming to see if her body had been found had only amped up my desire to lay waste to every one of them.

It was disgusting and infuriating enough to think of anyone doing what they did, but to know it was her family made it ten times worse in my book. Your family was supposed to love and protect you, not hurt you or try to kill you. I was so looking forward to taking them out. I didn't come out and say bluntly to her we were going to kill them, but I hoped, from all we said and Kimera's question, that she knew that. Those kinds of people you didn't send to prison because they either got out and came for revenge or they sent others after you while they were still behind bars. That meant that Andrik wouldn't get out or be left to issue hit orders to any minions they had or to the family back in Russia.

It was a waiting game now to see when they appeared. Spawn, with help from Crusher, went to the dump site and put up the trail cameras so we could make sure to capture them on video when they came. It was another warning system in case they slipped here without us knowing it. Spawn set some kind of alert on his computer to tell him if the camera was activated. I told him he'd be driven crazy by animals, but he assured me it would be fine. It wasn't on a big game trail or where people usually walked or hiked. It was too overgrown for that.

I was thankful every damn day that Alisse had caught a glimpse of the tarp and made Ink stop to check it out. If she hadn't, Troian would be dead, and I would've never met the love of my life. I believed God had a hand in it that day. He wanted me to find her and for us to build a life together. I also believed he wouldn't object to what we were about to do, but if he did, I'd gladly stand before him when I died to have judgment passed.

It was hard to leave her at the compound and go to work, but I did. I had Spawn's promise to call me as soon as he got any kind of alert. I had to fight to keep my mind on my job so I didn't create something subpar. That would piss me off more. I took pride in the work I did.

The past few nights, when I got home, besides spending time with her, I met with my brothers so we could iron out our game plan. One of the concerns raised was blowback from the Gusev relatives in Russia. Crusher was the one to lay that to rest. His grin last night had been huge when we talked about it.

A huge, slightly vindictive grin spread across Crusher's face as Reaper voiced his concern that the Russian Gusevs would come seeking revenge when we took out their American branch.

"We don't have to worry about them," Crusher said with deep satisfaction in his voice.

"Why not? You think they don't care for their cousins that much?" Ink asked.

"Oh, they care as much as a bunch of evil bastards like them can. That's not what I meant. It seems Kirill and the rest of my family have decided they've had enough of the whole damn family. They hate what they do, and they're not so connected or liked even in the homeland to have big allies. He said if we take care of the vermin here, they'll take care of the ones there. All he needs to know is once we've done it, and they'll make their move before they can rally anyone to avenge their scummy cousins."

"Shit, are you serious?" Ratchet asked in awe.

"Yep. They detest them. Now, all we gotta do is wait. I hope they don't procrastinate. I'm ready to get my hands on them," Crusher added. He looked at me. "And I know Lash is more than ready. You got your toys ready to go?"

I smirked at him. "You know it. They're thirsty for some blood, just like I am."

This had gotten them all laughing and talking about what they wanted to do to them. We'd finished up not long after that.

Remembering that made me smile.

"What put that smile on your face? Are you sexting with Troian?" came the amused remark from behind me. I turned to gaze at Tinker. He had a shit-eating grin on his face. There were others in the shop, and they were trying not to smile at what he said. He hadn't whispered it.

"Shut up about me and my woman. Even if we did sext, I wouldn't tell you, you pervert. What do you want? Besides driving me crazy, that is. Don't you have work to do, or are the rest of us the only ones who do that around here?" I jokingly asked.

Everyone knew Tinker worked his ass off, but it was fun to tease him that he sat back and watched. Before he could answer, I hit him with another. "Or did you need to stretch your legs before your next round of soap operas and bonbon eating in the office? You know it's not a secret, right? We all know what you do behind that closed door. All we ask is you better not be jerking off, too."

"Fucker," he shouted, then came after me. I was expecting it, so I darted away. I ran, and he chased me around the shop. The guys all laughed their asses off and yelled out encouragement for one or the other. Finally, I stopped and faced him with my fists up. "Bring it," I taunted him.

"Hell with that. I'll just wait and ask Troian if you do," he said with a laugh. This got me to chase him. In the end, we called a truce. We could do this all day but there was work to do. The others got back to work while Tinker came to stand next to me. In a low voice, so no one could hear him this time, he asked, "Thinking about the Gusevs?"

"You know it. I'm anxious for them to get their asses here so we can take out the trash. This waiting is driving me nuts."

"I get it. I do. How's it going with Troian? I didn't get a chance to ask last night. Is she still talking about leaving? What about her friend? What's going on there?"

"Troian hasn't said anything about leaving in the past few days. She's letting me spend time with her, and I've even gotten a few kisses. I'm hoping that means she'll forgive me. As for her friend, what do you mean?" I asked with a chuckle.

"You know damn well what I mean. Spawn has spent more time at your house than he's ever done at anyone's. I don't think he's coming to just see you, and if he was doing it to see Troian, he'd be dead. That means the little nurse has captured his attention. You think he's serious or just trying to get a piece?"

"Brother, you'll have to ask him to know for sure, but he did talk the other night about marrying her and how many kids they'd have. He kinda made a bet with her about proving our toughness at the fighting match. She treated it as a big joke like me and Troian, but I'm not sure Spawn was joking. He's into her. I can't imagine it's all just to have sex with her. He can get sex without going to that much trouble. The big bastard attracts women like flies," I reminded him.

"Yeah, he does. Not that any of us can't, but they seem to love that tall, nerdy, badass vibe he gives off. I admit, he's not the ugliest guy I know, but still," he agreed, and then we both laughed.

I snorted. I was one hundred percent

heterosexual, but I could admit when another guy was attractive. I thought all my brothers were, in different ways, but Spawn was really attractive. No skinny, glasses-wearing, wimpy guy there. I knew that was stereotyping, but I wasn't the only one guilty of it.

"Well, since you're done fighting with me, get back to work. I've got soaps and bonbons waiting," he joked. I mouthed *fuck you*. That made him laugh harder, the bastard, as he walked back to his office.

I forced myself to concentrate and finish out the rest of the day. I was about an hour away from being done, although I could leave whenever I wanted. I tried to work at least an eight-hour day most of the time. It was never much of a problem in the past, but with Troian in my life, I wanted to spend time with her. I was jerked out of the zone by my phone buzzing. Thinking it was Troian again, I smiled as I took it out of my pocket. My smile disappeared when I read the text.

Spawn: They're here. Just triggered the cameras at the site. They're losing it. Get back as soon as you can. I'll have them tracked with the other cameras in town. We'll figure out where they're staying and do our thing. See you in a bit.

It was a group text that went out to the entire club. I immediately answered back.

Me: I'm heading that way now.

Just as I hit send, I saw Tinker respond.

Tinker: Me too.

The door to his office swung open, and he rushed

out. His eyes met mine, and he gave me a chin lift. I nodded. He turned to the closest guy, Gentry. He'd been with us the longest, and we often left him in charge. "Lash and I have shit to do. We'll see you later. Make sure to lock up."

"Sure, got it. Go, boss," Gentry calmly replied. Things didn't often shake him. Taking him at his word, we both hightailed it out to our bikes and were off in a matter of a couple of minutes. We didn't ride like nuts, but I'd be lying if I said I wasn't speeding. We made it back to the compound within fifteen minutes of receiving the text. I saw some of our brothers were already there. Their bikes were parked outside the clubhouse. As much as I wanted to see Troian, I needed to do this first.

We parked and got our asses inside. The guys were milling around, talking to each other. Since it was close to the end of the workday, none of us would be going back to work, so a few had a beer in their hands. I knew they'd keep it to one and done since it was likely we'd be going hunting tonight. None of them would want to miss that or be impaired in any way.

I paced, and they let me. I got sympathetic looks, but they didn't disturb me. As the minutes passed, more and more of my brothers came. Finally, we were only waiting on Reaper and Spawn. I'd barely registered when they came striding from down the hall together. Reaper must've been in Spawn's office. Damn, why hadn't I gone there? My mind was too focused on revenge, I guess.

Reaper whistled to get everyone's attention, then

circled his finger in the air. We knew what that meant, so we all headed for church. He and Spawn were in the lead. Getting inside and taking our seats quickly, we waited. Reaper didn't waste our time.

"You know why we're here. Spawn has the Gusevs in Bristol. Show them the video," he ordered.

Within a minute, we were seeing images on the wall. It was of four men, not dressed for tromping through the woods and high grass. They were in suits, the idiots. They frantically searched the high grass. We could hear their conversation.

"Fuck, where is she? Do you think animals dragged off the body?" the one I knew to be Jarek asked. I'd studied their pictures so much I knew them all.

Kaz shrugged. *"I don't know. It's possible, but wouldn't we find pieces of her or the tarp if they did that? And what about clothing and bones?"*

Hearing them so casually talk about animals ripping her body to pieces made me clench my fists and seethe. I shook it off for the moment so I wouldn't miss anything.

"Dumbasses, she wasn't carried off by animals. If she had been, there'd be evidence of it. Someone found the body and removed it," Zandro snapped.

"So they have her at the morgue, or do you think they buried her in a pauper's grave?" Laszlo asked.

"I don't know! That's what we have to find out. Or she's out there walking around, waiting to blow up our whole goddamn world," Zandro snapped again. It was

obvious he had no patience.

"Come on, surely you don't think she survived it, do you? She was so badly beaten, and we left her here where no one should stumble across her. There's no way she got up and walked away," Jarek protested.

Zandro swung around and backhanded him. *"Fucking idiot. Why else wouldn't we have been able to find news about a body being found unless the cyka survived and is hiding? We have to find her and silence her and anyone she told."*

They searched in a broader area and then stomped off out of view. However, Spawn had them covered, as we saw when he switched us to another screen. We watched as they got into a dark blue Tahoe. As they drove off, the license plate was visible. I got excited. He shut it off after that.

"Please tell me you were able to pick them up in town?" I pleaded.

"I have, and that's being monitored by Smoke right now while I do this," he said smugly.

"How did you get so much video? I thought those only took short snapshots with the audio," Mayhem asked.

"I may have tinkered with it to make it work more like a normal video camera that would record longer and better. They rushed their asses to town. They didn't go to the morgue because that would raise too many questions. Right now, they're driving around. I don't know if they think they'll see her on the street or what.

It's obvious they don't know what to do. As soon as they stop for the night, we can put our final plan in motion."

"What if they don't stay in town?" Sandman asked.

"I don't see that happening. They're too anxious to finish this and make sure their operation isn't about to be blown to hell and back," Maniac said.

"I agree, which means we need to be ready to roll tonight. There's no use staying in this room and waiting. Spawn will notify us once he has their location, and then we'll meet back up and talk. Go relax. Have dinner, play with your kids, or hell, have sex. Whatever works for you," Reaper told us.

"Does that mean you're going home to have sex, Pres?" Romulus popped in to say with a grin.

Reaper gave him a smirk. "Of course I am. Now fuck off."

This made us laugh, along with Romulus. Knowing we were dismissed, we got up and filed out. I knew I had to see Troian and let her know what was happening. I only prayed this wouldn't make her say after they were gone that she was still leaving. If she did, I didn't think I could let her.

When I walked into my house a few minutes later, the first thing I saw was Kimera lounging on the couch with a book in her hand. She looked up and smiled when she saw it was me. I was taken aback. She was supposed to be at work. I'd been so preoccupied with what was happening that I didn't notice her car still outside the house. She parked it on the street.

"What're you doing at home? I thought you worked today, or did I get my days mixed up? I swear you weren't here this morning."

She laughed. "I wasn't. I went in, and then someone called off for on call tonight. I volunteered to do it, so they got someone else to come in to cover the rest of my shift. Then they got the night covered but asked me to be on-call in case someone else called off. It seems people don't like to come in at night if they have an emergency surgery case."

"And you don't mind, or is there another reason you did it?"

"I don't mind, and it's not a given you'll get called in. Plus, I get paid to be on call. If I do go in, I get paid a shift differential. I don't have a husband or kids like most of the others either."

"Makes sense. They're lucky you do it. Where's Troian? Asleep?"

"She was. She was tired and laid down a couple of hours ago."

"I'll go check on her. When she wakes up, I need to fill you ladies in on what's happening."

"You can do it now. I'm awake," Troian said groggily as she came into the room. She was rubbing her eyes and yawning. I thought she looked adorable, all rumpled from sleep, but I hated seeing her look tired.

I went to her and cuddled her close as I gave her

a kiss. She returned it eagerly. I reluctantly broke it a minute later. "I didn't mean to wake you up, baby. Let me tell you ladies what's planned. Then you can go back to bed."

"You're going after them tonight, aren't you?" was her immediate response.

I guided her to the big chair and sat, bringing her down on my lap. She curled up. I rubbed her arm as I nodded. "Yeah, we're just waiting to find out where they end up staying tonight. Spawn got the video of them walking the site where they left you. They weren't happy, and they're not convinced you're dead. Or at least not all of them are. Right now, they appear to be aimlessly driving around town, looking for you. Like they expect to see you walking down the sidewalk." I snorted at that ridiculous idea.

A brisk knock came from the front door, and then I heard it open. Around the corner walked Spawn. His gaze went to Kimera first. Yeah, he had it bad. Then he glanced at me and Troian. I gave him an amused look. He couldn't respond without getting questions from the women, so he didn't say or do anything like flip me off. He sat on the couch next to Kimera. "Did you tell them already?" he asked.

"I was just explaining it, yes. They know they're here, riding around town, and that we'll go tonight once we know where they're staying."

"Well, at least you're home tonight, and we don't have to worry about you going to work," he said to Kimera.

"Actually, I'm not off. I'm on call. If they call, I have to go in," she informed him like she had me.

He frowned. "You can't. We'll need all the guys here or with us. You'll have to tell them you can't do it."

She glared at him. "No, I won't. First of all, I was the one to say yes when someone called off. Secondly, this is my work. I have obligations. Thirdly, you don't tell me what to do. Fourthly, I don't need anyone to escort me. I've been telling you that. No one knows I even know Troi. There's no reason to target me."

"And what if we're wrong and someone saw you pick her up outside the hospital? And that someone just happens to get asked by one of her cousins, and they share it? It can happen, and it's not worth the risk."

"Spawn, you're talking crazy. The odds of that are a million to one, if that. No one saw me, and even if they did, why would they tell perfect strangers that information if asked? No, I'll be fine. You guys just take care of those bastards and protect the women and kids here. I'll be good. I have my gun if I need it."

I sat back and watched them bicker. I knew he wasn't gonna win this argument. She was adamant, and she was right. The odds were next to zero of it happening, but that was probably easier for me to admit and accept since she wasn't my woman. If it had been Troian, I'd be like him. Finally, they came to a stalemate. Neither was willing to compromise, so they sat there fuming. I was about to suggest we all get some dinner and try to relax until more information came in when Troian spoke up.

"Won't it be dangerous? More likely, someone might see you guys with them if you have to go into a hotel or someplace to get them?"

"It is, but we'll be careful," I assured her.

"Why risk it? Instead, why not get their attention while they're out riding around town and lead them somewhere private?"

"Babe, that's a good idea, but how would we do that?" I asked.

"You take me to town, and you let them spot me. As soon as they do, we leave town, and they follow us. We lead them to your brothers so you can ambush them," she said matter-of-factly.

Now, I was the one arguing with her like Spawn had Kimera. "There's no goddamn way I'm doing that! There's so much that could go wrong. Unlike Kimera, they know you. If they see you, what's to stop them from getting into a shootout in the middle of the street, trying to kill you or take you? If we ride around with you covered in men, they'll know it's a trap, and they won't follow you. That's if I was even willing to entertain the idea, which I'm not," I practically bellowed.

She eased away from me and crossed her arms over her chest. "Lash, don't you take that tone with me. I'm not your child, nor will I be yelled at."

"I'm sorry. I know you're not my child, and I didn't mean to yell, but you can't do it. It's too dangerous. Too many things could go wrong. Besides, you're still recovering from surgery." I was grasping at straws.

"In that case, let me do it. I'll call off and tell them I have a family emergency out of town and not go to work if you let me pretend to be her," Kimera said, stunning us.

"And how the hell do you think you can pull that off, woman? You're shorter than her, and you have a totally different hair color," Spawn said with a grunt.

"If I'm in the car, they won't notice a few inches less, and as for my hair, it's about the same length. I've got a box of hair color. At night, it'll fool them at a distance. I can have it done in an hour. I'll style it like hers and be ready to go."

"That's the dumbest idea I ever heard. No, you can't do it. Troian isn't either," Spawn snarled.

"Oh really, what's wrong with it? They won't get their hands on her, and she won't be out there, potentially risking her health so soon after surgery. I can use a gun, and if they get stupid, I can help. You won't need to surround the car with a bunch of men. Surely, you have guys stealthy enough to hide in plain sight." Kimera scoffed.

"We do have guys stealthy enough, but that's not the point. The point is, we don't let our women put themselves in harm's way. We protect them and eliminate threats to them," he told her.

"Well, I'm not one of your women, so I don't count," was her snappy comeback.

We weren't getting anywhere, but once we moved away from my woman helping, I found it kinda amusing to watch them spar. Not that I'd take Kimera up on her offer either. Spawn was right. We were the protectors.

"Did you forget we were talking about how many kids we want? I'd say that makes you one of our women," he reminded her.

She rolled her eyes. "I believe that was to be determined with a fighting match that you men have no hope of winning, so that's not going to happen. Even if you did win, I don't see you settling down, Studcake."

"Why the hell not?" he asked, sounding offended.

"You're a player and used to having women fall at your feet and giving it up at a snap of your fingers. You go for quantity. I need quality and monogamy. We're not compatible. Although, if all I wanted was sex once and then be done, I'd give you a whirl."

His sputtering was painful. He didn't know what to say at first. I knew it was time to stop this before she tried to hit him, shoot him, or both.

"As entertaining as this is, we've got to get serious here. We don't have much time. No one is going out disguised as anyone, nor will you play bait, Hurricane. You'll stay here where you're safe. Kimera, if you get called out to work, we'll have Colt designated to escort you. He's staying behind."

Neither woman looked happy, but I was, and I knew Spawn was. Or at least with this aspect of it. The things Kimera said to him, I foresaw him discussing with her again soon. I was no longer in any doubt that he was intent on making her his old lady. God help us.

Troian: Chapter 17

Two hours later, my one more attempt to get Lash to see that using me to bring out my cousins and lead them to a safe place to deal with them was soundly knocked down before he kissed me and said they were meeting for church and then heading out after them. I was left with the other old ladies and Kimera in the common room of the clubhouse with the kids and prospects. My stomach was tied in knots, imagining what could happen. It was bad enough I had to worry they'd get hurt or killed. Now, the added fear they would be seen and sent to prison was pushing me to hyperventilate. My panic must've been obvious because Alisse reached over and rubbed my arm.

"They'll be alright. You have to trust that they know what they're doing, and they take every precaution they can."

"Is Ink going or staying here? What about Reaper and Maniac?" I asked Chey and Lark.

"We don't know. They haven't said. Some may stay, or they all could go. As president and VP, Reaper and Maniac like to go on these kinds of missions. However, sometimes, one will stay behind for the sake of leading from here," Cheyenne said.

"You mean in case they get caught or killed, then

the club still has a designated leader. Oh my God, I'm going to vomit. They shouldn't be doing this. It's all my fault. They need to let me be seen around town. I know my family will follow. Someone will see them take my cousins, and the cops will arrest them," I moaned.

A light slap to my cheek jarred me out of it. I gave Alisse a wide-eyed look. "You slapped me. What the he-heck was that for?" I hissed. I caught myself just in time not to say hell in front of Flynn.

"You were becoming hysterical. It was the fastest way to snap you out of it. It works in books and the movies, so I thought I'd try it. It worked," she said with a grin.

"I'll remember that when I see you getting a little upset over something. Hope you like a love tap," I snapped at her.

She laughed. I stuck out my tongue at her when Flynn's head was turned.

"If they'd just let me dye my hair and pretend to be you, we could settle all the concerns and worry down. I told them that, but Studcake had to get all up in arms over it, and that made Lash say no," Kimera grumbled.

A spray of iced tea hit me half in the face. I jerked my head back and wiped at the wetness. It was Chey who spit on me. What was it with these women? She was gasping for air. As she choked, Alisse pounded her on the back. Finally, Chey gulped in air and was able to talk. "Studcake! Who is that?"

Kimera was sitting there with one of her cute

skull caps on her head. They had skulls and other fun things on them in bright colors. It contrasted with the pissed look on her face. "You know, Spawn. He keeps trying to tell me what to do. I told him he's not my boss and I'm not his old lady, no matter if we talked kids or not. He says it's a given. He's delusional. I don't care if he wins our bet or not. A man like that doesn't want a permanent woman in his life. Even if I am looking for a relationship, which I'm not. You know he has p-u-s-s-y thrown at him left, right, and center." She spelled it because of Flynn. I knew because she'd glanced at him before she did it.

"Oh my God. Spawn said you're his, and he's talked kids with you! Why are we just hearing this? Spill. Tell us everything," Annie shrieked. Apparently, they weren't taking any chances and had her come to the compound until this was over.

It took some cajoling, then outright threats, to get Kimera to tell them everything. I had to admit, it was a great distraction. The other ladies were ecstatic that Spawn had said all that stuff. They swore it could only mean he was ready to settle down, and Kim was the one. Kimera said they were crazy and needed help. She knew someone who could give it to them.

We were all still trying to convince her to give him a chance to prove it when her phone rang. Looking relieved, she picked it up and then excused herself, saying, "It's work."

She was gone maybe a minute or two. She came back, sighing. "Well, they need me. I gotta go. I just need to run to the house and grab my purse. Where's Colt?

He's supposed to go with me, according to Mr. Dictator. I swear, if he's not here when I get back, I'm going without him. See you in a minute," she told us.

I wasn't thrilled she'd be off the compound, but she'd be safe at the hospital. She was back in no time with her bag and keys. Thankfully, Alisse had texted Colt, and he was ready and waiting. After telling them to drive safe, we sat back to wait for the guys to get out of their pow-wow and tell us who was doing what.

I distracted myself by coloring with Flynn. Maybe ten minutes or so after Kimera left, the men came strolling into the common room. Lash was headed for me, just like Reaper, Ink, Maniac, and Spawn, and for some reason, Tinker was headed to our table. When they got to us, Spawn frowned and asked, as he looked around, "Where's Kimera? Did she go back to the house to sulk?"

"No, she got called into work. She left," I told him.

"What? When? Did she take Colt like I told her?" he growled.

"She took Colt. She's been gone for, I don't know, ten minutes maybe," Annie added. I noticed Tinker was standing next to her chair. He was watching her.

"Well, at least she listened for once. I swear, she's too—" Spawn didn't get to finish what he was saying because the front door crashed open, and in came Rhaines. He was half carrying a bloody Colt. Shouts of shock and outrage bellowed from the men. The women, although visibly upset, grabbed the kids. I knew they wanted to know if he was okay and what happened. The three moms swept them up and out the door. I stayed with Annie. My heart was pounding. I got out of my chair. This wasn't good.

Lash ran over to help get Colt to an empty chair. As he did, Spawn and the others encircled him. They were all shouting questions at once. It was crazy. A sharp whistle cut through the din, and they grew quiet. It must've been Reaper who whistled since he was the one to ask the questions. "What the hell happened? Did you wreck your bike? Where's Kimera? You were supposed to be escorting her to work."

"I-I'm sorry, Pres. I tried," he said hoarsely. Lash told Crusher to get his bag out of the treatment room they had set up for these kinds of things.

"Tried what?" Spawn asked.

"Tried to keep them from..." he paused and panted harder as Lash ripped the leg of his bloody jeans. There was a deep wound underneath. Colt hissed in pain. It took him a few seconds to regain his voice. "I tried to stop them from taking her. I didn't know she did it," he panted.

"Take her! Who did what?" Spawn shouted. He was hovering over him with his fists clenched.

"Spawn, dial it down. Give him a chance to breathe," Maniac ordered him.

I could tell Spawn was barely containing himself. I was shaking. I knew what he was going to say. "My cousins took her, didn't they?" I moaned softly, but not so softly they didn't hear me.

Colt met my gaze and nodded. "They did. They came out of nowhere and were on us so fast. They hit my rear wheel, and I flew off the bike. I saw her stop before I hit. By the time I came to, they were throwing her in a Tahoe. She was fighting them, but it was four to one. That's when I noticed her hat was off. She must've taken it off after we left. Her hair was down, and it was red. I think they thought it was you. When they realized it wasn't, they took her anyway."

"Why didn't you fucking call? How did you get here? Where did this happen?" Spawn shouted.

"Just before you get into town. I was behind her. I couldn't call because when I went down, I busted my phone. It was faster to ride back than dick around finding a phone to use. Thankfully, the bike still ran. They headed west. I'm sorry," he groaned before he slumped over. For a second, I thought he'd died, but then I saw his chest move. I sobbed. Annie was holding me while Lash worked on Colt.

Spawn finally lost his shit and started throwing things and smashing them. It took a few of the guys to get him subdued. Reaper went up and grabbed him behind the neck. He brought his forehead to his. "Take a deep breath. We need you. Kimera needs you. You have to get control and then get on your computer. You can find her. You already knew where we could find them. Let's see if they went there. If they didn't, your cameras should tell us something. What about her phone? Maybe she has it with her. Go," he ordered when Spawn straightened and got a determined look on his face. He raced out of the room and down the hallway.

It was too much for me. I had to sit down. All I could do was think about what was happening to my new friend. Lash gave me a helpless glance as he ordered Rhaines and Crusher to carry Colt to the treatment room. I wanted to go, but my shaky legs wouldn't hold me up. I rocked back and forth. "It's all my fault. It's all my fault."

"What's your fault?" Tinker asked as he hunkered down in front of me. Annie was next to me in the other chair.

"This. Kimmy was taken, and Colt was hurt. It's my fault. If I'd never gone to the cops with my information on Andrik, they would've never beaten and dumped me. You guys wouldn't have been pulled into my mess. Why didn't I stay quiet or leave as soon as I gave the evidence to them? I'm stupid."

"Cut that shit out right now!" he barked, making me jump in surprise. "That's bullshit. You did the right thing. Most people might've ignored it, but you didn't. It's not your fault your family is scum. Spawn will find her, and we'll get her back. You'd better not let your man hear you talking like that."

"But, Tinker, if—" I was cut off by Annie.

"He's right. No more of that. These guys have done some truly amazing things, even this one," she said as she flashed a grin at Tinker. He let a small growl slip out. "My point is, none of them will rest until they get Kimera back and make every single one of your disgusting cousins pay dearly. People can say anything they like about how awful bikers are. It's true in some cases, but not this bunch. I'd take them any day over the supposedly good, normal people out there," she finished saying.

"Good to know," Tinker said.

There was a tension in the air between them that I didn't know if I was imagining it or, if not if anyone else felt it. It helped to divert my attention for a few moments, which was a blessing. It didn't last, and the memories of what it was like for me those first several days after the club found me came rushing back. The pain and horror over not knowing who I was. The question that tumbled over and over in my brain. What had I done that was so terrible someone would want me dead? Knowing it was my own family made it ten times worse.

I jumped when Lash came rushing back into the common room. He was shirtless. He didn't waste time getting to me. He snatched me out of my chair and into his arms. His arms squeezed me so tightly it hurt for a moment, and then he must've remembered my recent surgery because he loosened his hold. He sat in my vacant chair with me on his lap. One hand gently smoothed down my hair while the other lifted my head with his finger.

He studied my face for a few moments, and then he spoke. "I want you to stop blaming yourself. And before you deny it or one of my brothers narc you out for it, I know you, Troian. You are, and it's not true. The only ones to blame are those animals."

"But they took her because of me."

"They took her because they saw a woman who sorta resembles you. Do you think they wouldn't have done it to some other woman with long red hair they caught a glimpse of? I do. They were seeing what they wanted to see. Should Kimera have taken that risk? No. However, that's what friends do for each other. She might be headstrong and won't listen to reason, but she's brave and loyal. Spawn will find her, and if he needs help doing it, we have the best hackers in the world a call away."

"How's Colt?" I changed the subject.

"He'll live. He bled like a stuck pig, but it's not as bad as the blood made it look. I knocked him out, and Alisse came in. She's working on her stitching skills."

"Alisse? I saw her leave with the others and the kids."

"She just got them outside, and then Lark and Chey took them. She came in the back way. She knew where I'd take him. Crusher is back there, and if she needs me, he'll come get me. I need to be out here right now."

"I'm alright. You can't keep me from worrying. You should be with him."

"I might not be able to stop you from worrying, but I can be here to comfort you. Besides, Spawn should come running in here any minute, yelling he found her. Once he does, we'll be riding out to get her back and to bring them to justice."

There was a grim look on his face that wasn't

nearly as frightening as the fire in his eyes. I felt the same fire burning low in my gut. I lifted my hand and pressed it to his jaw. "Promise me one thing, if at all possible."

"I'll be careful, I swear."

"That too, but that's not what I was gonna say. Promise, if you can do it safely and without risk to you guys, that you bring them back here."

"Why?" he asked slowly.

"So I can look them in the eyes and watch them suffer," I snapped. I was feeling a bit feral at the moment.

"Baby, we can do that. I was planning to do it so we can take our time, but I'm not sure you should see that. It'll be ugly. They'll suffer," he warned me.

"Good. They deserve it, and not just because of Kimera and me. I keep thinking of the people they hurt with their disgusting business." I stared at him for a long time. The others had faded into the background. Their conversations were just a dull murmur.

After a minute or so, he nodded. "Okay, I promise. However, if you change your mind once we get them here, don't hesitate to tell me. No one will think less of you if you prefer not to see them."

"I promise."

I laid my head on his chest and closed my eyes. Tears burned behind my eyelids, but I refused to let them fall. I had to start acting more like a biker's woman since that was who I was and who I planned to remain for the rest of my life. I jumped when I heard feet pounding closer. I opened them and sat up. Spawn came running into the room just like Lash said he would. He had a wildness about him. His hair was a mess. I waited, holding my breath.

"We've found them. They didn't go to the motel they checked into, but I didn't think they would. Something was interfering with her phone's signal, and then we got lucky. Load up, we're going." He didn't say more. He just headed for the door. I knew they'd packed hours ago, and their stuff was in vehicles and on bikes.

Lash stood and placed me on my feet, gave me a kiss, and then more than half of them left. Besides Colt and Crusher, Reaper, Ink, and Shadow remained behind. I dropped back down on my chair to wait. I gnawed on my thumbnail. It was gonna be a torturous wait. As I sat there, I kept saying prayers constantly, not only for Kimera but for the guys and Colt. I needed them all to come back to us.

Lash:

As we followed Spawn to where Kimera was being held, it was hard to keep up with him. He was speeding like a demon. He was barely keeping it this side of recklessness. Not that I could blame him. If it was Troian, I'd be the same. I had no doubt my brother felt something powerful for Kimera, even if we'd only known her a short while. She'd gotten to him like my woman got to me. I hoped we'd get her back and he could pursue it. No, wait, he would get her back. There was no room for doubt.

It was pitch black, and the air was brisk, but the sky was clear as we left. Not that it mattered if it was dark. We had night vision with us. We'd packed for every possibility earlier this evening. He was leading us out of town rather than back toward it. I wondered where they'd taken her. Had they had a second place already set up, or were they just running blind with her? If they hadn't expected to find her, maybe the latter. Hence why, the hotel was picked and then abandoned. It was hard to hold someone hostage when you had paper-thin walls and people all around you.

Maniac was keeping pace next to Spawn. I was behind them and next to Mayhem. We weren't bothering to ride in our normal order. As those two began to slow, the rest of us did. I saw a hand signal from Spawn. We all slowed more and then pulled off to the side of the road. The area we were in had no cars at night. It led to a very rural area with few homes, mostly farmland. We all shut off our engines and got off our bikes or out of the van and SUV Rhaines, Ratchet, Remus, and Romulus had ridden in. It was only then that it hit me that all the Rs had left their bikes behind. I snorted, which earned me a puzzled look. I shook my head. I'd tell them later. We gathered around Spawn.

He pulled out an iPad. Damn, even at a time like this, he came prepared. He tapped it a couple of times before holding it out. "This is where we are. This red dot is where her signal and the other one are coming from. They must've had their phones off for fear of being tracked, so that's why I couldn't find them initially, but then Laszlo turned his back on.

"As far as I can tell, there are no houses out here. They must have her in an old outbuilding, a barn, or something. It could be a cabin. We won't assume there's no more than the four of them, even if it's unlikely. We go in quiet, and we bring those fuckers out. I don't care how beat up they are, as long as they're still breathing and we get to spend time with them. Any questions?" he asked.

Usually, in this situation, Maniac would be briefing us, but we could see that he was happy to allow Spawn to do it. "You heard him. Grab your shit, and let's go. Pull your bikes off the road as much as you can to hide them. Rhaines, you stay here with them. We'll call when we need you to come get them and Kimera. We'll bring them back here and split them up between the vehicles," Maniac added after Spawn stopped talking.

Everyone nodded their heads.

As we got our stuff and headed out, excitement filled me. As crazy as it sounded, I loved it when we got a chance to use those skills we'd acquired over the years. Yeah, not all of us had served in the military, but every single one of us had hard-earned experience.

There were lots of trees, which made the trek even more hazardous on a night like this. Thank God for night vision. As we'd ridden, the clouds had moved in, and a slight cold drizzle began to come down.

By the time we got to where we were going, I was ready to hurt someone and get dry. What we found was an old, long-abandoned church, by the looks of it. It was one of those small one-room buildings they used to gather in a hundred years or more ago. It was barely visible from the road, so I had no idea how they found it. There was a faint light shining from one of the dirty windows.

Maniac gave us hand signals, and we split up. We surrounded it since we didn't know if there were sentries or another entrance. I stuck to the back. There was a door. I knew Spawn was going in the front with Maniac. As we fanned out, we heard arguing and thumping sounds. It was Kimera's scream that released us to kick in the doors and dive through the windows. It was filled with so much fear. Maniac gave the go order in our earpieces, cursing.

Coming through the door with my gun out and scanning around, I took in the scene. My stomach dropped. Three of the Gusevs had their pants undone and were arguing and shoving at each other. The fourth, Zandro, whipped around with his pants down and his hard cock in his hand. That wasn't the part that made me sick. It was Kimera. She was thrown over the back of an old pew. Her clothes were torn, and she had no pants on. She was sobbing and trying to fight even though her arms were tied behind her back.

An inhuman roar came tearing out of Spawn, and then he was on Zandro. He hit him again and again. The rest of us shook off our disgust and went after the other three. Since they'd obviously been too eager to rape her, they forgot to keep their guns within reach. They tried to get to them, but it was too late. We got there first. We slammed them face-first to the floor and zip-tied their hands and feet. They swore and made threats. A well-placed kick to the heads shut them up.

Seeing Spawn still going berserk on Zandro, I ran over and pulled him off. He swung at me. I yelled, "Spawn, stop! You can kill him later. Go take care of Kimera. She needs you."

This got his attention. She was still leaning over the pew. Her head was down, and she was sobbing and shaking. He slowly went to her. We turned our backs. She didn't need a bunch of men seeing her nakedness. I could hear Spawn murmuring to her, but it was so low, and her replies were even lower that I couldn't catch what they said. It was several minutes before he said anything loud enough for us to hear. While we waited, we kept our eyes on the men we'd incapacitated.

"Rhaines, come get us. Bring the SUV," Spawn ordered into his earpiece. He turned it off to talk to her and now switched it back on.

"I'll be right there," Rhaines immediately answered. He had been a steady guy over the past nine months he'd been prospecting with us. He was well on his way to patching in.

Deciding it was safe to turn around, I did. I found Kimera huddled on the pew. She had on Spawn's t-shirt. She was hanging her head with her arms around herself. He was next to her but not touching her. The fury and anguish on his face gutted me. That could be me with Troian just as easily. My stomach rolled at that thought and the next. God, had we gotten here too late? Had Zandro or one of the others already violated her?

We stood there, not knowing what to say. It was the moans of the men on the ground that got us to move. We cut strips off their expensive shirts and used them to gag them. No one wanted to hear what they had to say, at least not yet.

It wasn't long before Rhaines came running in. He did remember to tell us he was inbound before coming through the door. His eyes filled with anger as he took in the scene. Since the men had their pathetic cocks still hanging out, he easily registered what happened. He marched over, and as he passed each one, he kicked them in the crotch as he muttered, "Filthy fucking animals."

I grinned. Maniac started issuing orders. "Take Spawn, Kimera, and Remus back to where we parked. Remus, you bring the van for these four fucks. The rest of us will walk back or catch a ride with you. Let's get them out of here and back where we can have long and very painful discussions with them," he snarled.

The rest of it went down like clockwork. I saw Kimera flinch away from Spawn when he went to carry her. His face was a mask of hate. When we were all back to where the bikes were, Ratchet was told to ride Spawn's bike so he could stay with her. That came directly from Spawn. It was a somber group who rode back into the compound a short while later. This was gonna gut my woman. I dreaded telling her.

Troian: Chapter 18

The wait was agony for all of us but more so for me. When the guys eventually made it back, I burst into tears, seeing Kimera brought in, huddled in on herself, in only what appeared to be Spawn's shirt. I assumed it was his because he only wore his cut. She wouldn't look at anyone. Seeing her, I knew what it meant. I couldn't help it. I almost puked on the common room floor. Lash hurried over to me after telling Spawn to take her to the exam room. They'd moved Colt out to his room after Alisse was done patching him up.

I sobbed as she passed me without looking up. I wanted to hold her, but I didn't know if she'd let me. Spawn went with her. He didn't touch her, but he stayed only a few steps away from her. Lash brought me to his chest. He didn't seem to care if I had snot on me, not that I knew if I did or not. He hugged and rocked me from side to side.

"They raped her!" I bawled when I thought she was out of earshot.

"Shh, we don't know for sure. It's likely based on how we found them. I need you to calm yourself. She's going to need you. Can you do that?"

I took several shuddering breaths, then nodded. He eased away from me. "I need to clean myself up. She can't see me like this," I said.

"We'll take care of things here. You go clean up. The hall bathroom should have mouthwash and spare toothbrushes and toothpaste in there, too, if you need it. Go get yourself clean, then come back."

I nodded, then walked off on shaky legs. It didn't take me long to get it done. Lash took me right back in his arms. I wrapped my arms behind his back and gazed up at him. All the men had grim looks on their faces. That's when I noticed that Maniac and Rhaines weren't with them. I gasped. "Are Rhaines and Maniac okay?"

"Yeah, they're fine. They just had to do something."

"Tell me you brought those bastards back with you," I hissed as thoughts of my now ex-cousins filled my head.

"We did, all four of them, although it was close for one. Spawn almost beat him to death."

"Which one?"

"Babe," he protested. I glared at him. "It was Zandro," he admitted.

"He raped her," I said.

"You don't need to know that shit."

"Yes, I do. I need to know so I can help my friend if she ever speaks to me again. If she went through this, I can sure as hell hear it."

"We don't know for sure if he raped her or if the

others already had. He was the one pantless and behind her when we came in, and the others had their cocks out but their pants on," he said gruffly.

I choked back my sobs. Crying wouldn't do her or me any good. The only thing that would was to make those animals suffer and then die. To shut down the whole operation so they couldn't continue to hurt people or hurt future victims.

"Where are they?"

"They're secure elsewhere on the compound. Listen, I hate to leave you, but I need to go check on her and get Alisse. We need to make sure Kimera is okay. Do you want me to see if she wants you there? If not, don't take it personally. She's mixed up right now."

"Go do what you have to do. If she wants me, I'll come. If not, I'll just sit here and think of all the things those monsters have in store for them. Oh, and Lash, no starting the fun with them without me. Hear?"

He studied me and then slowly nodded. I sat back to wait to see if he came to get me. When he didn't, my heart sank. However, I concentrated on the hatred filling it. I'd make sure they paid in blood and pain. No one bothered me. I had no idea how long I sat there before he came back. He wasn't alone. Spawn was with him. He looked like hell. As the guys came to attention, Lash came to me.

"She's resting. Alisse is with her. So, you still want to do this?" he asked one more time. I nodded.

"Let's go."

I followed them out the door. I had news for them. I had no intention of just watching or telling those monsters off. I wanted to inflict some of the pain.

Lash:

My heart ached for both Kimera and Spawn. She was barely speaking and wouldn't make eye contact. When I tried to get her to let Alisse or me examine her, she freaked out. We backed off and didn't perform the rape exam. I had to force Spawn out into the hall while we talked to her about it. She refused to say one way or the other if they'd raped her. When I asked if she wanted to see Troian, she shook her head hard. I knew that would tear my Hurricane up, but I had to honor my patient's wishes. In the end, she let Alisse help her into a gown and let me give her a sedative. Alisse volunteered to stay with her. Spawn and the rest of us had work to do. He was practically vibrating.

Seeing Troian still so determined to go with us, I didn't argue. If she needed to leave, I'd make sure she got out of there. I figured she wanted to face them and maybe tell them off. I would, at a minimum, if I were in her shoes.

We didn't waste time getting to the bunker at the back of the compound. The two storage buildings back there not only hid underground bunkers from when this was used by the military, but our latest addition, a secure interrogation room, was there underground, too. We decided to make it a more formal area since we were growing up, and we didn't want to have our families witness us torturing people in the same rooms they had to live and sleep in if we ever had to put them there.

Spawn was the first to go through the door into the holding area. Maniac and Rhaines had the four men tied to chairs in the center of the room. I was happy to see they all had marks on them, although I knew the ones on Zandro were all from Spawn. As I brought Troian from behind my back to see them, she gasped. Their eyes widened.

I watched as her eyes narrowed. She stepped closer to them. They couldn't say anything since they were still gagged. She put a hand on Spawn's arm. He glanced at her. She motioned him down so he leaned over far enough that she could whisper in his ear. I wondered what she was saying. Whatever it was, when she was done, he whispered back to her. She looked at the rest of us. "Take off their gags, please. I want to hear what they have to say."

"Babe, they'll—" I started to say, but she held up her hand.

"I know they'll be ugly and disgusting. That's fine."

Maniac and Crusher waited. I gave them a chin lift, and then they removed the gags. The threats came first.

"You have no idea who you're messing with. You're all dead, including this whore. We'll slaughter every single one of you and your families," Laszlo snapped. Hatred burned in his eyes as he stared hard at her.

"Save your breath, Las, you're gonna need it. I can't wait to watch you beg, cry, puke, and suffer. It's the least you deserve for what you've done," she said quietly.

"The day our family took your sorry ass in was the worst day of our lives. All these years of supporting you, feeding you, taking care of you, and this is how you repay us? We should've sold your ass when your parents died," Kaz snarled at her.

"Why are you helping her? Because she's your whore? Hell, we should talk. We've got a great business going. We could use men like you," Jarek said next. There was a hopeful gleam in his eyes. I had to resist the urge to bury my fist down his throat and rip out his colon.

"I should've drowned you after I beat you, bitch. It felt so good pounding on you and hearing you scream and beg for mercy. It made me hard. I should've fucked you first, though. I've wanted to do that for years," Zandro growled out.

That set me off. I launched myself at him and began to pound on him. All I could see was her beaten body when we found her and the condition Kimera was in when we got to her. It was the hands pulling me back and shouting that brought me out of my berserker moment. It was Reaper's yelling in my ear that snapped the words into focus.

"Stop. Troian needs you. Fuck," he uttered.

I whipped around to face her behind me. She was

bent over at the waist. She was breathing hard, tears streaming down her face. Her mouth was open like she was screaming, only nothing was coming out. A look of horror and pain was on her face.

"Gag them," I yelled as I ran to her. I knew it would be too much to see them and hear their vile shit.

I bent over and wrapped her in my arms. "Baby, it's alright. They can't hurt you ever again," I told her. Her whole body shook. I rocked her, but she didn't respond. As the time stretched into a minute, then another, I grew alarmed. It was obvious she had gone into shock and needed to get out of there. I scooped her up, intent on getting her back to the house. I'd come back later to get in my licks.

"I'll be back. Save me some," I told my brothers. They were all watching her with concern and worry.

That's when she came alive. She struggled and moaned. "Shh, it's alright. I'm taking you to the house, Hurricane," I promised.

She slowly raised her head to meet my gaze. When she did, I knew. It was written there. "Put me down. I'm not done," she hissed.

I hesitated, and she jerked her body as if to jump out of my arms. I lowered her feet back to the ground. I held onto her until I was sure she was steady enough for me to let go. She slowly straightened up.

"Do you want to talk to me first?" I whispered so her cousins couldn't hear.

She shook her head no. "No, that can come later.

Right now, I have to do this."

"Are you sure? You remember everything, don't you?"

The blaze of retribution was written all over her face. "Oh yes, I remember. I recall every second of it." She stepped away from me and toward them. I followed her. She straightened and stood tall.

"Oh, I know exactly who I'm messing with, Las. A bunch of spineless, immoral flesh peddlers who think they rule the world. In reality, you're no one. You're insignificant. You won't be killing anyone. I can promise you that. And I've never been a whore."

She switched to the next one. She was meeting their eyes as she talked. "Kaz, you never supported, fed, or took care of me out of the goodness of your heart, and neither did your parents. I had to work my ass off to get the things you said you gave me. I was your housekeeper, cook, errand girl, and a hundred other things. You never let me forget I owed you, only I didn't. You got a servant. I started working and paying my way when I was fifteen, in case you forgot. I paid you rent and money for utilities and food starting then, too. As for selling my ass, well, you fucked up, didn't you?"

Next, she looked at Jarek. Each man was trying to look her in the face, but they kept shifting their gazes away from the intensity of hers. "I'm no man's whore. In fact, I've been with one man my whole life. This one. His name is Lash. I think you'll get to know him really well. Your offer to do business with them is laughable. These men are too honorable to do that. See, despite what you may think of bikers, they aren't all pieces of worthless shit like you four and Andrik."

They were mumbling around their gags and jerking on their restraints in agitation, but they couldn't be heard or get loose. I smiled at them. She then faced Zandro.

"Thank you, Zandro," she said, then paused. He appeared shocked. "See, you were idiots for coming here and trying to cover up your crime. I couldn't tell anyone that you were the ones who did it. Your beating left me without my memories. What we know has been pieced together mostly by Spawn." She pointed to my brother, who never looked away from them.

"They were almost a hundred percent positive you did it, and we've been waiting for you to make a move. I'm thanking you because your sweet words were the key that unlocked my memories. I remember it all now. Every hit and kick, all the ugly, disgusting things you said to me. I know you enjoyed it. These three got in their licks, but you were the one who did the bulk of it. As for fucking me, well, I felt how hard you got. What a pathetic excuse for a man. I bet you can only get hard if you're hurting a woman or have her tied down. Hell, I bet you even like that with the boys. Come on, I know you're secretly into men rather than women. It explains your need to hurt and degrade us. Luckily, I know what it's like to be with a real man, not a frustrated little boy." She smiled broadly as she finished her speech.

He howled behind his gag and jerked so hard to get loose it had to hurt. We all began to laugh and make fun of them, especially Zandro. He turned beet red.

After a minute or more of that, we quieted down. I went to say something, but she stopped me.

"As for Andrik, yes, I'm the one who turned him in and gave the authorities the evidence. I only regret I didn't find proof that the rest of you were involved, or you'd be right there with him. I hope he's being ass raped every day. It's only a small bit of justice for those poor women and girls you animals forced to be prostitutes all these years. It'll be a pleasure to see his end, too. Now, I think I'll watch for a while, and then I'll get back to you."

She nodded to me and swept her hand toward them as if to say, "They're all yours."

Spawn moved before I did. I had no problem letting him have his say. I knew how hard it was for him to keep quiet while Troian said her part. As infuriated as I was over what these men did to my woman, the woman I knew he wanted to be his old lady had most likely been raped by one, if not more, of these pathetic excuses for human beings. He had his fists clenched at his sides so tight they were white at the knuckles. Rage came off him in waves of energy you could feel.

He removed his cut and handed it off to Ink. Then he took off his shirt and threw it aside. Ink snatched it up. Now, all of us were big, muscular guys. Guys like Crusher and Tinker were wider than most. In Spawn's case, he might not be as wide in the shoulders as them, but he was huge and ripped. His height only made it more apparent, especially when he took off his shirt.

"You motherfuckers have no clue the hell you

released, but you will. I promise you that. We'll take more than a pound of flesh, but you…" He stopped in front of Zandro. "You, I'll really enjoy punishing. The woman you had naked just a while ago is mine. I'll make sure you live long enough to regret ever touching her or any other woman or girl. Hell, like Troi said, you've probably been doing it to boys too."

He turned to us. "Troi, if you don't wanna see their pathetic excuses for cocks, you'd better leave."

She waved her hand at him to proceed. I didn't necessarily want her to see them, but it was her call. I knew she needed this to fully heal. He didn't need to ask anyone to help him. Several brothers hurried forward with their knives out. They made short work of cutting and then ripping the clothes off our four prisoners. I saw Reaper go to the wall where the thermostat was. I knew what he was doing. He turned the air down as low as it would go.

"Now that we have that out of the way let's get them up and stretch them out. We need room to work. You know the drill, brothers," Reaper ordered.

This time, I helped them too. I manhandled Laszlo up from his chair. Spawn roughly jerked up Zandro even though I wanted him. I didn't bother to see who did the other two. Along the ceiling in this room was a track, and on it were multiple wheels with hooks attached. The hooks could be lowered to the height you needed, and hanging from them were manacles. You could move the hooks to where you wanted along the track as well. We spaced them so we could chain their arms above their heads and have room to walk between them. They struggled, not that it did them any good. Once they were hung up, we stood back. I heard Troi burst out laughing. I glanced over at her. She was grinning.

"What's so funny, baby?"

"Oh my God, it's true. They do have tiny ones. No wonder they're so hateful to women. Not one could really satisfy a woman, and I bet they've been laughed at a lot. Too bad you can't show them what a real one looks like." She giggled.

This made my brothers roar. They damn near fell to the floor laughing. Even Spawn smirked. Remus came forward. "Well, since you asked," he said with a smirk as he undid the snap on his jeans.

Before I could yell at him, she closed her eyes. "Okay, go for it. You all can, but I can't look. I don't think my man would like that, and I really don't want to know what yours looks like, just Lash's."

We laughed again. I was pleased she closed her eyes because if not, I'd have covered them. Not to be put off, Remus kept going and dropped his pants and underwear. He gripped his cock and held it up. "That's what a real one looks like, boys," he said with a grin.

Romulus joined him and did the same. "In case you need to see two." He snickered.

The rest of us kept ours tucked away, but I knew mine wasn't anything to sneeze at. I didn't typically go around looking at my brothers' cocks, but since they didn't seem to care who saw them getting sucked off or when they fucked in the open, I saw most, if not all, of them at one point or another. We were all way more endowed than those four fucks. Even if they were growers, they couldn't get big enough to be much. No wonder they were so ugly toward women.

I saw Troian's face turning red. Her eyes were still closed, but I couldn't resist whispering in her ear. "Are you peeking, Hurricane? You'd better not, or I'll have to remind you later how big mine is."

"No, I'm not. But I have to say, the way you're all laughing, it's hard not to," she confessed.

I nipped her ear with my teeth and growled, "I'll show you hard later. Behave," I ordered. The little minx giggled.

As the twins did up their pants, Spawn hissed, "Take off their gags. I want to hear their screams. It's time to get this show on the road. Troi, you can look, sweetheart."

She opened her eyes as the gags were removed. As expected, Zandro was the one to say something. He seemed to be the leader now that Andrik was gone. "You can't kill us. If you do, our family will slaughter every single one of you, including your families. You're fucking with the Bratva," he announced proudly.

Crusher was the one to chuckle the loudest. "You bastards aren't Bratva. Sure, your family in Russia is, but you're not."

"You don't know shit," Zandro snarled.

"*O, ya mnogo znayu. Ty polon der'ma. Imya Razina*

vam nichego ne govorit?" Crusher said. I watched as they paled.

Troian translated for us. "Oh, I know a lot. You're full of shit. Does the name Razin ring any bells?"

"Who are you?" Laszlo uttered hoarsely.

"I'm Damien Tatum. You might know of my cousin and godfather, Kirill Razin. He sure knows you and your so-called Bratva family in Russia. As we speak, he and the others are set to wipe them out, just like we plan to wipe you and your filth out here," he informed them with a grin.

It was hard to tell if they were shaking due to the temperature or his revelation. They went so white. They looked like they'd seen a ghost when they heard Kirill's name. Even though I was Crusher's cousin, I didn't know much about his mom's family. They hadn't ever been talked about around me. Growing up, I knew that she was from Russia and that the rest of her family mainly lived there. All I knew was she was my Aunt Zivka. She'd always been sweet and motherly toward me. No one had said anything about them being Bratva. I could see why, though.

"Y-you can't," Kaz stuttered, then shut up.

"What? Nothing to say?" Crusher taunted Zandro. He didn't respond. I think he knew there would be no mercy for them at that point, and any threats meant nothing. Nodding, Spawn moved even closer to Zandro.

He didn't say a word. He just let his fist fly. It took

Zandro in the ribs. We all heard the crack. He cried out in pain. The next blow was to the opposite side. Same sound again. This removed the restraint from the rest of us. I noticed Mayhem had taken Kaz, and Crusher was with Jarek. We rained blows all over them for several minutes before taking a break. I'd worked up the beginning of a sweat. My fists weren't taking too bad of a punishment. Busted knuckles would be a small price to pay to inflict pain on these bastards.

A soft hand on my arm made me turn. There stood Troian. She was holding several pairs of brass knuckles. I wasn't sure how she got those. "Use these. It'll hurt more and keep your hands from taking such a beating."

I nodded and took a pair. She handed out the rest. Before we could do more than that, she strolled around the hanging men, making a circle. She tapped a finger on her chin as she ran her gaze up and down them. She stopped when she was next to me. "I think you should give them a few more punches, then change things up. What do you think? If I remember correctly, not only did I have bruises all over me, but I had cuts too."

"You did, you're right, Hurricane. Hey, I need to start learning more Russian. How do you say hurricane in that?" I asked.

"*Uragan*," she said.

"*Uragan*, where would you like me to cut him?" I pointed to Laszlo, who looked about to piss himself.

"Choices, so many of them. I mean, the obvious is to put them in the same spots mine were. I know you remember where those were. Why don't you start there? You go first, and then the others can place theirs in the same spots on their carcasses," she said with a smile.

"Perfect," I purred before removing my blade from the sheath in the back of my pants. I moved closer and swiped my blade across his ribs. The others followed suit. It was a bloody game of follow-the-leader. We played until every cut on her was duplicated on each of them. Blood dripped on the floor. We hadn't cut deep enough that they were in jeopardy of bleeding to death, but we'd have to close the wounds at some point.

I admit, I was taken aback that my brothers were so willing to let her dictate so much of it. I knew it wouldn't last forever, but while it did, she could get her rage out. Was it the most therapeutic way to do it? Most likely not. But if it worked, I didn't give a damn.

"Hmm, these spots look so sore. I wonder if they can hurt more?" She sounded like she was almost talking to herself. She suddenly punched Zandro over top of one of his larger, deeper cuts. He shouted. I saw she had a pair of brass knuckles of her own. She did it a few more times and then calmly said, "You're so right, Zandro. It does feel good. I bet kicking would, too.

She drew back her leg and brought it up high, nailing him between the legs. His scream was decibels higher than his shout. My brothers and I all winced and hissed. She wasn't done. She went down the line, landing a kick to each man. Kaz vomited after she kicked him. She came back to me. "Thank you. Please go back to playing with your toys."

Right then, I knew I'd never love a woman as much as I loved her. And that I'd never treat one as well. If I didn't, I'd be lucky to wake up the next morning. My Hurricane was coming into her own, or maybe she was just coming back to herself. The real her that she had to keep hidden all her life, I bet.

"Babe, there's more that we plan to do. A lot more. It's gonna get bloodier and more gruesome. I'm not sure you want to stay for that," I told her softly, giving her an out and me a chance not to show her fully what her man was capable of doing to a person. There was a part of me that feared she would run from me. I felt like I'd made headway these past few days in winning her forgiveness for having her investigated. What if this ruined that?

"I can handle it. Are you worried I can't, or you don't want me to see what you're capable of?"

"Both, shit, mostly the latter. I can get very ugly, baby. I don't want you to fear me or be disgusted by me."

"That'll never happen. Keep going. If I feel it's becoming too much, I'll leave."

Staring at her for several moments, I let my civilized parts fall away. I gave her a kiss full of passion and tongue, then let her go. I took off my cut and shirt. She took them and laid them lovingly aside. It was time to get down and dirty.

Troian: Chapter 19:

No matter what he did, it wouldn't change how I felt about him. Even when I was trying to tell him we were through and I was leaving, I knew I wasn't going to be able to do it. I loved him, and short of him harming innocents, me, or our children, then I couldn't, wouldn't walk away.

"Why don't you let the rest of us get a little anger relief while you guys rest?" Reaper asked. Lash, Spawn, Crusher, and Mayhem all took a step back. Rhaines was right there with bottles of water for them. They ignored the blood on their hands and took one.

Time became a blur as the others took turns beating them and adding new ways to make them hurt. I saw nails ripped out, salt rubbed into open wounds, and more cuts made by much duller items than their knives. I knew they weren't showing me nearly everything they could do. That was apparent when I saw the things they had on the walls and locked up in drawers and cabinets.

Sometime later, they indicated that the original four could get back to work. When they did, I was startled when Spawn glanced over at Lash. "Lash, brother, do you want to show them how you got your name?"

Lash spared me a quick look, then nodded. He walked to a small cabinet on the wall. It hadn't been opened by anyone yet. He brought out a key, unlocked it, and then swung the doors open. Inside, I saw what looked like several different kinds of whips. I gasped. How he got his road name hit me. He raised a brow at me. I nodded my head. He rolled his shoulders and then fingered them. I recognized the standard bullwhip, and one I knew was called a cat o' nine-tails variety. I had no clue what the rest were called.

"I want to see you use the big one first, then this one," I said as I pointed out my two suggestions.

"Your wish is my command, my love," he said with a tiny smile. He reached in and took out the bullwhip. "Stand back. I don't want to accidentally hit you," he ordered me. I moved out of range like the others were.

Zandro and the others couldn't see what he held since he was behind them. They tried to turn but could only see part of him. He walked to the dead center between them and brought it out from behind his back. He gave it an experimental snap. The sound in the enclosed room was like a gunshot. They jumped and frantically tried to turn. He did it again, then slowly came to stand a bit closer to them but still a distance away.

"My name is Lash, and I got that name for a special, unusual skill I have. I like using a whip and seeing how I can mark things. It took years of practice to hone my skills. I'd like to show you how I do it. Plus, my beautiful woman wants to see me work. I can't say no," he said softly.

Their eyes practically bugged out of their sockets. The smell of piss hit my nose as all four pissed themselves. Even through the other things they did to them, only Laszlo had pissed himself up to this point.

"No! Please, we surrender. We won't bother you again," Kaz yelled.

"God no," Laszlo sobbed.

"Please," Jarek pleaded.

Even Zandro begged. "We'll do anything you want. Just stop."

"You seem to be under the impression there's anything in the world you can do or promise us that'll stop this and make us let you live. You're really stupid, aren't you? There's nothing you can say, do, promise, swear, or anything else that's gonna save your miserable lives. You're dead men," Spawn snarled.

I heard the cracking sound as Lash let loose with the bullwhip. It sang almost as it flew gracefully through the air and hit Zandro across the chest. In a blur, Lash hit the other three too. Each had a perfect line across their chest from nipple to nipple. They were so precise you would swear he drew them on with a marker and a ruler. Blood began to run as they cried out in pain.

He landed lash after lash, but it was always in a different spot on the front or back of them. When they had a dozen marks, he smiled at me. "Would you like me to switch now, my love?"

"I think you should," I said.

Before he could go get the other one, Reaper halted him. "I think you should give them one more. It should be..." he came up and whispered in his ear. Whatever he said made Lash chuckle darkly as he nodded.

"I think that's perfect, Pres," he said.

As soon as Reaper was out of range, Lash swung his arm, and *crack, crack, crack, crack*. He snapped it lightning fast. He was so quick. He had all four hits done before I heard the first scream. It took me a second or two to figure out where he hit them. When I did, I gasped and then laughed. Oh my God, it was a perfect punishment. He'd kissed the head of each of their cocks with the tip of the whip. It left a small, painful, and bloody cut right through the natural slit. All of his brothers moaned in empathy and winced as they cupped themselves and muttered.

He didn't waste time. He went and got my other choice as soon as he was done. My cousins were in agony, screaming and crying, and he wasn't done. He came back and snapped the new one. They shuddered, and between moans, they whimpered in terror and pain. I'd seen lots of these over the years when I watched movies, especially the old-time ones about pirates and the Royal Navy in England. It was the cat-o'-nine-tails. It was used in those times when severe punishment was needed.

They opened their mouths, I think to beg, but

no words would come out. He went behind them and laid into their backs. As sick as it might sound, the sight of him being so masterful was turning me on. Not the actual blood or pain he was inflicting but the fact he looked so damn sexy and commanding doing it. My panties actually grew damp. By the time he was done, their backs were a roadmap of cuts, and the blood poured.

Reaper called a halt. "That's enough, Lash. Take a rest. I think we need to stop the bleeding. Who wants to help do that?"

Ratchet, Ink, Tinker, and Sandman held up their hands faster than the rest. Maniac moved, and I saw while I was watching all the action that someone had started a fire in a burn barrel. Sticking out of it were pieces of iron with handles on them. The guys went over, and each grabbed one. The glowing tips were shaped like fire pokers. In stunned awe, I watched them touch them to the bigger wounds. The smell of burning flesh made me gag.

"Baby, why don't you step outside? It's gonna stink for a while in here," Lash said as he came to stand by me. His whips were on a bench along the wall. I knew he'd make sure they were cleaned before putting them back. Something told me he took care of his tools very carefully.

"I'll be fine. I've gotta tell you something, though. Come here," I told him as I wiggled my finger to get him to lean down. He did.

"What?" he asked warily.

"That was so damn sexy. You made me wet," I whispered in his ear before I edged closer and captured his mouth. I thrust my tongue inside and played with his. He groaned, then jerked me tight against him and kissed me harder. Wolf whistles came at us from all directions.

"Hey, hey, keep it clean until we're done here. Then you two can go home and celebrate," Mayhem called out. When Lash let go of me, I was blushing and had a huge grin on my face. I blew all of them kisses.

It wasn't long before we sobered back up and faced the meat sacks in front of us. Reaper spoke again. "What else do you want them to suffer?"

"They used their hands to touch women and girls, and God knows who else when they shouldn't have. I say we break them," Shadow growled darkly. The others seemed to agree. It wasn't long before they took turns individually breaking all ten fingers on each of them. They were barely conscious when the guys were done. I didn't know how long they'd be able to continue to breathe.

"Brothers, they don't look like they'll last much longer unless we give them rest and medical attention. Do we want to continue this later or finish it now?" Maniac yelled. They, as one, nodded to Lash and Spawn.

"It appears to be your call," Reaper stated.

Lash looked at me. "Troian, is there anything else you want me to do to them? You were hurt by them, left for dead. It's your call."

I thought for a couple of moments, then shook my head. "No, I'm good if you are, honey."

"I'm good," he replied. Everyone then glanced at Spawn.

He didn't say anything for almost a solid minute, and then he answered them. "There's one more thing I want to do, and then we can be done with this. If I didn't want to get back to Kimera and take care of her, I'd say let's keep going. However, they've breathed enough air."

"They're all yours," Lash told him.

We watched as Spawn went and got a pair of gloves. I wondered why. None of them had worn them so far. He put them on and then picked up his knife again. He flipped the serrated edge down, and then I figured out what he was doing. He went to Kaz first, sneered at him, then grasped his cock and sawed through it. The screams were like that of an animal in absolute agony. This set off my other cousins, causing them to scream as they watched. The guys all stood there stoically and never flinched as he worked. Spawn dropped the offending piece of flesh on the ground and moved to the next one. It wasn't until he got to Zandro that he said anything.

"This is for touching my woman and all the others before her."

"I didn't! I never raped her. I swear," Zandro yelled. I didn't know if he was telling the truth, and I didn't care.

"Even if you didn't, you were going to. Tell the

Devil I said hello and to make it extra hot for you in hell," he hissed. He never looked away from Zandro's eyes as he took his time sawing his cock off.

I wish I could say I was a badass to the very end, but I'd seen, heard, and done enough. As he dropped Zan's flaccid flesh to the floor and the screams reached new heights, my legs gave out. Lucky for me, Lash caught me. He swung me up in his arms. I didn't care that he was covered in blood. He said something to his brothers, but I didn't catch it, and then he was striding out into the fresh air. I took deep breaths and sighed. It was over. Or at least this part was. I knew they had more work to do. I wondered how they planned to accomplish it.

Lash:

Three days. That's how long it had been since we brought justice and revenge upon the Gusevs. Well, at least the ones here. There were still those in Russia and the one who was sitting on his ass in prison. Until they were all taken care of, I wouldn't be able to move on. I didn't want us to be looking over our shoulders for the rest of our lives.

Troian had been quiet. I tried to determine if it was because of what she saw when we tortured and killed her family. She kept denying it. I was praying she was telling the truth, and it was because of her worry about Kimera, as she said. That poor woman wasn't dealing well. She still refused to talk about what happened, even to Troian. She was staying at our house, and her screams at night woke us up. I wished there was some way to take away her nightmares.

Spawn haunted the house despite the fact she wouldn't talk to him or even let him get too close. My brother had it bad. If something didn't ease the tension and rage still inside of him soon, I was afraid he'd do something drastic. With that in mind, I spoke to Reaper, and we set up tonight.

It would be a good distraction for all of us as we waited for our plans for Andrik to be carried out. He wouldn't escape justice by being in prison. He'd pay. As for those back in Russia in the Bratva, Kirill and the rest of Crusher's family had them well in hand and were eliminating the threats. They were too busy trying to save their own necks to worry about trying to get revenge for distant cousins in America.

It took a lot of convincing, pleading, and even threats on Troian's part to get Kimera to leave the house and come outside. We had seating set up and space heaters, too, in case it got to be too cold. Troian knew what was about to happen, and she was smiling. Kimera was confused and was scanning the area. We'd set this up between the barbeque slash picnic area and the playground. In front of the seats was open ground, and we had sprayed a large square using white spray paint.

The other old ladies, Annie, and the kids, were seated. Troian and Kimera sat down near them. Seeing they were in place, I signaled my brothers. I was peeking out the back door facing the marked area. Rhaines moved up and pushed the door all the way open, and held it for us. Out marched me and my brothers. The women started booing and calling out taunts when they saw us.

We were stripped to the waist. We'd wrapped our hands for those planning to fight, which appeared to be all of us. It had been a long time since we'd had a good brawl, and every one of us was looking forward to it. That would've been enough to get us in the ring, but the added fact we had our male pride and honor as tough men to defend was icing on the cake. Spawn and I had told our brothers about what was said and the bet we made with the two women. They were more than ready to prove we could birth babies if it were possible.

Annie was sitting there with our women. She had a grin on her face. Troian was smiling at me and eating me alive with her eyes, if I wasn't mistaking the heat in her gaze. Kimera's pinched and defeated look of late was now one of disbelief. I saw her stop scanning us and stop her gaze on one man, Spawn. He was staring right back at her.

We lined the dirt ring and waited for Reaper to start it. He faced the women. "We're here tonight to settle a bet that was recently made. Two of you ladies challenged the manhood of the Iron Punishers in regard to our ability to handle pain. The exact charge was we wouldn't be able to stand the rigors of childbirth if we were able to have children. Troian and Kimera were adamant it wasn't possible, and I believe they said we'd curl up and whine or something to that effect."

The women snickered. He waited until they quieted, then continued. "Of course, there's no way we can give birth to prove it, so an all-out no-holds-barred fight was suggested. We men will engage in it and not hold back. The ladies will then judge when we're done if men could stand to have babies."

"What else do you get out of it if you win, other than your male pride?" Annie yelled.

"Well, for those of us just supporting our two brothers, it'll be pride and satisfaction as well as a damn good workout. As for Spawn and Lash, well, that's between them and those two." He pointed to the two instigators.

"We'd like to know what it is unless it's a secret," Annie insisted.

I wasn't about to blurt out that we'd bargained for total control in the bedroom. Instead, I answered them with the other half of the bet. "Part of it was we all put money down on the outcome. If the men win, we pick a worthy organization to receive the pot as a donation. The losers double the pot amount to make it a better donation. The other part of it is personal and between us and the ladies."

"Oh, I gotta hear that part. Ladies, we'll talk later," Annie teased them. The other old ladies were grinning and telling them they had to hear it, too. Both Kimera and Troian blushed.

"Enough talk. It's time to get this started. This is based on total honesty, so no cheating, just to be unified against the men. The rules are we won't permanently maim each other or use weapons other than our hands and feet. A match will go until it's called due to being pinned and unable to break loose, one man being unconscious, too hurt to continue, or one of the fighters tapping out. We won't kill each other either. Those are the rules. The refs for this will be Colt, me, and Mayhem. We'll take turns. Do you ladies agree to be unbiased?" Reaper added.

"Agreed," rang out from all of them.

"Good. We'll pull names out of this bag. The two names we draw will be the first match. We'll go from there. Settle in, ladies. It's gonna be a long night," he said with a smirk.

He held out the bag to Cheyenne. She reached in and pulled out a piece of paper, then drew out another one. He nodded to her. She opened them and read them out loud. "The first match is Shadow and Remus."

The rest of us moved back and let them enter the ring. Reaper rang an old-fashioned bell like you had at fights. He'd used the one from our gym inside the clubhouse in the basement. It had a roped-in ring for fights like this. The reason we weren't in there was we thought outside would be a nice change and help keep us cooler. Not only had we done this for sport and fun in the past, but it had been used when brothers had issues between them.

One that came to mind was when Reaper took Crusher there after he made Chey run away due to his insistence that we make sure she wasn't a spy for the Soldiers of Corruption, who tried to infiltrate our club to take it over. He'd only done it to ensure the club was safe, but he spoke of it where she overheard him. That's what earned him the match.

It took Reaper some talking to get her to come back and give him another chance. We should've learned from that mistake, but I turned around and did the same thing, and we were overheard. Making sure the fucking doors were closed to church and not speaking out of turn would be a priority from now on.

Both men came out and felt each other out for a minute or so, then got down to business. They didn't go easy on each other. We never did when it came to this. We enjoyed the workout and honing our skills.

There'd be a lot of aching men tonight, but it would be worth it. No one timed it. There was no time limit. They landed some wicked blows and kicks. They had the women gasping. In the end, it was Shadow who won by knocking Remus out. His brother helped carry him out of the ring and onto the sideline to recover. I checked him over, then let him be. He'd wake up soon.

The next match was drawn by Annie. She drew Ink and Tinker's names. This was another great match. Tinker had a couple of inches on Ink and a few pounds, but overall, they were evenly matched. Both took a beating, and it only ended when Tinker got Ink in a submission hold he couldn't break. He tried for a few minutes, then Reaper called it. They laughed and fist-bumped each other afterward. Alisse ran to her man to check him out while I checked on Tinker.

The third match was between Rhaines and Romulus. Alisse was the one to draw their names. I was interested to see how they did, especially Rhaines, to determine how he held up. He was a prospect and still proving himself. Romulus because he was one of the two latest patched members, like his twin. They were a bit less hardened than us. That wasn't to say they weren't tough and able to get the job done. I ended up impressed as hell, and I knew the others were too. Romulus won. In the end, after a hard fight, he made Rhaines tap out. Rhaines looked disgusted, but we all told him what a good job he did.

The next names were pulled by Lark. It was Reaper against Mayhem. This should be good. Our president was against our enforcer. Both were brutal fighters and had no backup in them. Since they were two of the three refs, Colt took over. He was still hurting from his accident, but he was out of bed and moving around. He couldn't fight, but he could referee. He was bummed to be missing out.

Mayhem and Reaper put on one helluva show. There was a lot of yelling and swearing. Thank God the little ones were sleeping through it mostly. The women had the cutest ear protection on them. I didn't know they made them that small. Both men were bloody and bruised and not giving an inch. In the end, Colt had no choice but to call it a draw. We agreed with him. They waved off anyone checking their wounds except Reaper, who couldn't keep Chey away. She fussed over him, and he ate it up even if he didn't need it.

The fifth round was Troian's picks of Maniac and Crusher. Lark sat on the sidelines, chewing on her thumbnail and flinching. Flynn, their son, watched in awe. He loved it. Maybe some people would say it was wrong to let kids see this, but he knew the rules of fighting even at his young age. Maniac was already working with him, and he knew it was either for defense or something like that. Never just to be a bully or his ass would be beaten when he got home. This one ended when it was called due to too much blood. You couldn't tell if either man was seriously getting hurt, and we didn't want to chance it. Mayhem called it.

Next was Ratchet and Sandman. Chey picked them. They tried to get Kimera to choose the names, but she refused. They didn't push her. I was glad to see she had stayed, to be honest. Spawn kept a close watch on her. That meant the last match would be me and him. That wasn't a coincidence. Our names had been excluded from the bag. We'd told the others we wanted to be matched up for last and why. They agreed.

Both men fought a good match. Lots of kicks and jabs were exchanged. They were overall very evenly matched. In the end, Ratchet lucked out and got Sandman in a hold he found impossible to break, so he eventually submitted. As they got up and walked off laughing and slapping each other on the backs, it was our turn.

Troian and Kimera looked pale. I winked at Troian, hoping to settle her concerns. Spawn walked over to Kimera and said something to her before he joined me. As he shook my hand, he said, "Good luck."

"Good luck to you too. Here's hoping we convince the women and we win the rest of our bet."

"You might, but I don't see that happening for me. She's so damaged from what happened, she'll never let another man near her," he said softly. I heard the pain in his voice.

"No, it just means you'll have to take your time and prove to her that not all men are like those animals. If you want her, and I mean want her as more than a fling or a conquest, then you'll put in the time and effort. If you only want that, then walk away and let some other man heal her."

His face grew furious. "Over my goddamn dead body is some other man making love to that woman. She's mine. I'm not looking for a fling or to just get my cock wet," he hissed.

I smiled at him. "That's what I thought. Get ready to win this, and then get started on winning your woman, brother. Let's do this."

He did grin this time, and then the bell rang. The man hit like a hammer. He made pain shoot through my body whenever he landed a blow or kick. I knew I was doing the same to him. Even if he was several inches taller than me, I was quicker and had a slightly longer reach. Exhilaration flowed through me as we fought. God, I loved this shit. It was almost as good as using my whips.

We were both taking a beating and loving it. Neither could get the other to submit or in a hold that couldn't be broken. Nor did we knock each other out. It was turning into a very long battle. I didn't know how it happened, but we were circling each other, and I threw a wicked right hook just as he stumbled. I landed the blow and hit him close to his temple. He fell to his knees. I gave him a second to recover, but it wasn't needed because we heard a scream and looked up.

Kimera was standing up, looking terrified. She was crying, and then she took off running. Spawn staggered to his feet and went after her. It wasn't the way I thought the match would end, but I knew he needed to comfort her. I made my way over to Troian. She wrapped me in her arms and gave me a kiss.

"I don't care what the others say. In my books, you proved your point. I'll pay my half of the bet."

"You mean you'll pay the money?" I teased.

She smirked. "Yeah, that and the other too. As soon as we're both healed, I'm yours for the night. Make me scream longer and harder than you ever have. Show me what you've been hiding."

"Oh, I can do that, Hurricane. I can so do that," I whispered right before I took her mouth. The others all faded away.

Troian: Chapter 20

Kimera was still not herself. She wouldn't tell me what happened nor what Spawn said to her the day of the fight when she ran off. It had been ten days since that. Her bruises and soreness had healed enough that she insisted she go back to work. We tried to talk her out of it and to take more time off, but she refused. She said they needed her, so she went back three days ago.

It had gone fine until last night. There was a big fight, and Spawn had lost his shit. He was spending time at the house every day. I knew why, and I didn't mind. I wasn't bringing her out of her funk, so if he could, more power to him. The fight started when she calmly announced after dinner that she planned to move back to her house.

Spawn lost his mind and started telling her why that wasn't going to happen. When she argued back, he informed her it wasn't safe for her, even with Toro. She came back with how she had her gun, not just Toro, and she'd be fine. That's when he threatened to lock her up here, which turned into a screaming match that ended in her crying and running to her room. He tried to follow her, but she locked him out. He sat in the hallway, talking through the door at her for a long time. We left them alone to talk. We knew he wanted to help her, and he might be the one to get through to her, even if she was angry at him.

This morning, she'd come downstairs very subdued, but she did talk a little. There was no more talk about leaving, and I didn't bring it up. As much as I liked her place, I didn't like the idea of her out there with no one close by to help if she needed it. Toro was great, and I knew she could shoot, but still.

Maybe I was so willing to not talk about it since I was tired. Lash had left in the middle of the night, saying he had a club matter to attend to and he'd be back sometime today. I hadn't been able to sleep even though I did get a few texts telling me he was fine.

It was afternoon when Lash came in. He had a serious expression on his face. I hurried over to him. "What's wrong? What was the club matter you had to take care of?"

He smiled tenderly at me. "That's why I'm here. We need you and Kimera to come to the clubhouse so we can fill you in. It's not bad, babe. I promise. Where is she?"

"She's in her room. Let me get her."

It didn't take me long to get her to join me. She had an apprehensive expression on her face as we went with him. I wondered briefly where Spawn was. When we arrived and walked into the clubhouse, the common room was filled with the other brothers. I didn't see any of the women, though. This made me nervous. He led us past them, and they fell in behind us. We were taken to church. My nerves increased tenfold. Spawn was sitting in there with Reaper. He looked fierce as he sat there.

He jumped to his feet and pulled out a chair next to him. He gestured to Kimera to sit, which she did slowly. I was further down next to Lash. The others all took seats. When they were seated and the door was shut, Reaper slammed a heavy hammer-like thing on the table.

"Ladies, welcome. Thanks for joining us. You have to be wondering why you're here. First, let me tell you, it's nothing bad. In fact, it's damn good. We wanted to tell you together. You need to know, as the newest members of our family, we don't make promises we don't keep, nor do we leave loose ends," Reaper informed us, then paused.

I didn't know if he was waiting for us to say something, but I did. "Thank you for telling us this, but I already knew that."

"Thank you for that, but actions speak louder than words. You were hurt by the people who were your family and should've protected you, Troian. And Kimera, you were hurt by those same people just for trying to help your friend. You have no idea how fucking sorry we are for that. It was our fault you got hurt. We should've had more than just one person with you," he added.

She stirred. "No, it wasn't your fault. I was the one who colored my hair and rode around like that. I got Colt hurt. He could've been killed. I'm the one who should be apologizing. You've been nice enough to let me stay here despite that, but I want you to know I plan to get out of your hair."

A growl came rumbling out of Spawn. He sent her a glare. She glared back. I guess stuff wasn't settled between them. It was just postponed. Damn. Reaper kept her from saying more.

"Sweetheart, yeah, you should've let us help you if you were going to do it anyway, but that doesn't mean it's your fault. We knew they were in town, and we should've had multiple men on all the women, not just one guard. We could debate all day, but that's not why we brought you here. You know that Crusher's family back in Russia was taking care of any loose ends there. That left us one here. Well, one of significance. We have some friends helping to make sure anyone still caught in that prostitution business is freed and given help to start over. That just left one bad seed to take care of," Reaper told her.

Butterflies erupted in my belly. Were they about to take care of Andrik? And if so, how? He was in prison. Lash squeezed my hand and smiled at me.

"I'll let Lash and Spawn tell you the rest," Reaper added, then got quiet. I saw Spawn give Lash a chin lift, and then my man started talking.

"Last night, Spawn and I made sure Andrik will never see daylight again. He met with an unfortunate accident which landed him in the infirmary of the prison."

"What kind of accident? And how will that keep him in prison? He only received a ten-year sentence," I said.

"He did, but then he took a hard tumble down the stairs," Lash said with a grin.

"How did he fall down those stairs?" Kimera asked softly.

"It seems someone started a rumor that he was not only in there for pandering but also because he liked the kiddies. Rumor was he not only pimped out women but kids too, and he sampled them," Spawn said abruptly.

"Who would do that?" I asked.

"A little thing appeared in his online records, and one of the inmates who likes to tell everything he sees when he works in the warden's office just happened to see it. It wasn't long before his entire cell block knew," Lash told us.

"How does this keep him there, though? Won't they just put him in protective custody? That's what they do to those filthy bastards," Kimera hissed.

"Usually, yes, but it seems his luck got worse once he got to the infirmary. See, there's an inmate who's in for life. He was a doctor. The warden lets him work there. Free labor, you see. It appears that recently, one of his nephews was molested. He's only ten years old. Suffice it to say, his uncle is furious that he's not able to do anything about it. I guess when a *cho mo* appeared in front of him, he couldn't resist," Spawn added.

"*Cho mo?*" I asked.

"That's prison slang for child molester. He beat

him and then strangled him to death. As they took him away, he was laughing. He said time in the hole and solitary was more than worth it. It wasn't like they could extend his sentence. All this might get him is death row, and he yelled he'd go to hell happy," Spawn said.

"How do you know all this? I don't understand," I cried.

"Babe, the record was changed by Spawn. He was the one who found out the guy in the infirmary was a lifer, and he figured he hated molesters after what happened to his nephew. He also made sure the cameras had a glitch in that cell block so no one was caught throwing his ass down the stairs or what was happening in the infirmary until it was too late.

"We have people on the inside. We got a message to one of them about what we needed. He told the doctor, let him know to expect a patient, and gave him the name. The rest was easy. We knew someone would at least beat his ass, if not kill him. The only thing we couldn't guarantee was they wouldn't outright kill him before he got to the doctor. The infirmary inmate took care of the rest of it. We didn't force him to do it. We just gave him the information and presented him with a chance," Lash said quietly.

I sat there stunned, not knowing what to feel. On the one hand, I was thrilled he was gone and had no chance of getting out and coming after me or doing the awful things he did before again. On the other, was it wrong that I felt like that and that it was a lie that got him killed? Not that I didn't think he deserved it for what he did to those women.

"What's bothering you?" Lash asked.

"I feel like I should be appalled that a lie got him killed, but I'm not," I confessed.

"It wasn't a lie. The court couldn't prove it when he went to trial. That didn't mean it wasn't true. I was able to find the proof they couldn't. It was buried deeper than the rest. I have it if you need to see it, but it's not pretty. He did sell kids to be used for sex, and he used them himself. He was a sick bastard, and you have no reason to feel anything but relieved and happy," Spawn snarled.

My stomach heaved at the thought. I shook my head no. I trusted him. I didn't need or want to see the proof. A sob caught our attention. We all looked at Kimera. She was crying and rocking in her seat. I tried to go to her, but Spawn got to her and lifted her out of her chair and onto his lap. He rocked her and whispered in her ear. She wasn't struggling to get away, so I stayed put. After about a minute, Reaper motioned for the rest of us to follow him. We quietly got up and left them alone.

Out in the common room, he had one final comment. "I think we should let them talk. You two, go home and celebrate the end of this nightmare. It's a damn good day. Go." He didn't have to tell us twice. The others were talking happily and grabbing drinks. Lash and I left them to it. We had things to talk about and a life to plan.

Lash:

Troian and I talked for hours about what we wanted together and how we would go forward. She'd fully forgiven me for the whole debacle over thinking she was involved and faking her memory loss. She'd been telling me a lot about her life. Most of it was lonely and sad, even in the middle of her supposed family. She was treated more as an afterthought than anything else. She helped pay bills, cook, clean, and take care of the kids.

None of the men we killed were married. There were three sisters, and they had husbands. Those men hadn't been trusted to be part of the family business, although the sisters might know where the money came from. Troian said she didn't think they did. Apparently, all five men treated women like airheaded nuisances, even their sisters and cousins. It would be up to their husbands to support their wives and kids without help now. I learned the sisters were named Ivanka, Vanda, and Dannica. They hadn't been much nicer to my woman than the men. They'd lose the family land and houses once the men didn't return and any search turned up nothing. Fitting, I thought.

Spawn made sure that the evidence he'd gotten to prove the four men were involved was sent to the authorities anonymously, of course. If anyone came looking for Troian, she had a lie waiting for them. We'd been seeing each other in secret for months, and when I asked her to come live with me, she jumped at the chance. She didn't say anything to her family since she knew they would disapprove, and she hadn't seen or talked to them in weeks.

Kimera had returned to the house hours ago after we left her with Spawn. She wasn't into talking, so we let her be. Spawn wasn't with her. I wondered what happened. I'd find out tomorrow. Tonight, I had to be here for my Hurricane. We fixed dinner together and then went to bed early. That was where we were now, and I had plans. She was completely healed from her surgery and me from my beating in the ring. Tonight was the night I'd make her pay the rest of her debt.

I'd been waiting for what seemed like forever to be with her again. I hungered for that woman like she was a drug and I was an addict. I'd thought a lot about what I wanted to do when I got my chance to have her totally at my mercy and her pleasure. I meant what I told her. I'd never do anything to hurt her, and it would only give her the utmost pleasure. She'd scream my name, I had no doubt. Just the thought made me hard.

She'd just come from her bath and slid into bed. She was dressed in a short nightgown. It reminded me more of a slip than a nightgown. It was a pale green and set off her glorious red hair and her contrasting tan skin. I was already done with my shower. I let her soak in the tub while I took it. I wanted to join her, but I didn't want to blow it before we had a chance to get started. She'd given me a puzzled look when I didn't join her.

She rolled over to face me. A tiny frown marred her face. "Is everything alright, Derrick? You didn't join me in the tub. Did I do something to upset you?"

I rubbed away the lines between her brows. "No, baby, you didn't do anything to upset me. I had a reason for not joining you. I need to ask you something before I tell you what that is."

"Go ahead."

"Do you hurt anywhere? Please don't say no if you have even the slightest soreness or pain."

"I feel terrific, and I'm not just saying that."

This put a smile on my face. She saw it. I moved closer. "Good, that means you're ready to pay off the other half of our bet. It's time to pay for doubting your man could endure childbirth. Remember what you promised me. I can do anything I want as long as I don't harm you, and it makes you scream louder and longer than ever before."

"Oh God," she moaned. It wasn't a moan of dread. It was one of pure desire. Glancing down, I saw her nipples were hard and pressing against her nightie. That was a good place to start. I gently pushed her onto her back.

"Stay there until I tell you to move. No touching me. If you do, I'll have to do something to prevent it. You can be as vocal as you want, but you can't ask for me to do things to you or to do things to me. I decide that. If I want your opinion, I'll ask. Understood?" I asked.

She shivered and nodded yes.

"Say it."

"I understand and agree, Derrick."

"Good." I didn't bother to say more. I'd let my actions speak for me for a bit.

I lowered my head and sucked on her left nipple through the fabric. I lashed it with my tongue. She moaned as I bit down, hard enough to make it sting but not to be unbearable pain, then I tugged, elongating it. While I kept my mouth busy on that one, I tugged and twisted the other one with my fingers. She cried out and slightly raised her back off the bed. I could've told her she disobeyed, but instead, I waited to see if she did it again.

I let go of her with my mouth and blew air over the wet fabric. She shivered. I switched breasts and repeated the process. I kept going back and forth a few times. When she broke and lifted her whole upper body off the bed and grasped the back of my head to hold me against her, I broke her grip and sat up.

"Nu-uh, that's not allowed. What did I tell you? No moving or touching me. You just did both. You know what that means." I had to fight not to smirk as I said it.

"Derrick, I'm sorry. I couldn't help it. It just felt so good. Let me try again," she pleaded.

"No, this is about you putting yourself completely in my hands. I know what you need. I can and will give it to you, but when I think you need it or can handle it. Put your arms up over your head."

She bit her bottom lip, but she did it, even though I saw a trace of apprehension in her brown eyes. I gave her a brief kiss on the lips. "I love you. You're safe with me, baby," I whispered. If she got too anxious or really upset, I'd stop. It wouldn't be fun for either of us if she couldn't let go.

"I love you too, honey," she said softly before raising her arms like I had asked. It made my chest hurt, in a good way, every time she told me she loved me. Before going further, I took time to take her nightie off. I sat back on my heels and admired her body. The small scars from her surgery or her beating didn't detract an ounce from how beautiful she was. I could spend hours just looking at her, but that would have to wait until much later. It had been too long since I had her.

Sliding my hand under my pillow, I brought out one of the things I'd staged in the room while she was bathing. Surprise registered on her face as she saw the lined leather cuffs I was holding up. I'd make sure she couldn't touch me until I was ready for her to do it. I reached up and wrapped them around her wrists and around one of the metal posts that made up the headboard. There were pieces of wood that alternated with metal twisted rods all the way across it.

"Are those comfortable? Wiggle your fingers for me," I told her. I could almost get a finger underneath the cuff part, but I wanted to be sure.

"They feel fine. God, I can't believe I just let you cuff me."

"If it makes you feel better, I'll let you cuff me one day." That was something I'd offered no woman, but I'd be willing to play at least once that way with her. Her smile was all the answer I needed.

"Deal. Show me what else you've got, my love."

I let out a growl and proceeded to show her. I tortured her breasts again, only this time when she was crying out, trying not to ask me for more. I added more bite to our play. She was responding so perfectly to the pain I was causing her that I hoped she might be able to take more. Before I tried, though, I had to make sure she knew there was a way to stop this. I should've told her before we began, but I was too excited.

"Baby, before we continue, I need you to listen carefully. If at any time you get scared or you want me to stop, I need you to tell me that. Not just because you're scared of how intense it is. That's not what I mean. I mean, if you're terrified or there's pain that you can't stand." I saw the apprehension again on her face as I said the last part about the pain.

I hurried to reassure her. "I'm not planning to subject you to real torture or shit. But there are degrees of discomfort and pain that can enhance pleasure to unbelievable heights. I want you to experience that."

"Why? What does it do for you? I can see how it might for me, but not you."

"Despite what you might've heard, some men like to see the woman they're with get off. Knowing we're the cause of it makes us enjoy it more. Our releases will be harder."

"So you've done this before and like it."

"Not like this, no. This is all us. There are things I want to do with you that I've never tried with anyone else. I've been teasing you but not letting you come. That's orgasm denial or maybe more like delay. When I finally let you come, it'll be explosive. When that happens, I want my mouth to be on your sweet pussy so I can taste all your sweetness. Then later, on my cock. I'm taking you again and again tonight. I want your screams, Troian. Show your man how good he makes you feel, and then show me how much you want me when the time comes," I growled. Just talking about it and imagining it was making me want to spread her legs and pound inside of her, but I wouldn't.

She sent me a smoldering look. "Then show me. Do it." She gestured with her chin at the items in my hand.

I gladly followed this one order. I lowered myself back down to work her nipples back into stiff peaks. Once I had them there, I placed the first clamp. They weren't the most intense ones out there. Hell, people had ones you added weights to, vibrated and more, or even used clothes pins. She wasn't at that level, and I wasn't sure if we'd go there, but this would drive her wild. Her nipples were so damn responsive to the slightest touch.

I tightened the right one until she hissed. I quickly did the same to the left. Once they were on, I flicked them with the tip of my finger. She cried out, "Oh fuck," and whimpered.

I kept going. Leaving them be for the moment, I kissed my way slowly toward her pussy. As I went, I licked and nipped at her soft skin. I left red marks from my teeth and whiskers on her. Marks of possession that made me want to howl. She was working hard not to move too much. A little wiggling was to be expected. If we kept playing like this, I'd become stricter with her.

Reaching her mound, I pushed her legs apart and inhaled. The scent of her pussy was strong. My mouth watered as I recalled how she tasted. I looked my fill. She was so wet, she was drenched. Lying down, I wedged myself between her thighs and ran my tongue from the bottom to the top of her slit, where I sucked hard on her clit. She moaned loudly.

I became lost in eating her pussy. I couldn't get enough of her. I lapped, flicked, nibbled, kissed, fingered, and blew on her. She was sobbing, and I refused to let her come. Every time she got close, I backed off and nibbled on her thighs. She was almost at the breaking point.

My cock was so hard I was grinding it into the bed. I forced myself to stop. I wasn't blowing my load in the sheets. Lifting up, I eased my lower half into a kneeling position as I lifted her ass up. I grabbed our pillows and shoved them underneath her. It would help me stay in control and to do the next part, which would make her break.

I reached up and tugged on her clamps. As she sobbed, I lapped at her folds and gathered her moisture on my pinky finger, then slipped it to her tiny forbidden hole. She tensed but didn't tell me no. We had a discussion one night about anal sex. She had questions about it and why some people enjoyed it. That had led her to ask if I'd ever done it. When I said yes, she wanted to know if I wanted that with her. I explained only if she wanted it. If not, then I'd be fine. She'd left it as something we could talk about again some other time. I thought it was time to see what she'd say.

I didn't breach her. I waited and lifted away to ask, "Troian, baby, are you alright with me fingering your ass? I'll go slow and only use one finger, but I'd like to see if you might like it. It'll burn. Bear down, it'll help. If you don't want to, you can say no to me. Or if we try and you hate it, you can stop it. Tell me."

She took a few seconds to answer. I waited. Finally, she answered me. "I'm scared it'll hurt badly, but I want to know if it can feel good like you said. I want to try. Just go slow."

I smiled at her. "Baby, I will. I think you should know. You're probably about to go off big time. I won't stop you this time. I want you to come hard and long. In fact, I'm gonna make you come more than once."

Before she could say anything more, I tugged on her breast clamp, which made her moan as I sucked on her hard nub, which made her legs shake. As she gave into those sensations, I pressed slowly but steadily on her asshole. She resisted, but I kept going. Slowly, I felt her relax a tiny bit.

I growled as I sucked harder and fluttered my

tongue inside her pussy. That's all it took to send her into a screaming orgasm. As she flooded my mouth and I lapped greedily, I slipped my finger all the way inside her ass and began to slowly fuck it. She wailed louder and jerked on her cuffs. I did it until she went limp underneath me, and then I kept going.

It didn't take me more than a minute to have her coming again. She squeezed my finger so tight in her ass I almost exploded, imagining that it was my cock. As she relaxed, I knew I had to be inside of her. I'd make it last longer on round two. Pulling my finger out of her ass, I sat up and yanked her bottom onto my thighs. She gave me a dazed look. I held her gaze as I pushed inside her soaking wet, tight snatch. I groaned loudly.

"Fuck, it's better than I remember. Yes, that's it. Squeeze me, Hurricane," I muttered. She tightened more, and I lost it. I set up a punishing pace. I hammered in and out of her like a jackhammer. Her screams got louder. Her legs wrapped around my waist, and she held me closer. I cupped her breasts and tugged hard on her clamps. She screeched and tightened like a vise as she came. I somehow found the strength not to come and kept going.

"Oh God, please, please, Derrick. Come for me. I need you to come, baby. Fuck me. Harder," she wailed.

"That's it. Take your man's cock. Come again. Take me with you," I snarled. I was breathing hard. It only took a few more strokes to send her into her next orgasm and have her pull the cum out of me. I roared as I came. As I did, I grew faint and imagined what else we could do when I rested a minute. That made me jerk and release more cum. As we both clung to each other and panted, I knew I'd never have this with anyone else but her. She was my Hurricane.

Troian: Epilogue- One Month Later

I watched as everyone celebrated the patching in of a new member. Colt had done his year, and the guys had voted him in. The joy and relief he felt was written all over his face. He was laughing and talking to Mayhem and Ratchet as they drank beer. Wait, I had to get used to calling him by his newly given road name, Gravel. When I asked why that name, they said it was to go along with his deep, gravelly voice. I could see it. They were mean and said it was because of all the gravel ground into his hide from going down on his bike. He flipped them off.

As I watched the others having fun, I tried not to be sad. There was so much to be happy about, but it was hard when I didn't see my friend Kimera here. She'd left two weeks ago despite everyone's objections. She argued there was no need for concern with all of my family gone. Spawn tried to force her to stay, but she refused.

Then, a week ago, when I went to see how she was doing, I found she was gone. She'd packed up Toro and had taken off. The hospital would only say she had a family emergency, and they didn't know when she would return. I thought Spawn was gonna lose his mind when he found out. He sat down and searched for her immediately. It wasn't long before he found her. However, he suddenly refused to go after her. He'd been walking around since like a thundercloud. Anyone speaking to him got their heads snapped off. I wondered why he'd changed his mind about her.

I asked Lash, and he told me to stay out of it and let his brother figure it out on his own. I would only be patient for so long. If she didn't come back soon, I'd go see why not. I'll be damned if any of them would keep me from going. Spawn wouldn't give me her address either, so I'd have to get her to give it to me. So far, she'd spoken to me twice, and both times said she was just recovering and needed time. She wouldn't tell me where she was.

Strong arms came around me from behind. I relaxed back against my man. As he kissed my neck, I tried to concentrate on him and the celebration. I was thrilled beyond words to be Lash's Hurricane and to be embarking on a life with him. Now, all I had to do was get my best friend back to where she belonged and find out what she was hiding. What had put that look on Spawn's face? Whatever it was, I knew it could be fixed. After finding Lash and the Iron Punishers, I could believe anything was possible.

The End Until Spawn's She-Wolf
Iron Punishers MC Book 5

Made in the USA
Las Vegas, NV
10 May 2024

89767021R00208